PENGUIN CLASSICS

THE BEST OF RICHARD MATHESON

RICHARD MATHESON (1926–2013) is the *New York Times* best-selling author of *I Am Legend, Hell House, Somewhere in Time, The Incredible Shrinking Man, A Stir of Echoes,* and *What Dreams May Come,* among other books. He was named a Grand Master of Horror by the World Horror Convention, and received the Bram Stoker Award for Lifetime Achievement. He also won the Edgar, the Spur, and the Writer's Guild awards. In 2010, he was inducted into the Science Fiction Hall of Fame. In addition to his novels, Matheson wrote screenplays, as well as sixteen *Twilight Zone* episodes, including "Nightmare at 20,000 Feet," based on his short story.

VICTOR LAVALLE is the award-winning author of four novels, *The Changeling, The Ecstatic, Big Machine,* and *The Devil in Silver,* and a collection of short stories, *Slapboxing with Jesus. Big Machine* was the winner of an American Book Award and the Shirley Jackson Award in 2010, and was selected as one of the best books of the year by the *Los Angeles Times, The Washington Post, Chicago Tribune, The Nation,* and *Publishers Weekly.* He teaches writing at Columbia University.

RICHARD MATHESON

The Best of
Richard Matheson

Edited with an Introduction by
VICTOR LAVALLE

PENGUIN BOOKS

PENGUIN BOOKS

An imprint of Penguin Random House LLC
375 Hudson Street
New York, New York 10014
penguin.com

LIBRARY OF CONGRESS CATALOGING-IN-PUBLICATION DATA
Names: Matheson, Richard, 1926–2013, author. | LaValle,
Victor D., 1972– editor.
Title: The best of Richard Matheson / edited with
an introduction by Victor LaValle.
Description: New York: Penguin Books, 2017. | Series: Penguin classics
Identifiers: LCCN 2017016393 (print) | LCCN 2017016915 (ebook) | ISBN
9781101993668 (ebook) | ISBN 9780143130178 (paperback)
Subjects: | BISAC: FICTION / Science Fiction / Short Stories. | FICTION /
Horror. | FICTION / Fantasy / Short Stories.
Classification: LCC PS3563.A8355 (ebook) | LCC PS3563.A8355 A6 2017 (print) |
DDC 813/.54—dc23
LC record available at https://lccn.loc.gov/2017016393

Printed in the United States of America

Set in Sabon LT Std Roman

Contents

Introduction by VICTOR LAVALLE   vii

THE BEST OF
RICHARD MATHESON

Born of Man and Woman   1
Prey   5
Witch War   18
Shipshape Home   24
Blood Son   44
Where There's a Will
    (written with Richard Christian Matheson)   53
Dying Room Only   61
Counterfeit Bills   79
Death Ship   82
Dance of the Dead   104
Man with a Club   121
Button, Button   129
Duel   138
Day of Reckoning   165
The Prisoner   171
Dress of White Silk   190
Haircut   195
Nightmare at 20,000 Feet   201
The Funeral   219

Third from the Sun   228
The Last Day   236
Long Distance Call   253
Deus ex Machina   266
One for the Books   275
Now Die in It   294
The Conqueror   306
The Holiday Man   324
No Such Thing as a Vampire   329
Big Surprise   338
A Visit to Santa Claus   345
Finger Prints   358
Mute   365
Shock Wave   395

Introduction

I've been asked to write an introduction to these stories by Richard Matheson—*The Best of Richard Matheson*—at least according to me. I had the enviable task of reading nearly every story he's ever written and selecting the thirty-three tales included here. This turned out to be like stepping into a time machine, transported back to the age when I started reading him. I was fourteen. The year was 1986. My introduction to his fiction, his short novel *I Am Legend*, was one of the first books that made me run up to my friends and tackle them so they'd all check it out, too. If you haven't read it (what the hell is wrong with you?), it manages to be a work of science fiction, a vampire story, a progenitor of the "biological plague" apocalyptic novel, and also an excellent thriller. All that in about 160 pages. I had to find out more. I dove into *The Shrinking Man* (the film added "Incredible") and *Hell House* and wow. I wish I had a more sophisticated way to describe my reaction to the seismic effect of Richard Matheson on my young mind, but "wow" gets at the raw, awestruck nature of the thing. And then I came to find out the man had written short stories. I tracked them down with gusto, with glee. And with time I began to relate to the man's writing in a way that seemed damn near mystical.

I want to explain exactly what I mean by that. There's a lot I need to say about Matheson, and the importance of his fiction, the reasons why this collection is so vital and worthwhile, but I

can't get to that directly. I will go there eventually. But first I
have to tell you about my Matheson moment. I don't mean that
I met the man. I mean I stepped into a story he could've written. I have to tell you about Cedric and his mother.

2

My mother made good when I turned fourteen. At least that's
how she saw it when she moved us out of an apartment in one
part of Queens and took us to a house she'd bought in another.
The woman emigrated from Uganda in her twenties and now,
in her forties, she'd worked like a machine to stop renting and
start owning. From a two-bedroom to a two-story home,
damn right my mother felt proud. Me, my sister, and my
grandmother were the grateful tagalongs.

We moved in over the summer and when September rolled
around I started going to school. The local public school was
Springfield Gardens High, and just before I arrived the place
had been outfitted with the newest, latest technology: metal
detectors. And with good reason. This was 1986, the Crack
Era, and as old news reports will tell you some people had a
propensity to shoot guns wildly in places where teens gathered. My mother took one look at the school where she was
meant to send her child and she made changes posthaste. This
woman was not about to have her kid ushered through those
contraptions every morning before heading to homeroom.
More to the point, she didn't want to get some phone call
about how I'd been caught by Stray Bullet Syndrome while
standing around outside. She found a private school out on
Long Island and before I could say "where the hell is Nassau
County" she'd gotten me enrolled on a scholarship. My mom
was no joke.

My mom also wasn't a car owner. She got to work and back
by taking a bus to the Long Island Rail Road and the train
into Manhattan. Suffice to say there weren't any such choices
at Woodmere Academy. People either got dropped off by their
parents (Mercedes, BMW, Audi) or they took a school bus.

Mom enrolled me in the pickup service and every morning, around 7:45, I'd go out and stand on the corner of 229th Street and 145th Avenue and there I'd wait for one of those long yellow buses to pick me up.

I waited in front of a single-family home with yellow aluminum siding. One morning, maybe around November or December, when the chill weather set in heavy, the front window of that house slipped up and a kid my age stuck his head out the window and called to me.

"Aye," he called. "Cheese bus."

I turned, baffled. He had an enormous round head and close haircut. This gave him a kind of Charlie Brown look. A brown Charlie Brown. He wore a white tank top. He was, by no definition, a skinny kid. In fact, me and him might've been body doubles.

"Cheese Bus," he said again, and I realized he'd given me a nickname. Before I could speak he reached one meaty hand out of the window and waved me away.

"Go stand down the block," he said. "Your bus is fucking up my vibe."

"You don't own the sidewalk," I said. Citing basic property law was the best I could do.

"You sound like a herb," he said. "Cheese, are you a herb?"

"Well how come you're not getting ready for school?" I said. What kind of kid treats cutting school like an insult? This one. And with that I cemented my herb status.

"I would try to help you," he said. "But I can't even guess where I'd start."

I walked up to the chain link fencing at the edge of his parents' property and leaned my elbows on it so that I was posed just like him.

"Seriously though," I said. "You're skipping?"

He thought about this a little bit. He sighed and said, "I've got company coming over."

"Like, you're having a party?"

"Party for two," he said, then he looked to his left and pointed, discreetly, with one finger.

When I looked up I saw two things: my bus—the cheese

bus—chugging toward me; and a girl, fourteen, moving down the block with much more grace. This would turn out to be Lianne, Cedric's sweetheart since seventh grade. They kissed sweetly when she reached him. He led her inside without even saying good-bye.

After that me and Cedric talked each morning. He'd lean out the window and gab with me before the bus showed up. I made nice, but not because I found him so charming. I'll admit I had ulterior motives. New in the neighborhood and being bused to a school miles away. How was I going to meet anyone? I wanted a girlfriend, too. Couldn't Lianne call in a friend for me?

3

It turned out to be surprisingly easy to cut school. Just don't be on the corner when the bus shows up. After two minutes the driver simply drove on. Meanwhile I'd been tucked inside Cedric's house, peeking out through the blinds like some secret agent at risk of having his cover blown. The bus left, then Cedric tapped me on the shoulder and said, "Stop hiding."

Easy to do when two young women knocked at the front door. Cedric went to let them in and I stood there in the living room feeling quite sure I'd ascended to some higher plane of existence. Or was about to. He opened the door and kissed Lianne, then stepped aside so she and her friend Tasha could slip in. The front door fed right into the living room where I stood. The living room fed right into the kitchen. Apparently there were two bedrooms elsewhere—Cedric's and his mom's. When I'd asked him if I could use hers—in case things went well with Tasha—he patted me on the arm and said, "Don't get ahead of yourself."

Now let me cut in with a message from me as a grown man, as a father. It is absolutely insane that four fourteen-year-olds were sneaking off to get intimate in the middle of the day; I can't pretend it wasn't. But at the time it felt wonderfully sane.

Anyway, I'm standing there and Tasha and Lianne are

coming through the doorway and then I heard it, a sound in the kitchen. Knocking. Not all that loud, but I was close to the kitchen and getting closer. By that I mean that Tasha and Lianne were taking off their coats and I ran away. Later I told Cedric I went to "get them water," but there's no other way to say it: I fled.

As soon as I entered the kitchen the knocking stopped. I figured it might be their boiler kicking in. It was winter after all. I knew I'd run away though so I came up with the water idea and went scrounging for cups. This led me on a chase through the cupboards as, in the other room, Cedric called for me. And then I reached their pantry door. This style of one-family home had a separate little pantry, about the size of a small walk-in closet. I found the door there and, still hunting for glasses, I tried the handle and found it locked. Then Cedric walked into the kitchen.

"Cheese," he said. "You making me look bad."

When he said it he didn't sound playful. He'd convinced his girlfriend to bring someone with her and then his boy had gone and run into the kitchen. But I also wondered if that was really the reason he seemed unhappy with me. He peeked at the pantry door then back to me.

"Cups is over here," he said, taking four down from a cupboard by the sink. Then he rushed me out of the kitchen.

He put on a movie. I definitely don't remember what it was. He closed the blinds so the living room went dim. Lianne leaned into him. Tasha and I hardly spoke. She was as nervous as me.

At some point Cedric went to the bathroom and left us alone in the living room. Lianne patted the cushion beside her and Tasha hopped over, the pair whispering and I sat there alone. Hadn't even sipped my water once. And then I heard it—that knocking—coming from the kitchen again. I didn't hesitate. Maybe I felt stupid sitting alone. I walked in there and went quiet.

The knocking, low and insistent, came from the other side of that pantry door. I checked for Cedric but he wasn't around. I tried the door but found it locked. Meanwhile the knocking kept on, regular if weak. It damn sure wasn't the boiler.

I whispered, "Who is it?"

When I spoke the knocking stopped. I mean instantly. What followed next was a scratching sound. Claws on the floor. I even thought I heard something panting softly.

A dog.

Cedric had a dog and he locked it up when company came over.

I got to my feet and laughed at myself and now thought only of how I would not fuck things up with Tasha, who—it turned out—was exactly as geeky as me. All I had to do was finally speak to her and find out. We finished the movie together in the living room, all four of us. By the time it was over even me and Tasha were kissing. At some point she mentioned a smell in the room. I almost laughed because I knew it was just the funk of four teenagers fucking around. But she persisted. It was worse than that. Could there be something going rotten in the fridge? In the walls? Maybe there was a mutt somewhere in the house, an animal that had had an accident.

Cedric hardly pulled away from Lianne's lips. He answered her casually, thoughtlessly. He said, "My mother would never let me have a dog."

I remember hearing those words and going utterly numb.

4

Which brings us to Richard Matheson.

If you've picked up this gorgeous book (don't you love that cover?) then you've probably already got a passing knowledge of the man. But just because you may have heard of him, read him, watched the countless shows and movies that he wrote or inspired, that doesn't mean you may have thought so much about his meaning in the history of the genres of science fiction and fantasy, horror and thrillers. Why bother hashing over all that when you could just dive into the tales themselves? A fine point. The best argument for stopping here and skipping ahead. I wouldn't blame you. Actually, I'd encourage such a thing.

I find it interesting to note that Matheson was the son of two Norwegian immigrants. I like to think on that because he is, to my mind, such an American writer, and it's always good to be reminded that for almost all of us that means, at some point, our people came from elsewhere and landed here. There's so much journeying in Matheson's writing—across time and space, across the threshold between life and death, across town to get to work on time (though of course you'll never get there safely)—as I read through all the stories I wondered how much the journeys of his parents meant to Matheson, the young man. It might be that as the son of a more recent immigrant my mother's course—her bravery, her drive—informs so much of what I imagine, what I write.

If nothing else he's written about how his parents came from Norway and found each other, then circled the wagons around family, fearful of the outside world and clinging to each other. Inside the walls sat a young, bookish Richard Matheson. They kept him close but his mind roamed.

We should get *The Twilight Zone* out of the way now. Yes, Richard Matheson wrote some of the most beloved and enduring episodes of that classic show. Let's rattle off just a few: "Third from the Sun," "Death Ship," "Nightmare at 20,000 Feet." You've seen them and loved them. You've sat down with some friend during a *Twilight Zone* marathon and giddily anticipated when one of them would play. But before they were on your screen they were in magazines, collected in books. I know this seems almost silly to say, but they were all stories first. And what's so remarkable, when you read them, is to see how perfect they were right from the start. The clarity of the language, the promise of a pleasing mystery, the mounting tension of the confrontation—the revelation—to come, and the cool satisfaction of seeing Matheson pull off this magic again and again and again (and again). Matheson regularly did the patient work of illustrating an ordinary existence only to have it smash directly into the monstrous, and this becomes the moment of a person's greatest test. Sometimes they triumph, sometimes they fail, but Matheson knew that in a way the pushing is the point. The stress and anxiety, the drama and fear, that's when humanity truly gets to understand itself, understand the world.

Matheson began his writing career with short stories. He worked that form for twenty years, and all were published between 1950 and 1970, a Golden Age for Matheson's fiction and also for the world of science fiction and fantasy magazines. He started with short stories and an industry existed to support him. Such an idea can seem like fantasy these days. But the pairing was auspicious. These genres were reaching a wider readership, so they'd better have some good content. And Richard Matheson was there. In many ways he was inventing the template that generations of writers would copy.

The problem with being a pioneer is that you often die out before your settlement thrives. You're in the ground for years before the village becomes a town; decades before the town becomes a city. Matheson, thankfully, got to see countless kinds of success. It's always nice to be able to say a writer enjoyed the fruits of his labor. How rare is that? Let's celebrate it.

But the other issue with being a pioneer is that the generations who come later may forget the ground you tilled, the innovations you brought into being. You hear Matheson's name on the lips of so many greats, from Stephen King to Joe Hill. (A little family joke I just couldn't resist.) But he deserves to be spoken of by so many more. His stories became the bedrock of many genres: thriller, horror, science fiction, fantasy, so essential it's almost impossible to really grasp how much he accomplished. How many people take a moment to give thanks for the sidewalks and highways? Yet most of us couldn't get anywhere without them.

The other reason this may be the case is that Matheson had such an effortless, clear writing style. He threw the reader into the story and made very little attempt to force attention on himself as Author. This is great for stories, but not so good for getting credit. Writing is like life: too often we praise the show-offs, the ones who wink at us when they toss out some abstruse word. Many tend to think of this as artistry, but I'm less inclined. Or maybe I only mean to highlight the grace, and confidence, of a writer like Richard Matheson. Clarity can be artistry as well. It implies confidence, too. You won't notice much of what he's doing the first time you tear through these stories, but on your second pass you should take your time.

His central concern is survival. What threatens your existence? Even more important, what will you do to get through? Think of the man in "Nightmare at 20,000 Feet" who risks popping open the emergency window of an airplane at cruising altitude so he can fire a gun at the being he's seen tearing at the plane's engine. He's nearly sucked out into the night sky, but he *must* do something. He, and the other passengers, must survive. The ordinary meets the monstrous and every life is at risk.

But let's not only talk of the classic stories, the ones you no doubt know; they're worth the price of admission alone, but Matheson has so much more here to offer. There's my personal favorite find, a story called "Witch War." Matheson plays out the idea of a conquering army powered only by the occult abilities of a handful of teenage girls. In between decimating the opposing army they talk smack about one another, they mock and joke, by the end they even revel in the fear they cause to the men they're meant to defend. It's a subtle and stunning little tale and it shows off another aspect of Matheson's talent: he can be wickedly funny.

Then there's "Dance of the Dead." I don't want to spoil anything for you, but it's straight up *disturbing*. It's a kind of postapocalyptic undead tale that also predates, even anticipates, the reprobates of *A Clockwork Orange*. (It was also made into a deeply troubling and memorable episode in the *Masters of Horror* anthology series, written by Matheson's son, Richard Christian Matheson, and directed by Tobe Hooper.) Where Richard Matheson often had his stories come out on the side of safety or triumph, this one has no time for such treacle. This one wants to hurt you. And it, too, is a product of the same singularly gifted mind.

The depth and variety of the man's imagination seem nearly unparalleled. His influence exists even for those who have never read him. He's in the DNA of too many other writers to count. When you enjoy science fiction and fantasy today, when you read modern horror, you are still reading Richard Matheson.

5

The next morning I decided not to skip school. This also had to do with the fact that Tasha—with whom I was now smitten— told me she couldn't cut twice in one week. So I showed up at my bus stop right around 7:45, and sure enough the cheese bus turned the corner a few blocks west, right on time. But then Cedric's living room window opened and he leaned out looking as blasé as always. Yet again he had on my Champion sweatshirt, one of many articles of clothing I'd lent him, never to be returned. He leaned on his elbows and watched me quietly for about the count of three.

"All right then," he said, keeping direct eye contact. "You want to see?"

Did I? In that moment I didn't really know.

Cedric opened the front door. I walked into the house with my head down, my curiosity tinged with dread.

The living room looked like it hadn't been cleaned—or even occupied—since me and Tasha had been there yesterday. The couch cushions still in disarray. Cedric walked ahead of me. He entered the kitchen and I hesitated.

"Well?" he called out.

I moved toward the kitchen, but I can't say it was my choice. I felt compelled to take a step. Pulled in, drawn closer. As I moved I heard the pantry door's lock click and a faint groan as it swung open. At the same time I smelled it again, what Tasha had been talking about the day before. A kind of rot so strong I experienced it as a wave of heat that made my eyes flutter. And still I stepped through the threshold and entered the kitchen.

"This is my mom," Cedric said.

There's a look to ships that have sunk to the bottom of the ocean and remained there for decades. When they're brought to the surface they're scaly with barnacles and orange with rust. They look vulnerable and indestructible, simultaneously. A sunken ship, now risen, Cedric's mother seemed much the same.

As I said, it was the Crack Era and I recognized what had torpedoed this woman. I tried to greet her but there wasn't time. Cedric's mother came at me, her hands dug into my coat pockets, she yanked my book bag off from where it dangled on one shoulder and, right in front of me, she unzipped it and tossed everything out on the floor.

"Ma!" Cedric shouted, but he didn't try to stop her. He'd never looked so young.

Each of us must've outweighed Cedric's mother by two hundred pounds but I knew I didn't have the strength to challenge her. She tossed through my things and sucked her teeth and both us boys just watched her.

"Ma," Cedric said again, but much softer this time. "Please, Ma."

Then she turned and leapt at him, her own child, and sent him flying backward. He went to the ground. She climbed right up onto his chest, that's how I remember it. She pulled at the sweatshirt, my sweatshirt, and I heard the fabric tear. I went down on a knee and tossed everything back into the bag and that's when Cedric cried out, I swear I thought it was an infant wailing from another room. When I looked up she'd torn open his sweatshirt and her hands dug at his flesh. I saw blood. I thought she might devour him right there.

And there I'd finally reached my Matheson moment. The ordinary was over. The monstrous was here. I wish I could say I helped him, but I didn't. I picked up my bag and I scurried backward. If someone was going to survive, better it be me. Even today I can still hear him whispering, pleading, that same single word. "Ma. Ma."

I got to the living room and crawled to the front door. I opened it and pulled the door shut behind me. I stopped skipping school after that. I told Tasha about what happened and, bless her, she believed me. But when I went back to the house, knocking for what seemed like hours, Cedric didn't answer. I'd never seen a place look so lifeless. Lianne told Tasha she couldn't reach him. She'd call the house, but the phone only rang and rang. I never saw him pop his head out his front window ever again.

Obviously I've turned this history into a story, my homage to Richard Matheson, to my old friend Cedric, and even to his mom. While some of this tale is indeed fiction, there really was a monster living in that house.

Which brings me back, one last time, to Richard Matheson. What did this son of Norwegian immigrants, who spent the majority of his life writing in California, know about the Crack Era nightmares of a black boy from Queens? On the surface I'd say nothing. Superficially he and I could hardly seem further apart. But then why, when I wrote out what happened between me and Cedric and his mother, did I hear the echoes of so many of Matheson's tales? I'm not talking about the plot points but the essence. The fight for survival, the monstrous breaking in on the ordinary, no one holds the sole rights to such real estate. But Richard Matheson tilled the soil long before me and, likely, long before you, too. He even built a house in which so many of us still dwell. All hail the architect! Now come on inside.

VICTOR LAVALLE

The Best of
Richard Matheson

BORN OF MAN
AND WOMAN

X—This day when it had light mother called me retch. You retch she said. I saw in her eyes the anger. I wonder what it is a retch.

This day it had water falling from upstairs. It fell all around. I saw that. The ground of the back I watched from the little window. The ground it sucked up the water like thirsty lips. It drank too much and it got sick and runny brown. I didnt like it.

Mother is a pretty I know. In my bed place with cold walls around I have a paper things that was behind the furnace. It says on it SCREENSTARS. I see in the pictures faces like of mother and father. Father says they are pretty. Once he said it.

And also mother he said. Mother so pretty and me decent enough. Look at you he said and didn't have the nice face. I touched his arm and said it is alright father. He shook and pulled away where I couldnt reach. Today mother let me off the chain a little so I could look out the little window. Thats how I saw the water falling from upstairs.

XX—This day it had goldness in the upstairs. As I know when I looked at it my eyes hurt. After I look at it the cellar is red.

I think this was church. They leave the upstairs. The big machine swallows them and rolls out past and is gone. In the back part is the little mother. She is much small than me. I am I can see out the little window all I like.

In this day when it got dark I had eat my food and some bugs. I hear laughs upstairs. I like to know why there are laughs for. I took the chain from the wall and wrapped it around me.

I walked squish to the stairs. They creak when I walk on them. My legs slip on them because I dont walk on stairs. My feet stick to the wood.

I went up and opened a door. It was a white palace. White as white jewels that come from upstairs sometime. I went in and stood quiet. I hear the laughing some more. I walk to the sound and look through to the people. More people that I thought was. I thought I should laugh with them.

Mother came out and pushed the door in. It hit me and hurt. I fell back on the smooth floor and the chain made noise. I cried. She made a hissing noise into her and put her hand on her mouth. Her eyes got big.

She looked at me. I heard father call. What fell he called. She said a iron board. Come help pick it up she said. He came and said how is *that* so heavy you need. He saw me and grew big. The anger came in his eyes. He hit me. I spilled some of the drip on the floor from one arm. It was not nice. It made ugly green on the floor.

Father told me to go to the cellar. I had to go. The light it hurt some now in my eyes. It is not so like that in the cellar.

Father tied my legs and arms up. He put me on my bed. Upstairs I heard laughing while I was quiet there looking on a black spider that was swinging down to me. I thought what father said. Ohgod he said. And only eight.

XXX—This day father hit in the chain again before it had light. I have to try pull it out again. He said I was bad to come upstairs. He said never do that again or he would beat me hard. That hurts.

XXXX—I got the chain from the wall out. Mother was upstairs. I heard little laughs very high. I looked out the window. I saw all little people like the little mother and little fathers too. They are pretty.

They were making nice noise and jumping around the ground. Their legs was moving hard. They are like mother and father. Mother says all right people look like they do.

One of the little fathers saw me. He pointed at the window. I let go and slid down the wall in the dark. I curled up as they would not see. I heard their talks by the window and foots running. Upstairs there was a door hitting. I heard the little mother call upstairs. I heard heavy steps and I rushed in my bed place. I hit the chain in the wall and lay down on my front.

I heard my mother come down. Have you been at the window she said. I heard the anger. *Stay* away from the window. You have pulled the chain out again.

She took the stick and hit me with it. I didnt cry. I cant do that. But the drip ran all over the bed. She saw it and twisted away and made a noise. Oh mygodmygod she said why have you *done* this to me? I heard the stick go bounce on the stone floor. She ran upstairs.

XXXXX—This day it had water again. When mother was upstairs I heard the little one come slow down the steps. I hidded myself in the coal bin for mother would have anger if the little mother saw me.

She had a little live thing with her. It walked on the arms and had pointing ears. She said things to it.

It was all right except the live thing smelled me. It ran up the coal and looked down at me. The hairs stood up. In the throat it made an angry noise. I hissed but it jumped on me.

I didnt want to hurt it. I got fear because it bit me harder than the rat does. I hurt and the little mother screamed. I grabbed the live thing tight. It made sounds I never heard. I pushed it all together. It was all lumpy and red on the black coal.

I hid there when mother called. I was afraid of the stick. She left. I crept over the coal with the thing. I hid it under my pillow and rested on it. I put the chain in the wall again.

X—This is another times. Father chained me tight. I hurt because he beat me. This time I hit the stick out of his hands and made noise. He went away and his face was white. He ran out of my bed place and locked the door.

I am not so glad. All day it is cold in here. The chain comes slow out of the wall. And I have a bad anger with mother and father. I will show them. I will do what I did that once.

I will screech and laugh loud. I will run on the walls. Last I will hang head down by all my legs and laugh and drip green all over until they are sorry they didn't be nice to me.

If they try to beat me again Ill hurt them. I will.

X—

PREY

Amelia arrived at her apartment at six-fourteen. Hanging her coat in the hall closet, she carried the small package into the living room and sat on the sofa. She nudged off her shoes while she unwrapped the package on her lap. The wooden box resembled a casket. Amelia raised its lid and smiled. It was the ugliest doll she'd ever seen. Seven inches long and carved from wood, it had a skeletal body and an oversized head. Its expression was maniacally fierce, its pointed teeth completely bared, its glaring eyes protuberant. It clutched an eight-inch spear in its right hand. A length of fine, gold chain was wrapped around its body from the shoulders to the knees. A tiny scroll was wedged between the doll and the inside wall of its box. Amelia picked it up and unrolled it. There was handwriting on it. *This is He Who Kills*, it began. *He is a deadly hunter*. Amelia smiled as she read the rest of the words. Arthur would be pleased.

The thought of Arthur made her turn to look at the telephone on the table beside her. After a while, she sighed and set the wooden box on the sofa. Lifting the telephone to her lap, she picked up the receiver and dialed a number.

Her mother answered.

"Hello, Mom," Amelia said.

"Haven't you left yet?" her mother asked.

Amelia steeled herself. "Mom, I know it's Friday night—" she started.

She couldn't finish. There was silence on the line. Amelia closed her eyes. Mom, please, she thought. She swallowed. "There's this man," she said. "His name is Arthur Breslow. He's a high-school teacher."

"You aren't coming," her mother said.

Amelia shivered. "It's his birthday," she said. She opened her eyes and looked at the doll. "I sort of promised him we'd . . . spend the evening together."

Her mother was silent. There aren't any good movies playing tonight, anyway, Amelia's mind continued. "We could go tomorrow night," she said.

Her mother was silent.

"Mom?"

"Now even Friday night's too much for you."

"Mom, I see you two, three nights a week."

"To *visit*," said her mother. "When you have your own room here."

"Mom, *let's not start on that again*," Amelia said. I'm not a child, she thought. Stop treating me as though I were a child!

"How long have you been seeing him?" her mother asked.

"A month or so."

"Without telling me," her mother said.

"I had every intention of telling you." Amelia's head was starting to throb. I will *not* get a headache, she told herself. She looked at the doll. It seemed to be glaring at her. "He's a nice man, Mom," she said.

Her mother didn't speak. Amelia felt her stomach muscles drawing taut. I won't be able to eat tonight, she thought.

She was conscious suddenly of huddling over the telephone. She forced herself to sit erect. *I'm thirty-three years old*, she thought. Reaching out, she lifted the doll from its box. "You should see what I'm giving him for his birthday," she said. "I found it in a curio shop on Third Avenue. It's a genuine Zuni fetish doll, extremely rare. Arthur is a buff on anthropology. That's why I got it for him."

There was silence on the line. All right, *don't talk*, Amelia thought. "It's a hunting fetish," she continued, trying hard to sound untroubled. "It's supposed to have the spirit of a Zuni hunter trapped inside it. There's a golden chain around it to prevent the spirit from—" She couldn't think of the word; ran a shaking finger over the chain. "—escaping, I guess," she said. "His name is He Who Kills. You should see his face." She felt warm tears trickling down her cheeks.

"Have a good time," said her mother, hanging up.

Amelia stared at the receiver, listening to the dial tone. Why is it always like this? she thought. She dropped the receiver onto its cradle and set aside the telephone. The darkening room looked blurred to her. She stood the doll on the coffee-table edge and pushed to her feet. I'll take my bath now, she told herself. I'll meet him and we'll have a lovely time. She walked across the living room. A lovely time, her mind repeated emptily. She knew it wasn't possible. Oh, *Mom!* she thought. She clenched her fists in helpless fury as she went into the bedroom.

In the living room, the doll fell off the table edge. It landed head down and the spear point, sticking into the carpet, braced the doll's legs in the air.

The fine, gold chain began to slither downward.

It was almost dark when Amelia came back into the living room. She had taken off her clothes and was wearing her terrycloth robe. In the bathroom, water was running into the tub.

She sat on the sofa and placed the telephone on her lap. For several minutes, she stared at it. At last, with a heavy sigh, she lifted the receiver and dialed a number.

"Arthur?" she said when he answered.

"Yes?" Amelia knew the tone—pleasant but suspecting. She couldn't speak.

"Your mother," Arthur finally said.

That cold, heavy sinking in her stomach. "It's our night together," she explained. "Every Friday—" She stopped and waited. Arthur didn't speak. "I've mentioned it before," she said.

"I know you've mentioned it," he said.

Amelia rubbed at her temple.

"She's still running your life, isn't she?" he said.

Amelia tensed. "I just don't want to hurt her feelings anymore," she said. "My moving out was hard enough on her."

"I don't want to hurt her feelings either," Arthur said. "But how many birthdays a year do I have? We *planned* on this."

"I know." She felt her stomach muscles tightening again.

"Are you really going to let her do this to you?" Arthur asked. "One Friday night out of the whole year?"

Amelia closed her eyes. Her lips moved soundlessly. I just can't hurt her feelings anymore, she thought. She swallowed. "She's my mother," she said.

"Very well," he said, "I'm sorry. I was looking forward to it, but—" He paused. "I'm sorry," he said. He hung up quietly.

Amelia sat in silence for a long time, listening to the dial tone. She started when the recorded voice said loudly, "Please hang up." Putting the receiver down, she replaced the telephone on its table. So much for my birthday present, she thought. It would be pointless to give it to Arthur now. She reached out, switching on the table lamp. She'd take the doll back tomorrow.

The doll was not on the coffee table. Looking down, Amelia saw the gold chain lying on the carpet. She eased off the sofa edge onto her knees and picked it up, dropping it into the wooden box. The doll was not beneath the coffee table. Bending over, Amelia felt around underneath the sofa.

She cried out, jerking back her hand. Straightening up, she turned to the lamp and looked at her hand. There was something wedged beneath the index fingernail. She shivered as she plucked it out. It was the head of a doll's spear. She dropped it into the box and put the finger in her mouth. Bending over again, she felt around more cautiously beneath the sofa.

She couldn't find the doll. Standing with a weary groan, she started pulling one end of the sofa from the wall. It was terribly heavy. She recalled the night that she and her mother had shopped for the furniture. She'd wanted to furnish the apartment in Danish modern. Mother had insisted on this heavy, maple sofa; it had been on sale. Amelia grunted as she dragged it from the wall. She was conscious of the water running in the bathroom. She'd better turn it off soon.

She looked at the section of carpet she'd cleared, catching sight of the spear shaft. The doll was not beside it. Amelia picked it up and set it on the coffee table. The doll was caught beneath the sofa, she decided; when she'd moved the sofa, she had moved the doll as well.

She thought she heard a sound behind her—fragile, skittering. Amelia turned. The sound had stopped. She felt a chill move up the backs of her legs. "It's He Who Kills," she said with a smile. "He's taken off his chain and gone—"

She broke off suddenly. There had definitely been a noise inside the kitchen, a metallic, rasping sound. Amelia swallowed nervously. What's going on? she thought. She walked across the living room and reached into the kitchen, switching on the light. She peered inside. Everything looked normal. Her gaze moved falteringly across the stove, the pan of water on it, the table and chair, the drawers and cabinet doors all shut, the electric clock, the small refrigerator with the cookbook lying on top of it, the picture on the wall, the knife rack fastened to the cabinet side—

—its small knife missing.

Amelia stared at the knife rack. Don't be silly, she told herself. She'd put the knife in the drawer, that's all. Stepping into the kitchen, she pulled out the silverware drawer. The knife was not inside it.

Another sound made her look down quickly at the floor. She gasped in shock. For several moments, she could not react; then, stepping to the doorway, she looked into the living room, her heartbeat thudding. Had it been imagination? She was sure she'd seen a movement.

"Oh, come on," she said. She made a disparaging sound. She hadn't seen a thing.

Across the room, the lamp went out.

Amelia jumped so startledly, she rammed her right elbow against the doorjamb. Crying out, she clutched the elbow with her left hand, eyes closed momentarily, her face a mask of pain.

She opened her eyes and looked into the darkened living room. "Come on," she told herself in aggravation. Three sounds plus a burned-out bulb did not add up to anything as idiotic as—

She willed away the thought. She had to turn the water off.

Leaving the kitchen, she started for the hall. She rubbed her elbow, grimacing.

There was another sound. Amelia froze. Something was coming across the carpet toward her. She looked down dumbly. No, she thought.

She saw it then—a rapid movement near the floor. There was a glint of metal, instantly, a stabbing pain in her right calf. Amelia gasped. She kicked out blindly. Pain again. She felt warm blood running down her skin. She turned and lunged into the hall. The throw rug slipped beneath her and she fell against the wall, hot pain lancing through her right ankle. She clutched at the wall to keep from falling, then went sprawling on her side. She thrashed around with a sob of fear.

More movement, dark on dark. Pain in her left calf, then her right again. Amelia cried out. Something brushed along her thigh. She scrabbled back, then lurched up blindly, almost falling again. She fought for balance, reaching out convulsively. The heel of her left hand rammed against the wall, supporting her. She twisted around and rushed into the darkened bedroom. Slamming the door, she fell against it, panting. Something banged against it on the other side, something small and near the floor.

Amelia listened, trying not to breathe so loudly. She pulled carefully at the knob to make sure the latch had caught. When there were no further sounds outside the door, she backed toward the bed. She started as she bumped against the mattress edge. Slumping down, she grabbed at the extension phone and pulled it to her lap. Whom could she call? The police? They'd think her mad. Mother? She was too far off.

She was dialing Arthur's number by the light from the bathroom when the doorknob started turning. Suddenly, her fingers couldn't move. She stared across the darkened room. The door latch clicked. The telephone slipped off her lap. She heard it thudding onto the carpet as the door swung open. Something dropped from the outside knob.

Amelia jerked back, pulling up her legs. A shadowy form was scurrying across the carpet toward the bed. She gaped at it. It isn't true, she thought. She stiffened at the tugging on her bedspread. *It was climbing up to get her.* No, she thought; *it isn't true.* She couldn't move. She stared at the edge of the mattress.

Something that looked like a tiny head appeared. Amelia twisted around with a cry of shock, flung herself across the bed and jumped to the floor. Plunging into the bathroom, she spun around and slammed the door, gasping at the pain in her ankle. She had barely thumbed in the button on the doorknob when something banged against the bottom of the door. Amelia heard a noise like the scratching of a rat. Then it was still.

She turned and leaned across the tub. The level of the water was almost to the overflow drain. As she twisted shut the faucets, she saw drops of blood falling into the water. Straightening up, she turned to the medicine-cabinet mirror above the sink.

She caught her breath in horror as she saw the gash across her neck. She pressed a shaking hand against it. Abruptly, she became aware of pain in her legs and looked down. She'd been slashed along the calves of both legs. Blood was running down her ankles, dripping off the edges of her feet. Amelia started crying. Blood ran between the fingers of the hand against her neck. It trickled down her wrist. She looked at her reflection through a glaze of tears.

Something in her aroused her, a wretchedness, a look of terrified surrender. *No*, she thought. She reached out for the medicine-cabinet door. Opening it, she pulled out iodine, gauze and tape. She dropped the cover of the toilet seat and sank down gingerly. It was a struggle to remove the stopper of the iodine bottle. She had to rap it hard against the sink three times before it opened.

The burning of the antiseptic on her calves made her gasp. Amelia clenched her teeth as she wrapped gauze around her right leg.

A sound made her twist toward the door. She saw the knife blade being jabbed beneath it. It's trying to stab my feet, she thought; it thinks I'm standing there. She felt unreal to be considering its thoughts. *This is He Who Kills*; the scroll flashed suddenly across her mind. *He is a deadly hunter.* Amelia stared at the poking knife blade. God, she thought.

Hastily, she bandaged both her legs, then stood and, looking into the mirror, cleaned the blood from her neck with a wash-rag. She swabbed some iodine along the edges of the gash, hissing at the fiery pain.

She whirled at the new sound, heartbeat leaping. Stepping to the door, she leaned down, listening hard. There was a faint metallic noise inside the knob.

The doll was trying to unlock it.

Amelia backed off slowly, staring at the knob. She tried to visualize the doll. Was it hanging from the knob by one arm, using the other to probe inside the knob lock with the knife? The vision was insane. She felt an icy prickling on the back of her neck. *I mustn't let it in,* she thought.

A hoarse cry pulled her lips back as the doorknob button popped out. Reaching out impulsively, she dragged a bath towel off its rack. The doorknob turned, the latch clicked free. The door began to open.

Suddenly the doll came darting in. It moved so quickly that its figure blurred before Amelia's eyes. She swung the towel down hard, as though it were a huge bug rushing at her. The doll was knocked against the wall. Amelia heaved the towel on top of it and lurched across the floor, gasping at the pain in her ankle. Flinging open the door, she lunged into the bedroom.

She was almost to the hall door when her ankle gave. She pitched across the carpet with a cry of shock. There was a noise behind her. Twisting around, she saw the doll come through the bathroom doorway like a jumping spider. She saw the knife blade glinting in the light. Then the doll was in the shadows, coming at her fast. Amelia scrabbled back. She glanced over her shoulder, saw the closet and backed into its darkness, clawing for the doorknob.

Pain again, an icy slashing at her foot. Amelia screamed and heaved back. Reaching up, she yanked a topcoat down. It fell across the doll. She jerked down everything in reach. The doll was buried underneath a mound of blouses, skirts and dresses. Amelia pitched across the moving pile of clothes. She forced herself to stand and limped into the hall as quickly as she could. The sound of thrashing underneath the clothes faded from her hearing. She hobbled to the door. Unlocking it, she pulled the knob.

The door was held. Amelia reached up quickly to the bolt. It had been shot. She tried to pull it free. It wouldn't budge. She clawed at it with sudden terror. It was twisted out of shape. "No," she muttered. *She was trapped.* "Oh, God." She started pounding on the door. "Please help me! *Help me!*"

Sound in the bedroom. Amelia whirled and lurched across the living room. She dropped to her knees beside the sofa, feeling for the telephone, but her fingers trembled so much that she couldn't dial the numbers. She began to sob, then twisted around with a strangled cry. The doll was rushing at her from the hallway.

Amelia grabbed an ashtray from the coffee table and hurled it at the doll. She threw a vase, a wooden box, a figurine. She couldn't hit the doll. It reached her, started jabbing at her legs. Amelia reared up blindly and fell across the coffee table. Rolling to her knees, she stood again. She staggered toward the hall, shoving over furniture to stop the doll. She toppled a chair, a table. Picking up a lamp, she hurled it at the floor. She backed into the hall and, spinning, rushed into the closet, slammed the door shut.

She held the knob with rigid fingers. Waves of hot breath pulsed against her face. She cried out as the knife was jabbed beneath the door, its sharp point sticking into one of her toes. She shuffled back, shifting her grip on the knob. Her robe hung open. She could feel a trickle of blood between her breasts. Her legs felt numb with pain. She closed her eyes. Please, someone help, she thought.

She stiffened as the doorknob started turning in her grasp. Her flesh went cold. It couldn't be stronger than she: It *couldn't* be. Amelia tightened her grip. *Please*, she thought. The side of her head bumped against the front edge of her suitcase on the shelf.

The thought exploded in her mind. Holding the knob with her right hand, she reached up, fumbling, with her left. The suitcase clasps were open. With a sudden wrench, she turned the doorknob, shoving at the door as hard as possible. It rushed away from her. She heard it bang against the wall. The doll thumped down.

Amelia reached up, hauling down her suitcase. Yanking open the lid, she fell to her knees in the closet doorway, holding the suitcase like an open book. She braced herself, eyes wide, teeth clinched together. She felt the doll's weight as it banged against the suitcase bottom. Instantly, she slammed the lid and threw the suitcase flat. Falling across it, she held it shut until her shaking hands could fasten the clasps. The sound of them clicking into place made her sob with relief. She shoved away the suitcase. It slid across the hall and bumped against the wall. Amelia struggled to her feet, trying not to listen to the frenzied kicking and scratching inside the suitcase.

She switched on the hall light and tried to open the bolt. It was hopelessly wedged. She turned and limped across the living room, glancing at her legs. The bandages were hanging loose. Both legs were streaked with caking blood, some of the gashes still bleeding. She felt at her throat. The cut was still wet. Amelia pressed her shaking lips together. She'd get to a doctor soon now.

Removing the ice pick from its kitchen drawer, she returned to the hall. A cutting sound made her look toward the suitcase. She caught her breath. The knife blade was protruding from the suitcase wall, moving up and down with a sawing motion. Amelia stared at it. She felt as though her body had been turned to stone.

She limped to the suitcase and knelt beside it, looking with revulsion at the sawing blade. It was smeared with blood. She tried to pinch it with the fingers of her left hand, pull it out. The blade was twisted, jerked down, and she cried out, snatching back her hand. There was a deep slice in her thumb. Blood ran down across her palm. Amelia pressed the finger to her robe. She felt as though her mind was going blank.

Pushing to her feet, she limped back to the door and started prying at the bolt. She couldn't get it loose. Her thumb began to ache. She pushed the ice pick underneath the bolt socket and tried to force it off the wall. The ice pick point broke off.

Amelia slipped and almost fell. She pushed up, whimpering. There was no time, no time. She looked around in desperation.

The window! She could throw the suitcase out! She visualized it tumbling through the darkness. Hastily, she dropped the ice pick, turning toward the suitcase.

She froze. The doll had forced its head and shoulders through the rent in the suitcase wall. Amelia watched it struggling to get out. She felt paralyzed. The twisting doll was staring at her. No, she thought, it isn't true. The doll jerked free its legs and jumped to the floor.

Amelia jerked around and ran into the living room. Her right foot landed on a shard of broken crockery. She felt it cutting deep into her heel and lost her balance. Landing on her side, she thrashed around. The doll came leaping at her. She could see the knife blade glint. She kicked out wildly, knocking back the doll. Lunging to her feet, she reeled into the kitchen, whirled, and started pushing shut the door.

Something kept it from closing. Amelia thought she heard a screaming in her mind. Looking down, she saw the knife and a tiny wooden hand. The doll's arm was wedged between the door and the jamb! Amelia shoved against the door with all her might, aghast at the strength with which the door was pushed the other way. There was a cracking noise. A fierce smile pulled her lips back and she pushed berserkly at the door. The screaming in her mind grew louder, drowning out the sound of splintering wood.

The knife blade sagged. Amelia dropped to her knees and tugged at it. She pulled the knife into the kitchen, seeing the wooden hand and wrist fall from the handle of the knife. With a gagging noise, she struggled to her feet and dropped the knife into the sink. The door slammed hard against her side; the doll rushed in.

Amelia jerked away from it. Picking up the chair, she slung it toward the doll. It jumped aside, then ran around the fallen chair. Amelia snatched the pan of water off the stove and hurled it down. The pan clanged loudly off the floor, spraying water on the doll.

She stared at the doll. It wasn't coming after her. It was trying to climb the sink, leaping up and clutching at the counter side with one hand. It wants the knife, she thought. It has to have its weapon.

She knew abruptly what to do. Stepping over to the stove, she pulled down the broiler door and twisted the knob on all the way. She heard the puffing detonation of the gas as she turned to grab the doll.

She cried out as the doll began to kick and twist, its maddened thrashing flinging her from one side of the kitchen to the other. The screaming filled her mind again and suddenly she knew it was the spirit in the doll that screamed. She slid and crashed against the table, wrenched herself around and, dropping to her knees before the stove, flung the doll inside. She slammed the door and fell against it.

The door was almost driven out. Amelia pressed her shoulder, then her back against it, turning to brace her legs against the wall. She tried to ignore the pounding scrabble of the doll inside the broiler. She watched the red blood pulsing from her heel. The smell of burning wood began to reach her and she closed her eyes. The door was getting hot. She shifted carefully. The kicking and pounding filled her ears. The screaming flooded through her mind. She knew her back would get burned, but she didn't dare to move. The smell of burning wood grew worse. Her foot ached terribly.

Amelia looked up at the electric clock on the wall. It was four minutes to seven. She watched the red second hand revolving slowly. A minute passed. The screaming in her mind was fading now. She shifted uncomfortably, gritting her teeth against the burning heat on her back.

Another minute passed. The kicking and the pounding stopped. The screaming faded more and more. The smell of burning wood had filled the kitchen. There was a pall of gray smoke in the air. That they'll see, Amelia thought. Now that it's over, they'll come and help. That's the way it always is.

She started to ease herself away from the broiler door, ready to throw her weight back against it if she had to. She turned around and got on her knees. The reek of charred wood made her nauseated. She had to know, though. Reaching out, she pulled down the door.

Something dark and stifling rushed across her and she heard the screaming in her mind once more as hotness flooded over her and into her. It was a scream of victory now.

Amelia stood and turned off the broiler. She took a pair of ice tongs from its drawer and lifted out the blackened twist of wood. She dropped it into the sink and ran water over it until the smoke had stopped. Then she went into the bedroom, picked up the telephone and depressed its cradle. After a moment, she released the cradle and dialed her mother's number.

"This is Amelia, Mom," she said. "I'm sorry I acted the way I did. I want us to spend the evening together. It's a little late, though. Can you come by my place and we'll go from here?" She listened. "Good," she said. "I'll wait for you."

Hanging up, she walked into the kitchen, where she slid the longest carving knife from its place in the rack. She went to the front door and pushed back its bolt, which now moved freely. She carried the knife into the living room, took off her bathrobe and danced a dance of hunting, of the joy of hunting, of the joy of the impending kill.

Then she sat down, cross-legged, in the corner. He Who Kills sat, cross-legged, in the corner, in the darkness, waiting for the prey to come.

WITCH WAR

Seven pretty little girls sitting in a row. Outside, night, pouring rain—war weather. Inside, toasty warm. Seven overalled little girls chatting. Plaque on the wall saying: P.G. CENTER.

Sky clearing its throat with thunder, picking and dropping lint lightning from immeasurable shoulders. Rain hushing the world, bowing the trees, pocking earth. Square building, low, with one wall plastic.

Inside, the buzzing talk of seven pretty little girls.

"So I say to him—'Don't give me *that*, Mr. High and Mighty.' So he says, 'Oh yeah?' And I say, 'Yeah!'"

"Honest, will I ever be glad when this thing's over. I saw the cutest hat on my last furlough. Oh, *what* I wouldn't give to wear it!"

"You too? Don't I *know* it! You just can't get your hair right. Not in *this* weather. Why don't they let us get rid of it?"

"*Men!* They make me sick."

Seven gestures, seven postures, seven laughters ringing thin beneath thunder. Teeth showing in girl giggles. Hands tireless, painting pictures in the air.

P.G. Center. Girls. Seven of them. Pretty. Not one over sixteen. Curls. Pigtails. Bangs. Pouting little lips—smiling, frowning, shaping emotion on emotion. Sparkling young eyes—glittering, twinkling, narrowing, cold or warm.

Seven healthy young bodies restive on wooden chairs. Smooth adolescent limbs. Girls—pretty girls—seven of them.

An army of ugly shapeless men, stumbling in mud, struggling along the pitchblack muddy road.

Rain a torrent. Buckets of it thrown on each exhausted man. Sucking sound of great boots sinking into oozy yellow-brown mud, pulling loose. Mud dripping from heels and soles.

Plodding men—hundreds of them—soaked, miserable, depleted. Young men bent over like old men. Jaws hanging loosely, mouth gasping at black wet air, tongues lolling, sunken eyes looking at nothing, betraying nothing.

Rest.

Men sink down in the mud, fall on their packs. Heads thrown back, mouths open, rain splashing on yellow teeth. Hands immobile—scrawny heaps of flesh and bone. Legs without motion—khaki lengths of worm-eaten wood. Hundreds of useless limbs fixed to hundreds of useless trunks.

In back, ahead, beside, rumble trucks and tanks and tiny cars. Thick tires splattering mud. Fat treads sinking, tearing at mucky slime. Rain drumming wet fingers on metal and canvas.

Lightning flashbulbs without pictures. Momentary burst of light. The face of war seen for a second—made of rusty guns and turning wheels and faces staring.

Blackness. A night hand blotting out the brief storm glow. Wind-blown rain flitting over fields and road, drenching trees and trucks. Rivulets of bubbly rain tearing scars from the earth. Thunder, lightning.

A whistle. Dead men resurrected. Boots in sucking mud again—deeper, closer, nearer. Approach to a city that bars the way to a city that bars the way to a . . .

An officer sat in the communication room of the P.G. Center. He peered at the operator, who sat hunched over the control board, phones over his ears, writing down a message.

The officer watched the operator. They are coming, he thought. Cold, wet and afraid they are marching at us. He shivered and shut his eyes.

He opened them quickly. Visions fill his darkened pupils— of curling smoke, flaming men, unimaginable horrors that shape themselves without words or pictures.

"Sir," said the operator, "from advance observation post. Enemy forces sighted."

The officer got up, walked over to the operator and took the message. He read it, face blank, mouth parenthesized. "Yes," he said.

He turned on his heel and went to the door. He opened it and went into the next room. The seven girls stopped talking. Silence breathed on the walls.

The officer stood with his back to the plastic window. "Enemies," he said, "two miles away. Right in front of you."

He turned and pointed out the window. "Right out there. Two miles away. Any questions?"

A girl giggled.

"Any vehicles?" another asked.

"Yes. Five trucks, five small command cars, two tanks."

"That's too easy," laughed the girl, slender fingers fussing with her hair.

"That's all," said the officer. He started from the room. "Go to it," he added, and, under his breath, "Monsters!"

He left.

"Oh, me," sighed one of the girls, "here we go again."

"What a bore," said another. She opened her delicate mouth and plucked out chewing gum. She put it under her chair seat.

"At least it stopped raining," said a redhead, tying her shoelaces.

The seven girls looked around at each other. *Are you ready?* Said their eyes. *I'm ready, I suppose.* They adjusted themselves on the chairs with girlish grunts and sighs. They hooked their feet around the legs of their chairs. All gum was placed in storage. Mouths were tightened into prudish fixity. The pretty little girls made ready for the game.

Finally they were silent on their chairs. One of them took a deep breath. So did another. They all tensed their milky flesh and clasped fragile fingers together. One quickly scratched her head to get it over with. Another sneezed prettily.

"Now," said a girl on the right end of the row.

Seven pairs of beady eyes shut. Seven innocent little minds began to picture, to visualize, to transport.

Lips rolled into thin gashes, faces drained of color, bodies shivered passionately. Their fingers twitching with concentration, seven pretty little girls fought a war.

The men were coming over the rise of a hill when the attack came. The leading men, feet poised for the next step, burst into flame.

There was no time to scream. Their rifles slapped down into the muck, their eyes were lost in fire. They stumbled a few steps and fell, hissing and charred, into the soft mud.

Men yelled. The ranks broke. They began to throw up their weapons and fire at the night. More troops puffed incandescently, flared up, were dead.

"Spread out!" screamed an officer as his gesturing fingers sprouted flame and his face went up in licking yellow heat.

The men looked everywhere. Their dumb terrified eyes searched for an enemy. They fired into the fields and woods. They shot each other. They broke into flopping runs over the mud.

A truck was enveloped in fire. Its driver leaped out, a two-legged torch. The truck went bumping over the road, turned, wove crazily over the field, crashed into a tree, exploded and was eaten up in blazing light. Black shadows flitted in and out of the aura of light around the flames. Screams rent the night.

Man after man burst into flame, fell crashing on his face in the mud. Spots of searing light lashed the wet darkness—screams—running coals, sputtering, glowing, drying—incendiary ranks—trucks cremated—tanks blowing up.

A little blonde, her body tense with repressed excitement. Her lips twitch, a giggle hovers in her throat. Her nostrils dilate. She shudders in giddy fright. She imagines, imagines . . .

A soldier runs headlong across a field, screaming, his eyes insane with horror. A gigantic boulder rushes at him from the black sky.

His body is driven into the earth, mangled. From the rock edge, fingertips protrude.

The boulder lifts from the ground, crashes down again, a shapeless trip hammer. A flaming truck is flattened. The boulder flies again to the black sky.

A pretty brunette, her face a feverish mask. Wild thoughts tumble through her virginal brain. Her scalp grows taut with ecstatic fear. Her lips draw back from clenching teeth. A gasp of terror hisses from her lips. She imagines, imagines . . .

A soldier falls to his knees. His head jerks back. In the light of burning comrades, he stares dumbly at the white-foamed wave that towers over him.

It crashes down, sweeps his body over the muddy earth, fills his lungs with salt water. The tidal wave roars over the field, drowns a hundred flaming men, tosses their corpses in the air with thundering whitecaps.

Suddenly the water stops, flies into a million pieces and disintegrates.

A lovely little redhead, hands drawn under her chin in tight bloodless fists. Her lips tremble, a throb of delight expands her chest. Her white throat contracts, she gulps in a breath of air. Her nose wrinkles with dreadful joy. She imagines, imagines. . . .

A running soldier collides with a lion. He cannot see in the darkness. His hands strike wildly at the shaggy mane. He clubs with his rifle butt.

A scream. His face is torn off with one blow of thick claws. A jungle roar billows in the night.

A red-eyed elephant tramples wildly through the mud, picking up men in its thick trunk, hurling them through the air, mashing them under driving black columns.

Wolves bound from the darkness, spring, tear at throats. Gorillas scream and bounce in the mud, leap at falling soldiers.

A rhinoceros, leather skin glowing in the light of living torches, crashes into a burning tank, wheels, thunders into blackness, is gone.

Fangs—claws—ripping teeth—shrieks—trumpeting—roars. The sky rains snakes.

Silence. Vast brooding silence. Not a breeze, not a drop of rain, not a grumble of distant thunder. The battle is ended.

Motionless trucks—silent tanks, wisps of oily smoke still

rising from their shattered hulks. Great death covering the field. Another battle in another war.

Victory—everyone is dead.

The girls stretched languidly. They extended their arms and rotated their round shoulders. Pink lips grew wide in pretty little yawns. They looked at each other and tittered in embarrassment. Some of them blushed. A few looked guilty.

Then they all laughed out loud. They opened more gumpacks, drew compacts from pockets, spoke intimately with schoolgirl whispers, with late-night dormitory whispers.

Muted giggles rose up fluttering in the warm room.

"Aren't we awful?" one of them said, powdering her pert nose.

Later they all went downstairs and had breakfast.

SHIPSHAPE HOME

"That janitor gives me the creeps," Ruth said when she came in that afternoon.

I looked up from the typewriter as she put the bags on the table and faced me. I was killing a second draft on a story.

"He gives you the creeps," I said.

"Yes, he does," she said. "That way he has of slinking around. He's like Peter Lorre or somebody."

"Peter Lorre," I said. I was still plotting.

"*Babe*," she implored. "I'm serious. The man is a creep."

I snapped out of the creative fog with a blink.

"Hon, what can the poor guy do about his face?" I said. "Heredity. Give him a break."

She plopped down in a chair by the table and started to take out groceries, stacking cans on the table.

"Listen," she said.

I could smell it coming. That dead serious tone of hers which she isn't even aware of anymore. But which comes every time she's about to make one of her "revelations" to me.

"Listen," she repeated. Dramatic emphasis.

"Yes, dear," I said. I leaned one elbow on the typewriter cover and gazed at her patiently.

"You get that look off your face," she said. "You always look at me as if I were an idiot child or something."

I smiled. Wanly.

"You'll be sorry," she said. "Some night when that man creeps in with an axe and dismembers us."

"He's just a poor man earning a living," I said. "He mops the halls, he stokes the furnaces, he . . ."

"We have oil heat," she said.

"If we had a furnace, the man would stoke it," I said. "Let us have charity. He labors like ourselves. I write stories. He mops floors. Who can say which is the greater act?"

She looked dejected.

"Okay," she said with a surrendering gesture. "Okay, if you don't want to face facts."

"Which are?" I prodded. I decided it was best to let it out of her before it burned a hole in her mind.

Her eyes narrowed. "You listen to me," she said. "That man has some design in being here. He's no janitor. I wouldn't be surprised if . . ."

"If this apartment house were just a front for a gambling establishment. A hideout for public enemies one through fifteen. An abortion mill. A counterfeiter's lair. A murderer's rendezvous."

She was already in the kitchen thumping cans and boxes into the cupboard.

"Okay," she said. "*Okay*." In that patient if-you-get-murdered-then-don't-come-to-me-for-sympathy voice. "Don't say I didn't try. If I'm married to a wall, I can't help it."

I came in and slid my arms around her waist. I kissed her neck.

"Stop that," she said. "You can't disconcert me. The janitor is . . ."

She turned. "You're serious," I said.

Her face darkened. "Honey, I *am*," she said. "The man looks at me in a funny way."

"How?"

"Oh," she searched. "In . . . in . . . *anticipation*."

I chuckled. "Can't blame the man."

"Be serious now."

"Remember the time you thought the milkman was a knife killer for the Mafia?" I said.

"I don't care."

"You read too many fantasy pulps," I said.

"You'll be sorry."

I kissed her neck again. "Let's eat," I said.

She groaned. "Why do I tell you anything?"

"Because you love me," I said.

She closed her eyes. "I give up," she said quietly, with the patience of a saint under fire.

I kissed her. "Come on, hon, we have enough troubles."

She shrugged. "Oh, all right."

"Good," I said. "When are Phil and Marge coming?"

"Six," she said. "I got pork."

"Roast?"

"Mmmmm."

"I'll buy that."

"You already did."

"In that case, back to the typewriter."

While I squeezed out another page I heard her muttering to herself in the kitchen. I didn't catch it all. All that came through was a grimly prophetic, "Murdered in our beds or something."

"No, it's flukey," Ruth analyzed as we all sat having dinner that night.

I grinned at Phil and he grinned back.

"I think so too," Marge agreed. "Whoever heard of charging only sixty-five a month for a five-room apartment furnished? Stove, refrigerator, washer—it's fantastic."

"Girls," I said. "Let's not quibble. Let's take advantage."

"*Oh!*" Ruth tossed her pretty blonde head. "If a man said—Here's a million dollars for you, old man—you'd probably take it."

"I most definitely would take it," I said. "I would then run like hell."

"You're naïve," she said. "You think people are . . . are . . ."

"Steady," I said.

"You think everybody is Santa Claus!"

"It *is* a little funny," Phil said. "Think about it, Rick."

I thought about it. A five-room apartment, brand new, furnished in the best manner, dishes . . . I pursed my lips. A guy can get lost in his typewriter. Maybe it was true. I nodded anyways. I could see their point. Of course I wouldn't say so. And spoil Ruth's and my little game of war? Never.

"I think they charge too much," I said.

"Oh . . . Lord!" Ruth was taking it straight, as she usually did. "Too much! Five rooms yet! Furniture, dishes, linens, a . . . a television set! What do you want—a swimming pool!"

"A small one?" I said meekly.

She looked at Marge and Phil.

"Let us discuss this thing quietly," she said. "Let us pretend that the fourth voice we hear is nothing but the wind in the eaves."

"I am the wind in the eaves," I said.

"Listen," Ruth re-spun her forbodings, "what if the place is a fluke? I mean what if they just want people here for a cover-up. That would explain the rent. You remember the rush on the place when they started renting?"

I remembered as well as Phil and Marge. The only reason we'd got our apartment was because we happened to be walking past the place when the janitor first put out the renting sign. We went right in. I remember our amazement, our delight, at the rental. We thought it was Christmas.

We were the first tenants. The next day was like the Alamo under attack. It's a little hard to get an apartment these days.

"I say there's something funny about it," Ruth finished. "And did you ever notice that janitor?"

"He's a creep," I contributed blandly.

"He *is*," Marge laughed. "My God, he's something out of a B-picture. Those eyes. He looks like Peter Lorre."

"See!" Ruth was triumphant.

"Kids," I said, raising a hand of weary conciliation, "if there's something foul going on behind our backs, let's allow it to go on. We aren't being asked to contribute or suffer by it. We are living in a nice spot for a nice rent. What are we going to do—look into it and try to spoil it?"

"What if there are designs on us?" Ruth said.

"What designs, hon?" I asked.

"I don't know," she said. "But I sense something."

"Remember the time you sensed the bathroom was haunted?" I said. "It was a mouse."

She started clearing off the dishes. "Are you married to a blind man too?" she asked Marge.

"Men are all blind," Marge said, accompanying my poor man's seer into the kitchen. "We must face it."

Phil and I lit cigarettes.

"No kidding now," I said, so the girls wouldn't hear. "Do you think there's anything wrong?"

He shrugged. "I don't know, Rick," he said. "I will say this—it's pretty strange to rent a furnished place for so little."

"Yeah," I said. Yeah, I thought—awake at last.

Strange it is.

I stopped for a chat with our strolling cop the next morning. Johnson walks around the neighborhood. There are gangs in the neighborhood, he told me, traffic is heavy and the kids need watching especially after three in the afternoon.

He's a good Joe, lots of fun. I chat with him everyday when I go out for anything.

"My wife suspects foul doings in our apartment house," I told him.

"This is my suspicion too," Johnson said, dead sober. "It is my unwilling conclusion that, within those walls, six-year-olds are being forced to weave baskets by candle light."

"Under the whip hand of a gaunt old hag," I added.

He nodded sadly. Then he looked around, plotter-like.

"You won't tell anyone, will you?" he said. "I want to crack the case all by myself."

I patted his shoulder. "Johnson," I said. "Your secret is locked behind these iron lips."

"I am grateful," he said.

We laughed.

"How's the missus?" he asked.

"Suspicious," I said. "Curious. Investigating."

"Much the same," he said. "Everything normal."

"Right," I said. "I think I'll stop letting her read those science-fiction magazines."

"What is it she suspects?" he asked.

"Oh," I grinned. "Just suppositions. She thinks the rent is too cheap. Everybody around here pays twenty to fifty dollars more, she says."

"Is that right?" Johnson said.

"Yeah," I said, punching his arm. "Don't *you* tell anybody. I don't want to lose a good deal."

Then I went to the store.

"I knew it," Ruth said. "I *knew* it."

She gazed intently at me over a dishpan of soggy clothes.

"You knew what, hon?" I said, putting down the package of second sheets I'd gone down the street to buy.

"This place is a fluke," she said. She raised her hand. "Don't say a word," she said. "You just listen to me."

I sat down. I waited. "Yes dear," I said.

"I found engines in the basement," she said.

"What kind of engines, dear? Fire engines?"

Her lips tightened. "Come on, now," she said, getting a little burned. "I saw the things."

She meant it.

"I've been down there too, hon," I said. "How come I never saw any engines?"

She looked around. I didn't like the way she did it. She looked as if she really thought someone might be lurking at the window, listening.

"This is *under* the basement," she said.

I looked dubious.

She stood up. "Damn it! You come on and I'll show you."

She held my hand as we went through the hall and into the elevator. She stood grimly by me as we descended, my hand tight in her grip.

"When did you see them?" I asked, trying to be nice.

"When I was washing in the laundry room down there," she said. "In the hallways, I mean, when I was bringing the clothes back. I was coming to the elevator and I saw a doorway. It was a little bit open."

"Did you go in?" I asked.

She looked at me. "You went in," I said.

"I went down the steps and it was light and . . ."

"And you saw engines."

"I saw engines."

"Big ones?"

The elevator stopped and the doors slid open. We went out.

"I'll show you how big," she said.

It was a blank wall. "It's here," she said.

I looked at her. I tapped the wall. "Honey," I said.

"Don't you dare say it!" she snapped. "Have you ever heard of doors in a wall?"

"Was this door in the wall?"

"The wall probably slides over it," she said starting to tap. It sounded solid to me. "Darn it!" she said, "I can just hear what you're going to say."

I didn't say it. I just stood there watching her.

"Lose something?"

The janitor's voice *was* sort of like Lorre's, low and insinuating. Ruth gasped, caught way off guard. I jumped myself.

"My wife thinks there's a—" I started nervously.

"I was showing him the right way to hang a picture," Ruth interrupted hastily. "*That's* the way, babe." She turned toward me. "You put the nail in at an angle, not straight in. Now, do you understand?" She took my hand.

The janitor smiled.

"See you," I said awkwardly. I felt his eyes on us as we walked back to the elevator.

When the doors shut, Ruth turned quickly.

"Good night!" she stormed. "What are you trying to do, get him on us?"

"Honey. What . . . ?" I was flabbergasted.

"Never mind," she said. "There are engines down there. *Huge* engines. I saw them. And he knows about them."

"Baby," I said. "Why don't . . ."

"Look at me," she said quickly.

I looked. Hard.

"Do you think I'm crazy?" she asked. "Come on, now. Never mind the hesitation."

I sighed. "I think you're imaginative," I said. "You read those . . ."

"Uh!" she muttered. She looked disgusted. "You're as bad as . . ."

"You and Galileo," I said.

"I'll show you those things," she said. "We're going down there again tonight when that janitor is asleep. If he's ever asleep."

I got worried then.

"Honey, cut it out," I said. "You'll get me going too."

"Good," she said. "*Good*. I thought it would take a hurricane."

I sat staring at my typewriter all afternoon, nothing coming out.

But concern.

I didn't get it. Was she actually serious? All right, I thought, I'll take it straight. She saw a door that was left open. Accidentally. That was obvious. If there were really huge engines under the apartment house as she said, then the people who built them darn sure wouldn't want anyone to know about them.

East 7th Street. An apartment house. And huge engines underneath it.

True?

"The janitor has three eyes!"

She was shaking. Her face was white. She stared at me like a kid who'd read her first horror story.

"Honey," I said. I put my arms around her. She was scared. I felt sort of scared myself. And not that the janitor had an extra eye either.

I didn't say anything at first. What can you say when your wife comes up with something like that?

She shook a long time. Then she spoke, in a quiet voice, a timid voice.

"I know," she said. "You don't believe me."

I swallowed. "Babe," I said helplessly.

"We're going down tonight," she said. "This is something important now. It's serious."

"I don't think we should . . ." I started.

"I'm going down there," she said. She sounded edgy now, a little hysterical. "I tell you there are engines down there. God-damn it, there are engines!"

She started crying now, shaking badly. I patted her head, rested it against my shoulder. "All right, baby," I said. "All right."

She tried to tell me through her tears. But it didn't work. Later when she'd calmed down, I listened. I didn't want to get her upset. I figured the safest way was just to listen.

"I was walking through the hall downstairs," she said. "I thought maybe there was some afternoon mail. You know once in a while the mailman will . . ."

She stopped. "Never mind that. What matters is what hap-pened when I walked past the janitor."

"What?" I said, afraid of what was coming.

"He smiled," she said. "You know the way he does. Sweet and murderous."

I let it go. I didn't argue the point. I still didn't think the jan-itor was anything but a harmless guy who had the misfortune to be born with a face that was strictly from Charles Addams.

"So?" I said. "Then what?"

"I walked past him. I felt myself shiver. Because he looked at me as if he knew something about me I didn't even know. I don't care what you say—that's the feeling I got. And then . . ."

She shuddered. I took her hand.

"Then?" I said.

"I felt him looking at me."

I'd felt that too when he found us in the basement. I knew what she meant. You just knew the guy was looking at you.

"All right," I said. "I'll buy that."

"You won't buy this," she said grimly. She sat stiffly a mo-ment, then said, "When I turned around to look he was walk-ing away from me."

I could feel it on the way. "I don't . . ." I started weakly.

"His head was turned but he was looking at me."

I swallowed. I sat there numbly, patting her hand without even knowing I was doing it.

"How, hon?" I heard myself asking.

"There was an eye in the back of his head."

"*Hon*," I said. I looked at her in—let's face it—fright. A mind on the loose can get awfully confused.

She closed her eyes. She clasped her hands after drawing away the one I was holding. She pressed her lips together. I saw a tear wriggle out from under her left eyelid and roll down her cheek. She was white.

"I saw it," she said quietly. "So help me God, I saw that eye."

I don't know why I went on with it. Self torture, I guess. I really wanted to forget the whole thing, pretend it never even happened.

"Why haven't we seen it before, Ruth?" I asked. "We've seen the back of the man's head before."

"Have we?" she said. "Have we?"

"Sweetheart, *somebody* must have seen it. Do you think there's never been anyone behind him?"

"His hair parted, Rick," she said, "and before I ran away I saw the hair going back over it, so you couldn't see it."

I sat there silently. What to say now?—I thought. What could a guy possibly say to his wife when she talks to him like that? You're nuts? You're loony? Or the old, tired, "You've been working too hard." She hadn't been working too hard.

Then again maybe she *had* been working overtime. With her imagination.

"Are you going down with me tonight?" she asked.

"All right," I said quietly. "All right, sweetheart. Now will you go and lie down?"

"I'm all right."

"Sweetheart, go and lie down," I said firmly. "I'll go with you tonight. But I want you to lie down now."

She got up. She went into the bedroom and I heard the bedsprings squeak as she sat down, then drew up her legs and fell back on the pillow.

I went in a little later to put a comforter over her. She was looking at the ceiling. I didn't say anything to her. I don't think she wanted to talk to me.

"What can I do?" I said to Phil.

Ruth was asleep. I'd sneaked across the hall.

"Maybe she saw them?" he said. "Isn't it possible?"

"Yeah, sure," I said. "And you know what else is possible too."

"Look, you want to go down and see the janitor. You want to . . ."

"No," I said. "There's nothing we can do."

"You're going down to the basement with her?"

"If she keeps insisting," I said. "Otherwise, no."

"Look," he said. "When you go, come and get us."

I looked at him curiously. "You mean the thing is getting to you, too?" I said.

He looked at me in a funny way. I saw his throat move.

"Don't . . . look, don't tell anyone," he said.

He looked around, then turned back.

"Marge told me the same thing," he said. "She said the janitor has three eyes."

I went down after supper for some ice cream. Johnson was walking around.

"They're working you overtime," I said as he started to walk beside me.

"They expect some trouble from the local gangs," he said.

"I never saw any gangs," I said distractedly.

"They're here," he said.

"Mmmm."

"How's your wife?"

"Fine," I lied.

"She still think the apartment house is a front?" he laughed.

I swallowed. "No," I said. "I've broken her of that. I think she was just kidding me all the time."

He nodded and left me at the corner. And for some reason I couldn't keep my hands from shaking all the way home. I kept looking over my shoulder too.

"It's time," Ruth said.

I grunted and rolled on my side. She nudged me. I woke up sort of hazy and looked automatically at the clock. The radium numbers told me it was almost four o'clock.

"You want to go *now*?" I asked, too sleepy to be tactful.

There was a pause. That woke me up.

"I'm going," she said quietly.

I sat up. I looked at her in the half darkness, my heart starting to do a drum beat too heavily. My mouth and throat felt dry.

"All right," I said. "Wait till I get dressed."

She was already dressed. I heard her in the kitchen making some coffee while I put on my clothes. There was no noise. I mean it didn't sound as if her hands were shaking. She spoke lucidly too. But when I stared into the bathroom mirror I saw a worried husband. I splashed cold water in my face and combed my hair.

"Thanks," I said as she handed me the cup of coffee. I stood there, nervous before my own wife.

She didn't drink any coffee. "Are you awake?" she asked. I nodded. I noticed the flashlight and the screwdriver on the kitchen table. I finished the coffee.

"All right," I said. "Let's get it over with."

I felt her hand on my arm.

"I hope you'll . . ." she started. Then turned her face.

"What?"

"Nothing," she said. "We'd better go."

The house was dead quiet as we went into the hall. We were halfway to the elevator when I remembered Phil and Marge. I told her.

"We can't wait," she said. "It'll be light soon."

"Just wait and see if they're up," I said.

She didn't say anything. She stood by the elevator door while I went down the hall and knocked quietly on the door of their apartment. There was no answer. I glanced up the hall.

She was gone.

I felt my heart lurch. Even though I was sure there was no danger in the basement, it scared me. "Ruth," I muttered and headed for the stairs.

"Wait a second!" I heard Phil call loudly from his door.

"I can't!" I called back, charging down.

When I got to the basement I saw the open elevator door and light streaming from the inside. Empty.

I looked around for a light switch but there wasn't any. I started to move along the dark passage as fast as I could.

"Hon!" I whispered urgently. "Ruth, where are you?"

I found her standing before a doorway in the wall. It was open.

"Now stop acting as if I were insane," she said coldly.

I gaped and felt a hand pressing against my cheek. It was my own. She was right. There were stairs. And it was lighted down there. I heard sounds. Sounds of metallic clickings and strange buzzings.

I took her hand. "I'm sorry," I said. "I'm sorry."

Her hand tightened in mine. "All right," she said. "Never mind that now. There's something flukey about all this."

I nodded. Then I said, "Yeah," realizing she couldn't see my nod in the darkness.

"Let's go down," she said.

"I don't think we better," I said.

"We've got to know," she said as if the entire problem had been assigned to us.

"But there must be someone down there," I said.

"We'll just peek," she said.

She pulled me. And I guess I felt too ashamed of myself to pull back. We started down. Then it came to me. If she was right about the doorway in the walls and the engines, she must be right about the janitor and he must really have . . .

I felt a little detached from reality. East 7th Street, I told myself again. An apartment house on East 7th Street. It's all real.

I couldn't quite convince myself.

We stopped at the bottom. And I just stared. Engines, all right. Fantastic engines. And, as I looked at them it came to me what kind of engines they were. I'd read about science too, the non-fiction kind.

I felt dizzy. You can't adapt quick to something like that. To be plunged from a brick apartment house into this . . . this storehouse of energy. It got me.

I don't know how long we were there. But suddenly I realized we had to get out of there, report this thing.

"Come on," I said. We moved up the steps, my mind working like an engine itself. Spinning out ideas, fast and furious. All of them crazy—all of them acceptable. Even the craziest one.

It was when we were moving down the basement hall we saw the janitor coming at us.

It was dark still, even with a little light coming from the early morning haze. I grabbed Ruth and we ducked behind a stone pillar. We stood holding our breaths, listening to the thud of his approaching shoes.

He passed us. He was holding a flashlight but he didn't play the beam around. He just moved straight for the open door.

Then it happened.

As he came into the patch of light from the open doorway he stopped. His head was turned away. The guy was facing the stairway.

But he was looking at us.

It knocked out what little breath I had left. I just stood there and stared at that eye in the back of his head. And, although there wasn't any face around it, that damned eye had a smile going with it. A nasty, self-certain and frightening smile. He saw us and he was amused and wasn't going to do anything about it.

He went through the doorway and the door thudded shut behind him, the stone wall segment slid down and shut it from view.

We stood there shivering.

"You saw it," she finally said.

"Yes."

"He knows we saw those engines," she said. "Still he didn't do anything."

We were still talking as the elevator ascended.

"Maybe there's nothing really wrong," I said. "Maybe . . ."

I stopped, remembering those engines. I knew what kind they were.

"What shall we do?" she asked. I looked at her. She was scared. I put my arm around her. But I was scared too.

"We'd better get out," I said. "Fast."

"We have nothing packed though," she said.

"We'll pack then," I said. "We'll leave before morning. I don't think they can do . . ."

"They?"

Why did I say that?—I wondered. They. It had to be a group though. The janitor didn't make those engines all by himself.

I think it was the third eye that capped my theory. And when we stopped to see Phil and Marge and they asked us what happened I told them what I thought. I don't think it surprised Ruth much. She undoubtedly thought it herself.

"I think the house is a rocket ship," I said.

They stared at me. Phil grinned; then he stopped when he saw I wasn't kidding.

"What?" Marge said.

"I know it sounds crazy," I said, sounding more like my wife than she did. "But those are rocket engines. I don't know how in the hell they got there but . . ." I shrugged helplessly at the whole idea.

"All I know is that they're rocket engines."

"That doesn't mean it's a . . . a ship?" Phil finished weakly, switching from statement to question in mid-sentence.

"Yes," said Ruth.

And I shuddered. That seemed to settle it. She'd been right too often lately.

"But . . ." Marge shrugged. "What's the point?"

Ruth looked at us. "I know," she said.

"What, baby?" I asked, afraid to be asking.

"That janitor," she said. "He's not a man. We know that. That third eye makes it . . ."

"You mean the guy *has* one?" Phil asked incredulously.

I nodded. "He has one. I saw it."

"Oh my God," he said.

"But he's not a man," Ruth said again. "Humanoid, yes, but not an earthling. He might look like he does actually—except for the eye. But he might be completely different, so different he had to change his form. Give himself that extra eye just to keep track of us when we wouldn't expect it."

Phil ran a shaking hand through his hair.

"This is crazy," he said.

He sank down into a chair. So did the girls. I didn't. I felt uneasy about sticking around. I thought we should grab our hats and run. They didn't seem to feel in immediate danger though. I finally decided it wouldn't hurt to wait until morning. Then I'd tell Johnson or something. Nothing could happen now.

"This is crazy," Phil said again.

"I saw those engines," I said. "They're really there. You can't get away from it."

"Listen," Ruth said, "they're probably extraterrestrials."

"What are you talking about?" Marge asked irritably. She was good and afraid, I saw.

"Hon," I contributed weakly, "you've been reading an awful lot of science-fiction magazines."

Her lips drew together. "Don't start in again," she said. "You thought I was crazy when I suspected this place. You thought so when I told you I saw those engines. You thought so when I told you the janitor had three eyes. Well, I was right all three times. Now, give me some credit."

I shut up. And she went on.

"What if they're from another planet," she rephrased for Marge's benefit. "Suppose they want some Earth people to experiment on. To *observe*," she amended quickly, I don't know for whose benefit. The idea of being experimented on by three-eyed janitors from another planet had nothing exciting about it.

"What better way," Ruth was saying, "of getting people than to build a rocket ship apartment house, rent it out cheap and get it full of people fast?"

She looked at us without yielding an inch.

"And then," she said, "just wait till some morning early when everybody was asleep and . . . goodbye Earth."

My head was whirling. It was crazy but what could I say? I'd been cleverly dubious three times. I couldn't afford to doubt now. It wasn't worth the risk. And, in my flesh, I sort of felt she was right.

"But the whole house," Phil was saying. "How could they get it . . . in the air?"

"If they're from another planet they're probably centuries ahead of us in space travel."

Phil started to answer. He faltered, then he said, "But it doesn't *look* like a ship."

"The house might be a shell over the ship," I said. "It probably is. Maybe the actual ship includes only the bedrooms.

That's all they'd need. That's where everybody would be in the early morning hours if . . ."

"No," Ruth said. "They couldn't knock off the shell without attracting much attention."

We were all silent laboring under a thick cloud of confusion and half-formed fears. Half formed because you can't shape your fears of something when you don't even know what it is.

"Listen," Ruth said.

It made me shudder. It made me want to tell her to shut up with her horrible forebodings. Because they made too much sense.

"Suppose it *is* a building," she said. "Suppose the ship is *outside* of it."

"But . . ." Marge was practically lost. She got angry because she was lost. "There's nothing outside the house, that's obvious!"

"Those people would be way ahead of us in science," Ruth said. "Maybe they've mastered invisibility of matter."

We all squirmed at once, I think. "Babe," I said.

"Is it possible?" Ruth asked strongly.

I sighed. "It's possible. *Just* possible."

We were quiet. Then Ruth said, "Listen."

"No," I cut in. "You listen. I think maybe we're going overboard on this thing. But there *are* engines in the basement and the janitor *does* have three eyes. On the basis of that I think we have reason enough to clear out. Now."

We all agreed on that anyways.

"We'd better tell everybody in the building," Ruth said. "We can't leave them here."

"It'll take too long," Marge argued.

"No, we have to," I said. "You pack, babe, I'll tell them."

I headed for the door and grabbed the knob.

Which didn't turn.

A bolt of panic drove through me. I grabbed at it and yanked hard. I thought for a second, fighting down fear, that it was locked on the inside. I checked.

It was locked on the outside.

"What is it?" Marge said in a shaking voice. You could sense a scream bubbling up in her.

"Locked," I said.

Marge gasped. We all stared at each other.

"It's true," Ruth said, horrified. "Oh, my God, it's all true then."

I made a dash for the window. Then the place started to vibrate as if we were being hit by an earthquake. Dishes started to rattle and fall off shelves. We heard a chair crash onto its side in the kitchen.

"What is it!" Marge cried again. Phil grabbed for her as she started to whimper. Ruth ran to me and we stood there, frozen, feeling the floor rock under our feet.

"The engines!" Ruth suddenly cried. "They're starting them!"

"They have to warm up!" I made a wild guess. "We can still get out!"

I let go of Ruth and grabbed a chair. For some reason I felt that the windows had been automatically locked too.

I hurled the chair through the glass. The vibrations were getting worse.

"Quick!" I shouted over the noise. "Out the fire escape! Maybe we can make it!"

Impelled by panic and dread, Marge and Phil came running over the shaking floor. I almost shoved them out through the gaping window hole. Marge tore her skirt. Ruth cut her fingers. I went last, dragging a glass dagger through my leg. I didn't even feel it I was so keyed up.

I kept pushing them, hurrying down the fire escape steps. Marge caught a slipper heel in between two gratings and it snapped off. Her slipper came off. She limped, half fell down the orange-painted metal steps, her face white and twisted with fear. Ruth in her loafers clattered down behind Phil. I came last, shepherding them frantically.

We saw other people at their windows. We heard windows crashing above and below. We saw an older couple crawl hurriedly through their window and start down. They held us up.

"Look out, will you!" Marge shouted at them in a fury.

They cast a frightened look over their shoulders.

Ruth looked back at me, her face drained of color. "Are you coming?" she asked quickly, her voice shaking.

"I'm here," I said breathlessly. I felt as if I were going to collapse on the steps. Which seemed to go on forever.

At the bottom was a ladder. We saw the old lady drop from it with a sickening thud, crying out in pain as her ankle twisted under her. Her husband dropped down and helped her up. The building was vibrating harshly now. We saw dust scaling out from between the bricks.

My voice joined the throng, all crying the same word, *"Hurry!"*

I saw Phil drop down. He half caught Marge, who was sobbing in fright. I heard her half-articulate "Oh, thank God!" as she landed and they started up the alleyway. Phil looked back over his shoulder at us but Marge dragged him on.

"Let me go first!" I snapped quickly. Ruth stepped aside and I swung down the ladder and dropped, feeling a sting in my insteps, a slight pain in my ankles. I looked up, extending my arms for her.

A man behind Ruth was trying to shove her aside so he could jump down.

"Look out!" I yelled like a raging animal, reduced suddenly by fear and concern. If I'd had a gun I'd have shot him.

Ruth let the man drop. He scrambled to his feet, breathing feverishly and ran down the alley. The building was shaking and quivering. The air was filled with the roar of the engines now.

"Ruth!" I yelled.

She dropped and I caught her. We regained our balance and started up the alley. I could hardly breathe. I had a stitch in my side.

As we dashed into the street we saw Johnson moving through the ranks of scattered people trying to herd them together.

"Here now!" he was calling. "Take it easy!"

We ran up to him. "Johnson!" I said. "The ship, it's . . ."

"Ship?" He looked incredulous.

"The house! It's a rocket ship! It's . . ." The ground shook wildly.

Johnson turned away to grab someone running past. My

breath caught and Ruth gasped, throwing her hands to her cheeks.

Johnson was still looking at us; with that third eye. The one that had a smile with it.

"No," Ruth said shakily. "No."

And then the sky, which was growing light, grew dark. My head snapped around. Women were screaming their lungs out in terror. I looked in all directions.

Solid walls were blotting out the sky.

"Oh my God," Ruth said. "We can't get out. *It's the whole block.*"

Then the rockets started.

BLOOD SON

The people on the block decided definitely that Jules was crazy when they heard about his composition.

There had been suspicions for a long time.

He made people shiver with his blank stare. His coarse guttural tongue sounded unnatural in his frail body. The paleness of his skin upset many children. It seemed to hang loose around his flesh. He hated sunlight.

And his ideas were a little out of place for the people who lived on the block.

Jules wanted to be a vampire.

People declared it common knowledge that he was born on a night when winds uprooted trees. They said he was born with three teeth. They said he'd used them to fasten himself on his mother's breast drawing blood with the milk.

They said he used to cackle and bark in his crib after dark. They said he walked at two months and sat staring at the moon whenever it shone.

Those were things that people said.

His parents were always worried about him. An only child, they noticed his flaws quickly.

They thought he was blind until the doctor told them it was just a vacuous stare. He told them that Jules, with his large head, might be a genius or an idiot. It turned out he was an idiot.

He never spoke a word until he was five. Then, one night coming up to supper, he sat down at the table and said "Death."

His parents were torn between delight and disgust. They finally settled for a place in between the two feelings. They decided that Jules couldn't have realized what the word meant.

But Jules did.

From that night on, he built up such a large vocabulary that everyone who knew him was astonished. He not only acquired every word spoken to him, words from signs, magazines, books; he made up his own words.

Like—*nightouch*. Or—*killove*. They were really several words that melted into each other. They said things Jules felt but couldn't explain with other words.

He used to sit on the porch while the other children played hopscotch, stickball and other games. He sat there and stared at the sidewalk and made up words.

Until he was twelve Jules kept pretty much out of trouble.

Of course there was the time they found him undressing Olive Jones in an alley. And another time he was discovered dissecting a kitten on his bed.

But there were many years in between. Those scandals were forgotten.

In general he went through childhood merely disgusting people.

He went to school but never studied. He spent about two or three terms in each grade. The teachers all knew him by his first name. In some subjects like reading and writing he was almost brilliant.

In others he was hopeless.

One Saturday when he was twelve, Jules went to the movies. He saw *Dracula*.

When the show was over he walked, a throbbing nerve mass, through the little girl and boy ranks.

He went home and locked himself in the bathroom for two hours.

His parents pounded on the door and threatened but he wouldn't come out.

Finally he unlocked the door and sat down at the supper table. He had a bandage on his thumb and a satisfied look on his face.

The morning after he went to the library. It was Sunday. He sat on the steps all day waiting for it to open. Finally he went home.

The next morning he came back instead of going to school.

He found *Dracula* on the shelves. He couldn't borrow it because he wasn't a member and to be a member he had to bring in one of his parents.

So he stuck the book down his pants and left the library and never brought it back.

He went to the park and sat down and read the book through. It was late evening before he finished.

He started at the beginning again, reading as he ran from street light to street light, all the way home.

He didn't hear a word of the scolding he got for missing lunch and supper. He ate, went in his room and read the book to the finish. They asked him where he got the book. He said he found it.

As the days passed Jules read the story over and over. He never went to school.

Late at night, when he had fallen into an exhausted slumber, his mother used to take the book into the living room and show it to her husband.

One night they noticed that Jules had underlined certain sentences with dark shaky pencil lines.

Like: "The lips were crimson with fresh blood and the stream had trickled over her chin and stained the purity of her lawn death robe."

Or: "When the blood began to spurt out, he took my hands in one of his, holding them tight and, with the other seized my neck and pressed my mouth to the wound . . ."

When his mother saw this, she threw the book down the garbage chute.

In the next morning when Jules found the book missing he screamed and twisted his mother's arm until she told him where the book was.

Then he ran down to the cellar and dug in the piles of garbage until he found the book.

Coffee grounds and egg yolk on his hands and wrists, he went to the park and read it again.

For a month he read the book avidly. Then he knew it so well he threw it away and just thought about it.

Absence notes were coming from school. His mother yelled. Jules decided to go back for a while.

He wanted to write a composition.

One day he wrote it in class. When everyone was finished writing, the teacher asked if anyone wanted to read their composition to the class.

Jules raised his hand.

The teacher was surprised. But she felt charity. She wanted to encourage him. She drew in her tiny jab of a chin and smiled.

"All right," she said. "Pay attention children. Jules is going to read us his composition."

Jules stood up. He was excited. The paper shook in his hands.

"My Ambition by . . ."

"Come to the front of the class, Jules, dear."

Jules went to the front of the class. The teacher smiled lovingly. Jules started again.

"My Ambition by Jules Dracula."

The smile sagged.

"When I grow up I want to be a vampire."

The teacher's smiling lips jerked down and out. Her eyes popped wide.

"I want to live forever and get even with everybody and make all the girls vampires. I want to smell of death."

"Jules!"

"I want to have a foul breath that stinks of dead earth and crypts and sweet coffins."

The teacher shuddered. Her hands twitched on her green blotter. She couldn't believe her ears. She looked at the children. They were gaping. Some of them were giggling. But not the girls.

"I want to be all cold and have rotten flesh with stolen blood in the veins."

"That will . . . hrrumph!"

The teacher cleared her throat mightily.

"That will be all Jules," she said.

Jules talked louder and desperately.

"I want to sink my terrible white teeth in my victim's necks. I want them to . . ."

"Jules! Go to your seat this instant!"

"I want them to slide like razors in the flesh and into the veins," read Jules ferociously.

The teacher jolted to her feet. Children were shivering. None of them were giggling.

"Then I want to draw my teeth out and let the blood flow easy in my mouth and run hot in my throat and . . ."

The teacher grabbed his arm. Jules tore away and ran to a corner. Barricaded behind a stool he yelled:

"And drip off my tongue and run out my lips down my victim's throats! I want to drink girls' blood!"

The teacher lunged for him. She dragged him out of the corner. He clawed at her and screamed all the way to the door and the principal's office.

"That is my ambition! That is my ambition! *That is my ambition!*"

It was grim.

Jules was locked in his room. The teacher and the principal sat with Jules's parents. They were talking in sepulchral voices.

They were recounting the scene.

All along the block parents were discussing it. Most of them didn't believe it at first. They thought their children made it up.

Then they thought what horrible children they'd raised if the children could make up such things.

So they believed it.

After that, everyone watched Jules like a hawk. People avoided his touch and look. Parents pulled their children off the street when he approached. Everyone whispered tales of him.

There were more absence notes.

Jules told his mother he wasn't going to school anymore. Nothing would change his mind. He never went again.

When a truant officer came to the apartment Jules would run over the roofs until he was far away from there.

A year wasted by.

Jules wandered the streets searching for something; he didn't know what. He looked in alleys. He looked in garbage cans. He looked in lots. He looked on the east side and the west side and in the middle.

He couldn't find what he wanted.

He rarely slept. He never spoke. He stared down all the time. He forgot his special words.

Then.

One day in the park, Jules strolled through the zoo.

An electric shock passed through him when he saw the vampire bat.

His eyes grew wide and his discolored teeth shone dully in a wide smile.

From that day on, Jules went daily to the zoo and looked at the bat. He spoke to it and called it the Count. He felt in his heart it was really a man who had changed.

A rebirth of culture struck him.

He stole another book from the library. It told all about wildlife.

He found the page on the vampire bat. He tore it out and threw the book away.

He learned the selection by heart.

He knew how the bat made its wound. How it lapped up the blood like a kitten drinking cream. How it walked on folded wing stalks and hind legs like a black furry spider. Why it took no nourishment but blood.

Month after month Jules stared at the bat and talked to it. It became the one comfort in his life. The one symbol of dreams come true.

One day Jules noticed that the bottom of the wire covering the cage had come loose.

He looked around, his black eyes shifting. He didn't see anyone looking. It was a cloudy day. Not many people were there.

Jules tugged at the wire.

It moved a little.

Then he saw a man come out of the monkey house. So he

pulled back his hand and strolled away whistling a song he had just made up.

Late at night, when he was supposed to be asleep he would walk barefoot past his parents' room. He would hear his father and mother snoring. He would hurry out, put on his shoes and run to the zoo.

Every time the watchman was not around, Jules would tug at the wiring.

He kept on pulling it loose.

When he was finished and had to run home, he pushed the wire in again. Then no one could tell.

All day Jules would stand in front of the cage and look at the Count and chuckle and tell him he'd soon be free again.

He told the Count all the things he knew. He told the Count he was going to practice climbing down walls head first.

He told the Count not to worry. He'd soon be out. Then, together, they could go all around and drink girls' blood.

One night Jules pulled the wire out and crawled under it into the cage.

It was very dark.

He crept on his knees to the little wooden house. He listened to see if he could hear the Count squeaking.

He stuck his arm in the black doorway. He kept whispering. He jumped when he felt a needle jab in his finger.

With a look of great pleasure on his thin face, Jules drew the fluttering hairy bat to him.

He climbed down from the cage with it and ran out of the zoo; out of the park. He ran down the silent streets.

It was getting late in the morning. Light touched the dark skies with gray. He couldn't go home. He had to have a place.

He went down an alley and climbed over a fence. He held tight to the bat. It lapped at the dribble of blood from his finger.

He went across a yard and into a little deserted shack.

It was dark inside and damp. It was full of rubble and tin cans and soggy cardboard and excrement.

Jules made sure there was no way the bat could escape.

Then he pulled the door tight and put a stick through the metal loop.

He felt his heart beating hard and his limbs trembling. He let go of the bat. It flew to a dark corner and hung on the wood.

Jules feverishly tore off his shirt. His lips shook. He smiled a crazy smile.

He reached down into his pants pocket and took out a little pen knife he had stolen from his mother.

He opened it and ran a finger over the blade. It sliced through the flesh.

With shaking fingers he jabbed at his throat. He hacked. The blood ran through his fingers.

"Count! Count!" he cried in frenzied joy. "Drink my red blood! Drink me! Drink me!"

He stumbled over the tin cans and slipped and felt for the bat. It sprang from the wood and soared across the shack and fastened itself on the other side.

Tears ran down Jules's cheeks.

He gritted his teeth. The blood ran across his shoulders and across his thin hairless chest.

His body shook in fever. He staggered back toward the other side. He tripped and felt his side torn open on the sharp edge of a tin can.

His hands went out. They clutched the bat. He placed it against his throat. He sank on his back on the cool wet earth. He sighed.

He started to moan and clutch at his chest. His stomach heaved. The black bat on his neck silently lapped his blood.

Jules felt his life seeping away.

He thought of all the years past. The waiting. His parents. School. Dracula. Dreams. For this. This sudden glory.

Jules's eyes flickered open.

The inside of the reeking shack swam about him.

It was hard to breathe. He opened his mouth to gasp in the air. He sucked it in. It was foul. It made him cough. His skinny body lurched on the cold ground.

Mists crept away in his brain.

One by one like drawn veils.

Suddenly his mind was filled with terrible clarity.

He felt the aching pain in his side.

He knew he was lying half naked on garbage and letting a flying bat drink his blood.

With a strangled cry, he reached up and tore away the furry throbbing bat. He flung it away from him. It came back, fanning his face with its vibrating wings.

Jules staggered to his feet.

He felt for the door. He could hardly see. He tried to stop his throat from bleeding so.

He managed to get the door open.

Then, lurching into the dark yard, he fell on his face in the long grass blades.

He tried to call out for help.

But no sounds save a bubbling mockery of words came from his lips.

He heard the fluttering wings.

Then, suddenly they were gone.

Strong fingers lifted him gently. Through dying eyes Jules saw the tall dark man whose eyes shone like rubies.

"My son," the man said.

WHERE THERE'S A WILL

Written with Richard Christian Matheson

He awoke.

It was dark and cold. Silent.

I'm thirsty, he thought. He yawned and sat up; fell back with a cry of pain. He'd hit his head on something. He rubbed at the pulsing tissue of his brow, feeling the ache spread back to his hairline.

Slowly, he began to sit up again but hit his head once more. He was jammed between the mattress and something over-head. He raised his hands to feel it. It was soft and pliable, its texture yielding beneath the push of his fingers. He felt along its surface. It extended as far as he could reach. He swallowed anxiously and shivered.

What in God's name was it?

He began to roll to his left and stopped with a gasp. The sur-face was blocking him there, as well. He reached to his right and his heart beat faster. It was on the other side, as well. He was surrounded on four sides. His heart compressed like a smashed soft-drink can, the blood spurting a hundred times faster.

Within seconds, he sensed that he was dressed. He felt trou-sers, a coat, a shirt and tie, a belt. There were shoes on his feet.

He slid his right hand to his trouser pocket and reached in. He palmed a cold, metal square and pulled his hand from the pocket, bringing it to his face. Fingers trembling, he hinged the top open and spun the wheel with his thumb. A few sparks glinted but no flame. Another turn and it lit.

He looked down at the orange cast of his body and shivered again. In the light of the flame, he could see all around himself.

He wanted to scream at what he saw.

He was in a casket.

He dropped the lighter and the flame striped the air with a yellow tracer before going out. He was in total darkness, once more. He could see nothing. All he heard was his terrified breathing as it lurched forward, jumping from his throat.

How long had he been here? Minutes? Hours? Days?

His hopes lunged at the possibility of a nightmare; that he was only dreaming, his sleeping mind caught in some kind of twisted vision. But he knew it wasn't so. He knew, horribly enough, exactly what had happened.

They had put him in the one place he was terrified of. The one place he had made the fatal mistake of speaking about to them. They couldn't have selected a better torture. Not if they'd thought about it for a hundred years.

God, did they loathe him that much? To do *this* to him.

He started shaking helplessly, then caught himself. He wouldn't let them do it. Take his life and his business all at once? No, goddamn them, *no!*

He searched hurriedly for the lighter. That was their mistake, he thought. Stupid bastards. They'd probably thought it was a final, fitting irony: A gold-engraved thank you for making the corporation what it was. On the lighter were the words: *To Charlie/Where there's a Will* . . .

"Right," he muttered. He'd beat the lousy sons of bitches. They weren't going to murder him and steal the business he owned and built. There *was* a will.

His.

He closed his fingers around the lighter and, holding it with a white-knuckled fist, lifted it above the heaving of his chest. The wheel ground against the flint as he spun it back with his thumb. The flame caught and he quieted his breathing as he surveyed what space he had in the coffin.

Only inches on all four sides.

How much air could there be in so small a space, he wondered? He clicked off the lighter. Don't burn it up, he told himself. Work in the dark.

Immediately, his hands shot up and he tried to push the lid up. He pressed as hard as he could, his forearms straining. The lid remained fixed. He closed both hands into tightly balled fists and pounded them against the lid until he was coated with perspiration, his hair moist.

He reached down to his left-trouser pocket and pulled out a chain with two keys attached. They had placed those with him, too. *Stupid bastards*. Did they really think he'd be so terrified he couldn't *think*? Another amusing joke on their part. A way to lock up his life completely. He wouldn't need the keys to his car and to the office again so why not put them in the casket with him?

Wrong, he thought. He *would* use them again.

Bringing the keys above his face, he began to pick at the lining with the sharp edge of one key. He tore through the threads and began to rip apart the lining. He pulled at it with the fingers until it popped free from its fastenings. Working quickly, he pulled at the downy stuffing, tugging it free and placing it at his sides. He tried not to breathe too hard. The air had to be preserved.

He flicked on the lighter and looking at the cleared area, above, knocked against it with the knuckles of his free hand. He sighed with relief. It was oak not metal. Another mistake on their part. He smiled with contempt. It was easy to see why he had always been so far ahead of them.

"Stupid bastards," he muttered, as he stared at the thick wood. Gripping the keys together firmly, he began to dig their serrated edges against the oak. The flame of the lighter shook as he watched small pieces of the lid being chewed off by the gouging of the keys. Fragment after fragment fell. The lighter kept going out and he had to spin the flint over and over, repeating each move, until his hands felt numb. Fearing that he would use up the air, he turned the light off again, and continued to chisel at the wood, splinters of it falling on his neck and chin.

His arm began to ache.

He was losing strength. Wood no longer coming off as steadily. He laid the keys on his chest and flicked on the lighter again. He could see only a tattered path of wood where he had dug but it was only inches long. It's not enough, he thought. It's not enough.

He slumped and took a deep breath, stopping halfway through. The air was thinning. He reached up and pounded against the lid.

"Open this thing, goddammit," he shouted, the veins in his neck rising beneath the skin. *"Open this thing and let me out!"*

I'll die if I don't do something more, he thought.

They'll win.

His face began to tighten. He had never given up before. Never. And they weren't going to win. There was no way to stop him once he made up his mind.

He'd show those bastards what willpower was.

Quickly, he took the lighter in his right hand and turned the wheel several times. The flame rose like a streamer, fluttering back and forth before his eyes. Steadying his left arm with his right, he held the flame to the casket wood and began to scorch the ripped grain.

He breathed in short, shallow breaths, smelling the butane and wool odor as it filled the casket. The lid started to speckle with tiny sparks as he ran the flame along the gouge. He held it to one spot for several moments then slid it to another spot. The wood made faint crackling sounds.

Suddenly, a flame formed on the surface of the wood. He coughed as the burning oak began to produce grey pulpy smoke. The air in the casket continued to thin and he felt his lungs working harder. What air was available tasted like gummy smoke, as if he were lying in a horizontal smokestack. He felt as though he might faint and his body began to lose feeling.

Desperately, he struggled to remove his shirt, ripping several of the buttons off. He tore away part of the shirt and wrapped it around his right hand and wrist. A section of the lid was beginning to char and had become brittle. He slammed his swathed fist and forearm against the smoking wood and it crumbled down on him, glowing embers falling on his face and neck. His arms scrambled frantically to slap them out. Several burned his chest and palms and he cried out in pain.

Now a portion of the lid had become a glowing skeleton of wood, the heating radiating downward at his face. He squirmed away from it, turning his head to avoid the falling pieces of wood. The casket was filled with smoke and he could breathe only the choking, burning smell of it. He coughed his throat hot and raw. Fine-powder ash filled his mouth and nose and he pounded at the lid with his wrapped fist. Come on, he thought. Come on.

"Come on!" he screamed.

The section of lid gave suddenly and fell around him. He slapped at his face, neck and chest but the hot particles sizzled on his skin and he had to bear the pain as he tried to smother them.

The embers began to darken, one by one and now he smelled something new and strange. He searched for the lighter at his side, found it, and flicked it on.

He shuddered at what he saw.

Moist, root laden soil packed firmly overhead.

Reaching up, he ran his fingers across it. In the flickering light, he saw burrowing insects and the whiteness of earthworms, dangling inches from his face. He drew down as far as he could, pulling his face from their wriggling movements.

Unexpectedly, one of the larva pulled free and dropped. It fell to his face and its jelly-like casing stuck to his upper lip. His mind erupted with revulsion and he thrust both hands upward, digging at the soil. He shook his head wildly as the larva were thrown off. He continued to dig, the dirt falling in on him. It poured into his nose and he could barely breathe. It stuck to his lips and slipped into his mouth. He closed his eyes tightly but he could feel it clumping on the lids. He held his breath as he pistoned his hands upward and forward like a maniacal digging machine. He eased his body up, a little at a time, letting the dirt collect under him. His lungs were laboring, hungry for air. He didn't dare open his eyes. His fingers became raw from digging, nails bent backward on several fingers, breaking off. He couldn't even feel the pain or the running blood but knew the dirt was being stained by its flow. The pain in his arms and lungs grew worse with each passing second until shearing agony filled his body. He continued to press himself upward, pulling his feet and knees closer to his chest. He began to wrestle himself into a kind of spasmed crouch, hands above his head, upper arms gathered around his face. He clawed fiercely at the dirt which gave way with each shoveling gouge of his fingers. Keep going, he told himself. *Keep going.* He refused to lose control. Refused to stop and die in the earth. He bit down hard, his teeth nearly breaking from the tension of his jaws. *Keep going,* he thought. *Keep going!* He pushed up harder and harder, dirt cascading over his body, gathering in his hair and on his shoulders. Filth surrounded him. His lungs felt ready to burst. It seemed like minutes since he'd taken a breath. He wanted to scream from his need for air but couldn't. His fingernails began to sting and throb, exposed cuticles and nerves rubbing against the granules of dirt. His mouth opened in pain and was filled with dirt, covering his tongue and gathering in his throat. His gag reflex jumped and he began retching, vomit and dirt mixing as it exploded from his mouth. His head began to empty of life as he felt himself breathing in more dirt, dying of asphyxiation. The clogging dirt began to fill his air passages, the beat of his heart doubled. *I'm losing!* he thought in anguish.

Suddenly, one finger thrust up through the crust of earth. Unthinkingly, he moved his hand like a trowel and drove it through to the surface. Now, his arms went crazy, pulling and punching at the dirt until an opening expanded. He kept thrashing at the opening, his entire system glutted with dirt. His chest felt as if it would tear down the middle.

Then his arms were poking themselves out of the grave and within several seconds he had managed to pull his upper body from the ground. He kept pulling, hooking his shredded fingers into the earth and sliding his legs from the hole. They yanked out and he lay on the ground completely, trying to fill his lungs with gulps of air. But no air could get through the dirt which had collected in his windpipe and mouth. He writhed on the ground, turning on his back and side until he'd finally raised himself to a forward kneel and began hacking phlegm-covered mud from his air passages. Black saliva ran down his chin as he continued to throw up violently, dirt falling from his mouth to the ground. When most of it was out he began to gasp, as oxygen rushed into his body, cool air filling his body with life.

I've *won*, he thought. I've beaten the bastards, *beaten* them! He began to laugh in victorious rage until his eyes pried open and he looked around, rubbing at his blood-covered lids. He heard the sound of traffic and blinding lights glared at him. They crisscrossed on his face, rushing at him from left and right. He winced, struck dumb by their glare, then realized where he was.

The cemetery by the highway.

Cars and trucks roared back and forth, tires humming. He breathed a sigh at being near life again; near movement and people. A grunting smile raised his lips.

Looking to his right, he saw a gas-station sign high on a metal pole several hundred yards up the highway.

Struggling to his feet, he ran.

As he did, he made a plan. He would go to the station, wash up in the rest room, then borrow a dime and call for a limo from the company to come and get him. No. Better a cab. That way he could fool those sons of bitches. Catch them by surprise. They undoubtedly assume he was long gone by now. Well, he had beat them. He knew it as he picked up the pace of his run. Nobody could stop you when you really wanted something, he told himself, glancing back in the direction of the grave he had just escaped.

He ran into the station from the back and made his way to the bathroom. He didn't want anyone to see his dirtied, bloodied state.

There was a pay phone in the bathroom and he locked the door before plowing into his pocket for change. He found two pennies and a quarter and deposited the silver coin, they'd even provided him with money, he thought; the stupid bastards.

He dialed his wife.

She answered and screamed when he told her what had happened. She screamed and screamed. What a hideous joke she said. Whoever was doing this was making a hideous joke. She hung up before he could stop her. He dropped the phone and turned to face the bathroom mirror.

He couldn't even scream. He could only stare in silence.

Staring back at him was a face that was missing sections of flesh. Its skin was grey, and withered yellow bone showed through.

The he remembered what else his wife had said and began to weep. His shock began to turn to hopeless fatalism.

It had been over seven months, she'd said.

Seven months.

He looked at himself in the mirror again, and realized there was nowhere he could go.

And, somehow all he could think about was the engraving on his lighter.

DYING ROOM ONLY

The café was a rectangle of brick and wood with an attached shed on the edge of the little town. They drove past it at first and started out into the heat-shimmering desert.

Then Bob said, "Maybe we'd better stop there. Lord knows how far it is to the next one."

"I suppose," Jean said without enthusiasm.

"I know it's probably a joint," Bob said, "but we have to eat something. It's been more than five hours since we had breakfast."

"Oh—all right."

Bob pulled over to the side of the road and looked back. There wasn't another car in sight. He made a quick U-turn and powered the Ford back along the road, then turned in and braked in front of the café.

"Boy, I'm starved," he said.

"So am I," Jean said. "I was starved last night, too, until the waitress brought that food to the table."

Bob shrugged. "So what can we do?" he said. "Is it better we starve and they find our bleached bones in the desert?"

She made a face at him and they got out of the car. "Bleached bones," she said.

The heat fell over them like a waterfall as they stepped into the sun. They hurried toward the café, feeling the burning ground through their sandals.

"It's so hot," Jean said, and Bob grunted.

The screen door made a groaning sound as they pulled it open. Then it slapped shut behind them and they were in the stuffy interior that smelled of grease and hot dust.

The three men in the café looked up at them as they entered. One, in overalls and a dirty cap, sat slumped in a back booth drinking beer. Another sat on a counter stool, a sandwich in his hand and a bottle of beer in front of him. The third man was behind the counter looking at them over a lowered newspaper. He was dressed in a white, short-sleeved shirt and wrinkled white ducks.

"Here we go," Bob whispered to her. "The Ritz-Carlton."

She enunciated slowly, "Ha-ha."

They moved to the counter and sat down on stools. The three men still looked at them.

"Our arrival in town must be an event," Bob said softly.

"We're celebrities," Jean said.

The man in the white ducks came over and drew a menu from behind a tarnished napkin holder. He slid it across the counter toward them. Bob opened it up and the two of them looked at it.

"Have you got any iced tea?" Bob asked.

The man shook his head. They looked at the menu again.

"What have you got that's cold?" Bob asked.

"Hi-Li Orange and Dr. Pepper," said the man in a bored voice.

Bob cleared his throat.

"May we have some water before we order. We've been—"

The man turned away and walked back to the sink. He ran water into two cloudy glasses and brought them back. They spilled over onto the counter as he set them down. Jean picked up her glass and took a sip. She almost choked on the water it was so brackish and warm. She put down the glass.

"Can't you get it any cooler?" she asked.

"This is desert country, ma'am," he said. "We're lucky we get any water at all."

He was a man in his early fifties, his hair steel-gray and dry, parted in the middle. The backs of his hands were covered with tiny swirls of black hair, and on the small finger of his right hand there was a ring with a red stone in it. He stared at them with lifeless eyes and waited for their order.

"I'll have a fried egg sandwich on rye toast and—" Bob started.

"No toast," said the man.

"All right, plain rye then."

"No rye."

Bob looked up. "What kind of bread have you got?" he asked.

"White."

Bob shrugged. "White then. And a strawberry malted. How about you, honey?"

The man's flat gaze moved over to Jean.

"I don't know," she said. She looked up at the man. "I'll decide while you're making my husband's order."

The man looked at her a moment longer, then turned away and walked back to the stove.

"This is awful," Jean said.

"I know, honey," Bob admitted, "but what can we do? We don't know how far it is to the next town."

Jean pushed away the cloudy glass and slid off the stool.

"I'm going to wash up," she said. "Maybe then I'll feel more like eating."

"Good idea," he said.

After a moment, he got off his stool, too, and walked to the front of the café where the two rest rooms were.

His hand was on the door knob when the man eating at the counter called, "Think it's locked, mister."

Bob pushed.

"No it isn't," he said and went in.

Jean came out of the washroom and walked back to her stool at the counter. Bob wasn't there. He must be washing up, too, she thought. The man who had been eating at the counter was gone.

The man in the white ducks left his small gas stove and came over.

"You want to order now?" he asked.

"What? Oh." She picked up the menu and looked at it for a moment. "I'll have the same thing, I guess."

The man went back to the stove and broke another egg on the edge of the black pan. Jean listened to the sound of the eggs frying. She wished Bob would come back. It was unpleasant sitting there alone in the hot, dingy café.

Unconsciously she picked up the glass of water again and took a sip. She grimaced at the taste and put down the glass.

A minute passed. She noticed that the man in the back booth was looking at her. Her throat contracted and the fingers of her right hand began drumming slowly on the counter. She felt her stomach muscles drawing in. Her right hand twitched suddenly as a fly settled on it.

Then she heard the door to the men's washroom open, and she turned quickly with a sense of body-lightening relief.

She shuddered in the hot café.

It wasn't Bob.

She felt her heart throbbing unnaturally as she watched the man return to his place at the counter and pick up his unfinished sandwich. She averted her eyes as he glanced at her. Then, impulsively, she got off the stool and went back to the front of the café.

She pretended to look at a rack of sunfaded postcards, but her eyes kept moving to the brownish-yellow door with the word MEN painted on it.

Another minute passed. She saw that her hands were starting to shake. A long breath trembled her body as she looked in nervous impatience at the door.

She saw the man in the back booth push himself up and plod slowly down the length of the café. His cap was pushed to the back of his head and his high-topped shoes clomped heavily on the floor boards. Jean stood rigidly, holding a postcard in her hands as the man passed her. The washroom door opened and closed behind him.

Silence. Jean stood there staring at the door, trying to hold herself under control. Her throat moved again. She took a deep breath and put the postcard back in place.

"Here's your sandwich," the man at the counter called.

Jean started at the sound of his voice. She nodded once at him but stayed where she was.

Her breath caught as the washroom door opened again. She started forward instinctively, then drew back as the other man walked out, his face florid and sweaty. He started past her.

"Pardon me," she said.

The man kept moving. Jean hurried after him and touched his arm, her fingers twitching at the feel of the hot, damp cloth.

"Excuse me," she said.

The man turned and looked at her with dull eyes. His breath made her stomach turn.

"Did you see my—my husband in there?"

"Huh?"

Her hands closed into fists at her sides.

"Was my husband in the washroom?"

He looked at her a moment as if he didn't understand her. Then he said, "No, ma'am," and turned away.

It was very hot in there, but Jean felt as if she'd suddenly been submerged in a pool of ice water. She stood numbly watching the man stumble back to his booth.

Then she found herself hurrying for the counter, for the man who sat drinking from his water-beaded bottle of beer.

He put down the bottle and turned to face her as she came up.

"Pardon me, but did you see my husband in the washroom before?"

"Your husband?"

She bit her lower lip. "Yes, my husband. You saw him when we came in. Wasn't he in the washroom when you were there?"

"I don't recollect as he was, ma'am."

"You mean you didn't see him in there?"

"I don't recollect seein' him, ma'am."

"Oh this—this is ridiculous," she burst out in angry fright. "He must have been in there."

For a moment they stood looking at each other. The man didn't speak; his face was blank.

"You're—sure?" she asked.

"Ma'am, I got no reason to lie to you."

"All right. Thank you."

She sat stiffly at the counter staring at the two sandwiches and milk shakes, her mind in desperate search of a solution. It was Bob—he was playing a joke on her. But he wasn't in the habit of playing jokes on her and this was certainly no place to start. Yet he must have. There must be another door to the washroom and—

Of course. It wasn't a joke. Bob hadn't gone into the washroom at all. He'd just decided that she was right; the place was awful and he'd gone out to the car to wait for her.

She felt like a fool as she hurried toward the door. The man might have told her that Bob had gone out. Wait till she told Bob what she'd done. It was really funny how a person could get upset over nothing.

As she pulled open the screen door she wondered if Bob had paid for what they'd ordered. He must have. At least the man didn't call after her as she went out.

She moved into the sunlight and started toward the car almost closing her eyes completely to shut out the glare on the windshield. She smiled to herself thinking about her foolish worrying.

"Bob," she murmured. "Bob, where—?"

In the stillness she heard the front screen door slap in its frame. Abruptly she started running up the side of the café building, heart hammering excitedly. Stifling heat waves broke over her as she ran.

At the edge of the building she stopped suddenly.

The man she'd spoken to at the counter was looking into the car. He was a small man in his forties, wearing a spotted fedora and a striped, green shirt. Black suspenders held up his dark, grease-spotted pants. Like the other man he wore high-top shoes.

She moved one step and her sandal scuffed on the dry ground. The man looked over at her suddenly, his face lean and bearded. His eyes were a pale blue that shone like milk spots in the leathery tan of his face.

The man smiled casually. "Thought I'd see if your husband was waitin' on you in your car," he said. He touched the brim of his hat and started back into the café.

"Are you—" Jean started, then broke off as the man turned. "Ma'am?"

"Are you sure he wasn't in the washroom?"

"Wasn't no one in there when I went in," he said.

She stood there shivering in the sun as the man went into the café and the screen door flapped closed. She could feel mindless dread filling her like ice water.

Then she caught herself. There had to be an explanation. Things like this just didn't happen.

She went back into the cafe, moved firmly across the floor and stopped before the counter. The man in the white ducks looked up from his paper.

"Would you please check the washroom?" she asked.

"The washroom?"

Anger tightened her.

"Yes, the washroom," she said. "I know my husband is in there."

"Ma'am, wasn't no one in there," said the man in the fedora.

"I'm sorry," she said tightly, refusing to allow his words. "My husband didn't just disappear."

The two men made her nervous with their silent stares.

"Well, are you going to look there?" she said, unable to control the break in her voice.

The man in the white ducks glanced at the man with the fedora and something twitched his mouth. Jean felt her hands jerk into angry fists. Then he moved down the length of the counter and she followed.

He turned the porcelain knob and held upon the spring-hinged door. Jean held her breath as she moved closer to look.

The washroom was empty.

"Are you satisfied?" the man said. He let the door swing shut.

"Wait," she said. "Let me look again."

The man pressed his mouth into a line.

"Didn't you see it was empty?" he said.

"I said I want to look again."

"Lady, I'm tellin' ya—"

Jean pushed at the door suddenly and it banged against the washroom wall.

"There!" she said. "There's a door there!"

She pointed to a door in the far wall of the washroom.

"That door's been locked for years, lady," the man said.

"It doesn't open?"

"Ain't got no reason to open it."

"It must open," Jean said. "My husband went in there and he didn't come out this door. And he didn't disappear!"

The man looked at her sullenly without speaking.

"What's on the other side of the door?" she asked.

"Nothing."

"Does it open on the outside?"

The man didn't answer.

"Does it?"

"It opens on a shed, lady, a shed no one's used for years," the man said angrily.

She stepped forward and gripped the knob of the door.

"I told you it didn't open." The man's voice was rising more.

"Ma'am?" Behind her Jean heard the cajoling voice of the man in the fedora and green shirt. "Ain't nothin' in that shed but old trash, ma'am. You want, I'll show it to you."

The way he said it, Jean suddenly realized that she was alone. Nobody she knew knew where she was; there was no way of checking if—

She moved out of the washroom quickly.

"Excuse me," she said as she walked by the man in the fedora, "I want to make a call first."

She walked stiffly to the wall phone, shuddering as she thought of them coming after her. She picked up the ear piece. There was no dial tone. She waited a moment, then tensed herself and turned to face the two watching men.

"Does—does it work?"

"Who ya call—" started the man in the white ducks, but the other man interrupted.

"You gotta crank it, ma'am," he said slowly. Jean noticed the other man glaring at him suddenly, and when she turned back to the phone, she heard their voices whispering heatedly.

She turned the crank with shaking fingers. *What if they come at me?* The thought wouldn't leave her.

"Yes?" a thin voice asked over the phone.

Jean swallowed. "Would you get me the marshal, please?" she asked.

"Marshal?"

"Yes, the—"

She lowered her voice suddenly, hoping the men wouldn't hear her. "The *marshal*," she repeated.

"There's no marshal, ma'am."

She felt close to screaming. "Who do I call?"

"You might want the sheriff, ma'am," the operator said.

Jean closed her eyes and ran her tongue over dry lips. "The sheriff then," she said.

There was a sputtering sound over the phone, a series of dull buzzes and then the sound of a receiver being lifted.

"Sheriff's office," said a voice.

"Sheriff, would you please come out to—"

"One second. I'll get the sheriff."

Jean's stomach muscles pulled in and her throat became taut. As she waited, she felt the eyes of the two men on her. She heard one of them move and her shoulders twitched spasmodically.

"Sheriff speaking."

"Sheriff, would you please come out to the—"

Her lips trembled as she realized suddenly that she didn't know the name of the café. She turned nervously and her heartbeat lurched when she saw the men looking at her coldly.

"What's the name of the café?"

"Why do you want to know?" asked the man in the white ducks.

He isn't going to tell me, she thought. *He's going to make me go out to look at the sign so that he can—*

"Are you going to—" she started to say, then turned quickly as the sheriff said, "Hello?"

"Please don't hang up," she said hurriedly. "I'm in a café on the edge of the town near the desert. On the western edge of town, I mean. I came here with my husband and now he's gone. He—just disappeared."

The sound of her own words made her shudder.

"You at The Blue Eagle?" the sheriff asked.

"I—I don't know," she said. "I don't know the name. They won't tell—"

Again she broke off nervously.

"Ma'am, if you want to know the name," said the man in the fedora, "it's The Blue Eagle."

"Yes, yes," she relayed to the mouth piece. "The Blue Eagle."

"I'll be right over," said the sheriff.

"What you tell her for?" the man in the white ducks spoke angrily behind her.

"Son, we don't want no trouble with the sheriff. We ain't done nothin'. Why shouldn't he come?"

For a long moment Jean leaned her forehead against the phone and drew in deep breaths. *They can't do anything now*, she kept telling herself. *I've told the sheriff and they have to leave me alone.* She heard one of the men moving to the door but no sound of the door opening.

She turned and saw that the man in the fedora was looking out the door while the other one stared at her.

"You tryin' to make trouble for my place?" he asked.

"I'm not trying to make trouble, but I want my husband back."

"Lady, we ain't done nothing with your husband!"

The man in the fedora turned around with a wry grin. "Looks like your husband lit out," he said blandly.

"He did not!" Jean said angrily.

"Then where's your car, ma'am?" the man asked.

There was a sudden dropping sensation in her stomach. Jean ran to the screen door and pushed out.

The car was gone.

"Bob!"

"Looks like he left you behind, ma'am," said the man.

She looked at the man with frightened eyes, then turned away with a sob and stumbled across the porch. She stood there in the over-hot shade crying and looking at the place where the car had been. The dust was still settling there.

She was still standing on the porch when the dusty blue patrol car braked in front of the café. The door opened and a tall, red-haired man got out, dressed in gray shirt and trousers, with a dull, metallic star pinned over his heart. Jean moved numbly off the porch to meet him.

"You the lady that called?" the man asked.

"Yes, I am."

"What's wrong now?"

"I told you. My husband disappeared."

"Disappeared?"

As quickly as possible she told him what had happened.

"You don't think he drove away then?" said the sheriff.

"He wouldn't leave me here like this."

The sheriff nodded. "All right, go on," he said.

When she was finished, the sheriff nodded again and they went inside. They went to the counter.

"This lady's husband go in the lavatory, Jim?" the sheriff asked the man in the white ducks.

"How should I know?" the man asked. "I was cooking. Ask Tom, he was in there." He nodded toward the man in the fedora.

"What about it, Tom?" asked the sheriff.

"Sheriff, didn't the lady tell you her husband just lit out before in their car?"

"That's not true!" Jean cried.

"You see the man driving the car away, Tom?" the sheriff asked.

"Sure I saw him. Why else would I say it?"

"No. No." Jean murmured the word with tiny, frightened shakes of her head.

"Why didn't you call after him if you saw him?" the sheriff asked Tom.

"Sheriff, ain't none of my business if a man wants to run out on—"

"He didn't run out!"

The man in the fedora shrugged his shoulders with a grin. The sheriff turned to Jean.

"Did you see your husband go in the lavatory?"

"Yes, of course I—well, no, I didn't exactly see him go in, but—"

She broke off into angry silence as the man in the fedora chuckled.

"I know he went in," she said, "because after I came out of the ladies' washroom I went outside and the car was empty. Where else could he have been? The café is only so big. There's

a door in that washroom. He said it hasn't been used in years."
She pointed at the man in the white ducks. "But I know it has.
I know my husband didn't just leave me here. He wouldn't do
it. I know him, and he wouldn't do it!"

"Sheriff," said the man in white ducks, "I showed the washroom to her when she asked. There wasn't nobody in there and
she can't say there was."

Jean twisted her shoulders irritably.

"He went through that other door," she said.

"Lady, that door ain't used!" the man said loudly. Jean
flinched and stepped back.

"All right, take it easy, Jim," the sheriff said. "Lady, if you
didn't see your husband go in that lavatory and you didn't see
if it was somebody else drivin' your car away, I don't see what
we got to go on."

"What?"

She couldn't believe what she'd heard. Was the man actually
telling her there was nothing to be done? For a second she
tightened in fury thinking that the sheriff was just sticking up
for his own townspeople against a stranger. Then the impact
of being alone and helpless struck her and her breath caught as
she looked at the sheriff with childlike, frightened eyes.

"Lady, I don't see what I can do," the sheriff said with a
shake of his head.

"Can't you—" She gestured timidly. "Can't you l-look in the
washroom for a clue or something? Can't you open that door?"

The Sheriff looked at her for a moment, then pursed his lips
and walked down to the washroom. Jean followed him closely,
afraid to stay near the two men.

She looked into the washroom as the sheriff was testing the
closed door. She shuddered as the man in the white ducks
came down and stood beside her.

"I told her it don't open," he said to the sheriff. "It's locked
on the other side. How could the man get out?"

"Someone might have opened it on the other side," Jean said
nervously.

The man made a sound of disgust.

"Anyone else been around here?" the sheriff asked Jim.

"Just Sam McComas havin' some beer before, but he went home about—"

"I mean in this shed."

"Sheriff, you know there ain't."

"What about big Lou?" the sheriff asked.

Jim was quiet a second and Jean saw his throat move.

"He ain't been around for months, Sheriff," Jim said. "He went up north."

"Jim, you better go around and open up this door," the sheriff said.

"Sheriff, ain't nothin' but an empty shed in there."

"I know, Jim, I know. Just want to satisfy the lady."

Jean stood there feeling the looseness around her eyes again, the sick feeling of being without help. It made her dizzy, as if everything were spinning away from her. She held one fist with her other hand and all her fingers were white.

Jim went out the screen door with a disgusted mutter and the door slapped shut behind him.

"Lady, come here," Jean heard the sheriff say quickly and softly. Her heart jumped as she moved into the washroom.

"You recognize this?"

She looked at the shred of cloth in his palm, then she gasped, "That's the color slacks he had on!"

"Ma'am, not so loud," the sheriff said. "I don't want them to think I know anything."

He stepped out of the washroom suddenly as he heard boots on the floor. "You goin' somewhere, Tom?" he asked.

"No, no, Sheriff," said the man in the fedora. "Just comin' down to see how you was gettin' on."

"Uh-huh. Well—stick around for a while will you, Tom?" said the sheriff.

"Sure, Sheriff, sure," Tom said broadly. "I ain't goin' nowhere."

They heard a clicking sound in the washroom, and in a moment the door was pulled open. The sheriff walked past Jean and down three steps into a dimly lit shed.

"Got a light in here?" he asked Jim.

"Nope, ain't got no reason to. No one ever uses it."

The sheriff pulled a light string, but nothing happened.

"Don't you believe me, Sheriff?" Jim said.

"Sure I do, Jim," said the sheriff. "I'm just curious."

Jean stood in the doorway looking down into the damp-smelling shed.

"Kinda beat up in here," said the sheriff looking at a knocked-over table and chair.

"No one's been here for years, Sheriff," Jim said. "Ain't no reason to tidy it up."

"Years, eh?" the sheriff said half to himself as he moved around the shed. Jean watched him, her hands numb at the fingertips, shaking. Why didn't he find out where Bob was? That shred of cloth—how did it get torn from Bob's slacks? She gritted her teeth hard. *I mustn't cry*, she ordered herself. *I just mustn't cry. I know he's all right. He's perfectly all right.*

The sheriff stopped and bent over to pick up a newspaper. He glanced at it casually, then folded it and hit it against one palm casually.

"Years, eh?" he said.

"Well, I haven't been here in years," Jim said hurriedly, licking his lips. "Could be that—oh, Lou or somebody been holin' up in here sometime the last year. I don't keep the outside door locked ya know."

"Thought you said Lou went up north," the sheriff said mildly.

"He did, he did. I say in the last year he might have—"

"This is yesterday's paper, Jim," the sheriff said.

Jim looked blank, started to say something and then closed his mouth without making a sound. Jean felt herself trembling without control now. She didn't hear the screen door close quietly in front of the café or the furtive footsteps across the porch boards.

"Well—I didn't say Lou was the only one who might have sneaked in here for a night," Jim said quickly. "Could have been any tramp passing by."

He stopped as the sheriff looked around suddenly, his gaze darting past Jean. "Where's Tom?" he asked loudly.

Jean's head snapped around. Then she backed away with a gasp as the Sheriff dashed up the steps and ran by her.

"Stick around, Jim!" the sheriff called over his shoulder.

Jean rushed out of the café after him. As she came out on the porch she saw the Sheriff shading his eyes with one hand and looking up the road. Her eyes jumped in the same direction, and she saw the man in the fedora running toward another man, a tall man.

"That'd be Lou," she heard the sheriff murmur to himself.

He started running; then, after a few steps, he came back and jumped into his car.

"Sheriff!"

He glanced out the window and saw the look of fright on her face. "All right, hurry up! Get in!"

She jumped off the porch and ran toward the car. The sheriff pushed open the door and Jean slid in beside him and pulled it shut. The sheriff gunned his car out past the café and it skidded onto the road in a cloud of dust.

"What is it?" Jean asked him breathlessly.

"Your husband didn't leave you," was all the sheriff said.

"Where is he?" she asked in a frightened voice.

But they were already overtaking the two men who had met and were now running into the brush.

The sheriff jerked the car off the road and slammed on the brakes. He pushed out of the car, quickly reaching down for his pistol.

"Tom!" he yelled. "Lou! Stop running!"

The men kept going. The sheriff leveled his pistol barrel and fired. Jean started at the explosion and saw, far out across the rocky desert, a spout of sand jump up near the men.

They both stopped abruptly, turned and held up their hands.

"Come on back!" yelled the sheriff. "And make it fast!"

Jean stood beside the car, unable to keep her hands from shaking. Her eyes were fastened on the two men walking toward them.

"All right, where is he?" the sheriff asked as they came up.

"Who you talkin' about, Sheriff?" asked the man in the fedora.

"Never mind that, Tom," the sheriff said angrily. "I'm not foolin' any more. This lady wants her husband back. Now where—"

"Husband!" Lou looked at the man in the fedora with angry eyes. "I thought we decided agin that!"

"Shut your mouth!" the man in the fedora said, his pleasant demeanor gone entirely now.

"You told me we wasn't gonna—" Lou started.

"Let's see what you got in your pockets, Lou," the sheriff said.

Lou looked at the sheriff blankly. "My pockets?" he said.

"Come on, come on." The sheriff waved his pistol impatiently. Lou started emptying his pockets slowly.

"Told me we wasn't gonna do that," he muttered aside to the man in the fedora. "Told me. Stupid jackass."

Jean gasped as Lou tossed the wallet on the ground. "That's Bob's," she murmured.

"Get his things, lady," the sheriff said.

Nervously she moved over at the feet of the men and picked up the wallet, the coins, the car keys.

"All right, where is he?" the sheriff asked. "And don't waste my time!" he said angrily to the man in the fedora.

"Sheriff, I don't know what you—" started the man.

The sheriff almost lunged forward. "So help me!" he raged. Tom threw up one arm and stepped back.

"I'll tell you for a fact, Sheriff," Lou broke in. "If I'd known this fella had his woman with him, I'd never've done it."

Jean stared at the tall, ugly man, her teeth digging into her lower lip. *Bob, Bob.* Her mind kept saying his name.

"Where is he, I said," the sheriff demanded.

"I'll show you, I'll show you," Lou said. "I told you I never would've done it if I'd known his woman was with him."

Again he turned to the man in the fedora. "Why'd you let him go in there?" he demanded. "Why? Answer me that?"

"Don't know what he's talkin' about, Sheriff," Tom said blandly. "Why, I—"

"Get on the road," the sheriff ordered. "Both of you. You take us to him or you're really in trouble. I'm followin' you in the car. Don't make any wrong move, not one."

The car moved slowly behind the two walking men.

"I been after these boys for a year," the sheriff told her.

"They set themselves up a nice little system robbin' men who come to the café, then dumpin' them in the desert and sellin' their car up north."

Jean hardly heard what he was saying. She kept staring at the road ahead, her stomach tight, her hands pressed tightly together.

"Never knew how they worked it though," the sheriff went on. "Never thought of the lavatory. Guess what they did was keep it locked for any man but one who was alone. They must've slipped up today. I guess Lou just jumped anyone who came in there. He's not any too bright."

"Do you think they—" Jean started hesitantly.

The sheriff hesitated. "I don't know, lady. I wouldn't think so. They ain't that dumb. Besides we had cases like this before and they never hurt no one worse than a bump on the head."

He honked the horn. "Come on, snap it up!" he called to the men.

"Are there snakes out there?" Jean asked.

The sheriff didn't answer. He just pressed his mouth together and stepped on the accelerator so the men had to break into a trot to keep ahead of the bumper.

A few hundred yards further on, Lou turned off and started down a dirt road.

"Oh my God, where did they take him?" Jean asked.

"Should be right down here," the sheriff said.

Then Lou pointed to a clump of trees and Jean saw their car. The sheriff stopped his coupe and they got out. "All right, where is he?" he asked.

Lou started across the broken desert ground. Jean kept feeling the need to break into a run. She had to tense herself to keep walking by the sheriff's side. Their shoes crunched over the dry desert soil. She hardly felt the pebbles through her sandals, so intently was she studying the ground ahead.

"Ma'am," Lou said, "I hope you won't be too hard on me. If I'd known you was with him, I'd've never touched him."

"Knock it off, Lou," the sheriff said. "You're both in up to your necks, so you might as well save your breath."

Then Jean saw the body lying out on the sand, and with a sob she ran past the men, her heart pounding.

"Bob—"

She held his head in her lap, and when his eyes fluttered open, she felt as if the earth had been taken off her back.

He tried to smile, then winced at the pain. "I been hit," he muttered.

Without a word, the tears came running down her cheeks. She helped him back to their car, and as she followed the sheriff's car, she held tightly to Bob's hand all the way back to town.

COUNTERFEIT BILLS

Mr. William O. Cook decided that afternoon—it was raining and he was coming home from work on the bus—that it would be pleasant to be two people. He was 41 ½, 5'7", semi-bald, oval-bellied and bored. Schedule depressed him; routine gave him a pain where he lived. If, he envisioned, one only had a spare self, one could assign all the duller activities of life—i.e. clerkship, husbandry, parenthood, etc.—to the double, retaining for one's own time, more pleasurable doings such as bleacher viewing, saloon haunting, corner ogling and covert visits to Madame Gogarty's pleasure pavilion across the tracks; except, of course, that, with a double, the visits wouldn't have to be covert.

Accordingly, Mr. Cook spent four years, six months, two days, $5,228.20, six thousand yards of wiring, three hundred and two radio tubes, a generator, reams of paper, dizzying mentation and the good will of his wife in assembling his duplication machine. This he completed one Sunday afternoon in autumn and, shortly after pot roast dinner with Maude and the five children, made a double of himself.

"Good evening," he said, extending his hand to the blinking copy.

His double shook hands with him and, shortly after, at Mr. Cook's request, went upstairs to watch television until bedtime while Mr. Cook climbed out the window over the coal bin, went to the nearest bar, had five fast, celebratory jolts, then took a cab to Madame Gogarty's where he enjoyed the blandishments of one Delilah Phryne, a red-headed former

blonde of some twenty-seven years, thirty-eight inches and di-
verse talents.

The plan set in motion, life became a song. Until one evening when Mr. Cook's double cornered him in the cellar work
room and demanded surcease with the words, "I can't stand it
anymore, dammit!"

It ensued that he was as bored with that drab portion of Mr.
Cook's life as Mr. Cook himself had been. No amount of reasonable threats prevailed. Faced with the prospect of being exposed by the sullen double, Mr. Cook—after discarding the
alternate course of murdering himself by proxy—hit upon the
idea of making a second duplicate in order to give the first one
a chance to live.

This worked admirably until the second duplicate grew
jaded and demanding. Mr. Cook tried to talk the two copies
into alternating painful duty with pleasurable diversion; but,
quite naturally, the first duplicate refused, enjoying the company of a Miss Gina Bonaroba of Madame Gogarty's too
much to be willing to spend part of his time performing the
mundane chores of everyday.

Cornered again, Mr. Cook reluctantly made a third duplicate; then a fourth, a fifth. The city, albeit large, soon became
thick with William O. Cooks. He would come upon himself at
corners, discover himself asking himself for lights, end up,
quite literally, beside himself. Life grew complex. Yet Mr.
Cook did not complain. Actually, he rather liked the company
of his facsimiles and they often enjoyed quite pleasant bowling
parties together. Then, of course, there was always Delilah
and her estimable charms.

Which was what, ultimately, brought about the disaster.

One evening, on arriving at Madame Gogarty's, Mr. Cook
found duplicate number seven in the willing arms of Delilah.
Protest as the poor girl would that she had no idea it wasn't
him, the infuriated Mr. Cook struck her, then as it were, himself. Meanwhile, down the hall, copy number three had come
upon copy number five in the overwhelming embrace of both
their favorite, a Miss Gertrude Leman. Another fist battle broke
out during which duplicates number two and four arrived and

joined in fiercely. The house soon rang with the cries of their composite battlings.

At this juncture, an incensed Madame Gogarty intervened. Following the breaking up of the brawl, she had Mr. Cook and his selves trailed to their house in the suburbs. That night, a trifle before midnight, there was an unexplained explosion in the cellar of that house. Arriving police and firemen found the ruins below strewn with bits mechanical and human. Mr. Cook, amidst hue and cry, was dragged to incarceration; Madame Gogarty was, grimly, satisfied. After all, she used to tell the girls over tea in later years, too many Cooks spoil the brothel.

DEATH SHIP

Mason saw it first.

He was sitting in front of the lateral viewer taking notes as the ship cruised over the new planet. His pen moved quickly over the graph-spaced chart he held before him. In a little while they'd land and take specimens. Mineral, vegetable, animal—if there were any. Put them in the storage lockers and take them back to Earth. There the technicians would evaluate, appraise, judge. And, if everything was acceptable, stamp the big, black INHABITABLE on their brief and open another planet for colonization from over-crowded Earth.

Mason was jotting down items about general topography when the glitter caught his eye.

"I saw something," he said.

He flicked the viewer to reverse lensing position.

"Saw what?" Ross asked from the control board.

"Didn't you see a flash?"

Ross looked into his own screen.

"We went over a lake, you know," he said.

"No, it wasn't that," Mason said, "this was in that clearing beside the lake."

"I'll look," said Ross, "but it probably was the lake."

His fingers typed out a command on the board and the big ship wheeled around in a smooth arc and headed back.

"Keep your eyes open now," Ross said. "Make sure. We haven't got any time to waste."

"Yes, sir."

Mason kept his unblinking gaze on the viewer, watching the earth below move past like a slowly rolled tapestry of woods and fields and rivers. He was thinking, in spite of himself, that maybe the moment had arrived at last. The moment in which Earthmen would come upon life beyond Earth, a race evolved from other cells and other muds. It was an exciting thought. 1997 might be the year. And he and Ross and Carter might now be riding a new *Santa Maria* of discovery, a silvery, bulleted galleon of space.

"There!" he said. "There it is!"

He looked over at Ross. The captain was gazing into his viewer plate. His face bore the expression Mason knew well. A look of smug analysis, of impending decision.

"What do you think it is?" Mason asked, playing the strings of vanity in his captain.

"Might be a ship, might not be," pronounced Ross.

Well, for God's sake, let's go down and see, Mason wanted to say, but knew he couldn't. It would have to be Ross's decision. Otherwise they might not even stop.

"I guess it's nothing," he prodded.

He watched Ross impatiently, watched the stubby fingers flick buttons for the viewer. "We might stop," Ross said. "We have to take samples anyway. Only thing I'm afraid of is . . ."

He shook his head. Land, man! The words bubbled up in Mason's throat. For God's sake, let's go down!

Ross evaluated. His thickish lips pressed together appraisingly. Mason held his breath.

Then Ross' head bobbed once in that curt movement which indicated consummated decision. Mason breathed again. He watched the captain spin, push and twist dials. Felt the ship begin its tilt to upright position. Felt the cabin shuddering slightly as the gyroscope kept it on an even keel. The sky did a ninety-degree turn, clouds appeared through the thick ports. Then the ship was pointed at the planet's sun and Ross switched off the cruising engines. The ship hesitated, suspended a split second, then began dropping toward the earth.

"Hey, we settin' down already?"

Mickey Carter looked at them questioningly from the port door that led to the storage lockers. He was rubbing greasy hands over his green jumper legs.

"We saw something down there," Mason said.

"No kiddin'," Mickey said, coming over to Mason's viewer. "Let's see."

Mason flicked on the rear lens. The two of them watched the planet billowing up at them.

"I don't know whether you can . . . oh, yes, there it is," Mason said. He looked over at Ross.

"Two degrees east," he said.

Ross twisted a dial and the ship then changed its downward movement slightly.

"What do you think it is?" Mickey asked.

"Hey!"

Mickey looked into the viewer with even greater interest. His wide eyes examined the shiny speck enlarging on the screen.

"Could be a ship," he said. "Could be."

Then he stood there silently, behind Mason, watching the earth rushing up.

"Reactors," said Mason.

Ross jabbed efficiently at the button and the ship's engines spouted out their flaming gasses. Speed decreased. The rocket eased down on its roaring fire jets. Ross guided.

"What do *you* think it is?" Mickey asked Mason.

"I don't know," Mason answered. "But if it's a ship," he added, half wishfully thinking, "I don't see how it could possibly be from Earth. We've got this run all to ourselves."

"Maybe they got off course," Mickey dampened without knowing.

Mason shrugged. "I doubt it," he said.

"What if it is a ship?" Mickey said. "And it's not ours?"

Mason looked at him and Carter licked his lips.

"Man," he said, "that'd be somethin'."

"Air spring," Ross ordered.

Mason threw the switch that set the air spring into operation. The unit which made possible a landing without them having to stretch out on thick-cushioned couches. They could stand on deck and hardly feel the impact. It was an innovation on the newer government ships.

The ship hit on its rear braces.

There was a sensation of jarring, a sense of slight bouncing. Then the ship was still, its pointed nose straight up, glittering brilliantly in the bright sunlight.

"I want us to stay together," Ross was saying. "No one takes any risks. That's an order."

He got up from his seat and pointed at the wall switch that let atmosphere into the small chamber in the corner of the cabin.

"Three to one we need our helmets," Mickey said to Mason.

"You're on," Mason said, setting into play their standing bet about the air or lack of it on every new planet they found. Mickey always bet on the need for apparatus, Mason for unaided lung use. So far, they'd come out about even.

Mason threw the switch, and there was a muffled sound of hissing in the chamber. Mickey got the helmet from his locker and dropped it over his head. Then he went through the double doors. Mason listened to him clamping the doors behind him. He kept wanting to switch on the side viewers and see if he could locate what they'd spotted. But he didn't. He let himself enjoy the delicate nibbling of suspense.

Through the intercom they heard Mickey's voice.

"Removing helmet," he said.

Silence. They waited. Finally, a sound of disgust.

"I lose again," Mickey said.

"God, did they hit!"

Mickey's face had an expression of dismayed shock on it. The three of them stood there on the greenish-blue grass and looked.

It *was* a ship. Or what was left of a ship for, apparently, it had struck the earth at terrible velocity, nose first. The main structure had driven itself about fifteen feet into the hard ground. Jagged pieces of superstructure had been ripped off by the crash and were lying strewn over the field. The heavy engines had been torn loose and nearly crushed the cabin. Everything was deathly silent, and the wreckage was so complete they could hardly make out what type of ship it was. It was as if some enormous child had lost fancy with the toy model and had dashed it to earth, stamped on it, banged on it insanely with a rock.

Mason shuddered. It had been a long time since he'd seen a rocket crash. He'd almost forgotten the everpresent menace of lost control, of whistling fall through space, of violent impact. Most talk had been about being lost in an orbit. This reminded him of the other threat in his calling. His throat moved unconsciously as he watched.

Ross was scuffing at a chunk of metal at his feet.

"Can't tell much," he said. "But I'd say it's our own."

Mason was about to speak, then changed his mind.

"From what I can see of that engine up there, I'd say it was ours," Mickey said.

"Rocket structure might be standard," Mason heard himself say, "everywhere."

"Not a chance," Ross said. "Things don't work out like that. It's ours all right. Some poor devils from Earth. Well, at least their death was quick."

"Was it?" Mason asked the air, visualizing the crew in their cabin, rooted with fear as their ship spun toward earth, maybe straight down like a fired cannon shell, maybe end-over-end like a crazy, fluttering top, the gyroscope trying in vain to keep the cabin always level.

The screaming, the shouted commands, the exhortations to a heaven they had never seen before, to a God who might be in another universe. And then the planet rushing up and blasting its hard face against their ship, crushing them, ripping the breath from their lungs. He shuddered again, thinking of it.

"Let's take a look," Mickey said.

"Not sure we'd better," Ross said. "We say it's ours. It might not be."

"Jeez, you don't think anything is still alive in there, do you?" Mickey asked the captain.

"Can't say," Ross said.

But they all knew he could see that mangled hulk before him as well as they. Nothing could have survived that.

The look. The pursed lips. As they circled the ship. The head movement, unseen by them.

"Let's try that opening there," Ross ordered. "And stay together. We still have work to do. Only doing this so we can let
the base know which ship this is." He had already decided it
was an Earth ship.

They walked up to a spot in the ship's side where the skin
had been laid open along the welded seam. A long, thick plate
was bent over as easily as a man might bend paper.

"Don't like this," Ross said. "But I suppose . . ."

He gestured with his head and Mickey pulled himself up to
the opening. He tested each handhold gingerly, then slid on his
work gloves as he found some sharp edge. He told the other
two and they reached into their jumper pockets. Then Mickey
took a long step into the dark maw of the ship.

"Hold *on*, now!" Ross called up. "Wait until I get there."

He pulled himself up, his heavy boot toes scraping up the
rocket skin. He went into the hole too. Mason followed.

It was dark inside the ship. Mason closed his eyes for a moment to adjust to the change. When he opened them, he saw
two bright beams searching up through the twisted tangle of beams and plates. He pulled out his own flash and
flicked it on.

"God, is this thing wrecked," Mickey said, awed by the sight
of metal and machinery in violent death. His voice echoed
slightly through the shell. Then, when the sound ended, an utter
stillness descended on them. They stood in the murky light and
Mason could smell the acrid fumes of broken engines.

"Watch the smell, now," Ross said to Mickey who was reaching up for support. "We don't want to get ourselves gassed."

"I will," Mickey said. He was climbing up, using one hand
to pull his thick, powerful body up along the twisted ladder.
He played the beam straight up.

"Cabin is all out of shape," he said, shaking his head.

Ross followed him up. Mason was last, his flash moving
around endlessly over the snapped joints, the wild jigsaw of
destruction that had once been a powerful new ship. He kept
hissing in disbelief to himself as his beam came across one violent distortion of metal after another.

"Door's sealed," Mickey said, standing on a pretzel-twisted

catwalk, bracing himself against the inside rocket wall. He grabbed the handle again and tried to pull it open.

"Give me your light," Ross said. He directed both beams at the door and Mickey tried to drag it open. His face grew red as he struggled. He puffed.

"No," he said, shaking his head. "It's stuck."

Mason came up beside them. "Maybe the cabin is still pressurized," he said softly. He didn't like the echoing of his own voice.

"Doubt it," Ross said, trying to think. "More than likely the jamb is twisted." He gestured with his head again. "Help Carter."

Mason grabbed one handle and Mickey the other. Then they braced their feet against the wall and pulled with all their strength. The door held fast. They shifted their grip, pulled harder.

"Hey, it slipped!" Mickey said. "I think we got it."

They resumed footing on the tangled catwalk and pulled the door open. The frame was twisted, the door held in one corner. They could only open it enough to wedge themselves in sideways.

The cabin was dark as Mason edged in first. He played his light beam toward the pilot's seat. It was empty. He heard Mickey squeeze in as he moved the light to the navigator's seat.

There was no navigator's seat. The bulkhead had been driven in there, the viewer, the table and the chair all crushed beneath the bent plates. There was a clicking in Mason's throat as he thought of himself sitting at a table like that, in a chair like that, before a bulkhead like that.

Ross was in now. The three beams of light searched. They all had to stand, legs braced, because the deck slanted.

And the way it slanted made Mason think of something. Of shifting weights, of *things* sliding down . . .

Into the corner where he suddenly played his shaking beam.

And felt his heart jolt, felt the skin on him crawling, felt his unblinking eyes staring at the sight. Then felt his boots thud him down the incline as if he were driven.

"Here," he said, his voice hoarse with shock.

He stood before the bodies. His foot had bumped into one

of them as he held himself from going down any further, as he shifted his weight on the incline.

Now he heard Mickey's footsteps, his voice. A whisper. A bated, horrified whisper.

"Mother of God."

Nothing from Ross. Nothing from any of them then but stares and shuddering breaths.

Because the twisted bodies on the floor were theirs, all three of them. And all three dead.

Mason didn't know how long they stood there, wordlessly, looking down at the still, crumpled figures on the deck.

How does a man react when he is standing over his own corpse? The question plied unconsciously at his mind. What does a man say? What are his first words to be? A poser, he seemed to sense, a loaded question.

But it was happening. Here he stood—and there he lay dead at his own feet. He felt his hands grow numb and he rocked unsteadily on the tilted deck.

"God."

Mickey again. He had his flash pointed down at his own face. His mouth twitched as he looked. All three of them had their flash beams directed at their own faces, and the bright ribbons of light connected their dual bodies.

Finally Ross took a shaking breath of the stale cabin air.

"Carter," he said, "find the auxiliary light switch, see if it works." His voice was husky and tightly restrained.

"Sir?"

"The light switch—the light switch!" Ross snapped.

Mason and the captain stood there, motionless, as Mickey shuffled up the deck. They heard his boots kick metallic debris over the deck surface. Mason closed his eyes, but was unable to take his foot away from where it pressed against the body that was his. He felt bound.

"I don't understand," he said to himself.

"Hang on," Ross said.

Mason couldn't tell whether it was said to encourage him or the captain himself.

Then they heard the emergency generator begin its initial whining spin. The lights flickered, went out. The generator coughed and began humming and the lights flashed on brightly.

They looked down now. Mickey slipped down the slight deck hill and stood beside them. He stared down at his own body. Its head was crushed in. Mickey drew back, his mouth a box of unbelieving terror.

"I don't get it," he said. "I don't get it. What *is* this?"

"Carter," Ross said.

"That's *me!*" Mickey said. "God, it's *me!*"

"Hold on!" Ross ordered.

"The three of us," Mason said quietly, "and we're all dead."

There seemed nothing to be said. It was a speechless nightmare. The tilted cabin all bashed in and tangled. The three corpses all doubled over and tumbled into one corner, arms and legs flopped over each other. All they could do was stare.

Then Ross said, "Go get a tarp. Both of you."

Mason turned. Quickly. Glad to fill his mind with a simple command. Glad to crowd out tense horror with activity. He took long steps up the deck. Mickey backed up, unable to take his unblinking gaze off the heavy-set corpse with the green jumper and the caved-in, bloody head.

Mason dragged a heavy, folded tarp from the storage locker and carried it back into the cabin, legs and arms moving in robotlike sequence. He tried to numb his brain, not think at all until the first shock had dwindled.

Mickey and he opened up the heavy canvas sheet with wooden motions. They tossed it out and the thick, shiny material fluttered down over the bodies. It settled, outlining the heads, the torsos, the one arm that stood up stiffly like a spear, bent over wrist and hand like a grisly pennant.

Mason turned away with a shudder. He stumbled up to the pilot's seat and slumped down. He stared at his outstretched legs, the heavy boots. He reached out and grabbed his leg and pinched it, feeling almost relief at the flaring pain.

"Come away," he heard Ross saying to Mickey, "I said, *come away!*"

He looked down and saw Ross half dragging Mickey up from a crouching position over the bodies. He held Mickey's arm and led him up the incline.

"We're dead," Mickey said hollowly. "That's us on the deck. We're *dead*."

Ross pushed Mickey up to the cracked port and made him look out.

"There," he said. "There's our ship over there. Just as we left it. This ship isn't ours. And those bodies. They . . . can't be ours."

He finished weakly. To a man of his sturdy opinionation, the words sounded flimsy and extravagant. His throat moved, his lower lip pushed out in defiance of this enigma. Ross didn't like enigmas. He stood for decision and action. He wanted action now.

"You saw yourself down there," Mason said to him. "Are you going to say it isn't you?"

"That's exactly what I'm saying," Ross bristled. "This may seem crazy, but there's an explanation for it. There's an explanation for everything."

His face twitched as he punched his bulky arm.

"This is me," he claimed. "I'm solid." He glared at them as if daring opposition. "I'm alive," he said.

They stared blankly at him.

"I don't get it," Mickey said weakly. He shook his head and his lips drew back over his teeth.

Mason sat limply in the pilot's seat. He almost hoped that Ross's dogmatism would pull them through this. That his staunch bias against the inexplicable would save the day. He wanted for it to save the day. He tried to think for himself, but it was so much easier to let the captain decide.

"We're all dead," Mickey said.

"Don't be a fool!" Ross exclaimed. "Feel yourself!"

Mason wondered how long it would go on. Actually, he began to expect a sudden awakening, him jolting to a sitting position on his bunk to see the two of them at their tasks as usual, the crazy dream over and done with.

But the dream went on. He leaned back in the seat and it

was a solid seat. From where he sat he could run his fingers over solid dials and buttons and switches. All real. It was no dream. Pinching wasn't even necessary.

"Maybe it's a vision," he tried, vainly attempting thought, as an animal mired tried hesitant steps to solid earth.

"That's enough," Ross said.

Then his eyes narrowed. He looked at them sharply. His face mirrored decision. Mason almost felt anticipation. He tried to figure out what Ross was working on. Vision? No, it couldn't be that. Ross would hold no truck with visions. He noticed Mickey staring open-mouthed at Ross. Mickey wanted the consoling of simple explanation too.

"Time warp," said Ross.

They still stared at him.

"What?" Mason asked.

"Listen," Ross punched out his theory. More than his theory, for Ross never bothered with that link in the chain of calculation. His certainty.

"Space bends," Ross said. "Time and space form a continuum. Right?"

No answer. He didn't need one.

"Remember they told us once in training of the possibility of circumnavigating time. They told us we could leave Earth at a certain time. And when we came back we'd be back a year earlier than we'd calculated. Or a year later.

"Those were just theories to the teachers. Well, I say it's happened to us. It's logical, it could happen. We could have passed right through a time warp. We're in another galaxy, maybe different space lines, maybe different time lines."

He paused for effect.

"I say we're in the future," he said.

Mason looked at him.

"How does that help us?" he asked, "if you're right."

"We're not dead?" Ross seemed surprised that they didn't get it.

"If it's in the future," Mason said quietly, "then we're going to die."

Ross gaped at him. He hadn't thought of that. Hadn't thought that his idea made things even worse. Because there was only one thing worse than dying. And that was knowing you were going to die. And where. And how.

Mickey shook his head. His hands fumbled at his sides. He raised one to his lips and chewed nervously on a blackened nail.

"No," he said weakly, "I don't get it."

Ross stood looking at Mason with jaded eyes. He bit his lips, feeling nervous with the unknown crowding him in, holding off the comfort of solid, rational thinking. He pushed, he shoved it away. He persevered.

"Listen," he said, "we're agreed that those bodies aren't ours."

No answer.

"Use your heads!" Ross commanded. "Feel yourself!"

Mason ran numbed fingers over his jumper, his helmet, the pen in his pocket. He clasped solid hands of flesh and bone. He looked at the veins in his arms. He pressed an anxious finger to his pulse. It's true, he thought. And the thought drove lines of strength back into him. Despite all, despite Ross' desperate advocacy, he was alive. Flesh and blood were his evidence.

His mind swung open then. His brow furrowed in thought as he straightened up. He saw a look almost of relief on the face of a weakening Ross.

"All right then," he said, "we're in the future."

Mickey stood tensely by the port. "Where does that leave us?" he asked.

The words threw Mason back. It was true, where did it leave them?

"How do we know how distant a future?" he said, adding weight to the depression of Mickey's words. "How do we know it isn't in the next twenty minutes?"

Ross tightened. He punched his palm with a resounding smack.

"How do we know?" he said strongly. "We don't go up, we can't crash. That's how we know."

Mason looked at him.

"Maybe if we went up," he said, "we might bypass our death altogether and leave it in this space-time system. We could get back to the space-time system of our own galaxy and . . ."

His words trailed off. His brain became absorbed with twisting thought.

Ross frowned. He stirred restlessly, licked his lips. What had been simple was now something else again. He resented the uninvited intrusion of complexity.

"We're alive now," he said, getting it set in his mind, consolidating assurance with reasonable words, "and there's only one way we can stay alive."

He looked at them, decision reached. "We have to stay here," he said.

They just looked at him. He wished that one of them, at least, would agree with him, show some sign of definition in their minds.

"But . . . what about our orders," Mason said vaguely.

"Our orders don't tell us to kill ourselves!" Ross said. "No, it's the only answer. If we never go up again, we never crash. We . . . we avoid it, we prevent it!"

His head jarred once in a curt nod. To Ross, the thing was settled.

Mason shook his head.

"I don't know," he said. "I don't . . ."

"I do," Ross stated. "Now let's get out of here. This ship is getting on your nerves."

Mason stood up as the captain gestured toward the door. Mickey started to move, then hesitated. He looked down at the bodies.

"Shouldn't we . . . ?" he started to inquire.

"What, what?" Ross asked, impatient to leave.

Mickey stared at the bodies. He felt caught up in a great, bewildering insanity.

"Shouldn't we . . . bury ourselves?" he said.

Ross swallowed. He would hear no more. He herded them out of the cabin. Then, as they started down through the wreckage, he looked in at the door. He looked at the tarpaulin with the jumbled mound of bodies beneath it. He pressed his lips together until they were white.

"I'm alive," he muttered angrily.

Then he turned out the cabin light with tight, vengeful fingers and left.

They all sat in the cabin of their own ship. Ross had ordered food brought out from the lockers, but he was the only one eating. He ate with a belligerent rotation of his jaw as though he would grind away all mystery with his teeth.

Mickey stared at the food.

"How long do we have to stay?" he asked, as if he didn't clearly realize that they were to remain permanently.

Mason took it up. He leaned forward in his seat and looked at Ross.

"How long will our food last?" he said.

"There's edible food outside, I've no doubt," Ross said, chewing.

"How will we know which is edible and which is poisonous?"

"We'll watch the animals," Ross persisted.

"They're a different type of life," Mason said. "What they can eat might be poisonous to us. Besides, we don't even know if there are any animals here."

The words made his lips raise in a brief, bitter smile. And he'd actually been hoping to contact another people. It was practically humorous.

Ross bristled. "We'll . . . cross each river as we come to it," he blurted out as if he hoped to smother all complaint with this ancient homily.

Mason shook his head. "I don't know," he said.

Ross stood up.

"Listen," he said. "It's easy to ask questions. We've all made a decision to stay here. Now let's do some concrete thinking about it. Don't tell me what we can't do. I know that as well as you. Tell me what we can do."

Then he turned on his heel and stalked over to the control board. He stood there glaring at blank-faced gauges and dials. He sat down and began scribbling rapidly in his log as if something of great note had just occurred to him. Later Mason looked at what Ross had written and saw that it was a long paragraph which explained in faulty but unyielding logic why they were all alive.

Mickey got up and sat down on his bunk. He pressed his large hands against his temples. He looked very much like a little boy who had eaten too many green apples against his mother's injunction and who feared retribution on both counts. Mason knew what Mickey was thinking. Of that still body with the skull forced in. The image of himself brutally killed in collision. He, Mason, was thinking of the same thing. And, behavior to the contrary, Ross probably was too.

Mason stood by the port looking out at the silent hulk across the meadow. Darkness was falling. The last rays of the planet's sun glinted off the skin of the crashed rocket ship. Mason turned away. He looked at the outside temperature gauge. Already it was seven degrees and it was still light. Mason moved the thermostat needle with his right forefinger.

Heat being used up, he thought. The energy of our grounded ship being used up faster and faster. The ship drinking its own blood with no possibility of transfusion. Only operation would recharge the ship's energy system. And they were without motion, trapped and stationary.

"How long can we last?" he asked Ross again, refusing to keep silence in the face of the question. "We can't live in this ship indefinitely. The food will run out in a couple of months. And a long time before that the charging system will go. The heat will stop. We'll freeze to death."

"How do we know the outside temperature will freeze us?" Ross asked, falsely patient.

"It's only sundown," Mason said, "and already it's . . . minus thirteen degrees."

Ross looked at him sullenly. Then he pushed up from his chair and began pacing.

"If we go up," he said, "we risk . . . *duplicating* that ship over there."

"But would we?" Mason wondered. "We can only die once. It seems we already have. In this galaxy. Maybe a person can die once in every galaxy. Maybe that's afterlife. Maybe . . ."

"Are you through?" asked Ross coldly.

Mickey looked up.

"Let's go," he said. "I don't want to hang around here."

He looked at Ross.

Ross said, "Let's not stick out our necks before we know what we're doing. Let's think this out."

"I have a wife!" Mickey said angrily. "Just because you're not married—"

"Shut up!" Ross thundered.

Mickey threw himself on the bunk and turned to face the cold bulkhead. Breath shuddered through his heavy frame. He didn't say anything. His fingers opened and closed on the blanket, twisting it, pulling it out from under his body.

Ross paced the deck, abstractedly punching at his palm with a hard fist. His teeth clicked together, his head shook as one argument after another fell before his bullheaded determination. He stopped, looked at Mason, then started pacing again. Once he turned on the outside spotlight and looked to make sure it was not imagination.

The light illumined the broken ship. It glowed strangely, like a huge, broken tombstone. Ross snapped off the spotlight with a soundless snarl. He turned to face them. His broad chest rose and fell heavily as he breathed.

"All right," he said. "It's *your* lives too. I can't decide for all of us. We'll hand vote on it. That thing out there may be something entirely different from what we think. If you two think it's worth the risk of our lives to go up, we'll . . . go up."

He shrugged. "Vote," he said. "I say we stay here."

"I say we go," Mason said.

They looked at Mickey.

"Carter," said Ross, "what's your vote?"

Mickey looked over his shoulder with bleak eyes.

"Vote," Ross said.

"Up," Mickey said. "Take us up. I'd rather die than stay here."

Ross's throat moved. Then he took a deep breath and squared his shoulders.

"All right," he said quietly. "We'll go up."

"God have mercy on us," Mickey muttered as Ross went quickly to the control board.

The captain hesitated a moment. Then he threw switches. The great ship began shuddering as gasses ignited and began to pour like channeled lightning from the rear vents. The sound was almost soothing to Mason. He didn't care anymore; he was willing, like Mickey, to take a chance. It had only been a few hours. It had seemed like a year. Minutes had dragged, each one weighted with oppressive recollections. Of the bodies they'd seen, of the shattered rocket—even more of the Earth they would never see, of parents and wives and sweethearts and children. Lost to their sight forever. No, it was far better to try to get back. Sitting and waiting was always the hardest thing for a man to do. He was no longer conditioned for it.

Mason sat down at his board. He waited tensely. He heard Mickey jump up and move over to the engine control board.

"I'm going to take us up easy," Ross said to them. "There's no reason why we should . . . have any trouble."

He paused. They snapped their heads over and looked at him with muscle-tight impatience.

"Are you both ready?" Ross asked.

"Take us up," Mickey said.

Ross jammed his lips together and shoved over the switch that read: *Vertical Rise.*

They felt the ship tremble, hesitate. Then it moved off the ground, headed up with increasing velocity. Mason flicked on the rear viewer. He watched the dark earth recede, tried not to look at the white patch in the corner of the screen, the patch that shone metallically under the moonlight.

"Five hundred," he read. "Seven-fifty . . . one thousand . . . fifteen hundred . . ."

He kept waiting. For explosion. For an engine to give out. For their rise to stop.

They kept moving up.

"Three thousand," Mason said, his voice beginning to betray the rising sense of elation he felt. The planet was getting farther and farther away. The other ship was only a memory now. He looked across at Mickey. Mickey was staring, open-mouthed, as if he were about ready to shout out *"Hurry!"* but was afraid to tempt the fates.

"Six thousand . . . *seven thousand*!" Mason's voice was jubilant. "We're *out* of it!"

Mickey's face broke into a great, relieved grin. He ran a hand over his brow and flicked great drops of sweat on the deck.

"God," he said, gasping, "my God."

Mason moved over to Ross's seat. He clapped the captain on the shoulder.

"We made it," he said. "Nice flying."

Ross looked irritated.

"We shouldn't have left," he said. "It was nothing all the time. Now we have to start looking for another planet." He shook his head. "It wasn't a good idea to leave," he said.

Mason stared at him. He turned away shaking his head, thinking . . . you can't win.

"If I ever see another glitter," he thought aloud, "I'll keep my big mouth shut. To hell with alien races anyways."

Silence. He went back to his seat and picked up his graph chart. He let out a long shaking breath. Let Ross complain, he thought, I can take anything now. Things are normal again. He began to figure casually what might have occurred down there on that planet.

Then he happened to glance at Ross.

Ross was thinking. His lips were pressed together. He said something to himself. Mason found the captain looking at him.

"Mason," he said.

"What?"

"Alien race, you said."

Mason felt a chill flood through his body. He saw the big head nod once in decision. Unknown decision. His hands started to shake. A crazy idea came. No, Ross wouldn't do that, not just to assuage vanity. Would he?

"I don't . . ." he started. Out of the corner of his eye he saw Mickey watching the captain too.

"*Listen*," Ross said. "I'll tell you what happened down there. I'll *show* you what happened!"

They stared at him in paralyzing horror as he threw the ship around and headed back.

"What are you doing?" Mickey cried.

"Listen," Ross said. "Didn't you understand me? Don't you see how we've been tricked?"

They looked at him without comprehension. Mickey took a step toward him.

"Alien race," Ross said. "That's the short of it. That time-space idea is all wet. But I'll tell you what idea isn't all wet. So we leave the place. What's our first instinct as far as reporting it? Saying it's uninhabitable? We'd do more than that. We wouldn't report it at all."

"Ross, you're not taking us back!" Mason said, standing up suddenly as the full terror of returning struck him.

"You bet I am!" Ross said, fiercely elated.

"You're crazy!" Mickey shouted at him, his body twitching, his hands clenched at his sides menacingly.

"Listen to me!" Ross roared at them. "Who would be benefited by us not reporting the existence of that planet?"

They didn't answer. Mickey moved closer.

"Fools!" he said. "Isn't it obvious? There *is* life down there. But life that isn't strong enough to kill us or chase us away with force. So what can they do? They don't want us there. So what can they do?"

He asked them like a teacher who cannot get the right answers from the dolts in his class.

Mickey looked suspicious. But he was curious now, too, and a little timorous as he had always been with his captain, except in moments of greatest physical danger. Ross had always led them, and it was hard to rebel against it even when it seemed he was trying to kill them all. His eyes moved to the viewer where the planet began to loom beneath them like a huge dark ball.

"We're alive," Ross said, "and I say there never *was* a ship down there. We saw it, sure. We *touched* it. But you can see anything if you believe it's there! All your senses can tell you there's something when there's nothing. All you have to do is *believe* it!"

"What are you getting at?" Mason asked hurriedly, too

frightened to realize. His eyes fled to the altitude gauge. Seventeen thousand . . . sixteen thousand . . . sixteen-fifty . . .

"Telepathy," Ross said, triumphantly decisive. "I say those men or whatever they are, saw us coming. And they didn't want us there. So they read our minds and saw the death fear, and they decided that the best way to scare us away was to show us our ship crashed and ourselves dead in it. And it worked . . . until now."

"So it worked!" Mason exploded. "Are you going to take a chance on killing us just to prove your damn theory?"

"It's *more* than a theory!" Ross stormed, as the ship fell, then added with the distorted argument of injured vanity, "my orders say to pick up specimens from every planet. I've always followed orders before and, by God, I still will!"

"You saw how cold it was!" Mason said. "No one can live there anyways! Use your head, Ross!"

"Damn it, *I'm* captain of this ship!" Ross yelled, "and I give the orders!"

"Not when our lives are in your hands!" Mickey started for the captain.

"Get back!" Ross ordered.

That was when one of the ship's engines stopped and the ship yawed wildly.

"You fool!" Mickey exploded, thrown off balance. "You *did* it, you *did* it!"

Outside the black night hurtled past.

The ship wobbled violently. *Prediction true* was the only phrase Mason could think of. His own vision of the screaming, the numbing horror, the exhortations to a deaf heaven— all coming true. That hulk would be this ship in a matter of minutes. Those three bodies would be . . .

"Oh . . . *damn*!" He screamed it at the top of his lungs, furious at the enraging stubbornness of Ross in taking them back, of causing the future to be as they saw—all because of insane pride.

"No, they're not going to fool us!" Ross shouted, still holding fast to his last idea like a dying bulldog holding its enemy fast in its teeth.

He threw switches and tried to turn the ship. But it wouldn't turn. It kept plunging down like a fluttering leaf. The gyroscope couldn't keep up with the abrupt variations in cabin equilibrium and the three of them found themselves being thrown off balance on the tilting deck.

"Auxiliary engines!" Ross yelled.

"It's no use!" Mickey cried.

"*Damn it!*" Ross clawed his way up the angled deck, then crashed heavily against the engine board as the cabin inclined the other way. He threw switches over with shaking fingers.

Suddenly Mason saw an even spout of flame through the rear viewer again. The ship stopped shuddering and headed straight down. The cabin righted itself.

Ross threw himself into his chair and shot out furious hands to turn the ship about. From the floor Mickey looked at him with a blank, white face. Mason looked at him too, afraid to speak.

"Now shut up!" Ross said disgustedly, not even looking at them, talking like a disgruntled father to his sons. "When we get down there you're going to see that it's true. That ship'll be gone. And we're going to go looking for those bastards who put the idea in our minds!"

They both stared at their captain numbly as the ship headed down backwards. They watched Ross's hands move efficiently over the controls. Mason felt a sense of confidence in his captain. He stood on the deck quietly, waiting for the landing without fear. Mickey got up from the floor and stood beside him, waiting.

The ship hit the ground. It stopped. They had landed again. They were still the same. And . . .

"Turn on the spotlight," Ross told them.

Mason threw the switch. They all crowded the port. Mason wondered for a second how Ross could possibly have landed in the same spot. He hadn't even appeared to be following the calculations made on the last landing.

They looked out.

Mickey stopped breathing. And Ross' mouth fell open.

The wreckage was still there.

They had landed in the same place and they had found the wrecked ship still there. Mason turned away from the port and stumbled over the deck. He felt lost, a victim of some terrible universal prank, a man accursed.

"You said . . ." Mickey said to the captain.

Ross just looked out of the port with unbelieving eyes.

"Now we'll go up again," Mickey said, grinding his teeth. "And we'll *really* crash this time. And we'll be killed. Just like those . . . those . . ."

Ross didn't speak. He stared out of the port at the refutation of his last clinging hope. He felt hollow, void of all faith in belief in sensible things.

Then Mason spoke.

"We're not going to crash—" he said somberly "—ever."

"What?"

Mickey was looking at him. Ross turned and looked too.

"Why don't we stop kidding ourselves?" Mason said. "We all know what it is, don't we?"

He was thinking of what Ross had said just a moment before. About the senses giving evidence of what was believed. Even if there was nothing there at all . . .

Then, in a split second, with the knowledge, he saw Ross and he saw Carter. As they were. And he took a short shuddering breath, a last breath until illusion would bring breath and flesh again.

"Progress," he said bitterly and his voice was an aching whisper in the phantom ship. "The Flying Dutchman takes to the universe."

DANCE OF THE DEAD

> *I wanna RIDE!*
> *With my Rota-Mota honey*
> *By my SIDE!*
> *As we whiz doing the highway*
> *We will HUG and SNUGGLE*
> *And we'll have a*
> *Little STRUGGLE!*

> *struggle* (strug` 'l), n., act of promiscuous loveplay;
> Usage evolved during WW III.

Double beams spread buttery lamplight on the highway. Rotor-Motors Convertible, Model C, 1997, rushed after it. Light spurted ahead, yellow glowing. The car pursued with a twelve-cylindered snarling pursuit. Night blotted in behind, jet and still. The car sped on. ST. LOUIS—10.

"I wanna FLY!" they sang, "with the Rota-Mota apple of my EYE!" they sang. "It's the only way of living . . ."

The quartet singing:

Len, 23.

Bud, 24.

Barbara, 20.

Peggy, 18.

Len with Barbara, Bud with Peggy.

Bud at the wheel, snapping around tilted curves, roaring up black-shouldered hills, shooting the car across silent flatlands. At the top of three lungs (the fourth gentler), competing with wind that buffeted their heads, that whipped their hair to lashing threads—singing:

"You can have your walkin' under MOONLIGHT
    BEAMS!
At a hundred miles an hour let me DREAM my
    DREAMS!"

Needle quivering at 130, two 5-mph notches from gauge's end. *A sudden dip!* Their young frames jolted and the thrown-up laughter of three was windswept into night. Around a curve, darting up and down a hill, flashing across a leveled—plain an ebony bullet skimming earth.

"In my ROTORY, MOTORY, FLOATERY, driving' machi-i-i-i-ine!"

YOU'LL BE A FLOATER IN YOUR ROTOR-MOTOR.
    In the back seat:
    "Have a jab, Bab."
    "Thanks, I had one after supper" (pushing away needle fixed to eye-dropper).
    In the front seat:
    "You meana tell me this is the first time you ever been t' Saint Loo!"
    "But I just started school in September."
    "Hey, you're a *frosh*!"
    Back seat joining front seat:
    "Hey, *frosh*, have a mussle-tussle."
    (Needle passed forward, eye bulb quivering amber juice.)
    "*Live* it, girl!"

mussle-tussle (Mus`'l-tus`'l), n., slang for the result of injecting a drug into a muscle; usage evolved during WW III.

Peggy's lips failed at smiling. Her fingers twitched.
    "No, thanks, I'm not . . ."
    "Come *on*, frosh!" Len leaning hard over the seat, white-browed

under black blowing hair. Pushing the needle at her face. "Live it, girl! Grab a li'l mussle-tussle!"

"I'd rather not," said Peggy. "If you don't—"

"What's 'at, frosh?" yelled Len and pressed his leg against the pressing leg of Barbara.

Peggy shook her head and golden hair flew across her cheeks and eyes. Underneath her yellow dress, underneath her white brassiere, underneath her young breast—a heart throbbed heavily. *Watch your step, darling, that's all we ask. Remember, you're all we have in the world now.* Mother words drumming at her; the needle making her draw back into the seat.

"*Come* on, frosh!"

The car groaned its shifting weight around a curve and centrifugal force pressed Peggy into Bud's lean hip. His hand dropped down and fingered at her leg. Underneath her yellow dress, underneath her sheer stocking—flesh crawled. Lips failed again; the smile was a twitch of red.

"Frosh, live it up!"

"Lay off, Len, jab your own dates."

"But we gotta teach frosh how to mussle-tussle!"

"Lay off, I said! She's my date!"

The black car roaring, chasing its own light. Peggy anchored down the feeling hand with hers. The wind whistled over them and grabbed down chilly fingers at their hair. She didn't want his hand there but she felt grateful to him.

Her vaguely frightened eyes watched the road lurch beneath the wheels. In back, a silent struggle began, taut hands rubbing, parted mouths clinging. Search for the sweet elusive at 120 miles-per-hour.

"*Rota-Mota honey,*" Len moaned the moan between salivary kisses. In the front seat a young girl's heart beat unsteadily. ST. LOUIS—6.

"No kiddin', you never been to Saint Loo?"

"No, I . . ."

"Then you never saw the loopy's dance?"

Throat contracting suddenly. "No, I . . . is that what . . . we're going to—?"

"Hey, frosh never saw the loopy's dance!" Bud yelled back.

Lips parted, slurping; skirt was adjusted with blasé aplomb.

"No kiddin!" Len fired up the words. "Girl, you haven't *lived*!"

"Oh, she's *got* to see *that*," said Barbara, buttoning a button.

"Let's go there then!" yelled Len. "Let's give frosh a thrill!"

"Good enough," said Bud and squeezed her leg. "Good enough up here, right Peg?"

Peggy's throat moved in the dark and the wind clutched harshly at her hair. She'd heard of it, she'd read of it but never had she thought she'd—

Choose your school friends carefully, darling. Be very careful.

But when no one spoke to you for two whole months? When you were lonely and wanted to talk and laugh and be alive? And someone spoke to you finally and asked you to go out with them?

"I yam Popeye, the sailor man!" Bud sang.

In back, they crowded artificial delight. Bud was taking a course in Pre-War Comics and Cartoons—2. This week the class was studying Popeye. Bud had fallen in love with the one-eyed seaman and told Len and Barbara all about him; taught them dialogue and song.

"I yam Popeye, the sailor man! I like to go swimmin' with bow-legged women! I yam Popeye, the sailor man!"

Laughter. Peggy smiled falteringly. The hand left her leg as the car screeched around a curve and she was thrown against the door. Wind dashed blunt coldness in her eyes and forced her back, blinking. 110—115—120 miles-per-hour. ST. LOUIS—3. *Be very careful, dear.*

Popeye cocked wicked eye.

"O, Olive Oyl, you is my sweet patootie."

Elbow nudging Peggy. "You be Olive Oyl—*you*."

Peggy smiled nervously. "I can't."

"Sure!"

In the back seat, Wimpy came up for air to announce, "I will gladly pay you Tuesday for a hamburger today."

Three fierce voices and a faint fourth raged against the howl of wind. "I fights to the *fin*-ish 'cause I eats my *spin*-ach! I yam Popeye, the sailor man! *Toot! Toot!*"

"I yam what I yam," reiterated Popeye gravelly and put his hand on the yellow-skirted leg of Olive Oyl. In the back, two members of the quartet returned to feeling struggle.

ST. LOUIS—1. The black car roared through the darkened suburbs. "On with the nosies!" Bud sang out. They all took out their plasticate nose-and-mouth pieces and adjusted them.

ANCE IN YOUR PANTS WOULD BE A PITY!
WEAR YOUR NOSIES IN THE CITY!!

ance (anse), n., slang for anticivilian germs; usage evolved during WW III.

"You'll like the loopy's dance!" Bud shouted to her over the shriek of wind. "It's sen-*saysh*!"

Peggy felt a cold that wasn't of the night or the wind. *Remember, darling, there are terrible things in the world today. Things you must avoid.*

"Couldn't we go somewhere else?" Peggy said but her voice was inaudible. She heard Bud singing, "I like to go swimmin' with bow-legged women!" She felt his hand on her leg again while, in the back, was the silence of grinding passion without kisses.

Dance of the dead. The words trickled ice across Peggy's brain.

ST. LOUIS.

The black car sped into the ruins.

It was a place of smoke and blatant joys. Air resounded with the bleating of revelers and there was a noise of sounding brass spinning out a cloud of music—1997 music, a frenzy of twisted dissonances. Dancers, shoe-horned into the tiny square of open floor, ground pulsing bodies together. A network of bursting sounds lanced through the mass of them; dancers singing:

"Hurt me! Bruise me! Squeeze me TIGHT!
Scorch my blood with hot DELIGHT!

Please abuse me every NIGHT!
LOVER, LOVER, LOVER, be a *beast-to-me*!"

Elements of explosion restrained within the dancing bounds—instead of fragmenting, quivering. "Oh, be a beast, beast, beast, *Beast*, BEAST to me!"

"How is *this*, Olive old goil?" Popeye inquired of the light of his eye as they struggled after the waiter. "Nothin' like this in Sykesville, eh?"

Peggy smiled but her hand in Bud's felt numb. As they passed by a murky lighted table, a hand she didn't see felt at her leg. She twitched and bumped against a hard knee across the narrow aisle. As she stumbled and lurched through the hot and smoky, thick aired room, she felt a dozen eyes disrobing her, abusing her. Bud jerked her along and she felt her lips trembling.

"Hey, how about that!" Bud exulted as they sat. "Right by the stage!"

From cigarette mists, the waiter plunged and hovered, pencil poised, beside their table.

"What'll it be!" His questioning shout cut through cacophony.

"Whiskey-water!" Bud and Len paralleled orders, then turned to their dates. "What'll it be!" the waiter's request echoes from their lips.

"*Green Swamp!*" Barbara said and, "*Green Swamp* here!" Len passed it along. Gin, Invasion Blood (1997 Rum), lime juice, sugar, mint spray, splintered ice—a popular college girl drink.

"What about you, honey?" Bud asked his date.

Peggy smiled. "Just some ginger ale," she said, her voice a fluttering frailty in the massive clash and fog of smoke.

"What?" asked Bud and, "What's that, didn't hear!" the waiter shouted.

"Ginger ale."

"*What!*"

"Ginger ale!"

"GINGER ALE!" Len screamed it out and the drummer, behind the raging curtain of noise that was the band's music, almost heard it. Len banged down his fist. *One—Two—Three!*

CHORUS: *Ginger Ale only twelve years old!*
Went to church and was as good as gold.
Till that day when—

"Come *on*, come *on*!" the waiter squalled. "Let's have that order, kids! I'm busy!"

"Two whiskey-waters and two Green Swamps!" Len sang out and the waiter was gone into the swirling maniac mist.

Peggy felt her young heart flutter helplessly. *Above all, don't drink when you're out on a date. Promise us that, darling, you must promise us that.* She tried to push away instructions etched in brain.

"How you like this place, honey? *Loopy*, ain't it?" Bud fired the question at her; a red-faced, happy-faced Bud.

loopy (lôô´pî), adj., common alter. of L.U.P.

She smiled at Bud, a smile of nervous politeness. Her eyes moved around, her face inclined and she was looking up at the stage. *Loopy*. The word scalpeled at her mind. *Loopy, loopy.*

The stage was five yards deep at the radius of its wooden semicircle. A waist-high rail girdled the circumference, two pale purple spotlights, unlit, hung at each end. Purple on white—the thought came. *Darling, isn't Sykesville Business College good enough: No! I don't want to take a business course, I want to major in art at the University!*

The drinks were brought and Peggy watched the disembodied waiter's arm thud down a high-green-looking glass before her. *Presto!*—the arm was gone. She looked into the murky green swamp depths and saw chipped ice bobbing.

"A toast! Pick up your glass, Peg!" Bud clarioned.

They all clinked glasses:

"To lust primordial!" Bud toasted.

"To beds intemperate!" Len added.

"To flesh insensate!" Barbara added a third link.

Their eyes zeroed in on Peggy's face, demanding. She didn't understand.

"*Finish it!*" Bud told her, plagued by freshman sluggishness.

"To . . . u-*us*," she faltered.

"How o-*ri*-ginal," stabbed Barbara and Peggy felt heat licking up her smooth cheeks. It passed unnoticed as three Youths of America with Whom the Future Rested gurgled down their liquor thirstily. Peggy fingered at her glass, a smile printed to lips that would not smile unaided.

"Come on, *drink*, girl!" Bud shouted to her across the vast distance of one foot. "Chuggalug!"

"Live it, girl," Len suggested abstractedly, fingers searching once more for soft leg. And finding, under the table, soft leg waiting.

Peggy didn't want to drink, she was afraid to drink. Mother words kept pounding—*never on a date, honey, never.* She raised the glass a little.

"Uncle Buddy will help, will help!"

Uncle Buddy leaning close, vapor of whiskey haloing his head. Uncle Buddy pushing cold glass to shaking young lips. "Come on, Olive Oyl, old goil! Down the hatch!"

Choking sprayed the bosom of her dress with green swamp droplets. Flaming liquid trickled into her stomach, sending offshoots of fire into her veins.

Bangity boom crash smash POW!! The drummer applied the *coup de grace* to what had been, in ancient times, a lover's waltz. Lights dropped and Peggy sat coughing and tear-eyed in the smoky cellar club.

She felt Bud's hand clamp strongly on her shoulder and, in the murk, she felt herself pulled off balance and felt Bud's hot wet mouth pressing at her lips. She jerked away and then the purple spots went on and a mottle-faced Bud drew back, gurgling, "I fights to the finish," and reaching for his drink.

"Hey, the loopy now, the loopy!" Len said eagerly, releasing exploratory hands.

Peggy's heart jolted and she thought she was going to cry

out and run thrashing through the dark, smoke-filled room. But a sophomore hand anchored her to the chair and she looked up in white-faced dread at the man who came out on the stage and faced the microphone which, like a metal spider, had swung down to meet him.

"May I have your attention, ladies and gentlemen," he said, a grim-faced, sepulchral-voiced man whose eyes moved out over them like flicks of doom. Peggy's breath was labored, she felt thin lines of green swamp water filtering hotly through her chest and stomach. It made her blink dizzily. *Mother.* The word escaped cells of the mind and trembled into conscious freedom. *Mother, take me home.*

"As you know, the act you are about to see is not for the faint of heart, the weak of will." The man plodded through the words like a cow enmired. "Let me caution those of you whose nerves are not what they ought to be—*leave now.* We make no guarantees of responsibility. We can't even afford to maintain a house doctor."

No laughter appreciative. "Cut the crap and get off stage," Len grumbled to himself. Peggy felt her fingers twitching.

"As you know," the man went on, his voice gilded with learned sonority, "This is not an offering of mere sensation but an honest scientific demonstration."

"*Loophole for Loopy's!*" Bud and Len heaved up the words with the thoughtless reaction of hungry dogs salivating at a bell.

It was, in 1997, a comeback so rigidly standard it had assumed the status of a catechism answer. A crenel in the postwar law allowed the LUP performance if it was orally prefaced as an exposition of science. Through this legal chink had poured so much abusing of the law that few cared any longer. A feeble government was grateful to contain infractions of the law at all.

When hoots and shoutings had evaporated in the smoke-clogged air, the man, his arms upraised in patient benediction, spoke again.

Peggy watched the studied movement of his lips, her heart swelling, then contracting in slow, spasmodic beats. An iciness was creeping up her legs. She felt it rising toward the thread-like fires in her body and her fingers twitched around the chilly moisture of the glass. *I want to go, please take me home*—Will-spent words were in her mind again.

"Ladies and gentlemen," the man concluded, "brace your-selves."

A gong sounded its hollow, shivering resonance, the man's voice thickened and slowed.

"The L.U. Phenomenon!"

The man was gone; the microphone had risen and was gone. Music began; a moaning brassiness, all muted. A jazzman's conception of *the palpable obscure*—mounted on a pulse of thumping drum. A dolor of saxophone, a menace of trom-bone, a harnessed bleating of trumpet—they raped the air with stridor.

Peggy felt a shudder plaiting down her back and her gaze dropped quickly to the murky whiteness of the table. Smoke and darkness, dissonance and heat surrounded her.

Without meaning to, but driven by an impulse of nervous fear, she raised the glass and drank. The glacial trickle in her throat sent another shudder rippling through her. Then fur-ther shoots of liquored heat budded in her veins and a numb-ness settled in her temples. Through parted lips, she forced out a shaking breath.

Now a restless, murmuring movement started through the room, the sound of it like willows in a soughing wind. Peggy dared not lift her gaze to the purpled silence of the stage. She stared down at the shifting glimmer of her drink, feeling mus-cle strands draw tightly in her stomach, feeling the hollow thumping of her heart. *I'd like to leave, please let's leave.*

The music labored toward a rasping dissonant climax, it's brass components struggling, in vain, for unity.

A hand stroked once at Peggy's leg and it was the hand of Popeye, the sailor man, who muttered roupily, "Olive Oyl, you is my goil." She barely felt or heard. Automatonlike, she raised the cold and sweating glass again and felt the chilling in her throat and then the flaring network of warmth inside her.

SWISH!

The curtain swept open with such a rush, she almost dropped her glass. It thumped down heavily on the table, swamp water cascading up its sides and raining on her hand. The music exploded shrapnel of ear-cutting cacophony and her body jerked. On the tablecloth, her hands twitched white on white while claws of uncontrollable demand pulled up her frightened eyes.

The music fled, frothing behind a wake of swelling drum rolls.

The nightclub was a wordless crypt, all breathing checked.

Cobwebs of smoke drifted in the purple light across the stage.

No sound except the muffled, rolling drum.

Peggy's body was a petrifaction in its chair, smitten to rock around her leaping heart, while, through the wavering haze of smoke and liquored dizziness, she looked up in horror to where it stood.

It had been a woman.

Her hair was black, a framing of snarled ebony for the tallow mask that was her face. Her shadow-rimmed eyes were closed behind lids as smooth and white as ivory. Her mouth, a lipless and unmoving line, stood like a clotted sword wound beneath her nose. Her throat, her shoulders and her arms were white, were motionless. At her sides, protruding from the sleeve ends of the green transparency she wore, hung alabaster hands.

Across this marble statue, the spotlights coated purple shimmer.

Still paralyzed, Peggy stared up at its motionless features, her fingers knitted in a bloodless tangle on her lap. The pulse of drumbeats in the air seemed to fill her body, its rhythm altering her heartbeat.

In the black emptiness behind her, she heard Len muttering, "I love my wife but, oh, you corpse," and heard the wheeze of helpless snickers that escaped from Bud and Barbara. The cold still rose in her, a silent tidal dread.

Somewhere in the smoke-fogged darkness, a man cleared viscid nervousness from his throat and a murmur of appreciative relief strained through the audience.

Still no motion on the stage, no sound but the sluggish cadence of the drum, thumping at the silence like someone seeking entrance at a far-off door. The thing that was a nameless victim of the plague stood palely rigid while the distillation sluiced through its blood-clogged veins.

Now the drum throbs hastened like the pulsebeat of a rising panic. Peggy felt the chill begin to swallow her. Her throat started tightening, her breathing was a string of lip-parted gasps.

The loopy's eyelid twitched.

Abrupt, black, straining silence webbed from the room. Even the breath choked off in Peggy's throat when she saw the pale eyes flutter open. Something creaked in the stillness; her body pressed back unconsciously against the chair. Her eyes were wide, unblinking circles that sucked into her brain the sight of the thing that had been a woman.

Music again; a brass-throated moaning from the dark, like some animal made of welded horns mewling its derangement in a midnight alley.

Suddenly, the right arm of the loopy jerked at its side, the tendons contracted. The left arm twitched alike, snapped out, then fell back and thudded in purple-white limpness against the thigh. The right arm out, the left arm out, the right, the left-right-left-right—like marionette arms twitching from an amateur's dangling strings.

The music caught the time, drum brushes scratching out a rhythm for the convulsions of the loopy's muscles. Peggy pressed back further, her body numbed and cold, her face a livid, staring mask in the fringes of the stage light.

The loopy's right foot moved now, jerking up inflexibly as the distillation constricted muscles in its leg. A second and a third contraction caused the leg to twitch, the left leg flung out in a violent spasm and then the woman's body lurched stiffly forward, filming the transparent silk to its light and shadow.

Peggy heard the sudden hiss of breath that passed the

clenching teeth of Bud and Len and a wave of nausea sprayed foaming sickness up her stomach walls. Before her eyes, the stage abruptly undulated with a watery glitter and it seemed as if the flailing loopy was headed straight for her.

Gasping dizzily, she pressed back in horror, unable to take her eyes from its now agitated face.

She watched the mouth jerk to a gaping cavity, then a twisted scar that split into a wound again. She saw the dark nostrils twitching, saw writhing flesh beneath the ivory cheeks, saw furrows dug and undug in the purple whiteness of the forehead. She saw one lifeless eye wink monstrously and heard the gasp of startled laughter in the room.

While music blared into a fit of grating noise, the woman's arms and legs kept jerking with convulsive cramps that threw her body around the purpled stage like a full-sized rag doll given spastic life.

It was nightmare in an endless sleep. Peggy shivered in helpless terror as she watched the loopy's twisting, leaping dance. The blood in her had turned to ice; there was no life in her but the endless, pounding stagger of her heart. Her eyes were frozen spheres staring at the woman's body writhing white and flaccid underneath the clinging silk.

Then, something went wrong.

Up till then, its muscular seizures had bound the loopy to an area of several yards before the amber flat which was the background for its paroxysmal dance. Now its erratic surging drove the loopy toward the stage-encircling rail.

Peggy heard the thump and creaking strain of wood as the loopy's hip collided with the rail. She cringed into a shuddering knot, her eyes still raised fixedly to the purple-splashed face whose every feature was deformed by throes of warping convulsion.

The loopy staggered back and Peggy saw and heard its leprous hands slapping with a fitful rhythm at its silk-scaled thighs.

Again it sprang forward like a maniac marionette and the woman's stomach thudded sickeningly into the railing wood.

The dark mouth gaped, clamped shut and then the loopy twisted through a jerking revolution and crashed back against the rail again, almost above the table where Peggy sat.

Peggy couldn't breathe. She sat rooted to the chair, her lips a trembling circle of stricken dread, a pounding of blood at her temples as she watched the loopy spin again, its arms a blur of flailing white.

The lurid bleaching of its face dropped toward Peggy as the loopy crashed into the waist-high rail again and bent across its top. The mask of lavender-rained whiteness hung above her, dark eyes twitching open into a hideous stare.

Peggy felt the floor begin to move and the livid face was blurred with darkness, then reappeared in a burst of luminosity. Sound fled on brass-shoed feet, then plunged into her brain again—a smearing discord.

The loopy kept on jerking forward, driving itself against the rail as though it meant to scale it. With every spastic lurch, the diaphanous silk fluttered like a film about its body and every savage collision with the railing tautened the green transparency across its swollen flesh. Peggy looked up in rigid muteness at the loopy's fierce attack on the railing, her eyes unable to escape the wild distortion of the woman's face with its black frame of tangled, snapping hair.

What happened then happened in a blurring passage of seconds.

The grim-faced man came rushing across the purple-lighted stage; the thing that had been a woman went crashing, twitching, flailing at the rail, doubling over it, the spasmodic hitching flinging up its muscle-knotted legs.

A clawing fall.

Peggy lurched back in her chair and the scream that started in her throat was forced back into a strangled gag as the loopy came crashing down onto the table, its limbs a thrash of naked whiteness.

Barbara screamed, the audience gasped and Peggy saw, on the fringe of vision, Bud jumping up, his face a twist of stunned surprise.

The loopy flopped and twisted on the table like a new-caught fish. The music stopped, grinding into silence; a rush of agitated murmur filled the room and blackness swept in brain-submerging waves across Peggy's mind.

Then the cold white hand slapped across her mouth, the dark eyes stared at her in purple light and Peggy felt the darkness flooding.

The horror-smoke room went turning on its side.

Consciousness. It flickered in her brain like gauze-veiled candle-light. A murmuring of sound, a blur of shadow before her eyes.

Breath dripped like syrup from her mouth.

"Here, Peg."

She heard Bud's voice and felt the chilly metal of a flask neck pressed against lips. She swallowed, twisting slightly at the trickle of fire in her throat and stomach, then coughed and pushed away the flask with deadened fingers.

Behind her, a rustling movement. "Hey, she's *back*," Len said. "Ol' Olive Oyl is back."

"You feel all right?" asked Barbara.

She felt all right. Her heart was like a drum hanging from piano wire in her chest, slowly, slowly beaten. Her hands and feet were numb, not with cold but with a sultry torpor. Thoughts moved with a tranquil lethargy, her brain a leisurely machine imbedded in swaths of woolly packing.

She felt all right.

Peggy looked across the night with sleepy eyes. They were on a hilltop, the braked convertible crouching on a jutting edge. Far below, the country slept, a carpet of light and shadow beneath the chalky moon.

An arm snake moved around her waist. "Where are we?" she asked him in a languid voice.

"Few miles outside school," Bud said. "How d'ya feel, honey?"

She stretched, her body a delicious strain of muscles. She sagged back, limp, against his arm.

"*Wonderful*," she murmured with a dizzy smile and scratched the tiny itching bump on her left shoulder. Warmth radiated through her flesh; the night was a sabled glow. There seemed—*somewhere*—to be a memory, but it crouched in secret behind folds of thick content.

"Woman, you were *out*," laughed Bud; and Barbara added and Len added, "*Were* you!" and "Olive Oyl went *plunko*!"

"Out?" Her casual murmur went unheard.

The flask went around and Peggy drank again, relaxing further as the liquor needled fire through her veins.

"Man, I never saw a loopy dance like that!" Len said.

A momentary chill across her back, then warmth again. "Oh," said Peggy, "that's right. I forgot."

She smiled.

"That was what I calls a grand finale!" Len said, dragging back his willing date, who murmured, "*Lenny* boy."

"LUP," Bud muttered, nuzzling at Peggy's hair. "Son of a gun." He reached out idly for the radio knob.

LUP (Lifeless Undead Phenomenon)—This freak of physiological abnormality was discovered during the war when, following certain germ-gas attacks, many of the dead troops were found erect and performing the spasmodic gyrations which later became know as the "loopy's" (LUP's) dance. The particular germ spray responsible was later distilled and is now used in carefully controlled experiments which are conducted only under the strictest of legal license and supervision.

Music surrounded them, its melancholy fingers touching at their hearts. Peggy leaned against her date and felt no need to curb exploring hands. Somewhere, deep within the jellied layers of her mind, there was something trying to escape. It fluttered like a frantic moth imprisoned in congealing wax, struggling wildly but only growing weaker in attempt as the chrysalis hardened.

Four voices sang softly in the night.

"If the world is here tomorrow
I'll be waiting, dear, for you
If the stars are there tomorrow
I'll be wishing on them too."

Four young voices singing, a murmur in immensity. Four bodies, two by two, slackly warm and drugged. A singing, an embracing—a wordless accepting.

"Star light, star bright
Let there be another night."

The singing ended but the song went on.
A young girl sighed.
"Isn't it romantic?" said Olive Oyl.

MAN WITH A CLUB

Jeez, wait'll I tell you what happened last night, Mack. I swear
you'll never believe it. You'll think I'm nuts. But I swear Mack,
I swear I seen it with my own eyes.

I was out with Dot. *You* know, the broad that lives down
near Prospect Park. Yeah, you remember her.

Well, we was going up the Paramount t'see Frankie Laine.
Sat'day night, you know. Puttin' on the dog. Show, feed, take her
home, give'er the old one two.

Well, anyway, I guess it was, oh, seven thirty when we come
up from the I.R.T. station. Forty secon' street. Time Square.
You know the place. Where they got stores down the stairs.
They sell jelly apples and stuff. Yeah, yeah, that's right.

So we come up the street, see? It's jus' like any time. You
know, all the t'eatres lit up, people walkin' around. I grab
Dot's arm and we head for Broadway.

Then I see a bunch o' guys across the street. So I figure it's
probably some drunk cuttin' up. *You* know. So I says to Dot—
come on let's go see what everybody's lookin' at.

So she says—Aw come on, we wantta get a good seat. So I
says . . . haah? Course I don't let no broad crack the whip over
me. *Come on* I say. So I pull her arm and we cross the street
even though she don't wanna.

So there's a big crowd there, see? There's so many people I
can't see what's up. So I taps a guy on the shoulder and I says—
what's goin' on? *He* don't know. He gives me a shrug. Is it
some guy drunk? I says to him. *He* don't know. He says he
thinks it's some guy who ain't got on no clothes. Yeah! That's
what the guy said. Woid fo' woid.

So Dot says—let's go, will ya? I give her the eye. *You* know. Cut it out I says. If there's a guy without no clothes, you'll be the first one'll wanna see it, I says. So she gets all snooty. You know, like all broads get. Sure.

So anyway, we stick around. I push more in the crowd so I can see. Everyone is kinda quiet. You know how crowds is when they're lookin' at somethin'. Like remember how quiet we all was when we was all watching old man Riley when the truck run over him? Yeah, that's right. Quiet like that.

So I keep shovin'. And Dot comes with me too. She knows what's good for 'er. She ain't givin' *me* up. Not with my dough she ain't. Bet your sweet . . . haah? Awright, awright, I'm tellin' ya, ain't I? Don't get 'em in a sling.

So we get up to the front practically and we see what's up.

It's a guy. Yeah. The guy had clothes on too. Yeah, ya slob, what didja think, I was gonna say he was bareass on Time Square? Haa haa, ya jerk!

So this guy has on like a bathin' suit see? Like made of fur. You know. Like Tarzan wears. But he don't look like no Tarzan. He looks like one of them apes Tarzan fights. Lots of muscles. Jeez he was more musclebound than them weight lifters down the "Y". Muscles all over 'im. *Covered* with 'em!

Covered with hair too. Like a ape. Ya know how cold it was last night? Well this guy wasn't even cold—that's how hairy he was.

But scared? Jeez, was he scared. Scared stiff. He had his back to a store window. You know the one, where they sell jewelry for ninety-nine cents. Yeah, near that t'eatre.

Inside the store this guy is starin' out at this other guy. This ape, this guy in Tarzan clothes. Yeah.

This guy has a club in his hand too. *Big* crappin' thing! Like a ballbat only lot fatter. Covered with bumps. Yeah. Like them cavemen used to carry. Yeah . . . haah? Wait a secon' will ya? I'll get to it. You ain't heard nothin' yet. This is a kick.

So we look at this jerk, see? Dot pulls back sort of. What's the matter I says to her, ya sorry he ain't got no clothes on? She don't say nothin'. Just looks white in the gills. Dames. You know.

So I turn to this old jerk next to me. I ask him—who is this guy? But he don't know.

Where'd he come from, I say to him. He shakes his head.

He looked cockeyed, this old jerk. He was staring at this other guy with the club. And his hands is closed like he was prayin' or somethin'. Yeah! Aah, ya meet 'em all over. 'Specially in Time Square. Ha! You said it Mack. Ain't it the truth?

So, anyway, where the hell am I? Haah? Oh, yeah.

So I ask this slob once more another question. I asks him how long he's standin' there. He turns and looks at me like he gonna jump me. Yeah. Jeez, Mack, no crap.

Then he says—just a little while. He turns away again and starts in starin' at the crazy guy with the club. He has a book under his arm too. Whattaya mean who? The old jerk I mean. He keeps starin' at this guy with the club.

So Dot pulls my arm. Come on, she says, let's go. I pull away. Let go woman, I says. I want to see what goes. So I look up front again.

This hairy guy is showin' his teeth at everybody, see? Yeah. Like an animal. Some broads in the crowd is pullin' their dates back. Come on, come on, they're sayin'. Jeez. Broads. Ya can't argue with 'em. They're too dumb. You know.

Then someone says—call a cop. So I figure things're gonna get hot soon. Maybe there'll be a good fight, I says to Dot. So what does she do? Come on Mickey, she says, let's go see Frankie Laine. Laine Schmaine. Aah, fo' Chrissakes anyway. What can ya expect from a dame?

Haah? So I says to her—in a couple o' minutes. Can'tch wait a couple o' minutes? A cop'll come soon I says to her. Cops always stick their noses in when there's a crowd.

So I turn to a guy on the other side of me and I says to him—where did this guy come from?

Who the hell knows? he says. All I know is, I was walkin' by, all of a sudden, *bang*! There he is, standin' by the window.

So we look at the guy. Would ya look at the guy, says this guy. Look at those teeth. He looks like a caveman.

I'm gettin' to that Mack. I'm *gettin'* to it. Hold your water.

So I look at the guy with the club, see? His eyes is small. His chin sticks way out. He looks like . . . you remember the time we cut school that day. What day? Shut up a second and I'll tell you what day!

You remember we went through Central Park and we went to that museum? You know, *way* up there. Around 8oth street or somethin'. *I* don't know. Anyway, you remember those cases o' heads?

No, ya jerk, don't ya remember? It was upstairs someplace. Well, what the hell. Anyway, the heads showed what men looked like from the time they was apes.

So what? So this guy looked like what men looked like t'ousands o' years ago. Or millions. Who knows? Anyway, this guy looks like a caveman. Yeah.

Let's see. Where was I? Oh, yeah.

So I hear some guy say—this is hideous.

Yeah! Ha! This guy says—this is *hideous*. Ain't that a kick? Well who the hell d'you think? The *old jerk*! With his bible. I *did* so tell ya it was a bible. Awright, so I said he had a book. So I meant it was a bible.

So I look at this guy see? The old guy.

He looks like one of those jerks you see down in the Square. You know, giving the crap about—comes the revolution! *You* know. Reds. Yeah.

Anyway I figure I'll humor the old fart. So I says—where do ya think the guy come from?

Well, *holy Jeez*, if this guy doesn't give me the eye like I spit on his old lady or something.

Don't you know? he says to me. Don't you *see*?

Yeah. How do ya like that? Don't I *see*. See what fo' crap's sake? That's what *I* wanna know.

So I look the old jerk over. Some goddam Commie I figure. I would've give him the knee if there wasn't so many guys around.

Well, to make a long story short, all of a sudden the crowd *jumps back*! I get almost knocked down. Dot yells blue murder. Look out! someone else yells.

So I look up front.

The crazy guy is tryin' to jump some broad up front. He's *growlin'* at her. Yeah! Look, was I there or wasn't I? Well, shut up then. I was there. I saw the bastid with my own eyes. Take my woid.

The guy even unloads his club and takes a swat at the broad.

Yeah! That's right. Boy, what a kick. It was like a crappin' movie.

Get a cop, get a cop! the broads start yellin', jumpin', out o' their pants. They're all the same. Somethin' happens and they go runnin' for cops.

Yeah, and some old character is standin' in an ashcan and yellin'—Police! Police! Help, police! Yeah! Ya shoulda seen the slob. You woulda died.

So everybody is excited and the crowd's breakin' it up. But there's more crowds pushin' in, see? To see what's goin' on. So everybody's shovin' and pushin', pushin' and shovin'. Scene from a crappin' movie.

What? The guy with the club? Aah, he's back against the window again. Sure. His eyes is rollin' around like crazy. All the time he's showin' his teeth. It was a riot Mack, take it from me.

So somebody *gets* a cop. No, wait a second. That ain't all.

This cop pushes through the crowd, see? *Big* son of a bitch. You know the kind. All right, *break* it up, *break* it up, he says. Same old crap all the time. *Break* it up.

He comes up to the guy with the club.

And who do you think *you* are, he says, Superman? He gives the guy a shove. Come on ya bum, he says, you're under . . .

And all of a sudden, boppo! The guy swings his club and whacks the bull over the nut. *Jeez did he slug him!* The cop goes down like a sack of potatoes. Blood comes out his ears.

Everyone gives a yell. Dot grabs my hand and pulls me down towards Eight Avenue.

But the guy isn't chasin' anybody. So I pulls away from Dot.

Come on Mickey, she says, let's go to the show. Is *she* scared. She's goin' in her . . . haah? Awright!

So I says I ain't missin' this for nothin'. What a broad.

You'd think a guy got a chance everyday to see a show like that.

She keeps whinin'. You *told* me you was takin' me to the Paramount, she says.

Look baby, I says, Look, you'll get to the Paramount, see? Just keep your pants on. Did I tell her right? What the hell. Ya can't let 'em walk on ya. Am I right or am I wrong?

Haah? Oh yeah.

Well I leave her down by the Automat down the street. I says I'll be right back. I just wanna get a good look at the knocked out cop.

So I go back. There isn't many people around. They was all scared I guess. Jeez how that guy cracked that cop! I could still hear it, Mack.

So the cop is out cold see? But there's *another* cop comin'. He has his gun out. Sure, whattaya think. You think they take a chance? Hell no. Pull out their rods. What do they care they might hit innocent bystanders. Aah, *you* know cops.

Stand back everybody! yells the cop. *Stand back!* Jeez. All the time! They say the same things.

So-o, I watch him move in on the guy with the club. He's still standin' by that store window. The caveman I'm talkin' about. Pay attention will ya!

So the cop says—*put down* that club if you value your life. Uh-huh. How do you like that?

Well this character just *growls*. He don't know what the hell the cop is talkin' about. He starts to *scream*. Like a animal. Gets down in a crouch like Godoy used to, remember? Yeah.

Does he drop the club? Are you kiddin'? He has it in his mitt so tight you couldn't drag it out with ten horses. Yeah.

And he's kinda *bouncin'* on his feet too. Yeah. Like that ape in the movies, what the hell's its name?

Anyway, bouncin' and puffin'. Yeah. Jeez, it was funny. Ooop, ooop, ooop, the guy is sayin'. You shoulda been there.

So the cop holds up his gun, see?

I'm *warnin'* ya, he says. You put down that club and come along peaceably or else.

The guy growls.

Then, *get this*, the store's front door opens all of a sudden.

Officer, officer! yells the guy. Don't you shoot out my brand new window!

Laugh! I t'ought I'd die.

But the cop keeps comin'. Everybody's quiet and watchin'. All the cars are stopped. Horns was honkin'. This big crowd all around watchin' the cop movin' in on this crazy guy. Yeah, a regular scene.

Drop that club! says the cop. He takes another step.

The crazy guy jumps!

Bang! goes the rod. Tears a hole out the guy's right shoulder. He goes floppin' back. Falls on the sidewalk. Squirmin' around. Blood all over the place. Jeez what a mess.

Get this though!

Even with half his shoulder shot off, this guy *starts gettin' up again*. Yeah! Jeez you never seen nothin' like it, I tell ya Mack. What stren'th!

Well the cop moves in fast and gives him a *whack* on the head with a butt. The guy goes down. But he gets up again! Honest I never seen such stren'th.

He takes a swing at the cop with his left arm. The cop gives him another on the head. The guy goes down for good. He's *out*.

No wait, there's some more.

After the ambulance comes and they all get carried away, I go back to Dot. Sure, she's still there. Whattaya think? No dame is gonna run out on dough. Am I right or wrong?

So we start back up the street. I see the blood on the sidewalk. The slob from the store is tryin' to mop it up. Kills his business, see?

Then I notice, who's walkin' beside me but the old jerk with the bible.

Well whattaya say? I says to him, kiddin' him along. *You* know.

He looks at me. Doesn't say nothin', just looks at me like he was tryin' to figure where the hell *I* come from. A real character.

Where do you think the guy come from? I says to him.

So he stares at me. And, *get this Mack*, he says:

From the past.

Yeah! How do you like that? Wait though. That ain't the best part.

I give him the once over, see? Then, just before we reach the corner I says—From the past haah? and give 'im an elbow in the rib.

And he says—get this—*Maybe from the future!*

Yeah! What do ya do with guys like that? Ya put 'em away. That's right.

So me and Dot went to the Paramount. Wait, I'll tell ya.

Boy, hey, *that Frankie Laine!*

BUTTON, BUTTON

The package was lying by the front door—a cube-shaped carton sealed with tape, the name and address printed by hand: MR. AND MRS. ARTHUR LEWIS, 217 E. 37TH STREET, NEW YORK, NEW YORK 10016. Norma picked it up, unlocked the door, and went into the apartment. It was just getting dark.

After she put the lamb chops in the broiler, she made herself a drink and sat down to open the package.

Inside the carton was a push-button unit fastened to a small wooden box. A glass dome covered the button. Norma tried to lift it off, but it was locked in place. She turned the unit over and saw a folded piece of paper Scotch-taped to the bottom of the box. She pulled it off: "Mr. Steward will call on you at eight p.m."

Norma put the button unit beside her on the couch. She sipped the drink and reread the typed note, smiling.

A few moments later, she went back into the kitchen to make the salad. The doorbell rang at eight o'clock. "I'll get it," Norma called from the kitchen. Arthur was in the living room, reading.

There was a small man in the hallway. He removed his hat as Norma opened the door. "Mrs. Lewis?" he inquired politely.

"Yes?"

"I'm Mr. Steward."

"Oh, yes." Norma repressed a smile. She was sure now it was a sales pitch.

"May I come in?" asked Mr. Steward.

"I'm rather busy," Norma said. "I'll get you your watchama-callit, though." She started to turn.

"Don't you want to know what it is?"

Norma turned back. Mr. Steward's tone had been offensive. "No, I don't think so," she said.

"It could prove very valuable," he told her.

"Monetarily?" she challenged.

Mr. Steward nodded. "Monetarily," he said.

Norma frowned. She didn't like his attitude. "What are you trying to sell?" she asked.

"I'm not selling anything," he answered.

Arthur came out of the living room. "Something wrong?"

Mr. Steward introduced himself.

"Oh, the . . ." Arthur pointed toward the living room and smiled. "What is that gadget, anyway?"

"It won't take long to explain," replied Mr. Steward. "May I come in?"

"If you're selling something . . ." Arthur said.

Mr. Steward shook his head. "I'm not."

Arthur looked at Norma. "Up to you," she said.

He hesitated. "Well, why not?" he said.

They went into the living room and Mr. Steward sat in Norma's chair. He reached into an inside coat pocket and withdrew a small sealed envelope. "Inside here is a key to the bell-unit dome," he said. He set the envelope on the chairside table. "The bell is connected to our office."

"What's it for?" asked Arthur.

"If you push the button," Mr. Steward told him, "somewhere in the world, someone you don't know will die. In return for which you will receive a payment of fifty thousand dollars."

Norma stared at the small man. He was smiling.

"What are you talking about?" Arthur asked him.

Mr. Steward looked surprised. "But I've just explained," he said.

"Is this a practical joke?" asked Arthur.

"Not at all. The offer is completely genuine."

"You aren't making sense," Arthur said. "You expect us to believe . . ."

"Whom do you represent?" demanded Norma.

Mr. Steward looked embarrassed. "I'm afraid I'm not at liberty to tell you that," he said. "However, I assure you the organization is of international scope."

"I think you'd better leave," Arthur said, standing.

Mr. Steward rose. "Of course."

"And take your button unit with you."

"Are you sure you wouldn't care to think about it for a day or so?"

Arthur picked up the button unit and the envelope and thrust them into Mr. Steward's hands. He walked into the hall and pulled open the door.

"I'll leave my card," said Mr. Steward. He placed it on the table by the door.

When he was gone, Arthur tore it in half and tossed the pieces onto the table. "God!" he said.

Norma was still sitting on the sofa. "What do you think it was?" she asked.

"I don't care to know," he answered.

She tried to smile but couldn't. "Aren't you curious at all?"

"No," he shook his head.

After Arthur returned to his book, Norma went back to the kitchen and finished washing the dishes.

"Why won't you talk about it?" Norma asked later.

Arthur's eyes shifted as he brushed his teeth. He looked at her reflection in the bathroom mirror.

"Doesn't it intrigue you?"

"It offends me," Arthur said.

"I know, but—" Norma rolled another curler in her hair "—doesn't it intrigue you, too?"

"You think it's a practical joke?" she asked as they went into the bedroom.

"If it is, it's a sick one."

Norma sat on the bed and took off her slippers.

"Maybe it's some kind of psychological research."

Arthur shrugged. "Could be."

"Maybe some eccentric millionaire is doing it."

"Maybe."

"Wouldn't you like to know?"

Arthur shook his head.

"Why?"

"Because it's immoral," he told her.

Norma slid beneath the covers. "Well, I think it's intriguing," she said.

Arthur turned off the lamp and leaned over to kiss her. "Good night," he said.

"Good night." She patted his back.

Norma closed her eyes. Fifty thousand dollars, she thought.

In the morning, as she left the apartment, Norma saw the card halves on the table. Impulsively, she dropped them into her purse. She locked the front door and joined Arthur in the elevator.

While she was on her coffee break, she took the card halves from her purse and held the torn edges together. Only Mr. Steward's name and telephone number were printed on the card.

After lunch, she took the card halves from her purse again and Scotch-taped the edges together. Why am I doing this? she thought.

Just before five, she dialed the number.

"Good afternoon," said Mr. Steward's voice.

Norma almost hung up but restrained herself. She cleared her throat. "This is Mrs. Lewis," she said.

"Yes, Mrs. Lewis." Mr. Steward sounded pleased.

"I'm curious."

"That's natural," Mr. Steward said.

"Not that I believe a word of what you told us."

"Oh, it's quite authentic," Mr. Steward answered.

"Well, whatever . . ." Norma swallowed. "When you said someone in the world would die, what did you mean?"

"Exactly that," he answered. "It could be anyone. All we guarantee is that you don't know them. And, of course, that you wouldn't have to watch them die."

"For fifty thousand dollars," Norma said.

"That is correct."

She made a scoffing sound. "That's crazy."

"Nonetheless, that is the proposition," Mr. Steward said. "Would you like me to return the button unit?"

Norma stiffened. "Certainly not." She hung up angrily.

The package was lying by the front door; Norma saw it as she left the elevator. Well, of all the nerve, she thought. She glared at the carton as she unlocked the door. I just won't take it in, she thought. She went inside and started dinner.

Later, she carried her drink to the front hall. Opening the door, she picked up the package and carried it into the kitchen, leaving it on the table.

She sat in the living room, sipping her drink and looking out the window. After awhile, she went back into the kitchen to turn the cutlets in the broiler. She put the package in a bottom cabinet. She'd throw it out in the morning.

"Maybe some eccentric millionaire is playing games with people," she said.

Arthur looked up from his dinner. "I don't understand you."

"What does that mean?"

"Let it go," he told her.

Norma ate in silence. Suddenly, she put her fork down. "Suppose it's a genuine offer," she said.

Arthur stared at her.

"Suppose it's a genuine offer."

"All right, suppose it is!" He looked incredulous. "What would you like to do? Get the button back and push it? Murder someone?"

Norma looked disgusted. "Murder."

"How would *you* define it?"

"If you don't even know the person?" Norma asked.

Arthur looked astounded. "Are you saying what I think you are?"

"If it's some old Chinese peasant ten thousand miles away? Some diseased native in the Congo?"

"How about some baby boy in Pennsylvania?" Arthur countered. "Some beautiful little girl on the next block?"

"Now you're loading things."

"The point is, Norma," he continued, "that *who* you kill makes no difference. It's still murder."

"The point is," Norma broke in, "if it's someone you've never seen in your life and never will see, someone whose death you don't even have to know about, you still wouldn't push the button?"

Arthur stared at her, appalled. "You mean you would?"

"Fifty thousand dollars, Arthur."

"What has the amount . . ."

"Fifty thousand dollars, Arthur," Norma interrupted. "A chance to take that trip to Europe we've always talked about."

"Norma, no."

"A chance to buy that cottage on the Island."

"Norma, no." His face was white. "For God's sake, no!"

She shuddered. "All right, take it easy," she said. "Why are you getting so upset? It's only talk."

After dinner, Arthur went into the living room. Before he left the table, he said, "I'd rather not discuss it anymore, if you don't mind."

Norma shrugged. "Fine with me."

She got up earlier than usual to make pancakes, eggs, and bacon for Arthur's breakfast.

"What's the occasion?" he asked with a smile.

"No occasion." Norma looked offended. "I wanted to do it, that's all."

"Good," he said. "I'm glad you did."

She refilled his cup. "Wanted to show you I'm not . . ." she shrugged.

"Not what?"

"Selfish."

"Did I say you were?"

"Well—" She gestured vaguely. "—last night . . ."

Arthur didn't speak.

"All that talk about the button," Norma said. "I think you—well, misunderstood me."

"In what way?" His voice was guarded.

"I think you felt—" She gestured again. "—that I was only thinking of myself."

"Oh."

"I wasn't."

"Norma."

"Well, I wasn't. When I talked about Europe, a cottage on the Island . . ."

"Norma, why are we getting so involved in this?"

"I'm not involved at all." She drew in a shaking breath. "I'm simply trying to indicate that . . ."

"What?"

"That I'd like for us to go to Europe. Like for us to have a nicer apartment, nicer furniture, nicer clothes. Like for us to finally have a baby, for that matter."

"Norma, we will," he said.

"When?"

He stared at her in dismay. "Norma . . ."

"When?"

"Are you—" He seemed to draw back slightly. "Are you really saying . . . ?"

"I'm saying that they're probably doing it for some research project!" she cut him off. "That they want to know what average people would do under such a circumstance! That they're just saying someone would die, in order to study reactions, see if there'd be guilt, anxiety, whatever! You don't really think they'd kill somebody, do you?"

Arthur didn't answer. She saw his hands trembling. After awhile, he got up and left.

When he'd gone to work, Norma remained at the table, staring into her coffee. I'm going to be late, she thought. She shrugged.

What difference did it make? She should be home anyways, not working in an office.

While she was stacking the dishes, she turned abruptly, dried her hands, and took the package from the bottom cabinet. Opening it, she set the button unit on the table. She stared at it for a long time before taking the key from its envelope and removing the glass dome. She stared at the button. How ridiculous, she thought. All this over a meaningless button.

Reaching out, she pressed it down. For us, she thought angrily.

She shuddered. Was it happening? A chill of horror swept across her.

In a moment, it had passed. She made a contemptuous noise. Ridiculous, she thought. To get so worked up over nothing.

She had just turned the supper steaks and was making herself another drink when the telephone rang. She picked it up. "Hello?"

"Mrs. Lewis?"

"Yes?"

"This is the Lenox Hill Hospital."

She felt unreal as the voice informed her of the subway accident, the shoving crowd. Arthur pushed from the platform in front of the train. She was conscious of shaking her head but couldn't stop.

As she hung up, she remembered Arthur's life insurance policy for $25,000, with double indemnity for—

"No." She couldn't seem to breathe. She struggled to her feet and walked in the kitchen numbly. Something cold pressed at her skull as she removed the button unit from the wastebasket. There were no nails or screws visible. She couldn't see how it was put together.

Abruptly, she began to smash it on the sink edge, pounding it harder and harder, until the wood split. She pulled the sides apart, cutting her fingers without noticing. There were no transistors in the box, no wires or tubes. The box was empty.

She whirled with a gasp as the telephone rang. Stumbling into the living room, she picked up the receiver.

"Mrs. Lewis?" Mr. Steward asked.

It wasn't her voice shrieking so; it couldn't be. "You said I wouldn't know the one that died!"

"My dear lady," Mr. Steward said, "do you really think you knew your husband?"

DUEL

At 11:32 a.m., Mann passed the truck.

He was heading west, en route to San Francisco. It was Thursday and unseasonably hot for April. He had his suitcoat off, his tie removed and shirt collar opened, his sleeve cuffs folded back. There was sunlight on his left arm and on part of his lap. He could feel the heat of it through his dark trousers as he drove along the two-lane highway. For the past twenty minutes, he had not seen another vehicle going in either direction.

Then he saw the truck ahead, moving up a curving grade between two high green hills. He heard the grinding strain of its motor and saw a double shadow on the road. The truck was pulling a trailer.

He paid no attention to the details of the truck. As he drew behind it on the grade, he edged his car toward the opposite lane. The road ahead had blind curves and he didn't try to pass until the truck had crossed the ridge. He waited until it started around a left curve on the downgrade, then, seeing that the way was clear, pressed down on the accelerator pedal and steered his car into the eastbound lane. He waited until he could see the truck front in his rearview mirror before he turned back into the proper lane.

Mann looked across the countryside ahead. There were ranges of mountains as far as he could see and, all around him, rolling green hills. He whistled softly as the car sped down the winding grade, its tires making crisp sounds on the pavement.

At the bottom of the hill, he crossed a concrete bridge and, glancing to the right, saw a dry stream bed strewn with rocks

and gravel. As the car moved off the bridge, he saw a trailer
park set back from the highway to his right. How can anyone
live out here? he thought. His shifting gaze caught sight of a
pet cemetery ahead and he smiled. Maybe those people in the
trailers wanted to be close to the graves of their dogs and cats.

The highway ahead was straight now. Mann drifted into a
reverie, the sunlight on his arm and lap. He wondered what
Ruth was doing. The kids, of course, were in school and would
be for hours yet. Maybe Ruth was shopping; Thursday was the
day she usually went. Mann visualized her in the supermarket,
putting various items into the basket cart. He wished he were
with her instead of starting on another sales trip. Hours of
driving yet before he'd reach San Francisco. Three days of hotel
sleeping and restaurant eating, hoped-for contacts and likely
disappointments. He sighed; then, reaching out impulsively, he
switched on the radio. He revolved the tuning knob until he
found a station playing soft, innocuous music. He hummed
along with it, eyes almost out of focus on the road ahead.

He started as the truck roared past him on the left, causing
his car to shudder slightly. He watched the truck and trailer
cut in abruptly for the westbound lane and frowned as he had
to brake to maintain a safe distance behind it. What's with
you? he thought.

He eyed the truck with cursory disapproval. It was a huge
gasoline tanker pulling a tank trailer, each of them having six
pairs of wheels. He could see that it was not a new rig but was
dented and in need of renovation, its tanks painted a cheap-
looking silvery color. Mann wondered if the driver had done
the painting himself. His gaze shifted from the word FLAM-
MABLE printed across the back of the trailer tank, red letters
on a white background, to the parallel reflector lines painted
in red across the bottom of the tank to the massive rubber
flaps swaying behind the rear tires, then back up again. The
reflector lines looked as though they'd been clumsily applied
with a stencil. The driver must be an independent trucker, he
decided, and not too affluent a one, from the looks of his
outfit. He glanced at the trailer's license plate. It was a California issue.

Mann checked his speedometer. He was holding steady at 55 miles an hour, as he invariably did when he drove without thinking on the open highway. The truck driver must have done a good 70 to pass him so quickly. That seemed a little odd. Weren't truck drivers supposed to be a cautious lot?

He grimaced at the smell of the truck's exhaust and looked at the vertical pipe to the left of the cab. It was spewing smoke, which clouded darkly back across the trailer. Christ, he thought. With all the furor about air pollution, why do they keep allowing that sort of thing on the highways?

He scowled at the constant fumes. They'd make him nauseated in a little while, he knew. He couldn't lag back here like this. Either he slowed down or he passed the truck again. He didn't have the time to slow down. He'd gotten a late start. Keeping it at 55 all the way, he'd just about make his afternoon appointment. No, he'd have to pass.

Depressing the gas pedal, he eased his car toward the opposite lane. No sign of anything ahead. Traffic on this route seemed almost nonexistent today. He pushed down harder on the accelerator and steered all the way into the eastbound lane.

As he passed the truck, he glanced at it. The cab was too high for him to see into. All he caught sight of was the back of the truck driver's left hand on the steering wheel. It was darkly tanned and square-looking, with large veins knotted on its surface.

When Mann could see the truck reflected in the rearview mirror, he pulled back over to the proper lane and looked ahead again.

He glanced at the rearview mirror in surprise as the truck driver gave him an extended horn blast. What was that? he wondered; a greeting or a curse? He grunted with amusement, glancing at the mirror as he drove. The front fenders of the truck were a dingy purple color, the paint faded and chipped; another amateurish job. All he could see was the lower portion of the truck; the rest was cut off by the top of his rear window.

To Mann's right, now, was a slope of shalelike earth with patches of scrub grass growing on it. His gaze jumped to the

clapboard house on top of the slope. The television aerial on
its roof was sagging at an angle of less than 40 degrees. Must
give great reception, he thought.

He looked to the front again, glancing aside abruptly at a sign
printed in jagged block letters on a piece of plywood: NIGHT
CRAWLERS—BAIT. What the hell is a night crawler? he wondered. It sounded like some monster in a low-grade Hollywood
thriller.

The unexpected roar of the truck motor made his gaze jump
to the rearview mirror. Instantly, his startled look jumped to
the side mirror. By God, the guy was passing him *again*. Mann
turned his head to scowl at the leviathan form as it drifted by.
He tried to see into the cab but couldn't because of its height.
What's with him, anyway? he wondered. What the hell are we
having here, a contest? See which vehicle can stay ahead the
longest?

He thought of speeding up to stay ahead but changed his
mind. When the truck and trailer started back into the west-
bound lane, he let up on the pedal, voicing a newly incredulous sound as he saw that if he hadn't slowed down, he would
have been prematurely cut off again. Jesus Christ, he thought.
What's *with* this guy?

His scowl deepened as the odor of the truck's exhaust
reached his nostrils again. Irritably, he cranked up the window
on his left. Damn it, was he going to have to breathe that
crap all the way to San Francisco? He couldn't afford to slow
down. He had to meet Forbes at a quarter after three and that
was that.

He looked ahead. At least there was no traffic complicating
matters. Mann pressed down on the accelerator pedal, drawing close behind the truck. When the highway curved enough
to the left to give him a completely open view of the route
ahead, he jarred down on the pedal, steering out into the opposite lane.

The truck edged over, blocking his way.

For several moments, all Mann could do was stare at it
in blank confusion. Then, with a startled noise, he braked,

returning to the proper lane. The truck moved back in front of him.

Mann could not allow himself to accept what apparently had taken place. It had to be a coincidence. The truck driver couldn't have blocked his way on purpose. He waited for more than a minute, then flicked down the turn-indicator lever to make his intentions perfectly clear and, depressing the accelerator pedal, steered again into the eastbound lane.

Immediately, the truck shifted, barring his way.

"Jesus Christ!" Mann was astounded. This was unbelievable. He'd never seen such a thing in twenty-six years of driving. He returned to the west-bound lane, shaking his head as the truck swung back in front of him.

He eased up on the gas pedal, falling back to avoid the truck's exhaust. Now what? he wondered. He still had to make San Francisco on schedule. Why in God's name hadn't he gone a little out of his way in the beginning, so he could have traveled by freeway? This damned highway was two lane all the way.

Impulsively, he sped into the eastbound lane again. To his surprise, the truck driver did not pull over. Instead, the driver stuck his left arm out and waved him on. Mann started pushing down on the accelerator. Suddenly, he let up on the pedal with a gasp and jerked the steering wheel around, raking back behind the truck so quickly that his car began to fishtail. He was fighting to control its zigzag whipping when a blue convertible shot by him in the opposite lane. Mann caught a momentary vision of the man inside it glaring at him.

The car came under his control again. Mann was sucking breath in through his mouth. His heart was pounding almost painfully. My God! he thought. *He wanted me to hit that car head on.* The realization stunned him. True, he should have seen to it himself that the road ahead was clear; that was his failure. But to wave him on . . . Mann felt appalled and sickened. Boy, oh, boy, oh, boy, he thought. This was really one for the books. That son of a bitch had meant for not only him to be killed but a totally uninvolved passer-by as well. The idea seemed beyond his comprehension. On a California highway on a Thursday morning? *Why?*

Mann tried to calm himself and rationalize the incident. Maybe it's the heat, he thought. Maybe the truck driver had a tension headache or an upset stomach; maybe both. Maybe he'd had a fight with his wife. Maybe she'd failed to put out last night. Mann tried in vain to smile. There could be any number of reasons. Reaching out, he twisted off the radio. The cheerful music irritated him.

He drove behind the truck for several minutes, his face a mask of animosity. As the exhaust fumes started putting his stomach on edge, he suddenly forced down the heel of his right hand on the horn bar and held it there. Seeing that the route ahead was clear, he pushed in the accelerator pedal all the way and steered into the opposite lane.

The movement of his car was paralleled immediately by the truck. Mann stayed in place, right hand jammed down on the horn bar. Get out of the way, you son of a bitch! he thought. He felt the muscles of his jaw hardening until they ached. There was a twisting in his stomach.

"Damn!" He pulled back quickly to the proper lane, shuddering with fury. "You miserable son of a bitch," he muttered, glaring at the truck as it was shifted back in front of him. What the hell is wrong with you? I pass your goddamn rig a couple of times and you go flying off the deep end? Are you nuts or something? Mann nodded tensely. Yes, he thought, he *is*. No other explanation.

He wondered what Ruth would think of all this, how she'd react. Probably, she'd start to honk the horn and would keep on honking it, assuming that, eventually, it would attract the attention of a policeman. He looked around with a scowl. Just where in hell *were* the policemen out here, anyway? He made a scoffing noise. What policemen? Here in the boondocks? They probably had a sheriff on horseback, for Christ's sake.

He wondered suddenly if he could fool the truck driver by passing on the right. Edging his car toward the shoulder, he peered ahead. No chance. There wasn't room enough. The truck driver could shove him through that wire fence if he wanted to, sure as hell, he thought.

Driving where he was, he grew conscious of the debris lying beside the highway: beer cans, candy wrappers, ice-cream containers, newspaper sections browned and rotted by the weather, a FOR SALE sign torn in half. Keep America beautiful, he thought sardonically. He passed a boulder with the name WILL JASPER painted on it in white. Who the hell is Will Jasper? he wondered. What would he think of this situation.

Unexpectedly, the car began to bounce. For several anxious moments, Mann thought that one of his tires had gone flat. Then he noticed that the paving along this section of highway consisted of pitted slabs with gaps between them. He saw the truck and trailer jolting up and down and thought: I hope it shakes your brains loose. As the truck veered into a sharp left curve, he caught a fleeting glimpse of the driver's face in the cab's side mirror. There was not enough time to establish his appearance.

"Ah," he said. A long, steep hill was looming up ahead. The truck would have to climb it slowly. There would doubtless be an opportunity to pass somewhere on the grade. Mann pressed down on the accelerator pedal, drawing as close behind the truck as safety would allow.

Halfway up the slope, Mann saw a turnout for the eastbound lane with no oncoming traffic anywhere in sight. Flooring the accelerator pedal, he shot into the opposite lane. The slow-moving truck began to angle out in front of him. Face stiffening, Mann steered his speeding car across the highway edge and curbed it sharply on the turnout. Clouds of dust went billowing up behind his car, making him lose sight of the truck. His tires buzzed and crackled on the dirt, then, suddenly, were humming on the pavement once again.

He glanced at the rearview mirror and a barking laugh erupted from his throat. He'd only meant to pass. The dust had been an unexpected bonus. Let the bastard get a sniff of something rotten smelling in *his* nose for a change! he thought.

He honked the horn elatedly, a mocking rhythm of bleats. Screw you, Jack!

He swept across the summit of the hill. A striking vista lay ahead: sunlit hills and flatland, a corridor of dark trees, quadrangles of cleared-off acreage and bright-green vegetables patches; far off, in the distance, a mammoth water tower. Mann felt stirred by the panoramic sight. Lovely, he thought. Reaching out, he turned the radio back on and started humming cheerfully with the music.

Seven minutes later, he passed a billboard advertising CHUCK'S CAFÉ. No thanks, Chuck, he thought. He glanced at a gray house nestled in a hollow. Was that a cemetery in its front yard or a group of plaster statuary for sale?

Hearing the noise behind him, Mann looked at the rearview mirror and felt himself go cold with fear. The truck was hurtling down the hill, pursuing him.

His mouth fell open and he threw a glance at the speedometer. He was doing more than 60! On a curving downgrade, that was not at all a safe speed to be driving. Yet the truck must be exceeding that by a considerable margin, it was closing the distance between them so rapidly. Mann swallowed, leaning to the right as he steered his car around a sharp curve. Is the man *insane*? he thought.

His gaze jumped forward searchingly. He saw a turnoff half a mile ahead and decided that he'd use it. In the rearview mirror, the huge square radiator grille was all he could see now. He stamped down on the gas pedal and his tires screeched unnervingly as he wheeled around another curve, thinking that, surely, the truck would have to slow down here.

He groaned as it rounded the curve with ease, only the sway of its tanks revealing the outward pressure of the turn. Mann bit trembling lips together as he whipped his car around another curve. A straight descent now. He depressed the pedal farther, glanced at the speedometer. Almost 70 miles an hour! He wasn't used to driving this fast!

In agony, he saw the turnoff shoot by on his right. He couldn't have left the highway at this speed, anyways; he'd have overturned. Goddamn it, what was wrong with that son of a bitch? Mann honked his horn in frightened rage. Cranking down the window suddenly, he shoved his left arm out to wave the truck back. "*Back!*" he yelled. He honked the horn again. "Get back, you crazy bastard!"

The truck was almost on him now. He's going to kill me! Mann thought, horrified. He honked the horn repeatedly, then had to use both hands to grip the steering wheel as he swept around another curve. He flashed a look at the rearview mirror. He could see only the bottom portion of the truck's radiator grille. He was going to lose control! He felt the rear wheels start to drift and let up on the pedal quickly. The tire treads bit in, the car leaped on, regaining its momentum.

Mann saw the bottom of the grade ahead, and in the distance there was a building with a sign that read CHUCK'S CAFÉ. The truck was gaining ground again. This is insane! he thought, enraged and terrified at once. The highway straightened out. He floored the pedal: 74 now—75. Mann braced himself, trying to ease the car as far to the right as possible.

Abruptly, he began to brake, then swerved to the right, raking his car into the open area in front of the café. He cried out as the car began to fishtail, then careened into a skid. *Steer with it!* Screamed a voice in his mind. The rear of the car was lashing from side to side, tires spewing dirt and raising clouds of dust. Mann pressed harder on the brake pedal, turning further into the skid. The car began to straighten out and he braked harder yet, conscious, on the sides of his vision, of the truck and trailer roaring by on the highway. He nearly sideswiped one of the cars parked in front of the café, bounced and skidded by it, going almost straight now. He jammed in the brake pedal as hard as he could. The rear end broke to the right and the car spun half around, sheering sideways to a neck-wrenching halt thirty yards beyond the café.

Mann sat in pulsing silence, eyes closed. His heartbeats felt like club blows in his chest. He couldn't seem to catch his breath. If he were ever going to have a heart attack, it would be now. After a while, he opened his eyes and pressed his right palm against his chest. His heart was still throbbing laboredly.

No wonder, he thought. It isn't every day I'm almost murdered by a truck.

He raised the handle and pushed out the door, then started forward, grunting in surprise as the safety belt held him in place. Reaching down with shaking fingers, he depressed the release button and pulled the ends of the belt apart. He glanced at the cafe. What had its patrons thought of his breakneck appearance? he wondered.

He stumbled as he walked to the front door of the café. TRUCKERS WELCOME, read a sign in the window. It gave Mann a queasy feeling to see it. Shivering, he pulled open the door and went inside, avoiding the sight of its customers. He felt certain they were watching him, but he didn't have the strength to face their looks. Keeping his gaze fixed straight ahead, he moved to the rear of the café and opened the door marked GENTS.

Moving to the sink, he twisted the right-hand faucet and leaned over to cup cold water in his palms and splash it on his face. There was a fluttering of his stomach muscles he could not control.

Straightening up, he tugged down several towels from their dispenser and patted them against his face, grimacing at the smell of the paper. Dropping the soggy towels into a wastebasket beside the sink, he regarded himself in the wall mirror. Still with us, Mann, he thought. He nodded, swallowing. Drawing out his metal comb, he neatened his hair. You never know, he thought. You just never know. You drift along, year after year, presuming certain values to be fixed; like being able to drive on a public thoroughfare without somebody trying to murder you. You come to depend on that sort of thing. Then something occurs and all bets are off. One shocking incident and all the years of logic and acceptance are displaced and, suddenly, the jungle is in front of you again. *Man, part animal, part angel.* Where had he come across that phrase? He shivered.

It was entirely an animal in that truck out there.

His breath was almost back to normal now. Mann forced a smile at his reflection. All right, boy, he told himself. It's over now. It as a goddamned nightmare, but it's over. You are on your way to San Francisco. You'll get yourself a nice hotel room, order a bottle of expensive Scotch, soak your body in a hot bath and forget. Damn right, he thought. He turned and walked out of the washroom.

He jolted to a halt, his breath cut off. Standing rooted, heartbeat hammering at his chest, he gaped through the front window of the café.

The truck and trailer were parked outside.

Mann stared at them in unbelieving shock. It wasn't possible. He'd seen them roaring by at top speed. The driver had won; he'd *won*! He'd had the whole damn highway to himself! *Why had he turned back?*

Mann looked around with sudden dread. There were five men eating, three along the counter, two in booths. He cursed himself for having failed to look at faces when he'd entered. Now there was no way of knowing who it was. Mann felt his legs begin to shake.

Abruptly, he walked to the nearest booth and slid in clumsily behind the table. Now wait, he told himself; just wait. Surely, he could tell which one it was. Masking his face with the menu, he glanced across its top. Was it that one in the khaki work shirt? Mann tried to see the man's hands but couldn't. His gaze flicked nervously across the room. Not that one in the suit, of course. Three remaining. That one in the front booth, square-faced, black-haired? If only he could see the man's hands, it might help. One of the two others at the counter? Mann studied them uneasily. Why hadn't he looked at faces when he'd come in?

Now *wait*, he thought. Goddamn it, *wait*! All right, the truck driver was in here. That didn't automatically signify that he meant to continue the insane duel. Chuck's Café might be the only place to eat for miles around. It *was* lunchtime, wasn't it? The truck driver had probably intended to eat here all the time. He'd just been moving too fast to pull into the parking lot before. So he'd slowed down, turned around and driven back, that was all. Mann forced himself to read the menu. Right, he thought. No point in getting so rattled. Perhaps a beer would help relax him.

The woman behind the counter came over and Mann ordered a ham sandwich on rye toast and a bottle of Coors. As the woman turned away, he wondered, with a sudden twinge of self-reproach, why he hadn't simply left the café, jumped into his car and sped away. He would have known immediately, then, if the truck driver was still out to get him. As it was, he'd have to suffer through an entire meal to find out. He almost groaned at his stupidity.

Still, what if the truck driver *had* followed him out and started after him again? He'd have been right back where he'd started. Even if he'd managed to get a good lead, the truck driver would have overtaken him eventually. It just wasn't in him to drive at 80 and 90 miles an hour in order to stay ahead. True, he might have been intercepted by a California Highway Patrol car. What if he weren't, though?

Mann repressed the plaguing thoughts. He tried to calm himself. He looked deliberately at the four men. Either of two seemed a likely possibility as the driver of the truck: the square-faced one in the front booth and the chunky one in the jumpsuit sitting at the counter. Mann had an impulse to walk over to them and ask which one it was, tell the man he was sorry he'd irritated him, tell him anything to calm him, since, obviously, he wasn't rational, was a manic-depressive, probably. Maybe buy the man a beer and sit with him awhile to try to settle things.

He couldn't move. What if the truck driver were letting the whole thing drop? Mightn't his approach rile the man all over again? Mann felt drained by indecision. He nodded weakly as the waitress set the sandwich and the bottle in front of him. He took a swallow of the beer, which made him cough. Was the truck driver amused by the sound? Mann felt a stirring of resentment deep inside himself. What right did that bastard have to impose this torment on another human being? It was a free country, wasn't it? Damn it, he had every right to pass the son of a bitch on a highway if he wanted to!

"Oh, hell," he mumbled. He tried to feel amused. He was making entirely too much of this. Wasn't he? He glanced at the pay telephone on the front wall. What was to prevent him from calling the local police and telling them the situation? But, then, he'd have to stay here, lose time, make Forbes angry, probably lose the sale. And what if the truck driver stayed to face them? Naturally, he'd deny the whole thing. What if the police believed him and didn't do anything about it? After they'd gone, the truck driver would undoubtedly take it out on him again, only worse. *God!* Mann thought in agony.

The sandwich tasted flat, the beer unpleasantly sour. Mann stared at the table as he ate. For God's sake, why was he just *sitting* here like this? He was a grown man, wasn't he? Why didn't he settle this damn thing once and for all?

His left hand twitched so unexpectedly, he spilled beer on his trousers. The man in the jump suit had risen from the counter and was strolling toward the front of the café. Mann felt his heartbeat thumping as the man gave money to the waitress, took his change and a toothpick from the dispenser and went outside. Mann watched in anxious silence.

The man did not get into the cab of the tanker truck.

It had to be the one in the front booth, then. His face took form in Mann's remembrance: square, with dark eyes, dark hair; the man who'd tried to kill him.

Mann stood abruptly, letting impulse conquer fear. Eyes fixed ahead, he started toward the entrance. Anything was preferable to sitting in that booth. He stopped by the cash register, conscious of the hitching of his chest as he gulped in air. Was the man observing him? he wondered. He swallowed, pulling out the clip of dollar bills in his right-hand trouser pocket. He glanced toward the waitress. Come *on*, he thought. He looked at his check and, seeing the amount, reached shakily into his trouser pocket for change. He heard a coin fall onto the floor and roll away. Ignoring it, he dropped a dollar and a quarter onto the counter and thrust the clip of bills into his trouser pocket.

As he did, he heard the man in the front booth get up. An icy shudder spasmed up his back. Turning quickly to the door, he shoved it open, seeing, on the edges of his vision, the square-faced man approach the cash register. Lurching from the café, he started toward his car with long strides. His mouth was dry again. The pounding of his heart was painful in his chest.

Suddenly, he started running. He heard the café door bang shut and fought away the urge to look across his shoulder. Was that a sound of other running footsteps now? Reaching his car, Mann yanked open the door and jarred in awkwardly behind the steering wheel. He reached into his trouser pocket for the keys and snatched them out, almost dropping them. His hand was shaking so badly he couldn't get the ignition key into its slot. He whined with mounting dread. Come on! he thought.

The key slid in, he twisted it convulsively. The motor started and he raced it momentarily before jerking the transmission shift to drive. Depressing the accelerator pedal quickly, he raked the car around and steered it toward the highway. From the corners of his eyes, he saw the truck and trailer being backed away from the café.

Reaction burst inside him. "No!" he raged and slammed his foot down on the brake pedal. This was idiotic! Why the hell should he run away? His car slid sideways to a rocking halt and, shouldering out the door, he lurched to his feet and started toward the truck with angry strides. *All right, Jack*, he thought. He glared at the man inside the truck. You want to punch my nose, okay, but no more goddamn tournament on the highway.

The truck began to pick up speed. Mann raised his right arm. "Hey!" he yelled. He knew the driver saw him. *"Hey!"* He started running as the truck kept moving, engine grinding loudly. It was on the highway now. He sprinted toward it with a sense of martyred outrage. The driver shifted gears, the truck moved faster. "Stop!" Mann shouted. "Damn it, *stop!*"

He thudded to a panting halt, staring at the truck as it receded down the highway, moved around a hill and disappeared. "You son of a bitch," he muttered. "You goddamn, miserable son of a bitch."

He trudged back slowly to this car, trying to believe that the truck driver had fled the hazard of a fistfight. It was possible, of course, but, somehow, he could not believe it.

He got into his car and was about to drive onto the highway when he changed his mind and switched the motor off. That crazy bastard might just be tooling along at 15 miles an hour, waiting for him to catch up. Nuts to that, he thought. So he blew his schedule; screw it. Forbes would have to wait, that was all. And if Forbes didn't care to wait, that was all right, too. He'd sit here for a while and let the nut get out of range, let him think he'd won the day. He grinned. You're the bloody Red Baron, Jack; you've shot me down. Now go to hell with my sincerest compliments. He shook his head. Beyond belief, he thought.

He really should have done this earlier, pulled over, waited. Then the truck driver would have had to let it pass. *Or picked on someone else,* the startling thought occurred to him. Jesus, maybe that was how the crazy bastard whiled away his work hours! Jesus Christ Almighty! Was it possible?

He looked at the dashboard clock. It was just past 12:30. Wow, he thought. All that in less than an hour. He shifted on the seat and stretched his legs out. Leaning back against the door, he closed his eyes and mentally perused the things he had to do tomorrow and the following day. Today was shot to hell, as far as he could see.

When he opened his eyes, afraid of drifting into sleep and losing too much time, almost eleven minutes had passed. The nut must be an ample distance off by now, he thought; at least 11 miles and likely more, the way he drove. Good enough. He wasn't going to try to make San Francisco on schedule now, anyways. He'd take it real easy.

Mann adjusted his safety belt, switched on the motor, tapped the transmission pointer into the drive position and pulled onto the highway, glancing back across his shoulder. Not a car in sight. Great day for driving. Everybody was staying at home. That nut must have a reputation around here. When Crazy Jack is on the highway, lock your car in the garage. Mann chuckled at the notion as his car began to turn the curve ahead.

Mindless reflex drove his right foot down against the brake pedal. Suddenly, his car had skidded to a halt and he was staring down the highway. The truck and trailer were parked on the shoulder less than 90 yards away.

Mann couldn't seem to function. He knew his car was blocking the west-bound lane, knew that he should either make a U-turn or pull off the highway, but all he could do was gape at the truck.

He cried out, legs retracting, as a horn blast sounded behind him. Snapping up his head, he looked at the rearview mirror, gasping as he saw a yellow station wagon bearing down on him at high speed. Suddenly, it veered off toward the eastbound lane, disappearing from the mirror. Mann jerked around and saw it hurtling past his car, its rear end snapping back and forth, its back tires screeching. He saw the twisted features of the man inside, saw his lips move rapidly with cursing.

Then the station wagon had swerved back into the westbound lane and was speeding off. It gave Mann an odd sensation to see it pass the truck. The man in that station wagon could drive on, unthreatened. Only he'd been singled out. What happened was demented. Yet it was happening.

He drove his car onto the highway shoulder and braked. Putting the transmission into neutral, he leaned back, staring at the truck. His head was aching again. There was a pulsing at his temples like the ticking of a muffled clock.

What was he to do? He knew very well that if he left his car to walk to the truck, the driver would pull away and repark farther down the highway. He may as well face the fact that he was dealing with a madman. He felt the tremor in his stomach muscles starting up again. His heartbeat thudded slowly, striking at his chest wall. Now what?

With a sudden, angry impulse, Mann snapped the transmission into gear and stepped down hard on the accelerator pedal. The tires of the car spun sizzlingly before they gripped; the car shot out onto the highway. Instantly, the truck began to move. He even had the motor on! Mann thought in raging fear. He floored the pedal, then, abruptly, realized he couldn't make it, that the truck would block his way and he'd collide with its trailer. A vision flashed across his mind, a fiery explosion and a sheet of flame incinerating him. He started braking fast, trying to decelerate evenly, so he wouldn't lose control.

When he'd slowed down enough to feel that it was safe, he steered the car onto the shoulder and stopped it again, throwing the transmission into neutral.

Approximately eighty yards ahead, the truck pulled off the highway and stopped.

Mann tapped his fingers on the steering wheel. *Now* what? He thought. Turn around and head east until he reached a cut-off that would take him to San Francisco by another route? How did he know the truck driver wouldn't follow him even then? His cheeks twisted as he bit his lips together angrily. No! He wasn't going to turn around!

His expression hardened suddenly. Well, he wasn't going to *sit* here all day, that was certain. Reaching out, he tapped the gearshift into drive and steered his car onto the highway once again. He saw the massive truck and trailer start to move but made no effort to speed up. He tapped at the brakes, taking a position about 30 yards behind the trailer. He glanced at his speedometer. Forty miles an hour. The truck driver had his left arm out of the cab window and was waving him on. What did that mean? Had he changed his mind? Decided, finally, that this thing had gone too far? Mann couldn't let himself believe it.

He looked ahead. Despite the mountain ranges all around, the highway was flat as far as he could see. He tapped a fingernail against the horn bar, trying to make up his mind. Presumably, he could continue all the way to San Francisco at this speed, hanging back just far enough to avoid the worst of the exhaust fumes. It didn't seem likely that the truck driver would stop directly on the highway to block his way. And if the truck driver pulled onto the shoulder to let him pass, he could pull off the highway, too. It would be a draining afternoon but a safe one.

On the other hand, outracing the truck might be worth just one more try. This was obviously what that son of a bitch wanted. Yet, surely, a vehicle of such size couldn't be driven with the same daring as, potentially, his own. The laws of mechanics were against it, if nothing else. Whatever advantage the truck had in mass, it had to lose in stability, particularly that of its trailer. If Mann were to drive at, say, 80 miles an hour and there were a few steep grades—as he felt sure there were—the truck would have to fall behind.

The question was, of course, whether he had the nerve to maintain such a speed over a long distance. He'd never done it before. Still, the more he thought about it, the more it appealed to him; far more than the alternative did.

Abruptly, he decided. *Right*, he thought. He checked ahead, then pressed down hard on the accelerator pedal and pulled into the eastbound lane. As he neared the truck, he tensed, anticipating that the driver might block his way. But the truck did not shift from the westbound lane. Mann's car moved along its mammoth side. He glanced at the cab and saw the name KELLER printed on its door. For a shocking instant, he thought it read KILLER and started to slow down. Then, glancing at the name again, he saw what it really was and depressed the pedal sharply. When he saw the truck reflected in the rearview mirror, he steered his car into the westbound lane.

He shuddered, dread and satisfaction mixed together, as he saw that the truck driver was speeding up. It was strangely comforting to know the man's intentions definitely again. That plus the knowledge of his face and name seemed, somehow, to reduce his stature. Before, he had been faceless, nameless, an embodiment of unknown terror. Now, at least he was an individual. All right, Keller, said his mind, let's see you beat me with that purple-silver relic now. He pressed down harder on the pedal. *Here we go*, he thought.

He looked at the speedometer, scowling as he saw that he was doing only 74 miles an hour. Deliberately, he pressed down on the pedal, alternating his gaze between the highway ahead and the speedometer until the needle turned past 80. He felt a flickering of satisfaction with himself. All right, Keller, you son of a bitch, top that, he thought.

After several moments, he glanced into the rearview mirror again. Was the truck getting closer? Stunned, he checked the speedometer. Damn it! He was down to 76! He forced in the accelerator pedal angrily. *He mustn't go less than 80!* Mann's chest shuddered with convulsive breath.

He glanced aside as he hurtled past a beige sedan parked on the shoulder underneath a tree. A young couple sat inside it, talking. Already they were far behind, their world removed from his. Had they even glanced aside when he'd passed? He doubted it.

He started as the shadow of an overhead bridge whipped across the hood and windshield. Inhaling raggedly, he glanced at the speedometer again. He was holding at 81. He checked the rearview mirror. Was it his imagination that the truck was gaining ground? He looked forward with anxious eyes. There had to be some kind of town ahead. To hell with time; he'd stop at the police station and tell them what had happened. They'd have to believe him. Why would he stop to tell them such a story if it weren't true? For all he knew, Keller had a police record in these parts. *Oh, sure, we're on to him,* he heard a faceless officer remark. *That crazy bastard's asked for it before and now he's going to get it.*

Mann shook himself and looked at the mirror. The truck *was* getting closer. Wincing, he glared at the speedometer. Goddamn it, pay attention! raged his mind. He was down to 74 again! Whining with frustration, he depressed the pedal. Eighty!—80! He demanded of himself. There was a murderer behind him!

His car began to pass a field of flowers; lilacs, Mann saw, white and purple stretching out in endless rows. There was a small shack near the highway, the words FIELD FRESH FLOWERS painted on it. A brown-cardboard square was propped against the shack, the word FUNERALS printed crudely on it. Mann saw himself, abruptly, lying in a casket, painted like some grotesque mannequin. The overpowering smell of flowers seemed to fill his nostrils. Ruth and the children sitting in the first row, heads bowed. All his relatives—

Suddenly, the pavement roughened and the car began to bounce and shudder, driving bolts of pain into his head. He felt the steering wheel resisting him and clamped his hands around it tightly, harsh vibrations running up his arms. He didn't dare look at the mirror now. He had to force himself to keep the speed unchanged. Keller wasn't going to slow down; he was sure of that. *What if he got a flat tire, though?* All control would vanish in an instant. He visualized the somersaulting of his car, its grinding, shrieking tumble, the explosion of its gas tank, his body crushed and burned and—

The broken span of pavement ended and his gaze jumped quickly to the rearview mirror. The truck was no closer, but it hadn't lost ground, either. Mann's eyes shifted. Up ahead were hills and mountains. He tried to reassure himself that upgrades were on his side, that he could climb them at the same speed he was going now. Yet all he could imagine were the downgrades, the immense truck close behind him, slamming violently into his car and knocking it across some cliff edge. He had a horrifying vision of dozens of broken, rusted cars lying unseen in the canyons ahead, corpses in every one of them, all flung to shattering deaths by Keller.

Mann's car went rocketing into a corridor of trees. On each side of the highway was a eucalyptus windbreak, each trunk three feet from the next. It was like speeding through a high-walled canyon. Mann gasped, twitching, as a large twig bearing dusty leaves dropped down across the windshield, then slid out of sight. Dear God! he thought. He was getting near the edge himself. If he should lose his nerve at this speed, it was over. Jesus! That would be ideal for Keller! He realized suddenly. He visualized the square-faced driver laughing as he passed the burning wreckage, knowing that he'd killed his prey without so much as touching him.

Mann started as his car shot out into the open. The route ahead was not straight now but winding up into the foothills. Mann willed himself to press down on the pedal even more. Eighty-three now, almost 84.

To his left was a broad terrain of green hills blending into mountains. He saw a black car on a dirt road, moving toward the highway. *Was its side painted white?* Mann's heartbeat lurched. Impulsively, he jammed the heel of his right hand down against the horn bar and held it there. The blast of horn was shrill and racking to his ears. His heart began to pound. Was it a police car? *Was it?*

He let the horn bar up abruptly. *No, it wasn't.* Damn! His mind raged. Keller must have been amused by his pathetic efforts. Doubtless, he was chuckling to himself right now. He heard the truck driver's voice in his mind, coarse and sly. *You think you gonna get a cop to save you, boy? Shee-it. You gonna die.* Mann's heart contorted with savage hatred. *You son of a bitch!* he thought. Jerking his right hand into a fist, he drove it down against the seat. Goddamn you, Keller! I'm going to kill you, if it's the last thing I do!

The hills were closer now. There would be slopes directly, long steep grades. Mann felt a burst of hope within himself. He was sure to gain a lot of distance on the truck. No matter how he tried, that bastard Keller couldn't manage 80 miles an hour on a hill. But *I* can! cried his mind with fierce elation. He worked up saliva in his mouth and swallowed it. The back of his shirt was drenched. He could feel sweat trickling down his sides. A bath and a drink, first order of the day on reaching San Francisco. A long, hot bath, a long, cold drink. Cutty Sark. He'd splurge, by Christ. He rated it.

The car swept up a shallow rise. Not steep enough, goddamn it! The truck's momentum would prevent its losing speed. Mann felt mindless hatred for the landscape. Already, he had topped the rise and tilted over to a shallow downgrade. He looked at the rearview mirror. *Square*, he thought, everything about the truck was square: the radiator grille, the fender shapes, the bumper ends, the outline of the cab, even the shape of Keller's hands and face. He visualized the truck as some great entity pursuing him, insentient, brutish, chasing him with instinct only.

Mann cried out, horror-stricken, as he saw the ROAD RE-PAIRS sign up ahead. His frantic gaze leaped down the highway. Both lanes blocked, a huge black arrow pointing toward the alternate route! He groaned in anguish, seeing it was dirt. His foot jumped automatically to the brake pedal and started pumping it. He threw a dazed look at the rearview mirror. The

truck was moving as fast as ever! It *couldn't*, though! Mann's
expression froze in terror as he started turning to the right.

He stiffened as the front wheels hit the dirt road. For an instant, he was certain that the back part of the car was going to
spin; he felt it breaking to the left. "No, don't!" he cried.
Abruptly, he was jarring down the dirt road, elbows braced
against his sides, trying to keep from losing control. His tires
battered at the ruts, almost tearing the wheel from his grip.
The windows rattled noisily. His neck snapped back and forth
with painful jerks. His jolting body surged against the binding
of the safety belt and slammed down violently on the seat. He
felt the bouncing of the car drive up his spine. His clenching
teeth slipped and he cried out hoarsely as his upper teeth
gouged deep into his lip.

He gasped as the rear end of the car began surging to the
right. He started to jerk the steering wheel to the left, then,
hissing, wrenched it in the opposite direction, crying out as the
right rear fender cracked a fence pole, knocking it down. He
started pumping at the brakes, struggling to regain control.
The car rear yawed sharply to the left, tires shooting out a
spray of dirt. Mann felt a scream tear upward in his throat. He
twisted wildly at the steering wheel. The car began careening
to the right. He hitched the wheel around until the car was on
course again. His head was pounding like his heart now, with
gigantic, throbbing spasms. He started coughing as he gagged
on dripping blood.

The dirt road ended suddenly, the car regained momentum
on the pavement and he dared to look at the rearview mirror.
The truck was slowed down but was still behind him, rocking
like a freighter on a storm-tossed sea, its huge tires scouring
up a pall of dust. Mann shoved in the accelerator pedal and his
car surged forward. A good, steep grade lay just ahead; he'd
gain that distance now. He swallowed blood, grimacing at the
taste, then fumbled in his trouser pocket and tugged out his
handkerchief. He pressed it to his bleeding lip, eyes fixed on
the slope ahead. Another fifty yards or so. He writhed his
back. His undershirt was soaking wet, adhering to his skin.

He glanced at the rearview mirror. The truck had just regained the highway. *Tough!* he thought with venom. Didn't get me, did you, Keller?

His car was on the first yards of the upgrade when steam began to issue from beneath its hood. Mann stiffened suddenly, eyes widening with shock. The steam increased, became a smoking mist. Mann's gaze jumped down. The red light hadn't flashed on yet but had to in a moment. How could this be happening? Just as he was set to get away! The slope ahead was long and gradual, with many curves. He knew he couldn't stop. Could he U-turn unexpectedly and go back down? the sudden thought occurred. He looked ahead. The highway was too narrow, bound by hills on both sides. There wasn't room enough to make an uninterrupted turn and there wasn't time enough to ease around. If he tried that, Keller would shift direction and hit him head on. "Oh, my God!" Mann murmured suddenly.

He was going to die.

He stared ahead with stricken eyes, his view increasingly obscured by steam. Abruptly, he recalled the afternoon he'd had the engine steam-cleaned at the local car wash. The man who'd done it had suggested he replace the water hoses, because steam-cleaning had a tendency to make them crack. He'd nodded, thinking that he'd do it when he had more time. *More time!* The phrase was like a dagger in his mind. He'd failed to change the hoses and, for that failure, he was now about to die.

He sobbed in terror as the dashboard light flashed on. He glanced at it involuntarily and read the word HOT, black on red. With a breathless gasp, he jerked the transmission into low. Why hadn't he done that right away! He looked ahead. The slope seemed endless. Already, he could hear a boiling throb inside the radiator. How much coolant was there left? Steam was clouding faster, hazing up the windshield. Reaching out, he twisted at a dashboard knob. The wipers started flicking back and forth in fan-shaped sweeps. There had to be enough coolant in the radiator to get him to the top. *Then* what? cried his mind. He couldn't drive without coolant, even downhill. He glanced at the rearview mirror. The truck was falling behind. Mann snarled with maddened fury. *If it weren't for that goddamned hose, he'd be escaping now!*

The sudden lurching of the car snatched him back to terror. If he braked now, he could jump out, run and scrabble up that slope. Later, he might not have the time. He couldn't make himself stop the car, though. As long as it kept on running, he felt bound to it, less vulnerable. God knows what would happen if he left it.

Mann started up the slope with haunted eyes, trying not to see the red light on the edges of his vision. Yard by yard, his car was slowing down. Make it, make it, pleaded his mind, even though he thought that it was futile. The car was running more and more unevenly. The thumping percolation of its radiator filled his ears. Any moment now, the motor would be choked off and the car would shudder to a stop, leaving him a sitting target. *No*, he thought. He tried to blank his mind.

He was almost to the top, but in the mirror he could see the truck drawing up on him. He jammed down on the pedal and the motor made a grinding noise. He groaned. It had to make the top! Please, God, help me! screamed his mind. The ridge was just ahead. Closer. Closer. Make it. "Make it." The car was shuddering and clanking, slowing down—oil, smoke and steam gushing from beneath the hood. The windshield wipers swept from side to side. Mann's head throbbed. Both his hands felt numb. His heartbeat pounded as he stared ahead. Make it, please, God, make it. Make it. *Make* it!

Over! Mann's lips opened in a cry of triumph as the car began descending and shaking uncontrollably, he shoved the transmission into neutral and let the car go into a glide. The triumph strangled in his throat as he saw that there was nothing in sight but hills and more hills. Never mind! He was on a downgrade now, a long one. He passed a sign that read, TRUCKS USE LOW GEARS NEXT 12 MILES. Twelve miles! Something would come up. It had to.

The car began to pick up speed. Mann glanced at the speedometer. Forty-seven miles an hour. The red light still burned.

He'd save the motor for a long time, too, though; let it cool for twelve miles, if the truck was far enough behind.

His speed increased. Fifty . . . 51. Mann watched the needle turning slowly toward the right. He glanced at the rearview mirror. The truck had not appeared yet. With a little luck, he might still get a good lead. Not as good as he might have if the motor hadn't overheated but enough to work with. There had to be some place along the way to stop. The needle edged past 55 and started toward the 60 mark.

Again, he looked at the rearview mirror, jolting as he saw that the truck had topped the ridge and was on its way down. He felt his lips begin to shake and crimped them together. His gaze jumped fitfully between the steam-obscured highway and the mirror. The truck was accelerating rapidly. Keller doubtless had the gas pedal floored. It wouldn't be long before the truck caught up to him. Mann's right hand twitched unconsciously toward the gearshift. Noticing, he jerked it back, grimacing, glanced at the speedometer. The car's velocity had just passed 60. Not enough! He had to use the motor now! He reached out desperately.

His right hand froze in mid-air as the motor stalled; then, shooting out the hand, he twisted the ignition key. The motor made a grinding noise but wouldn't start. Mann glanced up, saw that he was almost on the shoulder, jerked the steering wheel around. Again, he turned the key, but there was no response. He looked up at the rearview mirror. The truck was gaining on him swiftly. He glanced at the speedometer. The car's speed was fixed at 62. Mann felt himself crushed in a vise of panic. He stared ahead with haunted eyes.

Then he saw it, several hundred yards ahead: an escape route for trucks with burned-out brakes. There was no alternative now. Either he took the turnout or his car would be rammed from behind. The truck was frighteningly close. He heard the high-pitched wailing of its motor. Unconsciously, he started easing to the right, then jerked the wheel back suddenly. He mustn't give the move away! He had to wait until the last possible moment. Otherwise, Keller would follow him in.

Just before he reached the escape route, Mann wrenched the

steering wheel around. The car rear started breaking to the left, tires shrieking on the pavement. Mann steered with the skid, braking just enough to keep from losing all control. The rear tires grabbed and, at 60 miles an hour, the car shot up the dirt trail, tires slinging up a cloud of dust. Mann began to hit the brakes. The rear wheels sideslipped and the car slammed hard against the dirt bank to the right. Mann gasped as the car bounced off and started to fishtail with violent whipping motions, angling toward the trail edge. He drove his foot down on the brake pedal with all his might. The car rear skidded to the right and slammed against the bank again. Mann heard a grinding rend of metal and felt himself heaved downward suddenly, his neck snapped, as the car plowed to a violent halt.

As in a dream, Mann turned to see the truck and trailer swerving off the highway. Paralyzed, he watched the massive vehicle hurtle toward him, staring at it with a blank detachment, knowing he was going to die but so stupefied by the sight of the looming truck that he couldn't react. The gargantuan shape roared closer, blotting out the sky. Mann felt a strange sensation in his throat, unaware that he was screaming.

Suddenly, the truck began to tilt. Mann stared at it in choked-off silence as it started tipping over like some ponderous beast toppling in slow motion. Before it reached his car, it vanished from his rear window.

Hands palsied, Mann undid the safety belt and opened the door. Struggling from the car, he stumbled to the trail edge, staring downward. He was just in time to see the truck capsize like a foundering ship. The tanker followed, huge wheels spinning as it overturned.

The storage tank on the truck exploded first, the violence of its detonation causing Mann to stagger back and sit down clumsily on the dirt. A second explosion roared below, its shock wave buffeting across him hotly, making his ears hurt. His glazed eyes saw a fiery column shoot up toward the sky in front of him, then another.

Mann crawled slowly to the trail edge and peered down at the canyon. Enormous gouts of flame were towering upward, topped by thick, black, oily smoke. He couldn't see the truck or trailer, only flames. He gaped at them in shock, all feeling drained from him.

Then, unexpectedly, emotion came. Not dread, at first, and not regret; not the nausea that followed soon. It was a primeval tumult in his mind: the cry of some ancestral beast above the body of its vanquished foe.

DAY OF RECKONING

Dear Pa:

I am sending you this note under Rex's collar because I got to stay here. I hope this note gets to you all right.

I couldn't deliver the tax letter you sent me with because the Widow Blackwell is killed. She is upstairs. I put her on her bed. She looks awful. I wish you would get the sheriff and the coroner Wilks.

Little Jim Blackwell, I don't know where he is right now. He is so scared he goes running around the house and hiding from me. He must have got awful scared by whoever killed his ma. He don't say a word. He just runs around like a scared rat. I see his eyes sometimes in the dark and then they are gone. They got no electric power here you know.

I came out toward sundown bringing that note. I rung the bell but there was no answer so I pushed open the front door and looked in.

All the shades was down. And I heard someone running light in the front room and then feet running upstairs. I called around for the Widow but she didn't answer me.

I started upstairs and saw Jim looking down through the banister posts. When he saw me looking at him, he run down the hall and I ain't seen him since.

I looked around the upstairs rooms. Finally, I went in the Widow Blackwell's room and there she was dead on the floor in a puddle of blood. Her throat was cut and her eyes was wide open and looking up at me. It was an awful sight.

I shut her eyes and searched around some and I found the razor. The Widow has all her clothes on so I figure it were only robbery that the killer meant.

Well, Pa, please come out quick with the sheriff and the coroner Wilks. I will stay here and watch to see that Jim don't go running out of the house and maybe get lost in the woods. But come as fast as you can because I don't like sitting here with her up there like that and Jim sneaking around in the dark house.

LUKE

Dear George:

We just got back from your sister's house. We haven't told the papers yet so I'll have to be the one to let you know.

I sent Luke out there with a property tax note and he found your sister murdered. I don't like to be the one to tell you but somebody has to. The sheriff and his boys are scouring the countryside for the killer. They figure it was a tramp or something. She wasn't raped though and, far as we can tell, nothing was stolen.

What I mean more to tell you about is little Jim.

That boy is fixing to die soon from starvation and just plain scaredness. He won't eat nothing. Sometimes, he gulps down a piece of bread or a piece of candy but as soon as he starts to chewing, his face gets all twisted and he gets violent sick and throws up. I don't understand it at all.

Luke found your sister in her room with her throat cut ear to ear. Coroner Wilks says it was a strong, steady hand that done it because the cut is deep and sure. I am terribly sorry to be the one to tell you all this but I think it is better you know. The funeral will be in a week.

Luke and I had a long time rounding up the boy. He was like lightning. He ran around in the dark and squealed like a rat. He showed his teeth at us when we'd corner him with a lantern. His skin is all white and the way he rolls his eyes back and foams at his mouth is something awful to see.

We finally caught him. He bit us and squirmed around like

an eel. Then he got all stiff and it was like carrying a two-by-four, Luke said.

We took him into the kitchen and tried to give him something to eat. He wouldn't take a bite. He gulped down some milk like he felt guilty about it. Then, in a second, his face twists and he draws back his lips and the milk comes out.

He kept trying to run away from us. Never a single word out of him. He just squeaks and mutters like a monkey talking to itself.

We finally carried him upstairs to put him to bed. He froze soon as we touched him and I thought his eyes would fall out he opened them so wide. His jaw fell slack and he stared at us like we was boogie men or trying to slice open his throat like his ma's.

He wouldn't go into his room. He screamed and twisted in our hands like a fish. He braced his feet against the wall and tugged and pulled and scratched. We had to slap his face and then his eyes got big and he got like a board again and we carried him in his room.

When I took off his clothes, I got a shock like I haven't had in years, George. That boy is all scars and bruises on his back and chest like someone has strung him up and tortured him with pliers or hot irons or God knows what all. I got a downright chill seeing that. I know they said the widow wasn't the same in her head after her husband died, but I can't believe she done this. It is the work of a crazy person.

Jim was sleepy but he wouldn't shut his eyes. He kept looking around the ceiling and the window and his lips kept moving like he was trying to talk. He was moaning kind of low and shaky when Luke and I went out in the hall.

No sooner did we leave him than he's screaming at the top of his voice and thrashing in his bed like someone was strangling him. We rushed in and I held the lantern high but we couldn't see anything. I thought the boy was sick with fear and seeing things.

Then, as if it was meant to happen, the lantern ran out of oil and all of a sudden we saw white faces staring at us from the walls and ceiling and the window.

It was a shaky minute there, George, with the kid screaming out his lungs and twisting on his bed but never getting up. And Luke trying to find the door and me feeling for a match but trying to look at those horrible faces at the same time.

Finally, I found a match and I got it lit and we couldn't see the faces any more, just part of one on the window.

I sent Luke down to the car for some oil and when he come back we lit the lantern again and looked at the window and saw that the face was painted on it so's to light up in the dark. Same thing for the faces on the walls and the ceiling. It was enough to scare a man half out of his wits to think of anybody doing that inside a little boy's room.

We took him to another room and put him down to bed. When we left him he was squirming in his sleep and muttering words we couldn't understand. I left Luke in the hall outside the room to watch. I went and looked around the house some more.

In the Widow's room I found a whole shelf of psychology books. They was all marked in different places. I looked in one place and it told about a thing how they can make rats go crazy by making them think there is food in a place when there isn't. And another one about how they can make a dog lose its appetite and starve to death by hitting big pieces of pipe together at the same time when the dog is trying to eat.

I guess you know what I think. But it is so terrible I can hardly believe it. I mean that Jim might have got so crazy that he cut her. He is so small I don't see how he could.

You are her only living kin, George, and I think you should do something about the boy. We don't want to put him in an orphan home. He is in no shape for it. That is why I am telling you all about him so you can judge.

There was another thing. I played a record on a phonograph in the boy's room. It sounded like wild animals all making terrible noises and even louder than them was a terrible high laughing.

That is about all, George. We will let you know if the sheriff

finds the one who killed your sister because no one really be-
lieves that Jim could have done it. I wish you would take the
boy and try to fix him up.

Until I hear,

SAM DAVIS

Dear Sam:

I got your letter and am more upset than I can say.

I knew for a long time that my sister was mentally unbal-
anced after her husband's death, but I had no idea in the world
she was gone so far.

You see, when she was a girl she fell in love with Phil. There
was never anyone else in her life. The sun rose and descended
on her love for him. She was so jealous that, once, because he
had taken another girl to a party, she crashed her hands
through a window and nearly bled to death.

Finally, Phil married her. There was never a happier couple,
it seemed. She did anything and everything for him. He was
her whole life.

When Jim was born I went to see her at the hospital. She
told me she wished it had been born dead because she knew
that the boy meant so much to Phil and she hated to have Phil
want anything but her.

She never was good to Jim. She always resented him. And,
that day, three years ago, when Phil drowned saving Jim's life,
she went out of her mind. I was with her when she heard about
it. She ran into the kitchen and got a carving knife and took it
running through the streets, trying to find Jim so she could kill
him. She finally fainted in the road and we took her home.

She wouldn't even look at Jim for a month. Then she packed
up and took him to that house in the woods. Since then I never
saw her.

You saw yourself, the boy is terrified of everyone and everything. Except one person. My sister planned that. Step by step
she planned it—God help me for never realizing it before. In a
whole, monstrous world of horrors she built around that boy
she left him trust and need for only one person—*her*. She was
Jim's only shield against those horrors. She knew that, when

she died, Jim would go completely mad because there wouldn't be anyone in the world he could turn to for comfort.

I think you see now why I say there isn't any murderer.

Just bury her quick and send the boy to me. I'm not coming to the funeral.

GEORGE BARNES

THE PRISONER

When he woke up he was lying on his right side. He felt a prickly wool blanket against his cheek. He saw a steel wall in front of his eyes.

He listened. Dead silence. His ears strained for a sound. There was nothing.

He became frightened. Lines sprang into his forehead.

He pushed up on one elbow and looked over his shoulder. The skin grew taut and pale on his lean face. He twisted around and dropped his legs heavily over the side of the bunk.

There was a stool with a tray on it; a tray of half-eaten food. He saw untouched roast chicken, fork scrapes in a mound of cold mashed potatoes, biscuit scraps in a puddle of greasy butter, an empty cup. The smell of cold food filled his nostrils.

His head snapped around. He gaped at the barred window, at the thick-barred door. He made frightened noises in his throat.

His shoes scraped on the hard floor. He was up, staggering. He fell against the wall and grabbed at the window bars above him. He couldn't see out of the window.

His body shook as he stumbled back and slid the tray of food onto the bunk. He dragged the stool to the wall. He clambered up on it awkwardly.

He looked out.

Gray skies, walls, barred windows, lumpy black spotlights, a courtyard far below. Drizzle hung like a shifting veil in the air.

His tongue moved. His eyes were round with shock.

"Uh?" he muttered thinly.

He slipped off the edge of the stool as it toppled over. His right knee crashed against the floor, his cheek scraped against the cold metal wall. He cried out in fear and pain.

He struggled up and fell against the bunk. He heard footsteps. He heard someone shout.

"Shut up!"

A fat man came up to the door. He was wearing a blue uniform. He had an angry look on his face. He looked through the bars at the prisoner.

"What's the matter with *you*?" he snarled.

The prisoner stared back. His mouth fell open. Saliva ran across his chin and dripped onto the floor.

"Well, well, well," said the man, with an ugly smile, "So it got to you at last, haah?"

He threw back his thick head and laughed. He laughed at the prisoner.

"Hey, Mac," he called. "Come 'ere. This you gotta see."

More footsteps. The prisoner pushed up. He ran to the door.

"What am I doing here?" he asked, "Why am I here?"

The man laughed louder.

"Ha!" he cried, "Boy, did you crack."

"Shut up, will ya?" growled a voice down the corridor.

"Knock it off!" the guard yelled back.

Mac came up to the cell. He was an older man with graying hair. He looked in curiously. He saw the white-faced prisoner clutching the bars and staring out. He saw how white the prisoner's knuckles were.

"What is it?" he asked.

"Big boy has cracked," said Charlie, "Big boy has cracked wide open."

"What are you talking about?" asked the prisoner, his eyes flitting from one guard's face to the other. "Where am I? For God's sake, where am I?"

Charlie roared with laughter. Mac didn't laugh. He looked closely at the prisoner. His eyes narrowed.

"You know where you are, son," he said quietly, "Stop laughing, Charlie."

Charlie sputtered down.

"Man I can't help it. This bastard was so sure he wouldn't crack. Not *me* boy," he mimicked, "I'll sit in that goddamn chair with a smile on my face."

The prisoner's grayish lips parted.

"What?" he muttered. "What did you say?"

Charlie turned away. He stretched and grimaced, pushed a hand into his paunch.

"Woke me up," he said.

"What chair?" cried the prisoner, "What are you talking about?"

Charlie's stomach shook with laughter again.

"Oh, Christ, this is rich," he chuckled, "Richer than a Christmas cake."

Mac went up to the bars. He looked into the prisoner's face. He said, "Don't try to fool us, John Riley."

"Fool you?"

The prisoner's voice was incredulous. "What are you talking about? My name isn't John Riley."

The two men looked at each other. They heard Charlie plodding down the corridor talking to himself in amusement.

Mac turned aside.

"No," said the prisoner. "Don't go away."

Mac turned back.

"What are you trying to pull?" he asked, "You don't think you'll fool us, do you?"

The prisoner stared.

"Will you tell me where I am?" he asked, "For God's sake, tell me."

"You know where you are."

"I tell you . . ."

"Cut it, Riley!" commanded Mac, "You're wasting your time."

"I'm not Riley!" cried the prisoner. "For God's sake, I'm not Riley. My name is Phillip Johnson."

Mac shook his head slowly.

"And you was going to be so brave," he said.

The prisoner choked up. He looked as though he had a hundred things to say and they were all jumbled together in his throat.

174   THE BEST OF RICHARD MATHESON

"You want to see the priest again?" asked Mac.

"Again?" asked the prisoner.

Mac stepped closer and looked into the cell.

"Are you sick?" he asked.

The prisoner didn't answer. Mac looked at the tray.

"You didn't eat the food we brought," he said. "You asked for it and we went to all that trouble and you didn't eat it. Why not?"

The prisoner looked at the tray, at Mac, then at the tray again. A sob broke in his chest.

"What am I doing here?" he begged, "I'm not a criminal, I'm . . ."

"Shut up for chrissake!" roared another prisoner.

"All right, all right, pipe down," Mac called down the corridor.

"Whassa matter?" someone sneered, "Did big boy wet his pants?"

Laughter. The prisoner looked at Mac.

"Look, will you listen?" he said, the words trembling in his throat.

Mac looked at him and shook his head slowly.

"Never figured on this did you, Riley?" he said.

"I'm not Riley!" cried the man. "My name is Johnson."

He pressed against the door, painful eagerness on his features. He licked his dry lips.

"Listen," he said. "I'm a scientist."

Mac smiled bitterly and shook his head again.

"Can't take it like a man, can you?" he said, "You're like all the rest for all your braggin' and struttin'."

The prisoner looked helpless.

"Listen," he muttered hoarsely.

"You listen to *me*," said Mac. "You have two hours, Riley."

"I told you I'm not . . ."

"Cut it! You have two hours. See if you can be a man in those two hours instead of a whining dog."

The prisoner's face was blank.

"You want to see the priest again?" Mac asked.

"No, I . . ." started the prisoner. He stopped. His throat tightened.

"Yes," he said. "I want to see the priest. Call him, will you?"

Mac nodded.

"I'll call him," he said. "In the meantime, keep your mouth shut."

The prisoner turned and shuffled back to the bunk. He sank down on it and stared at the floor.

Mac looked at him for a moment and then started down the hall.

"Whassa matter?" called one of the prisoners mockingly. "Did big boy wet his pants?"

The other prisoners laughed. Their laughter broke in waves over the slumped prisoner.

He got up and started to pace. He looked at the sky through the window. He stepped up to the cell door and looked up and down the hall.

Suddenly he smiled nervously.

"All right," he called out. "All right. It's very funny. I appreciate it. Now let me out of this rat trap."

Someone groaned. "Shut up, Riley!" someone else yelled.

His brow contracted.

"A joke's a joke," he said loudly. "But now I have to . . ."

He stopped, hearing fast footsteps on the corridor floor. Charlie's ungainly body hurried up and stopped before the cell.

"Are you gonna shut up?" he threatened, his pudgy lips outthrust. "Or do we give you a shot?"

The prisoner tried to smile.

"All right," he said. "All right, I'm properly subdued. Now come on," his voice rose. "Let me out."

"Any more crap outta you and it's the hypo," Charlie warned. He turned away.

"Always knew you was yellow," he said.

"*Listen* to me, will you?" said the prisoner, "I'm Phillip Johnson. I'm a nuclear physicist."

Charlie's head snapped back and a wild laugh tore through his thick lips. His body shook.

"A nu-nucleeeee . . ." His voice died away in wheezing laughter.

"I tell you it's true," the prisoner shouted after him.

A mock groan rumbled in Charlie's throat. He hit himself on the forehead with his fleshy palm.

"What won't they think of next?" he said. His voice rang out down the corridor.

"You shut up too!" yelled another prisoner.

"Knock it off!" ordered Charlie, the smile gone, his face a chubby mask of belligerence.

"Is the priest coming?" he heard the prisoner call.

"Is the priest coming? Is the priest coming?" he mimicked. He pounded on his desk elatedly. He sank back in the revolving chair. It squeaked loudly as he leaned back. He groaned.

"Wake me up once more and you'll get the hypo!" he yelled down the corridor.

"Shut up!" yelled one of the other prisoners.

"Knock it off!" retorted Charlie.

The prisoner stood on the stool. He was looking out through the window. He watched the rain falling.

"Where am I?" he said.

Mac and the priest stopped in front of the cell. Mac motioned to Charlie and Charlie pushed a button on the control board. The door slid open.

"Okay, Father," said Mac.

The priest went into the cell. He was short and stout. His face was red. It had a kind smile on it.

"Say, wantta hand me that tray, Father?" Mac asked.

The priest nodded silently. He picked up the tray and handed it to Mac.

"Thank you kindly, Father."

"Certainly."

The door shut behind the guard. He paused.

"Call out if he gets tough," he said.

"I'm sure he won't," said Father Shane, smiling at the prisoner who was standing by the wall, waiting for Mac to go.

Mac stood there a moment.

"Watch your step, Riley," he warned.

He moved out of sight. His footsteps echoed down the corridor.

Father Shane flinched as the prisoner hurried to his side.

"Now, my son . . ." he started.

"I'm not going to hit you, for God's sake," the prisoner said. "Listen to me, Father . . ."

"Suppose we sit down and relax," said the priest.

"What? Oh, all right. All right."

The prisoner sat down on the bunk. The priest went over and picked up the stool. Slowly he carried it to the side of the bunk. He placed it down softly in front of the prisoner.

"Listen to me," started the prisoner.

Father Shane lifted a restraining finger. He took out his broad white handkerchief and studiously polished the stool surface. The prisoner's hands twitched impatiently.

"For God's sake," he entreated.

"Yes," smiled the priest. "For His sake."

He settled his portly form on the stool. The periphery of his frame ran over the edges.

"Now," he said comfortingly.

The prisoner bit his lower lip.

"Listen to me," he said.

"Yes, John."

"My name isn't John," snapped the prisoner.

The priest looked confused.

"Not . . ." he started.

"My name is Phillip Johnson."

The priest looked blank a moment. Then he smiled sadly.

"Why do you struggle, my son? Why can't you . . ."

"I tell you my name is Phillip Johnson. Will you listen?"

"But my son . . ."

"Will you!"

Father Shane drew back in alarm.

"Will you shut that bastard up!" a voice said slowly and loudly in another cell.

Footsteps.

"Please don't go," begged the prisoner. "Please stay."

"If you promise to speak quietly and not disturb these other poor souls."

Mac appeared at the door.

"I promise, I promise," whispered the prisoner.

"What's the matter now?" Mac asked. He looked inquisitively at the priest.

"You wanna leave, Father?" he asked.

"No, no," said Father Shane. "We'll be all right. Riley has promised to . . ."

"I told you I'm not . . ."

The prisoner's voice broke off.

"What's that?" asked the priest.

"Nothing, nothing," muttered the prisoner, "Will you ask the guard to go away?"

The priest looked toward Mac. He nodded once, a smile shooting dimples into his red cheeks.

Mac left. The prisoner raised his head.

"Now, my son," said Father Shane. "Why is your soul troubled? Is it penitence you seek?"

The prisoner twisted his shoulders impatiently.

"Listen," he said. "Will you listen to me. Without speaking? Just listen and don't say anything."

"Of course, my son," the priest said. "That's why I'm here. However . . ."

"All right," said the prisoner. He shifted on the bunk. He leaned forward, his face drawn tight.

"Listen to me," he said, "My name isn't John Riley. My name is Phillip Johnson."

The priest looked pained.

"My son," he started.

"You said you'd listen," said the prisoner.

The priest lowered his eyelids. A martyred print stamped itself on his face.

"Speak then," he said.

"I'm a nuclear physicist. I . . ."

He stopped.

"What year is this?" he asked suddenly.

The priest looked at him. He smiled thinly.

"But surely you . . ."

"Please. *Please.* Tell me."

The priest looked mildly upset. He shrugged his sloping shoulders.

"1954," he said.

"What?" asked the prisoner. "Are you sure?" He stared at the priest. "Are you sure?" he repeated.

"My son, this is of no purpose."

"1954?"

The priest held back his irritation. He nodded.

"Yes, my son," he said.

"Then it's true," said the man.

"What, my son."

"Listen," said the prisoner. "Try to believe me. I'm a nuclear physicist. At least, I was in 1944."

"I don't understand," said the priest.

"I worked in a secret fission plant deep in the Rocky Mountains."

"In the Rocky Mountains?"

"No one ever heard of it," said the prisoner. "It was never publicized. It was built in 1943 for experiments on nuclear fission."

"But Oak Ridge . . ."

"That was another one. It was strictly a limited venture. Mostly guesswork. Only a few people outside of the plant knew anything about it."

"But . . ."

"Listen. We were working with U-238."

The priest started to speak.

"That's an isotope of uranium. Constitutes the bulk of it; more than 99 percent. But there was no way to make it undergo fission. We were trying to make it do that. Do you understand . . ."

The priest's face reflected his confusion.

"Never mind," said the prisoner hurriedly. "It doesn't matter. What matters is that there was an explosion."

"An . . ."

"An explosion, an explosion."

"Oh. But . . ." faltered the priest.

"This was in 1944," said the prisoner. "That's . . . ten years ago. Now I wake up and I'm here in . . . where are we?"

"State Penitentiary," prompted the priest without thinking.

"Colorado?"

The priest shook his head.

"This is New York," he said.

The prisoner's left hand rose to his forehead. He ran nervous fingers through his hair.

"Two thousand miles," he muttered. "Ten years."

"My son . . ."

He looked at the priest.

"Don't you believe me?"

The priest smiled sadly. The prisoner gestured helplessly with his hands.

"What can I do to prove it? I know it sounds fantastic. Blown through time and space."

He knitted his brow.

"Maybe I didn't get blown through space and time. Maybe I was blown out of my mind. Maybe I became someone else. Maybe . . ."

"Listen to me, Riley."

The prisoner's face contorted angrily.

"I told you. I'm *not* Riley."

The priest lowered his head.

"Must you do this thing?" he asked, "Must you try so hard to escape justice?"

"Justice?" cried the prisoner. "For God's sake is this justice? I'm no criminal. I'm not even the man you say I am."

"Maybe we'd better pray together," said the priest.

The prisoner looked around desperately. He leaned forward and grasped the priest's shoulders.

"Don't . . ." started Father Shane.

"I'm not going to hurt you," said the prisoner impatiently. "Just tell me about this Riley. Who is he? All right, all right," he went on as the priest gave him an imploring look. "Who am I supposed to be? What's my background?"

"My son, why must you . . ."

"Will you *tell* me. For God's sake I'm to be execu—that's it isn't it? Isn't it?"

The priest nodded involuntarily.

"In less than two hours. Won't you do what I ask?"

The priest sighed.

"What's my education?" asked the prisoner.

"I don't know," said Father Shane. "I don't know your education, your background, your family, or . . ."

"But it's not likely that John Riley would know nuclear physics is it?" inquired the prisoner anxiously. "Not likely is it?"

The priest shrugged slightly.

"I suppose not," he said.

"What did he . . . what did I do?"

The priest closed his eyes.

"Please," he said.

"What did I do?"

The priest clenched his teeth.

"You stole," he said. "You murdered."

The prisoner looked at him in astonishment. His throat contracted. Without realizing it, he clasped his hands together until the blood drained from them.

"Well," he mumbled, "If I . . . if *he* did these things, it's not likely he's an educated nuclear physicist is it?"

"Riley, I . . ."

"*Is* it!"

"No, no, I suppose not. What's the purpose of asking?"

"I *told* you. I can give you facts about nuclear physics. I can tell you things that you admit this Riley could never tell you."

The priest took a troubled breath.

"Look," the prisoner hurriedly explained. "Our trouble stemmed from the disparity between theory and fact. In theory the U-238 would capture a neutron and form a new isotope U-239 since the neutron would merely add to the mass of . . ."

"My son, this is useless."

"Useless!" cried the prisoner. "Why? *Why*? You tell me Riley couldn't know these things. Well, *I* know them. Can't you see that it means I'm not Riley. And if I became Riley, it was because of loss of memory. It was due to an explosion ten years ago that I had no control over."

Father Shane looked grim. He shook his head.

"That's right isn't it?" pleaded the prisoner.

"You may have read these things somewhere," said the priest. "You may have just remembered them in this time of stress. Believe me I'm not accusing you of . . ."

"I've told the truth!"

"You must struggle against this unmanly cowardice," said Father Shane. "Do you think I can't understand your fear of death? It is universal. It is . . ."

"Oh God, is it possible," moaned the prisoner. "Is it possible?"

The priest lowered his head.

"They can't execute me!" the prisoner said, clutching at the priest's dark coat. "I tell you I'm not Riley. I'm Phillip Johnson."

The priest said nothing. He made no resistance. His body jerked in the prisoner's grip. He prayed.

The prisoner let go and fell back against the wall with a thud.

"My God," he muttered. "Oh, my God, is there no one?"

The priest looked up at him.

"There is God," he said. "Let Him take you to His bosom. Pray for forgiveness."

The prisoner stared blankly at him.

"You don't understand," he said in a flat voice. "You just don't understand. I'm going to be executed."

His lips began to tremble.

"You don't believe me," he said. "You think I'm lying. Everyone thinks I'm lying."

Suddenly he looked up. He sat up.

"Mary!" he cried. "My wife. What about my wife?"

"You have no wife, Riley."

"No wife? Are you telling me I have no wife?"

"There's no point in continuing this, my son."

The prisoner reached up despairing hands and drove them against his temples.

"My God, isn't there anyone to listen?"

"Yes," murmured the priest.

Footsteps again. There was loud grumbling from the other prisoners.

Charlie appeared.

"You better go, Father," he said. "It's no use. He don't want your help."

"I hate to leave the poor soul in this condition."

The prisoner jumped up and ran to the barred door. Charlie stepped back.

"Watch out," he threatened.

"Listen, will you call my wife?" begged the prisoner. "Will you? Our home is in Missouri, in St. Louis. The number is . . ."

"Knock it off."

"You don't understand. My wife can explain everything. She can tell you who I really am."

Charlie grinned.

"By God, this is the best I ever seen," he said appreciatively.

"Will you call her?" said the prisoner.

"Go on. Get back in your cell."

The prisoner backed away. Charlie signaled and the door slid open. Father Shane went out, head lowered.

"I'll come back," he said.

"Won't you call my wife?" begged the prisoner.

The priest hesitated. Then, with a sigh, he stopped and took out a pad and pencil.

"What's the number?" he asked wearily.

The prisoner scuttled to the door.

"Don't waste your good time, Father," Charlie said.

The prisoner hurriedly told Father Shane the number.

"Are you sure you have it right?" he asked the priest, "Are you positive?" He repeated the number. The priest nodded.

"Tell her I . . . tell her I'm all right. Tell her I'm well and I'll be home as soon as . . . hurry! There isn't time. Get word to the governor or somebody."

The priest put his hand on the man's shaking shoulder.

"If there's no answer when I call," he said. "If no one is there, then will you stop this talk?"

"There will be. She'll be there. I know she'll be there."

"If she isn't."

"She will be."

The priest drew back his hand and walked down the corridor slowly, nodding at the other prisoners as he passed them. The prisoner watched him as long as he could.

Then he turned back. Charlie was grinning at him.

"You're the best one yet, all right," said Charlie.

The prisoner looked at him.

"Once there was a guy," recalled Charlie. "Said he ate a bomb. Said he'd blow the place sky high if we electrocuted him."

He chuckled at the recollection.

"We X-rayed him. He didn't swallow nothing. Except electricity later."

The prisoner turned away and went back to his bunk. He sank down on it.

"There was another one," said Charlie, raising his voice so the others could hear him. "Said he was Christ. Said he couldn't be killed. Said he'd get up in three days and come walkin' through the wall."

He rubbed his nose with a bunched fist.

"Ain't heard from him since," he snickered. "But I always keep an eye on the wall just in case."

His chest throbbed with rumbling laughter.

"Now there was another one," he started. The prisoner looked at him with hate burning in his eyes. Charlie shrugged his shoulders and started back up the corridor. Then he turned and went back.

"We'll be giving you a haircut soon," he called in. "Any special way you'd like it?"

"Go away."

"Sideburns, maybe?" Charlie said, his fat face wrinkling in amusement. The prisoner turned his head and looked at the window.

"How about bangs?" asked Charlie. He laughed and turned back down the wall.

"Hey Mac, how about we give big boy some bangs?"

The prisoner bent over and pressed shaking palms over his eyes.

The door was opening.

The prisoner shuddered and his head snapped up from the bunk. He stared dumbly at Mac and Charlie and the third man. The third man was carrying something in his hand.

"What do you want?" he asked thickly.

Charlie snickered.

"Man, this is rich," he said, "What do we want?"

His face shifted into a cruel leer. "We come to give you a haircut big boy."

"Where's the priest?"

"Out priesting," said Charlie.

"Shut up," Mac said irritably.

"I hope you're going to take this easy son," said the third man.

The skin tightened on the prisoner's skull. He backed against the wall.

"Wait a minute," he said fearfully. "You have the wrong man."

Charlie sputtered with laughter and reached down to grab him. The prisoner pulled back.

"No!" he cried, "Where's the priest?"

"Come *on*," snapped Charlie angrily.

The prisoner's eyes flew from Mac to the third man.

"You don't understand," he said hysterically. "The priest is calling my wife in St. Louis. She'll tell you all who I am. I'm not Riley. I'm Phillip Johnson."

"Come on, Riley," said Mac.

"Johnson, Johnson!"

"Johnson, Johnson come and get your hair cut Johnson, Johnson," chanted Charlie, grabbing the prisoner's arm.

"Let go of me!"

Charlie jerked him to his feet and twisted his arm around. His face was taut with vicious anger.

"Grab him," he snapped to Mac. Mac took hold of the prisoner's other arm.

"For God's sake, what do I have to do!" screamed the prisoner, writhing in their grip. "I'm not Johnson. I mean I'm not Riley."

"We heard you the first time," panted Charlie. "Come on. Shave him!"

They slammed the prisoner down on the bunk and twisted his arms behind him. He screamed until Charlie backhanded him across the mouth.

"Shut up!"

The prisoner sat trembling while his hair fluttered to the floor in dark heaps. Tufts of hair stuck to his eyebrows. A trickle of blood ran from the edge of his mouth. His eyes were stricken with horror.

When the third man had finished on the prisoner's head, he bent down and slashed open his pants.

"Mmmm," he grunted. "Burned legs."

The prisoner jerked down his head and looked. His mouth formed soundless words. The he cried out.

"Flash burns! Can you see them? They're from an atomic explosion. *Now* will you believe me?"

Charlie grinned. They let go of the prisoner and he fell down on the bunk. He pushed up quickly and clutched at Mac's arm.

"You're intelligent," he said. "Look at my legs. Can't you see that they're flash burns?"

Mac picked the prisoner's fingers off his arm.

"Take it easy," he said.

The prisoner moved toward the third man.

"You saw them," he pleaded. "Don't you know a flash burn? Look. L-look. Take my word for it. It's a flash burn. No other kind of heat could make such scars. *Look at it!*"

"Sure, sure, sure," said Charlie moving into the corridor. "We'll take your word for it. We'll get your clothes and you can go right home to your wife in Saint Louis."

"I'm telling you they're flash burns!"

The three men were out of the cell. They slid the door shut. The prisoner reached through the bars and tried to stop them. Charlie punched his arm and shoved him back. The prisoner sprawled onto the bunk.

"For God's sake," he sobbed, his face twisted with childish frenzy. "What's the matter with you? Why don't you listen to me?"

He heard the men talking as they went down the corridor. He wept in the silence of his cell.

After a while the priest came back. The prisoner looked up and saw him standing at the door. He stood up and ran to the door. He clutched at the priest's arm.

"You reached her? You reached her?"

The priest didn't say anything.

"You did, didn't you?"

"There was no one there by that name."

"What?"

"There was no wife of Phillip Johnson there. Now will you listen to me?"

"Then she moved. Of course! She left the city after I . . . after the explosion. You have to find her."

"There's no such person."

The prisoner stared at him in disbelief.

"But I told you . . ."

"I'm speaking truth. You're making it all up in a vain hope to cheat . . ."

"I'm not making it up! For God's sake listen to me. Can't you . . . wait, wait."

He held his right leg up.

"Look," he said eagerly. "These are flash burns. From an atomic explosion. Don't you see what that means?"

"Listen to me, my son."

"Don't you understand?"

"Will you listen to me?"

"Yes but . . ."

"Even if what you say is true . . ."

"It *is* true."

"Even if it is. You still committed the crimes you're here to pay for."

"*But it wasn't me!*"

"Can you prove it?" asked the priest.

"I . . . I . . ." faltered the prisoner. "These legs . . ."

"They're no proof."

"My wife . . ."

"Where is she?"

"I don't know. But you can find her. She'll tell you. She can save me."

"I'm afraid there's nothing that can be done."

"But there has to be! Can't you look for my wife? Can't you get a stay of execution while you look for her? Look, I have friends, a lot of them. I'll give you all their addresses. I'll give you names of people who work for the government who . . ."

"What would I say, Riley?" interrupted the priest sharply.

"Johnson!"

"Whatever you wish to be called. What would I say to these people? I'm calling about a man who was in an explosion ten years ago? But he didn't die? He was blown into . . ."

He stopped.

"Can't you see?" he entreated. "You must face this. You're only making it more difficult for yourself."

"But . . ."

"Shall I come in and pray for you?"

The prisoner stared at him. Then the tautness sapped from his face and stance. He slumped visibly. He turned and staggered back to his bunk and fell down on it. He leaned against the wall and clutched his shirtfront with dead curled fingers.

"No hope," he said. "There's no hope. No one will believe me. No one."

He was lying down on his bunk when the other two guards came. He was staring, glassy-eyed, at the wall. The priest was sitting on the stool and praying.

The prisoner didn't speak as they led him down the corridor, only once he raised his head and looked around as though all the world was a strange incomprehensible cruelty.

Then he lowered his head and shuffled mutely between the guards. The priest followed, hands folded, head lowered, his lips moving in silent prayer.

Later, when Mac and Charlie were playing cards the lights went out. They sat there waiting. They heard the other prisoners in death row stirring restlessly.

Then the lights went on.

"You deal," said Charlie.

DRESS OF WHITE SILK

Quiet is here and all in me.

Granma locked me in my room and wont let me out. Because its happened she says. I guess I was bad. Only it was the dress. Mommas dress I mean. She is gone away forever. Granma says your momma is in heaven. I dont know how. Can she go in heaven is shes dead?

Now I hear granma. She is in mommas room. She is putting mommas dress down the box. Why does she always? And locks it too. I wish she didnt. Its a pretty dress and smells sweet so. And warm. I love to touch it against my cheek. But I cant never again. I guess that is why granma is mad at me.

But I amnt sure. All day it was only like everyday. Mary Jane came over to my house. She lives across the street. Everyday she comes to my house and play. Today she was.

I have seven dolls and a fire truck. Today granma said play with your dolls and it. Dont you go inside your mommas room now she said. She always says it. She just means not mess up I think. Because she says it all the time. Dont go in your mommas room. Like that.

But its nice in mommas room. When it rains I go there. Or when granma is doing her nap I do. I dont make noise. I just sit on the bed and touch the white cover. Like when I was only small. The room smells like sweet.

I make believe momma is dressing and I am allowed in. I smell her white silk dress. Her going out for night dress. She called it that I dont remember when.

I hear it moving if I listen hard. I make believe to see her sitting at the dressing table. Like touching on perfume or something I mean. And see her dark eyes. I can remember.

Its so nice if it rains and I see eyes on the window. The rain sounds like a big giant outside. He says shushshush so every one will be quiet. I like to make believe that in mommas room.

What I like almost best is to sit at mommas dressing table. It is like pink and big and smells sweet too. The seat in front has a pillow sewed in it. There are bottles and bottles with bumps and have colored perfume in them. And you can see almost your whole self in the mirror.

When I sit there I make believe to be momma. I say be quiet mother I am going out and you can not stop me. It is something I say I dont know why like I hear it in me. And oh stop your sobbing mother they will not catch me I have my magic dress.

When I pretend I brush my hair long. But I only use my own brush from my room. I didnt never use mommas brush. I dont think granma is mad at me for that because I never use mommas brush. I wouldnt never.

Sometimes I did open the box up. Because I know where granma puts the key. I saw her once when she wouldnt know I saw her. She puts the key on the hook in mommas closet. Behind the door I mean.

I could open the box lots of times. Thats because I like to look at mommas dress. I like best to look at it. It is so pretty and feels soft and like silky. I could touch it for a million years.

I kneel on the rug with roses on it. I hold the dress in my arms and like breathe from it. I touch it against my cheek. I wish I could take it to sleep with me and hold it. I like to. Now I cant. Because granma says. And she says I should burn it up but I loved her so. And she cries about the dress.

I wasnt never bad with it. I put it back neat like it was never touched. Granma never knew. I laughed that she never knew before. But she knows now I did it I guess. And shell punish me. What did it hurt her? Wasnt it my mommas dress?

What I like real best in mommas room is look at the picture of momma. It has a gold thing around it. Frame is what granma says. It is on the wall on top the bureau.

Momma is pretty. Your momma was pretty granma says. Why does she? I see momma there smiling on me and she *is* pretty. For always.

Her hair is black. Like mine. Her eyes are even pretty like black. Her mouth is red so red. I like the dress and its the white one. It is all down on her shoulders. Her skin is white almost white like the dress. And so are her hands. She is so pretty. I love her even if she is gone away forever. I love her so much.

I guess I think thats what made me bad. I mean to Mary Jane.

Mary Jane came from lunch like she does. Granma went to do her nap. She said dont forget now no going to your mommas room. I told her no granma. And I was saying the truth but then Mary Jane and I was playing fire truck. Mary Jane said I bet you havent no mother I bet you made up it all she said.

I got mad at her. I have a momma I know. She made me mad at her to say I made up it all. She said Im a liar. I mean about the bed and the dressing table and the picture and the dress even and every thing.

I said well Ill show you smarty.

I looked into granmas room. She was doing her nap still. I went down and said Mary Jane to come on because granma wont know.

She wasnt so smart after then. She giggled like she does. Even she made a scaredy noise when she hit into the table in the hall upstairs. I said youre a scaredy cat to her. She said back well *my* house isnt so dark like this. Like that was so much.

We went in mommas room. It was more dark than you could see. I said this is my mommas room I suppose I made up it all.

She was by the door and she wasnt smart then either. She didnt say any word. She looked around the room. She jumped when I got her arm. Well come on I said.

I sat on the bed and said this is my mommas bed see how soft it is. She didnt say nothing. Scaredy cat I said. Am not she said like she does.

I said to sit down how can you tell if its soft if you dont sit down. She sat down by me. I said feel how soft it is. Smell how sweet it is.

I closed my eyes but funny it wasnt like always. Because Mary Jane was there. I told her to stop feeling the cover. You said to she said. Well stop it I said.

See I said and I pulled her up. Thats the dressing table. I took her and brought her there. She said let go. It was so quiet and like always. I started to feel bad. Because Mary Jane was there. Because it was in my mommas room and momma wouldnt like Mary Jane there.

But I had to show her the things because. I showed her the mirror. We looked at each other in it. She looked white. Mary Jane is a scaredy cat I said. Am not am not she said anyways nobodys house is so quiet and dark inside. Anyways she said it smells.

I got mad at her. No it doesnt smell I said. Does so she said and you said it did. I got madder too. It smells like sugar she said. It smells like sick people in your mommas room.

Dont say my mommas room is like sick people I said to her.

Well you didnt show me no dress and youre lying she said there isnt no dress. I felt all warm inside so I pulled her hair. Ill show you I said youre going to see my mommas dress and youll better not call me a liar.

I made her stand still and I got the key off the hook. I kneeled down. I opened the box with the key.

Mary Jane said pew that smells like garbage.

I put my nails in her and she pulled away and got mad. Dont you pinch me she said and she was all red. Im telling my mother on you she said. And anyways its not a white dress its dirty and ugly she said.

Its not dirty I said. I said it so loud I wonder why granma didnt hear. I pulled out the dress from the box. I held it up to show her how its white. It fell open like the rain whispering and the bottom touched on the rug.

It is too white I said all white and clean and silky.

No she said she was so mad and red it has a hole in it. I got more madder. If my momma was here shed show you I said. You got no momma she said all ugly. I hate her.

I have. I said it way loud. I pointed my finger to mommas picture. Well who can see in this stupid dark room she said. I pushed her hard and she hit against the bureau. See then I said mean look at the picture. Thats my momma and shes the most beautiful lady in the world.

Shes ugly she has funny hands Mary Jane said. She hasnt I said shes the most beautiful lady in the world!

Not not she said *she has buck teeth.*

I dont remember then. I think the dress moved in my arms. Mary Jane screamed. I dont remember what. It got dark and the curtains were closed I think. I couldnt see anyway. I couldnt hear nothing except buck teeth funny hands buck teeth funny hands even when no one was saying it.

There was something else because I think I heard some one call *dont let her say that!* I couldnt hold to the dress. And I had it on me I cant remember. Because I was grown up strong. But I was a little girl still I think. I mean outside.

I think I was terrible bad then.

Granma took me away from there I guess. I dont know. She was screaming god help us its happened its happened. Over and over. I dont know why. She pulled me all the way here to my room and locked me in. She wont let me out. Well Im not so scared. Who cares if she locks me in a million billion years? She doesnt have to even give me supper. Im not hungry anyway.

Im full.

HAIRCUT

Angelo was down the block having lunch at Temple's Cafeteria and Joe was alone, sitting in one of the barber chairs reading the morning paper.

It was hot in the shop. The air seemed heavy with the smell of lotions and tonics and shaving soap. There were dark swirls of hair lying on the tiles. In the stillness, a big fly buzzed around in lazy circles. **HEAT WAVE CONTINUES**, Joe read.

He was rubbing at his neck with a handkerchief when the screen door creaked open and shut with a thud. Joe looked across the shop at the man who was moving toward him.

"Yes, sir," Joe said automatically, folding the newspaper and sliding off the black leather of the chair.

As he put the newspaper on one of the wireback chairs along the wall, the man shuffled over to the chair and sat down on it, his hands in the coat pockets of his wrinkled brown gabardine suit. He slumped down in the chair, waiting, as Joe turned around.

"Yes, sir," Joe said again, looking at the man's sallow, dry-skinned face. He took a towel from the glass-floored cabinet. "Like to take your coat off, sir?" he asked, "Pretty hot today."

The man said nothing. Joe's smile faltered for a moment, then returned.

"Yes, sir," he said, tucking the towel under the collar of the man's faded shirt, feeling how dry and cool his skin was. He put the striped cloth over the man's coat and pinned it in place.

"Looks like we're havin' another scorcher," he said.

The man was silent. Joe cleared his throat.

"Shave?" he asked.

The man shook his head once.

"Haircut," Joe said and the man nodded slowly.

Joe picked up the electric shaver and flicked it on. The high-pitched buzzing filled the air.

"Uh . . . could you sit up a little, sir?" Joe asked.

Without a sound or change of expression, the man pressed his elbows down on the arms of the chair and raised himself a little.

Joe ran the shaver up the man's neck, noticing now white the skin was where the hair had been. The man hadn't been to a barber in a long time; for a haircut anyway.

"Well, it sure looks like the heat ain't plannin' to leave," Joe said.

"Keeps growing," the man said.

"You said it," Joe answered, "Gets hotter and hotter. Like I told the missus the other night . . ."

As he talked, he kept shaving off the hair on the back of the man's neck. The lank hair fluttered darkly down onto the man's shoulders.

Joe put a different head on the electric shaver and started cutting again.

"You want it short?" he asked.

The man nodded slowly and Joe had to draw away the shaver to keep from cutting him.

"It keeps growing," the man said.

Joe chuckled self-consciously. "Ain't it the way?" he said. Then his face grew studious. "Course hair always grows a lot faster in the summertime. It's the heat. Makes the glands work faster or somethin'. Cut it short, I always say."

"Yes," the man said, "short." His voice was flat and without tone.

Joe put down the shaver and pulled the creased handkerchief from his back trouser pocket. He mopped at his brow.

"*Hot,*" he said and blew out a heavy breath.

The man said nothing and Joe put away his handkerchief.

He picked up the scissors and comb and turned back to the chair. He clicked the scissor blades a few times and started trimming. He grimaced a little as he smelled the man's breath. Bad teeth, he thought.

"And my nails," the man said.

"Beg pardon?" Joe asked.

"They keep growing," the man said.

Joe hesitated a moment, glancing up at the mirror on the opposite wall. The man was staring into his lap.

Joe swallowed and started cutting again. He ran the thin comb through the man's hair and snipped off bunches of it. The dark, dry hair fell down on the striped cloth. Some of it fluttered down to the floor.

"Out?" the man said.

"What's that?" Joe asked.

"My nails," the man answered.

"Oh. No. We ain't got no manicurist," Joe said. He laughed apologetically. "We ain't that high-class."

The man's face didn't change at all and Joe's smile faded.

"You want a manicure, though," he said, "There's a big barber shop up on Atlantic Avena in the bank. They got a manicurist there."

"They keep growing," the man said.

"Yeah," Joe said distractedly, "Uh . . . you want any off the top?"

"I can't stop it," the man said.

"Huh?" Joe looked across the way again at the reflection of the man's unchanging face. He saw how still the man's eyes were, how sunken.

He went back to his cutting and decided not to talk anymore.

As he cut, the smell kept getting worse. It wasn't the man's breath, Joe decided, it was his body. The man probably hadn't taken a bath in weeks. Joe breathed through gritted teeth. If there's anything I can't stand, he thought.

In a little while, he finished cutting with the scissors and comb. Laying them down on the counter, he took off the striped cloth and shook the dark hair onto the floor.

He rearranged the towel and pinned the striped cloth on again. Then he flicked on the black dispenser and let about an inch and a half of white lather push out onto the palm of his left hand.

He rubbed it into the men's temples and around the ears, his fingers twitching at the cool dryness of the man's flesh. He's *sick*, he thought worriedly, hope to hell it isn't contagious. Some people just ain't got no consideration at all.

Joe stropped the straight razor, humming nervously to himself while the man sat motionless in the chair.

"Hurry," the man said.

"Yes, sir," Joe said, "right away." He stropped the razor blade once more, then let go of the black strap. It swung down and bumped once against the back of the chair.

Joe drew the skin taut and shaved around the man's right ear.

"I should have stayed," the man said.

"Sir?"

The man said nothing. Joe swallowed uneasily and went on shaving, breathing through his mouth in order to avoid the smell which kept getting worse.

"Hurry," the man said.

"Goin' as fast as I can," Joe said, a little irritably.

"I should have stayed."

Joe shivered for some reason. "Be finished in a second," he said. The man kept staring at his lap, his body motionless on the chair, his hands still in his coat pockets.

"Why?" the man said.

"What?" Joe asked.

"Does it keep growing?"

Joe looked blank. He glanced at the man's reflection again, feeling something tighten in his stomach. He tried to grin.

"That's life," he said, weakly, and finished up with the shaving as quickly as he could. He wiped off the lather with a clean towel, noticing how starkly white the man's skin was where the hair had been shaved away.

He started automatically for the water bottle to clean off the man's neck and around the ears. Then he stopped himself and turned back. He sprinkled powder on the brush and spread it around the man's neck. The sweetish smell of the clouding powder mixed with the other heavier smell.

"Comb it wet or dry?" Joe asked.

The man didn't answer. Nervously, trying not to breathe anymore than necessary, Joe ran the comb through the man's hair without touching it with his fingers. He parted it on the left side and combed and brushed it back.

Now, for the first time, the man's lifeless eyes raised and he looked into the mirror at himself.

"Yes," he said slowly. "That's better."

With a lethargic movement, he stood up and Joe had to move around the chair to get the towel and the striped cloth off.

"Yes, sir," he said, automatically.

The man started shuffling for the door, his hands still in the side pockets of his coat.

"Hey, wait a minute," Joe said, a surprised look on his face.

The man turned slowly and Joe swallowed as the dark-circled eyes looked at him.

"That's a buck-fifty," he said, nervously.

The man stared at him with glazed, unblinking eyes.

"What?" he said.

"A buck-fifty," Joe said again. "For the cut."

A moment more, the man looked at Joe. Then, slowly, as if he weren't sure he was looking in the right place, the man looked down at his coat pockets.

Slowly, jerkingly, he drew out his hands.

Joe felt himself go rigid. He caught his breath and moved back a step, eyes staring at the man's white hands, at the nails which grew almost an inch past the finger tips.

"But I have no money," the man said as he slowly opened his hands.

Joe didn't even hear the gasp that filled his throat.

He stood there, staring open-mouthed at the black dirt sifting through the man's white fingers.

He stood there, paralyzed, until the man had turned and, with a heavy shuffle, walked to the screen door and left the shop.

Then, he walked numbly to the doorway and out onto the sun-drenched sidewalk.

He stood there for a long time, blank-faced, watching the man hobble slowly across the street and walk up toward Atlantic Avenue and the bank.

NIGHTMARE AT 20,000 FEET

"Seat belt, please," said the stewardess cheerfully as she passed him.

Almost as she spoke, the sign above the archway which led to the forward compartment lit up—FASTEN SEAT BELT—with, below, its attendant caution—NO SMOKING. Drawing in a deep lungful, Wilson exhaled it in bursts, then pressed the cigarette into the armrest tray with irritable stabbing motions.

Outside, one of the engines coughed monstrously, spewing out a cloud of fume which fragmented into the night air. The fuselage began to shudder and Wilson, glancing through the window, saw the exhaust of flame jetting whitely from the engine's nacelle. The second engine coughed, then roared, its propeller instantly a blur of revolution. With a tense submissiveness, Wilson fastened the belt across his lap.

Now all the engines were running and Wilson's head throbbed in unison with the fuselage. He sat rigidly, staring at the seat ahead as the DC-7 taxied across the apron, heating the night with the thundering blast of its exhausts.

At the edge of the runway, it halted. Wilson looked out through the window at the leviathan glitter of the terminal. By late morning, he thought, showered and cleanly dressed, he would be sitting in the office of one more contact discussing one more specious deal the net result of which would not add one jot of meaning to the history of mankind. It was all so damned—

Wilson gasped as the engines began their warm-up race preparatory to takeoff. The sound, already loud, became deafening—waves of sound that crashed against Wilson's ears like club blows.

He opened his mouth as if to let it drain. His eyes took on the glaze of a suffering man, his hands drew in like tensing claws.

He started, legs retracting, as he felt a touch on his arm. Jerking aside his head, he saw the stewardess who had met him at the door. She was smiling down at him.

"Are you all right?" he barely made out her words.

Wilson pressed his lips together and agitated his hand at her as if pushing her away. Her smile flared into excess brightness, then fell as she turned and moved away.

The plane began to move. At first lethargically, like some behemoth struggling to overthrow the pull of its own weight. Then with more speed, forcing off the drag of friction. Wilson, turning to the window, saw the dark runway rushing by faster and faster. On the wing edge, there was a mechanical whining as the flaps descended. Then, imperceptibly, the giant wheels lost contact with the ground, the earth began to fall away. Trees flashed underneath, buildings, the darting quicksilver of car lights. The DC-7 banked slowly to the right, pulling itself upward toward the frosty glitter of the stars.

Finally, it leveled off and the engines seemed to stop until Wilson's adjusting ear caught the murmur of their cruising speed. A moment of relief slackened his muscles, imparting a sense of wellbeing. Then it was gone. Wilson sat immobile, staring at the NO SMOKING sign until it winked out, then, quickly, lit a cigarette. Reaching into the seat-back pocket in front of him, he slid free his newspaper.

As usual, the world was in a state similar to his. Friction in diplomatic circles, earthquakes and gunfire, murder, rape, tornadoes and collisions, business conflicts, gangsterism. God's in his heaven, all's right with the world, thought Arthur Jeffrey Wilson.

Fifteen minutes later, he tossed the paper aside. His stomach felt awful. He glanced up at the signs beside the two lavatories. Both, illuminated, read OCCUPIED. He pressed out his third cigarette since takeoff and, turning off the overhead light, stared out through the window.

Along the cabin's length, people were already flicking out their lights and reclining their chairs for sleep. Wilson glanced at his watch. Eleven-twenty. He blew out tired breath. As he'd anticipated, the pills he'd taken before boarding hadn't done a bit of good.

He stood abruptly as the woman came out of the lavatory and, snatching up his bag, he started down the aisle.

His system, as expected, gave no cooperation. Wilson stood with a tired moan and adjusted his clothing. Having washed his hands and face, he removed the toilet kit from the bag and squeezed a filament of paste across his toothbrush.

As he brushed, one hand braced for support against the cold bulkhead, he looked out through the port. Feet away was the pale blue of the inboard propeller. Wilson visualized what would happen if it were to tear loose and, like a tri-bladed cleaver, come slicing in at him.

There was a sudden depression in his stomach. Wilson swallowed instinctively and got some paste-stained saliva down his throat. Gagging, he turned and spat into the sink, then, hastily, washed out his mouth and took a drink. Dear God, if only he could have gone by train; had his own compartment, taken a casual stroll to the club car, settled down in an easy chair with a drink and a magazine. But there was no such time or fortune in this world.

He was about to put the toilet kit away when his gaze caught on the oilskin envelope in the bag. He hesitated, then, setting the small briefcase on the sink, drew out the envelope and undid it on his lap.

He sat staring at the oil-glossed symmetry of the pistol. He'd carried it around with him for almost a year now. Originally, when he'd thought about it, it was in terms of money carried, protection from holdup, safety from teenage gangs in the cities he had to attend. Yet, far beneath, he'd always known there was no valid reason except one. A reason he thought more of every day. How simple it would be—here, now—

Wilson shut his eyes and swallowed quickly. He could still taste the toothpaste in his mouth, a faint nettling of peppermint on the buds. He sat heavily in the throbbing chill of the lavatory, the oily gun resting in his hands. Until, quite suddenly, he began to shiver without control. God, let me go! His mind cried out abruptly.

"Let me go, *let me go*." He barely recognized the whimpering in his ears.

Abruptly, Wilson sat erect. Lips pressed together, he re-wrapped the pistol and thrust it into his bag, putting the brief-case on top of it, zipping the bag shut. Standing, he opened the door and stepped outside, hurrying to his seat and sitting down, sliding the overnight bag precisely into place. He in-dented the armrest button and pushed himself back. He was a business man and there was business to be conducted on the morrow. It was as simple as that. The body needed sleep, he would give it sleep.

Twenty minutes later, Wilson reached down slowly and de-pressed the button, sitting up with the chair, his face a mask of vanquished acceptance. Why fight it? he thought. It was obvi-ous he was going to stay awake. So that was that.

He had finished half of the crossword puzzle before he let the paper drop to his lap. His eyes were too tired. Sitting up, he rotated his shoulders, stretching the muscles of his back. Now what? he thought. He didn't want to read, he couldn't sleep. And there were still—he checked his watch—seven to eight hours left before Los Angeles was reached. How was he to spend them? He looked along the cabin and saw that, ex-cept for a single passenger in the forward compartment, every-one was asleep.

A sudden, overwhelming fury filled him and he wanted to scream, to throw something, to hit somebody. Teeth jammed together so rabidly it hurt his jaws, Wilson shoved aside the curtains with a spastic hand and stared out murderously through the window.

Outside, he saw the wing lights blinking off and on, the lurid flashes of exhaust from the engine cowlings. Here he was, he thought; twenty-thousand feet above the earth, trapped in a howling shell of death, moving through polar night toward—

Wilson twitched as lightning bleached the sky, washing its false daylight across the wing. He swallowed. Was there going to be a storm? The thought of rain and heavy winds, of the plane a chip in the sea of sky was not a pleasant one. Wilson was a bad flyer. Excess motion always made him ill. Maybe he should have taken another few Dramamines to be on the safe side. And, naturally, his seat was next to the emergency door. He thought about it opening accidentally; about himself sucked from the plane, falling, screaming.

Wilson blinked and shook his head. There was a faint tingling at the back of his neck as he pressed close to the window and stared out. He sat there motionless, squinting. He could have sworn—

Suddenly, his stomach muscles jerked in violently and he felt his eyes strain forward. There was something crawling on the wing.

Wilson felt a sudden, nauseous tremor in his stomach. Dear God, had some dog or cat crawled onto the plane before take-off and, in some way managed to hold on? It was a sickening thought. The poor animal would be deranged with terror. Yet, how, on the smooth, wind-blasted surface, could it possibly discover gripping places? Surely that was impossible. Perhaps, after all, it was only a bird or—

The lightning flared and Wilson saw that it was a man.

He couldn't move. Stupefied, he watched the black form crawling down the wing. *Impossible.* Somewhere, cased in layers of shock, a voice declared itself but Wilson did not hear. He was conscious of nothing but the titanic, almost muscle-tearing leap of his heart—and of the man outside.

Suddenly, like ice-filled water thrown across him, there was a reaction; his mind sprang for the shelter of explanation. A mechanic had, through some incredible oversight, been taken up with the ship and had managed to cling to it even though the wind had torn his clothes away, even though the air was thin and close to freezing.

Wilson gave himself no time for refutation. Jarring to his feet, he shouted: "Stewardess! Stewardess!" his voice a hollow, ringing sound in the cabin. He pushed the button for her with a jabbing finger.

"Stewardess!"

She came running down the aisle, her face tightened with alarm. When she saw the look on his face, she stiffened in her tracks.

"There's a man out there! A man!" cried Wilson.

"*What?*" Skin constricted on her cheeks, around her eyes.

"Look, *look*!" Hand shaking, Wilson dropped back into his seat and pointed out the window. "He's crawling on the—"

The words ended with a choking rattle in his throat. There was nothing on the wing.

Wilson sat there trembling. For a while, before he turned back, he looked at the reflection of the stewardess on the window. There was a blank expression on her face.

At last, he turned and looked up at her. He saw her red lips part as though she meant to speak but she said nothing, only placing the lips together again and swallowing. An attempted smile distended briefly at her features.

"I'm sorry," Wilson said. "It must have been a—"

He stopped as though the sentence were completed. Across the aisle a teenage girl was gaping at him with sleepy curiosity.

The stewardess cleared her throat. "Can I get you anything?" she asked.

"A glass of water," Wilson said.

The stewardess turned and moved back up the aisle.

Wilson sucked in a long breath of air and turned away from the young girl's scrutiny. He felt the same. That was the thing that shocked him most. Where were the visions, the cries, the pummeling of fists on temples, the tearing out of hair?

Abruptly he closed his eyes. There had been a man, he thought. There had, actually, been a man. That's why he felt the same. And yet, there couldn't have been. He knew that clearly.

Wilson sat with his eyes closed, wondering what Jacqueline would be doing now if she were in the seat beside him. Would she be silent, shocked beyond speaking? Or would she, in the more accepted manner, be fluttering around him, smiling, chattering, pretending that she hadn't seen? What would his sons think? Wilson felt a dry sob threatening in his chest. Oh, God—

Behind him, as he sat with the untouched cup of water in his hand, he heard the muted voices of the stewardess and one of the passengers. Wilson tightened with resentment. Abruptly, he reached down and, careful not to spill the water, pulled out the overnight bag. Unzipping it, he removed the box of sleeping capsules and washed two of them down. Crumpling the empty cup, he pushed it into the seat-pocket in front of him, then, not looking, slid the curtains shut. There—it was ended. One hallucination didn't make insanity.

Wilson turned onto his right side and tried to set himself against the fitful motion of the ship. He had to forget about this, that was the most important thing. He mustn't dwell on it. Unexpectedly, he found a wry smile forming on his lips. Well, by God, no one could accuse him of mundane hallucinations anyway. When he went at it, he did a royal job. A naked man crawling down a DC-7's wing at twenty-thousand feet— there was a chimera worthy of the noblest lunatic.

The humor faded quickly. Wilson felt chilled. It had been so clear, so vivid. How could the eyes see such a thing when it did not exist? How could what was in his mind make the physical act of seeing work to its purpose so completely? He hadn't been groggy, in a daze—nor had it been a shapeless, gauzy vision. It had been sharply three-dimensional, fully a part of the things he saw which he *knew* were real. That was the frightening part of it. It had not been dreamlike in the least. He had looked at the wing and—

Impulsively, Wilson drew aside the curtain.

He did not know, immediately, if he would survive. It seemed as if all the contents of his chest and stomach were bloating horribly, the excess pushing up into his throat and head, choking away breath, pressing out his eyes. Imprisoned in this swollen mass, his heart pulsed strickenly, threatening to burst its case as Wilson sat, paralyzed.

Only inches away, separated from him by the thickness of a piece of glass, the man was staring at him.

It was a hideously malignant face, a face not human. Its skin was grimy, of a wide-pored coarseness; its nose a squat, discolored lump; its lips misshapen, cracked, forced apart by teeth of a grotesque size and crookedness; its eyes recessed and small— unblinking. All framed by shaggy, tangled hair which sprouted, too in furry tufts from the man's ears and nose, in birdlike down across his cheeks.

Wilson sat riven to his chair, incapable of response. Time

stopped and lost its meaning. Function and analysis ceased. All were frozen in an ice of shock. Only the beat of heart went on—alone, a frantic leaping in the darkness. Wilson could not so much as blink. Dull-eyed, breathless, he returned the creature's vacant stare.

Abruptly then, he closed his eyes and his mind, rid of the sight, broke free. It isn't there, he thought. He pressed his teeth together, breath quavering in his nostrils. It isn't there, *it simply is not there.*

Clutching at the armrests with pale-knuckled fingers, Wilson braced himself. There is no man out there, he told himself. It was impossible that there should be a man out there crouching on the wing looking at him.

He opened his eyes—

—to shrink against the seat back with a gagging inhalation. Not only was the man still there but he was grinning. Wilson turned his fingers in and dug the nails into his palms until pain flared. He kept it there until there was no doubt in his mind that he was fully conscious.

Then, slowly, arm quivering and numb, Wilson reached up for the button which would summon the stewardess. He would not make the same mistake again—cry out, leap to his feet, alarm the creature into flight. He kept reaching upward, a tremor of aghast excitement in his muscles now because the man was watching him, the small eyes shifting with the movement of his arm.

He pressed the button carefully once, twice. Now come, he thought. Come with your objective eyes and see what I see— but hurry.

In the rear of the cabin, he heard a curtain being drawn aside and, suddenly, his body stiffened. The man had turned his caliban head to look in that direction. Paralyzed, Wilson stared at him. Hurry, he thought. For God's sake, *hurry!*

It was over in a second. The man's eyes shifted back to Wilson, across his lips a smile of monstrous cunning. Then with a leap, he was gone.

"Yes, sir?"

For a moment, Wilson suffered the fullest anguish of madness. His gaze kept jumping from the spot where the man had

NIGHTMARE AT 20,000 FEET

stood to the stewardess's questioning face, then back again. Back to the stewardess, to the wing, to the stewardess, his breath caught, his eyes stark with dismay.

"What *is* it?" asked the stewardess.

It was the look on her face that did it. Wilson closed a vise on his emotions. She couldn't possibly believe him. He realized it in an instant.

"I'm—I'm sorry," he faltered. He swallowed so dryly that it made a clicking noise in his throat. "It's nothing. I—apologize."

The stewardess obviously didn't know what to say. She kept leaning against the erratic yawing of the ship, one hand holding on to the back of the seat beside Wilson's, the other stirring limply along the seam of her skirt. Her lips were parted slightly as if she meant to speak but could not find the words.

"Well," she said finally and cleared her throat, "if you—need anything."

"Yes, yes. Thank you. Are we—going into a storm?"

The stewardess smiled hastily. "Just a small one," she said. "Nothing to worry about."

Wilson nodded with little twitching movements. Then, as the stewardess turned away, breathed in suddenly, his nostrils flaring. He felt certain that she already thought him mad but didn't know what to do about it because, in her course of training, there had been no instruction on the handling of passengers who thought they saw small men crouching on the wing.

Thought?

Wilson turned his head abruptly and looked outside. He stared at the dark rise of the wing, the spouting flare of the exhausts, the blinking lights. He'd *seen* the man—to that he'd swear. How could he be completely aware of everything around him—be, in all ways, sane and still imagine such a thing? Was it logical that the mind, in giving way, should, instead of distorting all reality, insert, within the still intact arrangement of details, one extraneous sight?

No, not logical at all.

Suddenly, Wilson thought about war, about the newspaper stories which recounted the alleged existence of creatures in

the sky who plagued the Allied pilots in their duties. They
called them gremlins, he remembered. Were there, actually,
such beings? Did they, truly, exist up here, never falling, riding
on the wind, apparently of bulk and weight, yet impervious to
gravity?

He was thinking that when the man appeared again.

One second the wing was empty. The next, with an arcing
descent, the man came jumping down to it. There seemed no
impact. He landed almost fragilely, short, hairy arms outstretched as if for balance. Wilson tensed. Yes, there was
knowledge in his look. The man—was he to think of it as a
man?—somehow understood that he had tricked Wilson into
calling the stewardess in vain. Wilson felt himself tremble with
alarm. How could he prove the man's existence to others? He
looked around desperately. That girl across the aisle. If he
spoke to her softly, woke her up, would she be able to—

No, the man would jump away before she could see. Probably to the top of the fuselage where no one could see him, not
even the pilots in their cockpit. Wilson felt a sudden burst of
self-condemnation that he hadn't gotten that camera Walter
had asked for. Dear Lord, he thought, to be able to take a picture of the man.

He leaned in close to the window. What was the man doing?

Abruptly, darkness seemed to leap away as the wing was
chalked with lightning and Wilson saw. Like an inquisitive
child, the man was squatted on the hitching wing edge, stretching out his right hand toward one of the whirling propellers.

As Wilson watched, fascinatedly appalled, the man's hand
drew closer and closer to the blurring gyre until, suddenly, it
jerked away and the man's lips twitched back in a soundless
cry. He's lost a finger! Wilson thought, sickened. But, immediately, the man reached forward again, gnarled finger extended,
the picture of some monstrous infant trying to capture the
spin of a fan blade.

If it had not been so hideously out of place it would have
been amusing for, objectively seen, the man, at that moment,
was a comic sight—a fairy tale troll somehow come to life,

wind whipping at the hair across his head and body, all of his attention centered on the turn of the propeller. How could this be madness? Wilson suddenly thought. What self-revelation could this farcical little horror possibly bestow on him?

Again and again, as Wilson watched, the man reached forward. Again and again jerked back his fingers, sometimes, actually, putting them in his mouth as if to cool them. And, always, apparently checking, he kept glancing back across at his shoulder looking at Wilson. *He knows*, thought Wilson. Knows that this is a game between us. If I am able to get someone else to see him, then he loses. If I am the only witness, then he wins. The sense of faint amusement was gone now. Wilson clenched his teeth. Why in hell didn't the pilots see!

Now the man, no longer interested in the propeller, was settling himself across the engine cowling like a man astride a bucking horse. Wilson stared at him. Abruptly a shudder plaited down his back. The little man was picking at the plates that sheathed the engine, trying to get his nails beneath them.

Impulsively, Wilson reached up and pushed the button for the stewardess. In the rear of the cabin, he heard her coming and, for a second, thought he'd fooled the man, who seemed absorbed with his efforts. At the last moment, however, just before the stewardess arrived, the man glanced over at Wilson. Then, like a marionette jerked upward from its stage by wires, he was flying up into the air.

"Yes?" She looked at him apprehensively.

"Will you—sit down, please?" he asked.

She hesitated. "Well, I—"

"Please."

She sat down gingerly on the seat beside his.

"What is it, Mr. Wilson?" she asked.

He braced himself.

"That man is still outside," he said.

The stewardess stared at him.

"The reason I'm telling you this," Wilson hurried on, "is that he's starting to tamper with one of the engines."

She turned her eyes instinctively toward the window.

"No, no, don't look," he told her. "He isn't there now." He cleared his throat viscidly. "He—jumps away whenever you come here."

A sudden nausea gripped him as he realized what she must be thinking. As he realized what he, himself, would think if someone told him such a story. A wave of dizziness seemed to pass across him and he thought—I *am* going mad!

"The point is this," he said, fighting off the thought. "If I'm not imagining this thing, the ship is in danger."

"Yes," she said.

"I know," he said. "You think I've lost my mind."

"Of course not," she said.

"All I ask is this," he said, struggling against the rise of anger. "Tell the pilots what I've said. Ask them to keep an eye on the wings. If they see nothing—all right. But if they do—"

The stewardess sat there quietly, looking at him. Wilson's hands curled into fists that trembled in his lap.

"*Well?*" he asked.

She pushed to her feet. "I'll tell them," she said.

Turning away, she moved along the aisle with a movement that was, to Wilson, poorly contrived—too fast to be normal yet, clearly, held back as if to reassure him that she wasn't fleeing. He felt his stomach churning as he looked out at the wing again.

Abruptly, the man appeared again, landing on the wing like some grotesque ballet dancer. Wilson watched him as he set to work again, straddling the engine casing with his thick, bare legs and picking at the plates.

Well, what was he so concerned about? thought Wilson. That miserable creature couldn't pry up rivets with his fingernails. Actually, it didn't matter if the pilots saw him or not—at least so far as the safety of the plane was concerned. As for his own personal reasons—

It was at that moment that the man pried up one edge of a plate.

Wilson gasped. "Here, quickly!" he shouted, noticing, up ahead, the stewardess and the pilot coming through the cockpit doorway.

The pilot's eyes jerked up to look at Wilson, then abruptly, he was pushing past the stewardess and lurching up the aisle.

"*Hurry!*" Wilson cried. He glanced out the window in time to see the man go leaping upward. That didn't matter now. There would be evidence.

"What's going on?" the pilot asked, stopping breathlessly beside his seat.

"He's torn up one of the engine plates!" said Wilson in a shaking voice.

"He's what?"

"The man outside!" said Wilson. "I tell you he's—!"

"Mister Wilson, keep your voice down!" ordered the pilot.

Wilson's jaw went slack.

"I don't know what's going on here," said the pilot, "But—"

Drawing in an agitated breath, the pilot bent over. In a moment, his gaze shifted coldly to Wilson's. "Well?" he asked.

Wilson jerked his head around. The plates were in their normal position.

"Oh, now wait," he said before the dread could come. "I saw him pry that plate up."

"Mister Wilson, if you don't—"

"*I said I saw him pry it up,*" said Wilson.

The pilot stood there looking at him in the same withdrawn, almost aghast way as the stewardess had. Wilson shuddered violently.

"Listen, I *saw* him!" he cried. The sudden break in his voice appalled him.

In a second, the pilot was down beside him. "Mister Wilson, please," he said. "All right, you saw him. But remember there are other people aboard. We mustn't alarm them."

Wilson was too shaken to understand at first.

"You—mean you've *seen* him then?" he asked.

"Of course," the pilot said, "but we don't want to frighten the passengers. You can understand that."

"Of course, of course. I don't want to—"

Wilson felt a spastic coiling in his groin and lower stomach. Suddenly, he pressed his lips together and looked at the pilot with malevolent eyes.

"I understand," he said.

"The thing we have to remember—" began the pilot.

"You can stop now," Wilson said.

"Sir?"

Wilson shuddered. "Get out of here," he said.

"Mister Wilson, what—?"

"Will you stop?" Face whitening, Wilson turned from the pilot and stared out at the wing, eyes like stone.

He glared back suddenly.

"Rest assured I'll not say another word!" he snapped.

"Mr. Wilson, try to understand our—"

Wilson twisted away and stared out venomously at the engine. From a corner of his vision, he saw two passengers standing in the aisle looking at him. *Idiots!* his mind exploded. He felt his hands begin to tremble and, for a few seconds, was afraid that he was going to vomit. It's the motion, he told himself. The plane was bucking in the air now like a storm-tossed boat.

He realized that the pilot was still talking to him and, refocusing his eyes, he looked at the man's reflection in the window. Beside him, mutely somber, stood the stewardess. Blind idiots, both of them, thought Wilson. He did not indicate his notice of their departure. Reflected on the window, he saw them heading toward the rear of the cabin. They'll be discussing me now, he thought. Setting up plans in case I grow violent.

He wished now that the man would reappear, pull off the cowling plate and ruin the engine. It gave him a sense of vengeful pleasure to know that only he stood between catastrophe and the more than thirty people aboard. If he chose, he could allow that catastrophe to take place. Wilson smiled without humor. There would be a royal suicide, he thought.

The little man dropped down again and Wilson saw that what he'd thought was correct—the man had pressed the plate back into place before jumping away. For, now, he was prying it up again and it was raising easily, peeling back like skin excised by some grotesque surgeon. The motion of the wing was very broken but the man seemed to have no difficulty staying balanced.

Once more Wilson felt panic. What was he to do? No one believed him. If he tried to convince them any more they'd probably restrain him by force. If he asked the stewardess to sit by him it would be, at best, only a momentary reprieve. The second she departed or, remaining, fell asleep, the man would return. Even if she stayed awake beside him, what was to keep the man from tampering with the engines on the other wing? Wilson shuddered, a coldness of dread misting along his bones.

Dear God, there was nothing to be done.

He twitched as, across the window through which he watched the little man, the pilot's reflection passed. The insanity of the moment almost broke him—the man and the pilot within feet of each other, both seen by him yet not aware of one another. No, that was wrong. The little man had glanced across his shoulder as the pilot passed. As if he knew there was no need to leap off any more, that Wilson's capacity for interfering was at an end. Wilson suddenly trembled with mind-searing rage. I'll kill you! he thought. You filthy little animal, I'll *kill* you!

Outside, the engine faltered.

It lasted only for a second, but, in that second, it seemed to Wilson as if his heart had, also, stopped. He pressed against the window, staring. The man had bent the cowling plate far back and now was on his knees, poking a curious hand into the engine.

"Don't." Wilson heard the whimper of his own voice begging. "*Don't . . .*"

Again, the engine failed. Wilson looked around in horror. Was everyone deaf? He raised his hand to press the button for the stewardess, then jerked it back. No, they'd lock him up, restrain him somehow. And he was the only one who knew what was happening, the only one who could help.

"*God . . .*" Wilson bit his lower lip until the pain made him whimper. He twisted around again and jolted. The stewardess was hurrying down the rocking aisle. She'd heard it! He watched her fixedly and saw her glance at him as she passed his seat.

She stopped three seats down the aisle. Someone else had heard! Wilson watched the stewardess as she leaned over, talking to the unseen passenger. Outside, the engine coughed again.

Wilson jerked his head around and looked out with horror-pinched eyes.

"*Damn you!*" he whined.

He turned again and saw the stewardess coming back up the aisle. She didn't look alarmed. Wilson stared at her with unbelieving eyes. It wasn't possible. He twisted around to follow her swaying movement and saw her turn in at the kitchen.

"*No.*" Wilson was shaking so badly now he couldn't stop. No one had heard.

No one knew.

Suddenly, Wilson bent over and slid his overnight bag out from under the seat. Unzipping it, he jerked out his briefcase and threw it on the carpeting. Then, reaching in again, he grabbed the oilskin envelope and straightened up. From the corners of his eyes, he saw the stewardess coming back and pushed the bag beneath the seat with his shoes, shoving the oilskin envelope beside himself. He sat there rigidly, breath quavering in his chest, as she went by.

Then he pulled the envelope into his lap and untied it. His movements were so feverish that he almost dropped the pistol. He caught it by the barrel, then clutched at the stock with white-knuckled fingers and pushed off the safety catch. He glanced outside and felt himself grow cold.

The man was looking at him.

Wilson pressed his shaking lips together. It was impossible that the man knew what he intended. He swallowed and tried to catch his breath. He shifted his gaze to where the stewardess was handing some pills to the passenger ahead, then looked back at the wing. The man was turning to the engine once again, reaching in. Wilson's grip tightened on the pistol. He began to raise it.

Suddenly, he lowered it. The window was too thick. The bullet might be deflected and kill one of the passengers. He shuddered and stared out at the little man. Again the engine failed and Wilson saw an eruption of sparks cast light across the man's animal features. He braced himself. There was only one answer.

He looked down at the handle of the emergency door. There

was a transparent cover over it. Wilson pulled it free and dropped it. He looked outside. The man was still there, crouched and probing at the engine with his hand. Wilson sucked in trembling breath. He put his left hand on the door handle and tested. It wouldn't move downward. Upward there was play.

Abruptly, Wilson let go and put the pistol in his lap. No time for argument, he told himself. With shaking hands, he buckled the belt across his thighs. When the door was opened, there would be a tremendous rushing out of air. For the safety of the ship, he must not go with it.

Now. Wilson picked the pistol up again, his heartbeat staggering. He'd have to be sudden, accurate. If he missed, the man might jump onto the other wing—worse, onto the tail assembly where, inviolate, he could rupture wires, mangle flaps, destroy the balance of the ship. No, this was the only way. He'd fire low and try to hit the man in the chest or stomach. Wilson filled his lungs with air. Now, he thought. *Now.*

The stewardess came up the aisle as Wilson started pulling at the handle. For a moment, frozen in her steps, she couldn't speak. A look of stupefied horror distended her features and she raised one hand as if imploring him. Then, suddenly, her voice was shrilling above the noise of the engines.

"Mr. Wilson, no!"

"Get back!" cried Wilson and he wrenched the handle up.

The door seemed to disappear. One second it was by him, in his grip. The next, with a hissing roar, it was gone.

In the same instant, Wilson felt himself enveloped by a monstrous suction which tried to tear him from his seat. His head and shoulders left the cabin and, suddenly, he was breathing tenuous, freezing air. For a moment, eardrums almost bursting from the thunder of the engines, eyes blinded by the arctic winds, he forgot the man. It seemed he heard a prick of screaming in the maelstrom that surrounded him, a distant shout.

Then Wilson saw the man.

He was walking across the wing, gnarled from leaning forward, talon-twisted hands outstretched in eagerness. Wilson flung his arm up, fired. The explosion was like a popping in the roaring violence of the air. The man staggered, lashed out and Wilson felt a streak of pain across his head. He fired again at immediate range and saw the man go flailing backward— then, suddenly, disappear with no more solidity than a paper doll swept in a gale. Wilson felt a bursting numbness in his brain. He felt the pistol torn from failing fingers.

Then all was lost in winter darkness.

He stirred and mumbled. There was a warmness trickling in his veins, his limbs felt wooden. In the darkness, he could hear a shuffling sound, a delicate swirl of voices. He was lying, face up, on something—moving, joggling. A cold wind sprinkled on his face, he felt the surface tilt beneath him.

He sighed. The plane was landed and he was being carried off on a stretcher. His head wound, likely, plus an injection to quiet him.

"Nuttiest way of tryin' to commit suicide *I* ever heard of," said a voice somewhere.

Wilson felt the pleasure of amusement. Whoever spoke was wrong, of course. As would be established soon enough when the engine was examined and they checked his wound more closely. Then they'd realize that he'd saved them all.

Wilson slept without dreams.

THE FUNERAL

Morton Silkline was in his office musing over floral arrangements for the Fenton obsequies when the chiming strains of "I Am Crossing o'er the Bar to Join the Choir Invisible" announced an entrant into Clooney's Cut-Rate Catafalque.

Blinking mediation from his liver-colored eyes, Silkline knit his fingers to a placid clasp, then settled back against the sable leather of his chair, a smile of funereal welcome on his lips. Out in the stillness of the hallways, footsteps sounded on the muffling carpet, moving with a leisured pace and, just before the tall man entered, the desk clock buzzed a curt acknowledgement to 7:30.

Rising as if caught in the midst of a tête-à-tête with death's bright angel, Morton Silkline circled the glossy desk on whispering feet and extended one flaccid-fingered hand.

"Ah, good evening, sir," he dulceted, his smile a precise compendium of sympathy and welcome, his voice a calculated drip of obeisance.

The man's handshake was cool and bone-cracking but Silkline managed to repress reaction to a momentary flicker of agony in his cinnamon eyes.

"Won't you be seated?" he murmured, fluttering his bruised hand toward The Grieved One's chair.

"Thank you," said the man, his voice a baritoned politeness as he seated himself, unbuttoning the front of his velvet-collared overcoat and placing his dark homburg on the glass top of the desk.

"My name is Morton Silkline," Silkline offered as he recircled to his chair, settling on the cushion like a diffident butterfly.

"Asper," said the man.

"May I say that I am proud to meet you, Mister Asper?" Silkline purred.

"Thank you," said the man.

"Well, now," Silkline said, getting down to the business of bereavement, "what can Clooney's do to ease your sorrow?"

The man crossed his dark-trousered legs. "I should like," he said, "to make arrangements for a funeral service."

Silkline nodded once with an I-am-here-to-succor smile.

"Of course," he said, "you've come to the right place, sir." His gaze elevated a few inches beyond the pale. "*When loved ones lie upon that lonely couch of everlasting sleep,*" he recited, "*let Clooney draw the coverlet.*"

His gaze returned and he smiled with a modest subservience. "Mrs. Clooney," he said, "made that up. We like to pass it along to those who come to us for comfort."

"Very nice," the man said. "Extremely poetic. But to details: I'd like to engage your largest parlor."

"I see," Silkline answered, restraining himself, only with effort, from the rubbing together of hands. "That would be our Eternal Rest Room."

The man nodded affably. "Fine. And I would also like to buy your most expensive casket."

Silkline could barely restrain a boyish grin. His cardiac muscle flexing vigorously, he forced back folds of sorrowful solicitude across his face.

"I'm sure," he said, "that can be effected."

"With gold trimmings?" the man said.

"Why . . . yes," said Director Silkline, clicking audibly as he swallowed. "I'm certain that Clooney's can satisfy your every need in this time of grievous loss. Naturally——" His voice slipped a jot from the condoling to the fiduciary "——it will entail a bit more expenditure than might, otherwise, be——"

"The cost is of no importance," said the man, waving it away. "I want only the best of everything."

"It will be so, sir, it *will* be so," declared a fervent Morton Silkline.

"Capital," said the man.

"Now," Silkline went on, briskly, "will you be wishing our Mr. Mossmound to deliver his sermon *On Crossing the Great Divide* or have you a denominational ceremony in mind?"

"I think not," said the man, shaking his head, thoughtfully. "A friend of mine will speak at the services."

"Ah," said Silkline, nodding, "I see."

Reaching forward, he plucked the gold pen from its onyx holder, then with two fingers of his left hand, drew out an application form from the ivory box on his desk top. He looked up with the accredited expression for the Asking of Painful Questions.

"And," he said, "what is the name of the deceased, may I ask?"

"Asper," said the man.

Silkline glanced up, smiling politely. "A relative?" he inquired.

"Me," said the man.

Silkline's laugh was a faint coughing.

"I beg your pardon?" he said. "I thought you said—"

"*Me*," the man repeated.

"But, I don't—"

"You see," the man explained, "I never had a proper going off. It was catch-as-catch-can, you might say; all improvised. Nothing—how shall I put it?—*tasty*." The man shrugged his wide shoulders. "I always regretted that," he said. "I always intended to make up for it."

Morton Silkline had returned the pen to its holder with a decisive jabbing of the hand and was on his feet, pulsing with a harsh distemper.

"Indeed, sir," he commented. *"Indeed."*

The man looked surprised at the vexation of Morton Silkline.

"I—" he began.

"I am as fully prepared as the next fellow for a trifling badinage," Silkline interrupted, "but *not* during work hours. I think you fail to realize, sir, just where you are. This is Clooney's, a much respected ossuary; not a place for trivial joking or—"

He shrank back and stared, open-mouthed, at the black-garbed man who was suddenly on his feet, eyes glittering with a light most unseemly.

"This," the man said, balefully, "is not a joke."

"Is not—" Silkline could manage no more.

"I came here," said the man, "with a most serious purpose in mind." His eyes glowed now like cherry-bright coals. "And I expect this purpose to be gratified," he said. "Do you understand?"

"I—"

"On Tuesday next," the man continued, "at 8:30 p.m., my friends and I will arrive here for the service. You will have everything prepared by then. Full payment will be made directly following the exequies. Are there any questions?"

"I—"

"I need hardly remind you," said the man, picking up his homburg, "that this affair is of the utmost importance to me." He paused potently before allowing his voice to sink to a forbidding basso profundo. "I expect all to go well."

Bowing a modicum from the waist, the man turned and moved in two regal strides across the office, pausing a moment at the door.

"Uh . . . one additional item," he said. "That mirror in the foyer . . . *remove* it. And, I might add, any others that my friends and I might chance upon during our stay in your parlors."

The man raised one gray-gloved hand. "And now good night."

When Morton Silkline reached the hall, his customer was just flapping out a small window. Quite suddenly, Morton Silkline found the floor.

They arrived at 8:30, conversing as they entered the foyer of Clooney's to be met by a tremble-legged Morton Silkline about whose eyes hung the raccoon circles of sleepless nights.

"Good evening," greeted the tall man, noting, with a pleased nod, the absence of the wall mirror.

"Good—" was the total of Silkline's wordage.

His vocal cords went slack and his eyes, embossed with daze, moved from figure to figure in the tall man's coterie—the gnarl-faced hunchback whom Silkline heard addressed as Ygor; the peak-hatted crone upon whose ceremented shoulder a black cat crouched; the hulking hairy-handed man who clicked yellow teeth together and regarded Silkline with markedly more than casual eyes; the waxen-featured little man who licked his lips and smiled at Silkline as though he possessed some inner satisfaction; the half-dozen men and women in evening dress, all cherry-eyed and -lipped and—Silkline cringed—superbly toothed.

Silkline hung against the wall, mouth a circular entranceway, hands twitching feebly at his sides as the chatting assemblage passed him by, headed for the Eternal Rest Room.

"Join us," the tall man said.

Silkline stirred fitfully from the wall and stumble-wove an erratic path down the hallway, eyes still saucer-round with stupor.

"I trust," the man said pleasantly, "everything is well prepared."

"Oh," Silkline squeaked. "Oh—oh, yes."

"Sterling," said the man.

When the two of them entered the room, the others were grouped in an admiring semicircle about the casket.

"Is good," the hunchback was muttering to himself. "Is good box."

"Aye, be that a casket or be that a casket, Delphinia?" cackled the ancient crone and Delphinia replied, "Mrrrrow."

While the others nodded, smiling felicitous smiles and murmuring, "Ah. Ah."

Then one of the evening-dressed women said, "Let Ludwig see," and the semicircle split open so the tall man could pass.

He ran his long fingers over the gold work on the sides and top of the casket, nodding appreciatively. "Splendid," he murmured, voice husky with emotion. "Quite splendid. Just what I always wanted."

"You picked a beauty, lad," said a tall white-haired gentleman.

"Well, try it on fer size!" the chuckling crone declared.

Smiling boyishly, Ludwig climbed into the casket and wriggled into place. "A perfect fit," he said, contentedly.

"Master look good," mumbled Ygor, nodding crookedly. "Look good in box."

Then the hairy-handed man demanded they begin because

he had an appointment at 9:15, and everyone hurried to their chairs.

"Come, duck," said the crone, waving a scrawny hand at the ossified Silkline. "Sit by my side. I likes the pretty boys, I do, eh, Delphinia?" Delphinia said, "Mrrrrrow."

"Please, Jenny," Ludwig Asper asked her, opening his eyes a moment. "Be serious. You know what this means to me."

The crone shrugged. "Aye. Aye," she muttered, then pulled off her peaked hat and fluffed at dank curls as the zombie-stiff Silkline quivered into place beside her, aided by the guiding hand of the little waxen-faced man.

"Hello, pretty boy," the crone whispered, leaning over and jabbing a spear-point elbow into Silkline's ribs.

Then the tall white-haired gentleman from the Carpathian zone rose and the service began.

"Good friends," said the gentleman, "we have gathered ourselves within these bud-wreathed walls to pay homage to our comrade, Ludwig Asper, whom the pious and unyielding fates have chosen to pluck from existence and place within that bleak sarcophagus of all eternity."

"*Ci-git*," someone murmured. "*Chant du cygne*," another. Ygor wept and the waxen-featured little man, sitting on the other side of Morton Silkline, leaned over to murmur, "*Tasty*," but Silkline wasn't sure it was in reference to the funeral address.

"And thus," the gentleman from Carpathia went on, "we collect our bitter selves about this, our comrade's bier; about this litter of sorrow, this cairn, this cromlech, this unhappy tumulus—"

"*Clearer, clearer*," demanded Jenny, stamping one pointy-toed and petulant shoe. "Mrrrrrow," said Delphinia and the crone winked one blood-laced eye at Silkline who shrank away only to brush against the little man who gazed at him with berry eyes and murmured once again, "*Tasty*."

The white-haired gentleman paused long enough to gaze down his royal nose at the crone. Then he continued, "—this mastaba, this sorrowing tope, this ghat, this dread dokhma—"

"What did he say?" asked Ygor, pausing in mid-sob. "What, what?"

"This ain't no declamation tourney, lad," the crone declared. "Keep it crisp, I say."

Ludwig raised his head again, a look of pained embarrassment on his face. "Jenny," he said. "*Please.*"

"Aaaaah . . . *toad's teeth!*" snapped the crone jadedly, and Delphinia moaned.

"*Requiescas in pace*, dear brother," the Count went on, testily. "The memory of you shall not perish with your untimely sepulture. You are, dear friend, not so much out of the game as playing on another field."

At which the hairy-handed man rose and hulked from the room with the guttural announcement, "*Go*," and Silkline felt himself rendered an icicle as he heard a sudden padding of clawed feet on the hallway rug and a baying which echoed back along the walls.

"Ullgate says he has a dinner appointment," the little man asided with a bright-eyed smile. Silkline's chair creaked with shuddering.

The white-haired gentleman stood tall and silent, his red eyes shut, his mouth tight-lipped with aristocratic pique.

"*Count*," pleaded Ludwig. "Please."

"Am I to endure these vulgar calumnies?" asked the Count. "These—"

"Well, *la-de-da*," crooned Jenny to her cat.

"Silence, woman!" roared the Count, his head disappearing momentarily in a white, trailing vapor, then reappearing as he gained control.

Ludwig sat up, face a twist of aggravation. "Jenny," he declared, "I think you'd better leave."

"You think to throw old Jenny of Boston out?" the crone challenged. "Well, you got a think that's coming then!"

And, as a shriveling Silkline watched, the crone slapped on her pointed hat and sprouted minor lightning at the fingertips. A snail-backed Delphinia bristled ebony hairs as the Count stepped forward, hand outstretched, to clamp onto the crone's shoulder, then stiffened in mid-stride as sizzling fire ringed him.

"Haa!" crowed Jenny while a horror-stricken Silkline gagged, "My rug!"

"Jen-*ny!*" Ludwig cried, clambering out. The crone gestured and all the flowers in the room began exploding like popcorn.

"*No-o,*" moaned Silkline as the curtains flared and split. Chairs were overthrown. The Count bicarbonated to a hissing stream of white which flew at Jenny—who flung up her arms and vanished, cat and all, in an orange spume as the air grew thick with squeaks and rib-winged flapping.

Just before the bulbous-eyed Morton Silkline toppled forward, the waxen-faced man leaned over, smiling toothfully, squeezed the Director's numbed arm and murmured, "*Tasty.*"

Then Silkline was at one with the rug.

Morton Silkline slumped in his sable-leathered chair, still twitching slightly even though a week had passed since the nerve-splitting event. On his desk lay the note that Ludwig Asper had left pinned to his unconscious chest.

Sir, it read. *Accept, in addition to this bag of gold (which I trust will cover all costs) my regrets that full decorum was not effected by the guests at my funeral. For, save for that, the entire preparation was most satisfactory to me.*

Silkline put down the note and grazed a loving touch across the hill of glinting coins on his desk. Through judicious inquiry, he had gleaned the information that a connection in Mexico (namely, a cosmetician nephew in Carillo's Cut-Rate Catacomb) could safely dispose of the gold at mutual profit. All things considered, the affair had not been really as bad as all—

Morton Silkline looked up as something entered his office.

He would have chosen to leap back screaming and vanish in the flowered pattern of the wallpaper but he was too petrified. Once more gape-mouthed, he stared at the huge, tentacled, ocher-dripping shapelessness that weaved and swayed before him.

"A friend," it said politely, "recommended you to me."

Silkline sat bug-eyed for a lengthy moment but then his twitching hand accidently touched the gold again. And he found strength.

"You've come," he said, breathing through his mouth, "to

the right place—uh . . . *sir. Pomps*—" He swallowed mightily
and braced himself "—*for all circumstances*."

He reached for his pen, blowing away the yellow-green
smoke which was beginning to obscure his office.

"Name of the deceased?" he asked, businesslike.

THIRD FROM THE SUN

His eyes were open five seconds before the alarm was set to go off. There was no effort in waking. It was sudden. Coldly conscious, he reached out his left hand in the dark and pushed in the stop. The alarm glowed a second, then faded.

At his side, his wife put her hand on his arm.

"Did you sleep?" he asked.

"No, did you?"

"A little," he said. "Not much."

She was silent for a few seconds. He heard her throat contract. She shivered. He knew what she was going to say.

"We're still going?" she asked.

He twisted his shoulders on the bed and took a deep breath.

"Yes," he said, and he felt her fingers tighten on his arm.

"What time is it?" she asked.

"About five."

"We'd better get ready."

"Yes, we'd better."

They made no move.

"You're sure we can get on the ship without anyone noticing?" she asked.

"They think it's just another test flight. Nobody will be checking."

She didn't say anything. She moved a little closer to him. He felt how cold her skin was.

"I'm afraid," she said.

He took her hand and held it in a tight grip. "Don't be," he said. "We'll be safe."

"It's the children I'm worried about."

"We'll be safe," he repeated.

She lifted his hand to her lips and kissed it gently.

"All right," she said.

They both sat up in the darkness. He heard her stand. Her night garment rustled to the floor. She didn't pick it up. She stood still, shivering in the cold morning air.

"You're sure we don't need anything else with us?" she asked.

"No, nothing. I have all the supplies we need in the ship. Anyways . . ."

"What?"

"We can't carry anything past the guard," he said. "He has to think you and the kids are just coming to see me off."

She began dressing. He threw off the covering and got up. He went across the cold floor to the closet and dressed.

"I'll get the children up," she said.

He grunted, pulling clothes over his head. At the door she stopped. "Are you sure . . ." she began.

"What?"

"Won't the guard think it's funny that . . . that our neighbors are coming down to see you off, too?"

He sank down on the bed and fumbled for the clasps on his shoes.

"We'll have to take that chance," he said. "We need them with us."

She sighed. "It seems so cold. So calculating."

He straightened up and saw her silhouette in the doorway.

"What else can we do?" he asked intensely. "We can't interbreed our own children."

"No," she said. "It's just . . ."

"Just what?"

"Nothing, darling. I'm sorry."

She closed the door. Her footsteps disappeared down the hall. The door to the children's room opened. He heard their two voices. A cheerless smile raised his lips. You'd think it was a holiday, he thought.

He pulled on his shoes. At least the kids didn't know what was happening. They thought they were going to take him down to the field. They thought they'd come back and tell all their schoolmates about it. They didn't know they'd never come back.

He finished clasping his shoes and stood up. He shuffled over to the bureau and turned on the light. It was odd, such an undistinguished looking man planning this.

Cold. Calculating. Her words filled his mind again. Well, there was no other way. In a few years, probably less, the whole planet would go up with a blinding flash. This was the only way out. Escaping, starting all over again with a few people on a new planet.

He stared at the reflection.

"There's no other way," he said.

He glanced around the bedroom. Goodbye, this part of my life. Turning off the lamp was like turning off a light in his mind. He closed the door gently behind him and slid his fingers off the worn handle.

His son and daughter were going down the ramp. They were talking in mysterious whispers. He shook his head in slight amusement.

His wife waited for him. They went down together, holding hands.

"I'm not afraid, darling," she said. "It'll be all right."

"Sure," he said. "Sure it will."

They all went in to eat. He sat down with his children. His wife poured out juice for them. Then she went to get the food.

"Help your mother, doll," he told his daughter. She got up.

"Pretty soon, haah, pop?" his son said. "Pretty soon, haah?"

"Take it easy," he cautioned. "Remember what I told you. If you say a word of it to anybody I'll have to leave you behind."

A dish shattered on the floor. He darted a glance at his wife. She was staring at him, her lips trembling.

She averted her eyes and bent down. She fumbled at the pieces, picked up a few. Then she dropped them all, stood up and pushed them against the wall with her shoe.

"As if it mattered," she said nervously. "As if it mattered whether the place is clean or not."

The children were watching her in surprise.

"What is it?" asked the daughter.

"Nothing, darling, nothing," she said. "I'm just nervous. Go back to the table. Drink your juice. We have to eat quickly. The neighbors will be here soon."

"Pop, why are the neighbors coming with us?" asked his son.

"Because," he said vaguely, "they want to. Now forget it. Don't talk about it so much."

The room was quiet. His wife brought their food and set it down. Only her footsteps broke the silence. The children kept glancing at each other, at their father. He kept his eyes on the plate. The food tasted flat and thick in his mouth and he felt his heart thudding against the wall of his chest. Last day. This is the last day.

"You'd better eat," he told his wife.

She sat down to eat. As she lifted the eating utensil the door buzzer sounded. The utensil skidded out of her nerveless fingers and clattered on the floor. He reached out quickly and put his hand on hers.

"All right, darling," he said. "It's all right." He turned to the children. "Go answer the door," he told them.

"Both of us?" his daughter asked.

"Both of you."

"But . . ."

"Do as I say."

They slid off their chairs and left the room, glancing back at their parents.

When the sliding door shut off their view, he turned back to his wife. Her face was pale and tight; she had her lips pressed together.

"Darling, please," he said. "Please. You know I wouldn't take you if I wasn't sure it was safe. You know how many times I've flown the ship before. And I know just where we're going. It's safe. Believe me it's safe."

She pressed his hand against her cheek. She closed her eyes and large tears ran out under her lids and down her cheeks.

"It's not that so m-much," she said. "It's just . . . leaving, never coming back. We've been here all our lives. It isn't like . . . like moving. We can't come back. Ever."

"Listen, darling," his voice was tense and hurried. "You

know as well as I do. In a matter of years, maybe less, there's going to be another war, a terrible one. There won't be a thing left. We have to leave. For our children, for ourselves . . ."

He paused, testing the words in his mind.

"For the future of life itself," he finished weakly. He was sorry he said it. Early in the morning, over prosaic food, that kind of talk didn't sound right. Even if it was true.

"Just don't be afraid," he said. "We'll be all right."

She squeezed his hand.

"I know," she said quietly. "I know."

There were footsteps coming toward them. He pulled out a tissue and gave it to her. She hastily dabbed at her face.

The door slid open. The neighbors and their son and daughter came in. The children were excited. They had trouble keeping it down.

"Good morning," the neighbor said.

The neighbor's wife went to his wife and the two of them went over to the window and talked in low voices. The children stood around, fidgeted and looked nervously at each other.

"You've eaten?" he asked his neighbor.

"Yes," his neighbor said. "Don't you think we'd better be going?"

"I suppose so," he said.

They left all the dishes on the table. His wife went upstairs and got garments for the family.

He and his wife stayed on the porch a moment while the rest went out to the ground car.

"Should we lock the door?" he asked.

She smiled helplessly and ran a hand through her hair. She shrugged. "Does it matter?" she said and turned away.

He locked the door and followed her down the walk. She turned as he came up to her.

"It's a nice house," she murmured.

"Don't think about it," he said.

They turned their backs on their home and got in the ground car.

"Did you lock it?" asked the neighbor.

"Yes."

The neighbor smiled wryly. "So did we," he said. "I tried not to, but then I had to go back."

They moved through the quiet streets. The edges of the sky were beginning to redden. The neighbor's wife and the four children were in back. His wife and the neighbor were in front with him.

"Going to be a nice day," said the neighbor.

"I suppose so," he said.

"Have you told your children?" the neighbor asked softly.

"Of course not."

"I haven't, I haven't," insisted his neighbor. "I was just asking."

"Oh."

They rode in silence a while.

"Do you ever get the feeling that we're . . . running out?" asked the neighbor.

He tightened. "No," he said. His lips pressed together. "No."

"I guess it's better not to talk about it," his neighbor said hastily.

"Much better," he said.

As they drove up to the guardhouse at the gate, he turned to the back.

"Remember," he said. "Not a word from any of you."

The guard was sleepy and didn't care. The guard recognized him right away as the chief test pilot for the new ship. That was enough. The family was coming down to watch him off, he told the guard. That was all right. The guard let them drive to the ship's platform.

The car stopped under the huge columns. They all got out and stared up.

Far above them, its nose pointed toward the sky, the great metal ship was beginning to reflect the early morning glow.

"Let's go," he said. "Quickly."

As they hurried toward the ship's elevator, he stopped for a moment to look back. The guardhouse looked deserted. He looked around at everything and tried to fix it all in his memory.

He bent over and picked up some dirt. He put it in his pocket.

"Goodbye," he whispered.

He ran to the elevator.

The doors shut in front of them. There was no sound in the rising cubicle but the hum of the motor and a few self-conscious coughs from the children. He looked at them. To be taken so young, he thought, without a chance to help.

He closed his eyes. His wife's arm rested on his arm. He looked at her. Their eyes met and she smiled at him.

"It's all right," she whispered.

The elevator shuddered to a stop. The doors slid open and they went out. It was getting lighter. He hurried them along the enclosed platform.

They all climbed through the narrow doorway in the ship's side. He hesitated before following them. He wanted to say something fitting the moment. It burned in him to say something fitting the moment.

He couldn't. He swung in and grunted as he pulled the door shut and turned the wheel tight.

"That's it," he said. "Come on, everybody."

Their footsteps echoed on the metal decks and ladders as they went up to the control room.

The children ran to the ports and looked out. They gasped when they saw how high they were. Their mothers stood behind them, looking down at the ground with frightened eyes.

He went up to them.

"So high," said his daughter.

He patted her head gently. "So high," he repeated.

Then he turned abruptly and went over to the instrument panel. He stood there hesitantly. He heard someone come up behind him.

"Shouldn't we tell the children?" asked his wife. "Shouldn't we let them know it's their last look?"

"Go ahead," he said. "Tell them."

He waited to hear her footsteps. There were none. He turned. She kissed him on the cheek. Then she went to tell the children.

He threw over the switch. Deep in the belly of the ship, a spark ignited the fuel. A concentrated rush of gas flooded from the vents. The bulkheads began to shake.

He heard his daughter crying. He tried not to listen. He extended a trembling hand toward the lever, then glanced back suddenly. They were all staring at him. He put his hand on the lever and threw it over.

The ship quivered a brief second and then they felt it rush along the smooth incline. It flashed up into the air, faster and faster. They all heard the wind rushing past.

He watched the children turn to the ports and look out again.

"Goodbye," they said. "Goodbye."

He sank down wearily at the control panel. Out of the corner of his eyes he saw his neighbor sit down next to him.

"You know just where we're going?" his neighbor asked.

"On that chart there."

His neighbor looked at the chart. His eyebrows raised.

"In another solar system," he said.

"That's right. It has an atmosphere like ours. We'll be safe there."

"The race will be safe," said his neighbor.

He nodded once and looked back at his and his neighbor's family. They were still looking out the ports.

"What?" he asked.

"I said," the neighbor repeated, "which one of these planets is it?"

He leaned over the chart, pointed.

"That small one over there," he said. "Near that moon."

"This one, third from the sun?"

"That's right," he said. "That one. Third from the sun."

THE LAST DAY

He woke up and the first thing he thought was—*the last night is gone*.

He had slept through half of it.

He lay there on the floor and looked up at the ceiling. The walls still glowed reddish from the outside light. There was no sound in the living room but that of snoring.

He looked around.

There were bodies sprawled out all over the room. They were on the couch, slumped on chairs, curled up on the floor. Some were covered with rugs. Two of them were naked.

He raised up on one elbow and winced at the shooting pains in his head. He closed his eyes and held them tightly shut for a moment. Then he opened them again. He ran his tongue over the inside of his dry mouth. There was still a stale taste of liquor and food in his mouth.

He rested on his elbow as he looked around the room again, his mind slowly registering the scene.

Nancy and Bill lying in each other's arms, both naked. Norman curled up in an arm chair, his thin face taut as he slept. Mort and Mel lying on the floor, covered with dirty throw rugs. Both snoring. Others on the floor.

Outside the red glow.

He looked at the window and his throat moved. He blinked. He looked down over his long body. He swallowed again.

I'm alive, he thought, and it's all true.

He rubbed his eyes. He took a deep breath of the dead air in the apartment.

He knocked over a glass as he struggled to his feet. The

liquor and soda sloshed over the rug and soaked into the dark blue weave.

He looked around at the other glasses, broken, kicked over, hurled against the wall. He looked at the bottles all over, all empty.

He stood staring around the room. He looked at the record player overturned, the albums all strewn around, jagged pieces of records in crazy patterns on the rug.

He remembered.

It was Mort who had started it the night before. He had suddenly rushed to the playing record machine and shouted drunkenly.

"What the hell is music anymore! Just a lot of noise!"

And he had driven the point of his shoe against the front of the record player and knocked it against the wall. He had lurched over and down on his knees. He had struggled up with the player in his beefy arms and heaved the entire thing over on its back and kicked it again.

"The hell with music!" he had yelled. "I hate the crap anyway!"

Then he'd started to drag records out of their jackets and snap them over his kneecap.

"Come on!" he'd yelled to everybody. "Come on!"

And it had caught on. The way all crazy ideas had caught on in those last few days.

Mel had jumped up from making love to a girl. He had flung records out the windows, scaling them far across the street. And Charlie had put aside his gun for a moment to stand at the windows too and try to hit people in the street with thrown records.

Richard had watched the dark saucers bounce and shatter on the sidewalks below. He'd even thrown one himself. Then he'd just turned away and let the others rage. He'd taken Mel's girl into the bedroom and had sex with her.

He thought about that as he stood waveringly in the reddish light of the room.

He closed his eyes a moment.

Then he looked at Nancy and remembered taking her too sometime in the jumble of wild hours that had been yesterday and last night.

She looked vile now, he thought. She'd always been an animal. Before, though, she'd had to veil it. Now, in the final twilight of everything she could revel in the only thing she'd ever really cared about.

He wondered if there were any people left in the world with real dignity. The kind that was still there when it no longer was necessary to impress people with it.

He stepped over the body of a sleeping girl. She had on only a slip. He looked down at her tangled hair, at her red lips smeared, the tight unhappy frown printed on her face.

He glanced into the bedroom as he passed it. There were three girls and two men in the bed.

He found the body in the bathroom.

It was thrown carelessly in the tub and the shower curtain torn down to cover it. Only the legs showed, dangling ridiculously over the front rim of the tub.

He drew back the curtain and looked at the blood-soaked shirt, at the white, still face.

Charlie.

He shook his head, then turned away and washed his face and hands at the sink. It didn't matter. Nothing mattered. As a matter of fact, Charlie was one of the lucky ones now. A member of the legion who had put their heads into ovens, or cut their wrists or taken pills or done away with themselves in the accepted fashions of suicide.

As he looked at his tired face in the mirror he thought of cutting his wrists. But he knew he couldn't. Because it took more than just despair to incite self-destruction.

He took a drink of water. Lucky, he thought, there's still water running. He didn't suppose there was a soul left to run the water system. Or the electric system or the gas system or the telephone system or any system for that matter.

What fool would work on the last day of the world?

Spencer was in the kitchen when Richard went in.

He was sitting in his shorts at the table looking at his hands. On the stove some eggs were frying. The gas was working then too, Richard thought.

"Hello," he said to Spencer.

Spencer grunted without looking up. He stared at his hands. Richard let it go. He turned the gas down a little. He took bread out of the cupboard and put it in the electric toaster. But the toaster didn't work. He shrugged and forgot about it.

"What time is it?"

Spencer was looking at him with the question.

Richard looked at his watch.

"It stopped," he said.

They looked at each other.

"Oh," Spencer said. Then he asked, "What day is it?"

Richard thought. "Sunday, I think," he said.

"I wonder if people are at church," Spencer said.

"Who cares?"

Richard opened the refrigerator.

"There aren't any more eggs," Spencer said.

Richard shut the door.

"No more eggs," he said dully. "No more chickens. No more anything."

He leaned against the wall with a shuddering breath and looked out the window at the red sky.

Mary, he thought. Mary, who I should have married. Who I let go. He wondered where she was. He wondered if she were thinking about him at all.

Norman came trudging in, groggy with sleep and hangover. His mouth hung open. He looked dazed.

"Morning," he slurred.

"Good morning, merry sunshine," Richard said, without mirth.

Norman looked at him blankly. Then he went over to the sink and washed out his mouth. He spit the water down the drain.

"Charlie's dead," he said.

"I know," Richard said.

"Oh. When did it happen?"

"Last night," Richard told him. "You were unconscious. You remember how he kept saying he was going to shoot us all? Put us out of our misery?"

"Yeah," Norman said. "He put the muzzle against my head. He said feel how cool it is."

"Well he got in a fight with Mort," Richard said. "The gun went off." He shrugged. "That was it."

They looked at each other without expression.

Then Norman turned his head and looked out the window. "It's still up there," he muttered.

They looked up at the great flaming ball in the sky that crowded out the sun, the moon, the stars.

Norman turned away, his throat moving. His lips trembled and he clamped them together.

"Jesus," he said. "It's *today*."

He looked up at the sky again.

"Today," he repeated. "*Everything*."

"Everything," said Richard.

Spencer got up and turned off the gas. He looked down at the eggs for a moment. Then he said, "What the hell did I fry these for?"

He dumped them into the sink and they slid greasily over the white surface. The yolks burst and spurted smoking, yellow fluid over the enamel.

Spencer bit his lips. His face grew hard.

"I'm taking her again," he said, suddenly.

He pushed past Richard and dropped his shorts off as he turned the corner into the hallways.

"There goes Spencer," Richard said.

Norman sat down at the table. Richard stayed at the wall.

In the living room they heard Nancy suddenly call out at the top of her strident voice.

"Hey, wake up everybody! Watch me do it! Watch me everybody, *watch me!*"

Norman looked at the kitchen doorway for a moment. Then something gave inside of him and he slumped his head forward on his arms on the table. His thin shoulders shook.

"I did it too," he said brokenly. "I did it too. Oh God, what did I come here for?"

"Sex," Richard said. "Like all the rest of us. You thought you could end your life in carnal, drunken bliss."

Norman's voice was muffled.

"I can't die like that," he sobbed. "I can't."

"A couple of billion people are doing it," Richard said. "When the sun hits us, they'll still be at it. What a sight."

The thought of a world's people indulging themselves in one last orgy of animalism made him shudder. He closed his eyes and pressed his forehead against the wall and tried to forget.

But the wall was warm.

Norman looked up from the table.

"Let's go home," he said.

Richard looked at him. "Home?" he said.

"To our parents. My mother and father. Your mother."

Richard shook his head.

"I don't want to," he said.

"But I can't go alone."

"Why?"

"Because . . . I can't. You know how the streets are full of guys just *killing* everybody they meet."

Richard shrugged.

"Why don't you?" Norman asked.

"I don't want to see her."

"Your *mother*?"

"Yes."

"You're crazy," Norman said. "Who else is there to . . ."

"No."

He thought of his mother at home waiting for him. Waiting for him on the last day. And it made him ill to think of him dallying, of maybe never seeing her again.

But he kept thinking—How can I go home and have her try to make me pray? Try to make me read from the Bible, spend these last hours in a muddle of religious absorption?

He said it again for himself.

"*No.*"

Norman looked lost. His chest shook with a swallowed sob.

"I want to see my mother," he said.

"Go ahead," Richard said, casually.

But his insides were twisting themselves into knots. To never see her again. Or his sister and her husband and her daughter.

Never to see any of them again.

He sighed. It was no use fighting it. In spite of everything, Norman was right. Who else was there in the world to turn to? In a wide world, about to be burned, was there any other person who loved him above all others?

"Oh . . . all right," he said. "Come on. Anything to get out of this place."

The apartment house hall smelled of vomit. They found the janitor dead drunk on the stairs. They found a dog in the foyer with its head kicked in.

They stopped as they came out of the entrance of the building. Instinctively they looked up.

At the red sky, like molten slag. At the fiery wisps that fell like hot rain drops through the atmosphere. At the gigantic ball of flame that kept coming closer and closer that blotted out the universe.

They lowered their watering eyes. It hurt to look. They started walking along the street. It was very warm.

"December," Richard said. "It's like the tropics."

As they walked along in silence, he thought of the tropics, of the poles, of all the world's countries he would never see. Of all the things he would never do.

Like hold Mary in his arms and tell her, as the world was ending, that he loved her very much and was not afraid.

"*Never*," he said, feeling himself go rigid with frustration.

"What?" Norman said.

"Nothing. Nothing."

As they walked, Richard felt something heavy in his jacket pocket. It bumped against his side. He reached in and drew out the object.

"What's that?" Norman asked.

"Charlie's gun," Richard said. "I took it last night so nobody else would get hurt."

His laughter was harsh.

"So nobody else would get hurt," he said bitterly. "Jesus, I ought to be on the stage."

He was about to throw it away when he changed his mind. He slid it back into his pocket.

"I may need it," he said.

Norman wasn't listening.

"Thank God nobody stole my car. Oh . . . !"

Somebody had thrown a rock through the windshield.

"What's the difference?" Richard said.

"I . . . none, I suppose."

They got into the front seat and brushed the glass off the cushion. It was stuffy in the car. Richard pulled off his jacket and threw it out. He put the gun in his side pants pocket.

As Norman drove downtown, they passed people in the street.

Some were running around wildly, as if they were searching for something. Some were fighting with each other. Strewn all over the sidewalks were bodies of people who had leaped from windows and been struck down by speeding cars. Buildings were on fire, windows shattered from the explosions of unlit gas jets.

There were people looting stores.

"What's the matter with them?" Norman asked, miserably. "Is that how they want to spend their last day?"

"Maybe that's how they spent their whole life," Richard answered.

He leaned against the door and gazed at the people they passed. Some of them waved at him. Some cursed and spat. A few threw things at the speeding car.

"People die the way they lived," he said. "Some good, some bad."

"*Look out!*"

Norman cried out as a car came careening down the street on the wrong side. Men and women hung out of the window shouting and singing and waving bottles.

Norman twisted the wheel violently and they missed the car by inches.

"Are they crazy!" he said.

Richard looked out through the back window. He saw the car skid, saw it get out of control and go crashing into a store front and turn over on its side, the wheels spinning crazily.

He turned back front without speaking. Norman kept looking ahead grimly, his hands on the wheel, white and tense.

Another intersection.

A car came speeding across their path. Norman jammed on
the brakes with a gasp. They crashed against the dashboard,
getting their breath knocked out.

Then, before Norman could get the car started again, a
gang of teenage boys with knives and clubs came dashing into
the intersection. They'd been chasing the other car. Now they
changed direction and flung themselves at the car that held
Norman and Richard.

Norman threw the car into first and gunned across the street.

A boy jumped on the back of the car. Another tried for the
running board, missed and went spinning over the street. Another jumped on the running board and grabbed the door
handle. He slashed at Richard with a knife.

"Gonna kill ya bastids!" yelled the boy. "Sonsabitches!"

He slashed again and tore open the back of the seat as Richard jerked his shoulder to the side.

"Get out of here!" Norman screamed, trying to watch the
boy and the street ahead at the same time.

The boy tried to open the door as the car wove wildly up
Broadway. He slashed again but the car's motion made him miss.

"I'll *get ya*!" he screamed in a fury of brainless hate.

Richard tried to open the door and knock the boy off, but
he couldn't. The boy's twisted white face thrust in through the
window. He raised his knife.

Richard had the gun now. He shot the boy in the face.

The boy flung back from the car with a dying howl and landed
like a sack of rocks. He bounced once, his left leg kicked and
then he lay still.

Richard twisted around.

The boy on the back was still hanging on, his crazed face
pressed against the back window. Richard saw his mouth
moving as the boy cursed.

"Shake him off!" he said.

Norman headed for the sidewalk, then suddenly veered back

into the street. The boy hung on. Norman did it again. The boy still clung to the back..

Then on the third time he lost his grip and went off. He tried to run along the street but his momentum was too great and he went leaping over the curb and crashing into a plate glass window, arms stuck up in front of him to ward off the blow.

They sat in the car, breathing heavily. They didn't talk for a long while. Richard flung the gun out the window and watched it clatter on the concrete and bounce off a hydrant. Norman started to say something about it, then stopped.

The car turned onto Fifth Avenue and started downtown at sixty miles an hour. There weren't many cars.

They passed churches. People were packed inside them. They overflowed out onto the steps.

"Poor fools," Richard muttered, his hands still shaking.

Norman took a deep breath.

"I wish I was a poor fool," he said. "A poor fool who could believe in something."

"Maybe," Richard said. Then he added, "I'd rather spend the last day believing what I think is true."

"The last day," Norman said, "I . . ."

He shook his head. "I can't believe it," he said. "I read the papers. I see that . . . thing up there. I know it's going to happen. But, God! The *end?*"

He looked at Richard for a split second.

"Nothing afterward?" he said.

Richard said, "I don't know."

At 14th Street, Norman drove to the East Side, then sped across the Manhattan Bridge. He didn't stop for anything, driving around bodies and wrecked cars. Once he drove over a body and Richard saw his face twitch as the wheel rolled over the dead man's leg.

"They're all lucky," Richard said. "Luckier than we are."

They stopped in front of Norman's house in downtown Brooklyn. Some kids were playing ball in the street. They didn't seem to realize what was happening. Their shouts sounded very loud in the silent street. Richard wondered if their parents knew where the children were. Or cared.

Norman was looking at him.

"Well . . . ?" he started to say.

Richard felt his stomach muscles tightening. He couldn't answer.

"Would you . . . like to come in for a minute?" Norman asked.

Richard shook his head.

"No," he said. "I better get home. I . . . should see her. My mother, I mean."

"Oh."

Norman nodded. Then he straightened up. He forced a momentary calm over himself.

"For what it's worth, Dick," he said, "I consider you my best friend and . . ."

He faltered. He reached out and gripped Richard's hand. Then he pushed out of the car, leaving the keys in the ignition.

"So long," he said hurriedly.

Richard watched his friend run around the car and move for the apartment house. When he had almost reached the door, Richard called out.

"Norm!"

Norman stopped and turned. The two of them looked at each other. All the years they had known each other seemed to flicker between them.

Then Richard managed to smile. He touched his forehead in a last salute.

"So long, Norm," he said.

Norman didn't smile. He pushed through the door and was gone.

Richard looked at the door for a long time. He started the motor. Then he turned it off again thinking that Norman's parents might not be home.

After a while he started it again and began the trip home.

As he drove, he kept thinking.

The closer he got to the end, the less he wanted to face it. He wanted to end it now. Before the hysterics started.

Sleeping pills, he decided. It was the best way. He had some at home. He hoped there were enough left. There might not be any left in the corner drug store. There'd been a rush for sleeping pills during those last few days. Entire families took them together.

He reached the house without event. Overhead the sky was an incandescent crimson. He felt the heat on his face like waves from a distant oven. He breathed in the heated air.

He unlocked the front door and walked in slowly.

I'll probably find her in the front room, he thought. Surrounded by her books, praying, exhorting invisible powers to succor her as the world prepared to fry itself.

She wasn't in the front room.

He searched the house. And, as he did so, his heart began to beat quickly and when he knew she really wasn't there he felt a great hollow feeling in his stomach. He knew that his talk about not wanting to see her had been just talk. He loved her. And she was the only one left now.

He searched for a note in her room, in his, in the living room.

"Mom," he said, "Mom, where are you?"

He found the note in the kitchen. He picked it up from the table.

Richard, Darling.

I'm at your sister's house. Please come there. Don't make me spend the last day without you. Don't make me leave this world without seeing your dear face again. Please.

The last day.

There it was in black and white. And, of all people, it had been his mother to write down the words. She who had always been so skeptical of his taste for material science. Now admitting that science's last prediction.

Because she couldn't doubt anymore. Because the sky was filled with flaming evidence and no one could doubt anymore.

The whole world going. The staggering detail of evolutions and revolutions, of strifes and clashes, of endless continuities of centuries streaming back into the clouded past, of rocks and trees and animals and men. All to pass. In a flash, in a moment. The pride, the vanity of man's world incinerated by a freak of astronomical disorder.

What point was there to all of it then? None, none at all. Because it was all ending.

He got some sleeping pills from the medicine cabinet and left. He drove to his sister's house thinking about his mother as he passed through the streets littered with everything from empty bottles to dead people.

If only he didn't dread the thought of arguing with his mother on this last day. Of disputing with her about her God and her conviction.

He made up his mind not to argue. He'd force himself to make their last day a peaceful one. He would accept her simple devotion and not hack at her faith anymore.

The front door was locked at Grace's house. He rang the bell and, after a moment, heard hurried steps inside.

He heard Ray shout inside, "Don't open it Mom! It may be that gang again!"

"It's Richard, I know it is!" his mother called back.

Then the door was open and she was embracing him and crying happily.

He didn't speak. Finally he said softly, "Hello Mom."

His niece Doris played all afternoon in the front room while Grace and Ray sat motionless in the living room looking at her.

If I were with Mary, Richard kept thinking. If only we were together today. Then he thought they might have had children. And he would have to sit like Grace and know that the few years his child had lived would be its only years.

The sky grew brighter as evening approached. It flowed with violent crimson currents. Doris stood quietly at the window and looked at it. She hadn't laughed all day or cried. And Richard thought to himself—she *knows*.

And thought too that at any moment his mother would ask them all to pray together. To sit and read the Bible and hope for divine charity.

But she didn't say anything. She smiled. She made supper. Richard stood with her in the kitchen as she made supper.

"I may not wait," he told her. "I . . . may take sleeping pills."

"Are you afraid, son?" she asked.

"Everybody is afraid," he said.

She shook her head. "Not everybody," she said.

Now, he thought, it's coming. That smug look, the opening line.

She gave him a dish with the vegetable and they all sat down to eat.

During supper none of them spoke except to ask for food. Doris never spoke once. Richard sat looking at her from across the table.

He thought about the night before. The crazy drinking, the fighting, the carnal abuses. He thought of Charlie dead in the bathtub. Of the apartment in Manhattan. Of Spencer driving himself into a frenzy of lust at the climax of his life. Of the boy lying dead in the New York gutter with a bullet in his brain.

They all seemed very far away. He could almost believe it had all never happened. Could almost believe that this was just another evening meal with his family.

Except for the cherry glow that filled the sky and flooded in through the windows like an aura from some fantastic fireplace.

Near the end of the meal Grace went and got a box. She sat down at the table with it and opened it. She took out white pills. Doris looked at her, her large eyes searching.

"This is dessert," Grace told her. "We're all going to have white candy for dessert."

"Is it peppermint?" Doris asked.

"Yes," Grace said. "It's peppermint."

Richard felt his scalp crawling as Grace put pills in front of Doris. In front of Ray.

"We haven't enough for all of us," she said to Richard.

"I have my own," he said.

"Have you enough for Mom?" she asked.

"I won't need any," her mother said.

In his tenseness, Richard almost shouted at her. Shouted— Oh stop being so damned noble! But he held himself. He stared in fascinated horror at Doris holding the pills in her small hand.

"This isn't peppermint," she said. "Momma this isn't . . ."

"*Yes it is.*" Grace took a deep breath. "Eat it, darling."

Doris put one in her mouth. She made a face. Then she spit it into her palm.

"It *isn't* peppermint," she said, upset.

Grace threw up her hand and buried her teeth in the white knuckles. Her eyes moved frantically to Ray.

"Eat it, Doris," Ray said. "Eat it, it's good."

Doris started to cry. "No, I don't like it."

"*Eat it!*"

Ray turned away suddenly, his body shaking. Richard tried to think of some way to make her eat the pills but he couldn't. Then his mother spoke.

"We'll play a game, Doris," she said. "We'll see if you can swallow all the candy before I count ten. If you do I'll give you a dollar."

Doris sniffed. "A dollar?" she said.

Richard's mother nodded.

"One," she said.

Doris didn't move.

"Two," said Richard's mother. "A *dollar*?"

"Yes, darling. Three, four, hurry up."

Doris reached for the pills.

"Five . . . six . . . seven . . ."

Grace had her eyes shut tightly. Her cheeks were white.

"Nine . . . ten . . ."

Richard's mother smiled but her lips trembled and there was a glistening in her eyes.

"There," she said cheerfully. "You've won the game."

Grace suddenly put pills into her mouth and swallowed them in fast succession. She looked at Ray. He reached out one trembling hand and swallowed his pills. Richard put his hand in his pocket for his pills but took it out again. He didn't want his mother to watch him take them.

Doris got sleepy almost immediately. She yawned and couldn't keep her eyes open. Ray picked her up and she rested against his shoulder, her small arms around his neck. Grace got up and the three of them went back into the bedroom.

Richard sat there while his mother went back and said good-bye to them. He sat staring at the white table cloth and the remains of food.

When his mother came back she smiled at him.

"Help me with the dishes," she said.

"The . . . ?" he started. Then he stopped. What difference did it make what they did?

He stood with her in the redlit kitchen, feeling a sense of sharp unreality as he dried the dishes they would never use again and put them in the closet that would be no more in a matter of hours.

He kept thinking about Ray and Grace in the bedroom. Finally he left the kitchen without a word and went back. He opened the door and looked in. He looked at the three of them for a long time. Then he shut the door again and walked slowly back to the kitchen. He stared at his mother.

"They're . . ."

"All right," his mother said.

"Why didn't you say anything to them?" he asked her. "How come you let them do it without saying anything?"

"Richard," she said, "everyone has to make his own way on this day. No one can tell others what to do. Doris was their child."

"And I'm yours . . . ?"

"You're not a child any longer," she said.

He finished up the dishes, his fingers numb and shaking.

"Mom, about last night," he said.

"I don't care about it," she said.

"But . . ."

"It doesn't matter," she said. "This part is ending."

Now, he thought, almost with pain. *This* part. Now she would talk about afterlife and heaven and reward for the just and eternal penitence for the sinning.

She said, "Let's go out and sit on the porch."

He didn't understand. He walked through the quiet house with her. He sat next to her on the porch steps and thought. I'll never see Grace again. Or Doris. Or Norman or Spencer or Mary or anybody . . .

He couldn't take it all in. It was too much. All he could do was sit there woodenly and look at the red sky and the huge sun about to swallow them. He couldn't even feel nervous any more. Fears were blunted by endless repetition.

"Mom," he said after a while, "why . . . why haven't you spoken about religion to me? I know you must want to."

She looked at him and her face was very gentle in the red glow.

"I don't have to, darling," she said. "I know we'll be together when this is over. You don't have to believe it. I'll believe for both of us."

And that was all. He looked at her, marveling at her confidence and her strength.

"If you want to take those pills now," she said, "it's all right. You can go to sleep in my lap."

He felt himself tremble. "You wouldn't mind?"

"I want you to do what you think is best."

He didn't know what to do until he thought of her sitting there alone when the world ended.

"I'll stay with you," he said impulsively.

She smiled.

"If you change your mind," she said, "you can tell me."

They were quiet for a while. Then she said, "It *is* pretty."

"*Pretty*?" he asked.

"Yes," she said, "God closes a bright curtain on our play."

He didn't know. But he put his arm around her shoulders and she leaned against him. And he did know one thing.

They sat there in the evening of the last day. And, though there was no actual point to it, they loved each other.

LONG DISTANCE CALL

Just before the telephone rang, storm winds toppled the tree outside her window and jolted Miss Keene from dreaming sleep. She flung herself up with a gasp, her frail hands crumpling twists of sheet in either palm. Beneath her fleshless chest the heart jerked taut, the sluggish blood spurred. She sat in rigid muteness, her eyes staring at the night.

In another second, the telephone rang.

Who on earth? The question shaped unwittingly in her brain. Her thin hand faltered in the darkness, the fingers searching a moment and then Miss Elva Keene drew the cool receiver to her ear.

"Hello," she said.

Outside a cannon of thunder shook the night, twitching Miss Keene's crippled legs. *I've missed the voice,* she thought, *the thunder has blotted out the voice.*

"Hello," she said again.

There was no sound. Miss Keene waited in expectant lethargy. Then she repeated. "Hel-*lo*," in a cracking voice. Outside the thunder crashed again.

Still no voice spoke, not even the sound of a phone being disconnected met her ears. Her wavering hand reached out and thumped down the receiver with an angry motion.

"Inconsideration," she muttered, thudding back on her pillow. Already her infirm back ached from effort of sitting.

She forced out a weary breath. Now she'd have to suffer through the whole tormenting process of going to sleep again—the composing of jaded muscles, the ignoring of abrasive pain in her legs, the endless, frustrating struggle to turn off the faucet in her brain and keep unwanted thoughts from dripping. Oh, well, it had to be done; Nurse Phillips insisted on proper rest. Elva Keene breathed slowly and deeply, drew the covers to her chin and labored hopefully for sleep.

In vain.

Her eyes opened and, turning her face to the window, she watched the storm move off on lightning legs. *Why can't I sleep,* she fretted, *why must I always lie here awake like this?*

She knew the answer without effort. When a life was dull, the smallest element added seemed unnaturally intriguing. And life for Miss Keene was the sorry pattern of lying flat or being propped on pillows, reading books which Nurse Phillips brought from the town library, getting nourishment, rest, medication, listening to her tiny radio—and waiting, *waiting* for something different to happen.

Like the telephone call that wasn't a call.

There hadn't even been the sound of a receiver replaced in its cradle. Miss Keene didn't understand that. Why would anyone call her exchange and then listen silently while she said, "Hello," over and over again? *Had* it actually been anyone calling?

What she should have done, she realized then, was to keep listening until the other person tired of the joke and put down the receiver. What she should have done was to speak out forcefully about the inconsideration of a prankish call to a crippled maiden lady in the middle of a stormy night. Then, if there had been someone listening, whoever it was would have been properly chastened by her angry words and . . .

"Well, of course."

She said it aloud in the darkness, punctuating the sentence with a cluck of somewhat relieved disgust. Of course, the telephone was out of order. Someone had tried to contact her, perhaps Nurse Phillips to see if she was all right. But the other end of the line had broken down in some way, allowing her phone to ring but no verbal communication to be made. Well, of course, that was the case.

Miss Keene nodded once and closed her eyes gently. Now to sleep, she thought. Far away, beyond the country, the storm

cleared its murky throat. *I hope no one is worrying*, Elva
Keene thought, *that would be too bad*.

She was thinking that when the telephone rang again.

There, she thought, *they are trying to reach me again*. She
reached out hurriedly in the darkness, fumbled until she felt
the receiver, then pulled it to her ear.

"Hello," said Miss Keene.

Silence.

Her throat contracted. She knew what was wrong, of course,
but she didn't like it, no, not at all.

"Hello?" she said tentatively, not yet certain that she was
wasting breath.

There was no reply. She waited a moment, then spoke a
third time, a little impatiently now, loudly, her shrill voice
ringing in the dark bedroom. "*Hello!*"

Nothing. Miss Keene had the sudden urge to fling the receiver away. She forced down that curious instinct—no, she
must wait; wait and listen to hear if anyone hung up the phone
on the other end of the line.

So she waited.

The bedroom was very quiet now, but Elva Keene kept
straining to hear; either the sound of a receiver going down or
the buzz which usually follows. Her chest rose and fell in delicate lurches, she closed her eyes in concentration, then opened
them again and blinked at the darkness. There was no sound
from the telephone; not a click, not a buzz, not a sound of
someone putting down a receiver.

"Hello!" she cried suddenly, then pushed away the receiver.

She missed her target. The receiver dropped and thumped
once on the rug. Miss Keene nervously clicked on the lamp,
wincing as the leprous bulb light filled her eyes. Quickly, she
lay on her side and tried to reach the silent, voiceless telephone.

But she couldn't stretch far enough and crippled legs pre-
vented her from rising. Her throat tightened. My God, must
she leave it there all night, silent and mystifying?

Remembering then, she reached out abruptly and pressed
the cradle arm. On the floor, the receiver clicked, then began

to buzz normally. Elva Keene swallowed and drew in a shaking breath as she slumped back on her pillow.

She threw out hooks of reason then and pulled herself back from panic. *This is ridiculous*, she thought, *getting upset over such a trivial and easily explained incident. It was the storm, the night, the way in which I'd been shocked from sleep. (What was it that had awakened me?) All these things piled on the mountain of teeth-grinding monotony that's my life. Yes, it was bad, very bad.* But it wasn't the incident that was bad. It was her reaction to it.

Miss Elva Keene numbed herself to further premonitions. *I shall sleep now*, she ordered her body with a petulant shake. She lay very still and relaxed. From the floor she could hear the telephone buzzing like the drone of far-off bees. She ignored it.

Early the next morning, after Nurse Phillips had taken away the breakfast dishes, Elva Keene called the telephone company.

"This is Miss Elva," she told the operator.

"Oh, yes, Miss Elva," said the operator, a Miss Finch. "Can I help you?"

"Last night my telephone rang twice," said Elva Keene. "But when I answered it, no one spoke. And I didn't hear my receiver drop. I didn't even hear a dial tone—just silence."

"Well, I'll tell you, Miss Elva," said the cheery voice of Miss Finch, "that storm last night just about ruined half our service. We're being flooded with calls about knocked down lines and bad connections. I'd say you're pretty lucky your phone is working at all."

"Then you think it was probably a bad connection," prompted Miss Keene, "caused by the storm?"

"Oh yes, Miss Elva, that's all."

"Do you think it will happen again?"

"Oh, it *may*," said Miss Finch. "It *may*. I really couldn't tell you, Miss Elva. But if it does happen again, you just call me and then I'll have one of our men check on it."

"All right," said Miss Elva. "Thank you, dear."

She lay on her pillows all morning in a relaxed torpor. *It gives one a satisfied feeling,* she thought, *to solve a mystery, slight as it is. It had been a terrible storm that caused the bad connection. And no wonder when it had even knocked down the ancient oak tree beside the house. That was the noise that had awakened me of course, and a pity it was that the dear tree had fallen. How it shaded the house in hot summer months. Oh, well, I suppose I should be grateful,* she thought, *that the tree fell across the road and not across the house.*

The day passed uneventfully, an amalgam of eating, reading Angela Thirkell and the mail (two throw-away advertisements and the light bill), plus brief chats with Nurse Phillips. Indeed, routine had set in so properly that when the telephone rang early that evening, she picked it up without even thinking.

"Hello," she said.

Silence.

It brought her back for a second. Then she called Nurse Phillips.

"What is it?" asked the portly woman as she trudged across the bedroom rug.

"This is what I was telling you about," said Elva Keene, holding out the receiver. "Listen."

Nurse Phillips took the receiver in her hand and pushed back gray locks with the earpiece. Her placid face remained placid. "There's nobody there," she observed.

"That's right," said Miss Keene. "That's right. Now you just listen and see if you can hear a receiver being put down. I'm sure you won't."

Nurse Phillips listened for a moment, then shook her head. "I don't hear anything," she said and hung up.

"Oh, wait!" Miss Keene said hurriedly. "Oh, well, it doesn't matter," she added, seeing it was already done. "If it happens too often, I'll just call Miss Finch and they'll have a repairman check on it."

"I see," Nurse Phillips said and went back to the living room.

Nurse Phillips left the house at eight, leaving on the bedside table, as usual, an apple, a cookie, a glass of water and the bottle of pills. She puffed up the pillows behind Miss Keene's fragile back, moved the radio and telephone a little closer to the bed, looked around complacently, then turned for the door, saying, "I'll see you tomorrow."

It was fifteen minutes later when the telephone rang. Keene picked up the receiver quickly. She didn't bother saying hello this time—she just listened.

At first it was the same—an absolute silence. She listened a moment more, impatiently. Then, on the verge of replacing the receiver, she heard the sound. Her cheek twitched, she jerked the telephone back to her ear.

"Hello?" she asked tensely.

A murmuring, a dull humming, a rustling sound—what was it? Miss Keene shut her eyes tightly, listening hard, but she couldn't identify the sound; it was too soft, too undefined. It deviated from a sort of whining vibration . . . to an escape of air . . . to a bubbling sibilance. *It must be the sound of the connection,* she thought, *it must be the telephone itself making the noise. Perhaps a wire blowing in the wind somewhere, perhaps . . .*

She stopped thinking then. She stopped breathing. The sound had ceased. Once more, silence rang in her ears. She could feel the heartbeats stumbling in her chest again, the walls of her throat closing in. *Oh, this is ridiculous,* she told herself. *I've already been through this—it was the storm, the storm!*

She lay back on her pillows, the receiver pressed to her ear, nervous breaths faltering from her nostrils. She could feel unreasoning dread rise like a tide within her, despite all attempts at sane deduction. Her mind kept slipping off the glassy perch of reason; she kept falling deeper and deeper.

Now she shuddered violently as the sounds began again. They couldn't *possibly* be human sounds, she knew, and yet there was something about them, some inflection, some almost identifiable arrangement of . . .

Her lips shook and a whine began to hover in her throat. But she couldn't put down the telephone, she simply couldn't. The sounds held her hypnotized. Whether they were the rise and fall of the wind or the muttering of faulty mechanisms, she didn't know, but they would not let her go.

"Hello?" she murmured, shakily.

The sounds rose in volume. They rattled and shook in her brain.

"H-e-l-l-o," answered a voice on the telephone. Then Miss Keene fainted dead away.

"Are you certain it was someone saying *hello*?" Miss Finch asked Miss Elva over the telephone. "It might have been the connection, you know."

"I tell you it was a *man*!" a shaking Elva Keene cried. "It was the same man who kept listening to me say hello over and over and over again without answering me back. The same one who made terrible noises over the telephone!"

Miss Finch cleared her throat politely. "Well, I'll have a man check your line, Miss Elva, as soon as he can. Of course, the men are very busy now with all the repairs on storm wreckage, but as soon as it's possible . . ."

"And what am I going to do if this—this *person* calls again?"

"You just hang up on him, Miss Elva."

"But he keeps calling!"

"Well." Miss Finch's affability wavered. "Why don't you find out who he is, Miss Elva. If you can do that, why, we can take immediate action, you see and . . ."

After she'd hung up, Miss Keene lay against the pillows tensely, listening to Nurse Phillips sing husky love songs over the breakfast dishes. Miss Finch didn't believe her story, that was apparent. Miss Finch thought she was a nervous old woman falling prey to imagination. Well, Miss Finch would find out differently.

"I'll just keep calling her and calling her until she *does*," she said irritably to Nurse Phillips just before afternoon nap.

"You just do that," said Nurse Phillips. "Now take your pill and lie down."

Miss Keene lay in grumpy silence, her vein-rutted hands knotted at her sides. It was after two and, except for the bubbling of Nurse Phillips's front-room snores, the house was silent in the October afternoon. *It makes me angry*, thought Elva Keene, *that no one will take this seriously. Well*—her thin lips pressed together—*the next time the telephone rings I'll make sure that Nurse Phillips listens until she does hear something.*

Exactly then the phone rang.

Miss Keene felt a cold tremor lace down her body. Even in the daylight with sunbeams speckling her flowered coverlet, the strident ringing frightened her. She dug porcelain teeth into her lower lip to steady it. *Shall I answer it*? The question came and then, before she could even think to answer, her hand picked up the receiver. A deep ragged breath; she drew the phone slowly to her ear. She said, "Hello?"

The voice answered back, "Hello?"—hollow and inanimate.

"Who is this?" Miss Keene asked, trying to keep her throat clear.

"Hello?"

"Who's calling, please?"

"Hello?"

"Is anyone there!"

"Hello?"

"Please . . . !"

"Hello?"

Miss Keene jammed down the receiver and lay on her bed trembling violently, unable to catch her breath. *What is it*, begged her mind, *what in God's name is it?*

"Margaret!" she cried. "*Margaret!*"

In the front room she heard Nurse Phillips grunt abruptly and then start coughing.

"Margaret, please . . . !"

Elva Keene heard the large-bodied woman rise to her feet and trudge across the living room floor. *I must compose myself*, she told herself, fluttering hands to her fevered cheeks. *I must tell her exactly what happened, exactly.*

"What is it?" grumbled the nurse. "Does your stomach ache?"

Miss Keene's throat drew in tautly as she swallowed. "He just called again," she whispered.

"Who?"

"That man!"

"What man?"

"The one who keeps calling!" Miss Keene cried. "He keeps saying hello over and over again. That's all he says—hello, hello, hel . . ."

"Now stop this," Nurse Phillips scolded stolidly. "Lie back and . . ."

"I don't *want* to lie back!" she said frenziedly. "I want to know who this terrible person is who keeps frightening me!"

"Now don't work yourself into a state," warned Nurse Phillips. "You know how upset your stomach gets."

Miss Keene began to sob bitterly. "I'm afraid. I'm afraid of him. Why does he keep calling me?"

Nurse Phillips stood by the bed looking down in bovine inertia. "Now, what did Miss Finch tell you?" she said softly.

Miss Keene's shaking lips could not frame the answer.

"Did she tell you it was the connection?" the nurse soothed. "Did she?"

"But it isn't! It's a man, a *man*!"

Nurse Phillips expelled a patient breath. "If it's a man," she said, "then just hang up. You don't have to talk to him. Just hang up. Is that so hard to do?"

Miss Keene shut tear-bright eyes and forced her lips into a twitching line. In her mind the man's subdued and listless voice kept echoing. Over and over, the inflection never altering, the question never deferring to her replies—just repeating itself endlessly in doleful apathy. *Hello? Hello?* Making her shudder to the heart.

"Look," Nurse Phillips spoke.

She opened her eyes and saw the blurred image of the nurse putting the receiver down on the table.

"There," Nurse Phillips said, "nobody can call you now. You leave it that way. If you need anything all you have to do is dial. Now isn't that all right? Isn't it?"

Miss Keene looked bleakly at her nurse. Then, after a moment, she nodded once. Grudgingly.

She lay in the dark bedroom, the sound of the dial tone humming in her ear; keeping her awake. *Or am I just telling myself that?* she thought. *Is it really keeping me awake? Didn't I sleep that first night with the receiver off the hook? No, it wasn't the sound, it was something else.*

She closed her eyes obdurately. *I won't listen*, she told

herself, *I just won't listen to it*. She drew in trembling breaths of the night. But the darkness would not fill her brain and blot away the sound.

Miss Keene felt around the bed until she found her jacket. She draped it over the receiver, swathing its black smoothness in woolly turns. Then she sank back again, stern breathed and taut. *I will sleep*, she demanded, *I will sleep*.

She heard it still.

Her body grew rigid and, abruptly, she unfolded the receiver from its thick wrappings and slammed it down angrily on the cradle. Silence filled the room with a delicious peace. Miss Keene fell back on the pillow with a feeble groan. *Now to sleep*, she thought.

The telephone rang.

Her breath snuffed off. The ringing seemed to permeate the darkness, surrounding her in a cloud of ear-lancing vibration. She reached out to put the receiver on the table again, then jerked her hand back with a gasp, realizing she would hear the man's voice again.

Her throat pulsed nervously. *What I'll do*, she planned, *what I'll do is take off the receiver very quickly—very quickly—and put it down, then push down on the arm and cut off the line. Yes, that's what I'll do!*

She tensed herself and spread her hand out cautiously until the ringing phone was under it. Then, breath held, she followed her plan, slashed off the ring, reached quickly for the cradle arm . . .

And stopped, frozen, as the man's voice reached out through darkness to her ears. "Where are you?" he asked. "I want to talk to you."

Claws of ice clamped down on Miss Keene's shuddering chest. She lay petrified, unable to cut off the sound of the man's dull, expressionless voice, asking, "Where are you? I want to talk to you."

A sound from Miss Keene's throat, thin and fluttering.

And the man said, "Where are you? I want to talk to you."

"No, no," sobbed Miss Keene.

"Where are you? I want . . ."

She pressed the cradle arm with taut white fingers. She held it down for five minutes before letting it go.

"I tell you I won't have it!"

Miss Keene's voice was a frayed ribbon of sound. She sat inflexibly on the bed, straining her frightened anger through the mouthpiece vents.

"You say you hang up on this man and he still calls?" Miss Finch inquired.

"I've *explained* all that!" Elva Keene burst out. "I had to leave the receiver off the phone all night so he wouldn't call. And the buzzing kept me awake. I didn't get a *wink* of sleep! Now, I want this line checked, do you hear me? I want you to stop this terrible thing!"

Her eyes were like hard, dark beads. The phone almost slipped from her palsied fingers.

"All right, Miss Elva," said the operator. "I'll send a man out today."

"Thank you, dear, thank you," Miss Keene said. "Will you call me when . . ."

Her voice stopped abruptly as a clicking sound started on the telephone.

"The line is busy," she announced.

The clicking stopped and she went on. "To repeat, will you let me know when you find out who this terrible person is?"

"Surely, Miss Elva, surely. And I'll have a man check your telephone this afternoon. You're at 127 Mill Lane, aren't you?"

"That's right, dear. You will see to it, won't you?"

"I promise faithfully, Miss Elva. First thing today."

"Thank you, dear," Miss Keene said, drawing in relieved breath.

There were no calls from the man all that morning, none that afternoon. Her tightness slowly began to loosen. She played a game of cribbage with Nurse Phillips and even managed a little laughter. It was comforting to know that the telephone company was working on it now. They'd soon catch that awful man and bring back her peace of mind.

But when two o'clock came, then three o'clock—and still no repairman at her house—Miss Keene began worrying again.

"What's the *matter* with that girl?" she said pettishly. "She promised me faithfully that a man would come this afternoon."

"He'll be here," Nurse Phillips said. "Be patient."

Four o'clock arrived and no man. Miss Keene would not play cribbage, read her book or listen to her radio. What had begun to loosen was tightening again, increasing minute by minute until five o'clock, when the telephone rang, her hand spurted out rigidly from the flaring sleeve of her bed jacket and clamped down like a claw on the receiver. *If the man speaks*, raced her mind, *if he speaks I'll scream until my heart stops*.

She pulled the receiver to her ear. "Hello?"

"Miss Elva, this is Miss Finch."

Her eyes closed and breath fluttered through her lips. "Yes?" she said.

"About those calls you say you've been receiving."

"Yes?" In her mind, Miss Finch's words cutting—"those calls you *say* you've been receiving."

"We sent a man out to trace them," continued Miss Finch. "I have his report here."

Miss Keene caught her breath. "Yes?"

"He couldn't find anything."

Elva Keene didn't speak. Her gray head lay motionless on the pillow, the receiver pressed to her ear.

"He says he traced the—the difficulty to a fallen wire on the edge of town."

"Fallen—wire?"

"Yes, Miss Elva." Miss Finch did not sound happy.

"You're telling me I didn't hear anything?"

Miss Finch's voice was firm. "There's no way anyone could have phoned you from that location," she said.

"I tell you a *man* called me!"

Miss Finch was silent and Miss Keene's fingers tightened convulsively on the receiver.

"There must be a phone there," she insisted. "There must be *some* way that man was able to call me!"

"Miss Elva, there's no one out there."

"Out where, *where?*"

The operator said, "Miss Elva, it's the cemetery."

In the black silence of her bedroom, a crippled maiden lady lay waiting. Her nurse would not remain for the night; her nurse had patted her and scolded her and ignored her.

She was waiting for a telephone call.

She could have disconnected the phone, but she had not the will. She lay there waiting, waiting, thinking.

Of the silence—of ears that had not heard, seeking to hear again. Of sounds bubbling and muttering—the first stumbling attempts at speech by one who had not spoken—how long? Of—*hello? Hello?*—first greeting by one long silent. Of—*where are you?* Of (that which made her lie so rigidly) the clicking and the operator speaking her address. Of—

The telephone ringing.

A pause. Ringing. The rustle of a nightgown in the dark.

The ringing stopped.

Listening.

And the telephone slipping from white fingers, the eyes staring, the thin heartbeats slowly pulsing.

Outside, the cricket-rattling night.

Inside, the words still sounding in her brain—giving terrible meaning to the heavy, choking silence.

"Hello, Miss Elva. I'll be right over."

DEUS EX MACHINA

It began when he cut himself with a razor.

Until then, Robert Carter was typical. He was thirty-four, an accountant with a railroad firm. He lived in Brooklyn with his wife, Helen, and their two daughters, Mary, ten, and Ruth. Ruth was five and not tall enough to reach the bathroom sink. A box for her to stand on was kept under the sink. Robert Carter shifted his feet as he leaned in toward the mirror to shave his throat, stumbled on the box and fell. As he did, his arms flailed out for balance, his grip clamping on the straight razor. He grunted as his knee banged on the tile floor. His forehead hit the sink. And his throat was driven against the hair-thin edge of the razor.

He lay sprawled and gasping on the floor. Out in the hall, he heard running feet.

"*Daddy*?" asked Mary.

He said nothing because he was staring at his reflection, at the wound on his throat. Vision seemed composed of overlays. In one, he saw blood running. In the other—

"Daddy?" Her voice grew urgent.

"I'm all right," he said. The overlays had parted now. Carter heard his daughter walk back to the bedroom as he watched the reddish-brown oil pulse from his neck and spatter on the floor.

Suddenly, with a convulsive shudder, he pulled a towel off its rack and pressed it to the wound. There was no pain. He drew the towel away, and in the moment before bubbling oil obscured the wound again, he saw red-cased wires as thin as threads.

Robert Carter staggered back, eyes round with shock. Reaction made him jerk away the towel again. Wires still, and metal.

Robert Carter looked around the bathroom dazedly. The details of reality crowded him in—the sink, the mirror-faced cabinet, the wooden bowl of shaving soap, its edge still frothed, the brush dripping snowy lather, the bottle of green lotion. All real.

Tight-faced, he wrapped the wound with jerking motions and pushed to his feet.

The face he saw in the mirror looked the same. He leaned in close, searching for some sign of difference. He prodded at the sponginess of his cheeks, ran a forefinger along the length of his jawbone. He pressed at the softness of this throat caked with drying lather. Nothing was different.

Nothing?

He twisted away from the mirror and stared at the wall through a blur of tears. Tears? He touched the corner of an eye.

It was a drop of oil on his finger.

Reaction hit him violently. He began to shake without control. Downstairs, he could hear Helen moving in the kitchen. In their room, he could hear the girls talking as they dressed. It was like any other morning—all of them preparing for another day. Yet it wasn't just another day. The night before he'd been a businessman, a father, husband, man. This morning—

"Bob?"

He twitched as Helen called up from the foot of the stairs. His lips moved as though he were about to answer her.

"Almost seven-fifteen," she said, and he heard her start back for the kitchen. "Hurry up, Mary!" she called before the kitchen door swung shut behind her.

It was then that Robert Carter had his premonition. Abruptly, he was on his knees, mopping at the oil with another towel. He wiped until the floor was spotless. He cleaned off the smeared razor blade. Then he opened the hamper and pushed the towel to the bottom of the clothes pile.

He jumped as they banged against the door.

"Daddy, I have to get in!" they said.

"Wait a second," he heard himself reply. He looked into the mirror. Lather. He wiped it off. There was still the bluish-dark beard on his face. *Or was it wire?*

"Daddy, I'm *late*," said Mary.

"All right." His voice was very calm as he drew the neck of his robe over the cut on his throat, flattening the makeshift bandage so it wouldn't be seen. He drew in a deep breath—could it be called breath?—and opened the door.

"I have to wash first," said Mary, pushing to the sink. "I have to go to school."

Ruth pouted. "Well, I have a lot of work to do," she said.

"That's enough," he told them. The words were leftovers from the yesterdays when he was their human father. "Behave," he said.

"Well, I have to wash first," Mary said, twisting the HOT faucet.

Carter stood looking at his children.

"What's that, Daddy?" asked Ruth.

He twitched in surprise. She was looking at the drops of oil on the side of the bathtub. He'd missed them.

"I cut myself," he said. If he wiped them away fast enough they couldn't see that they weren't drops of blood. He mopped at them with a piece of tissue paper and dropped it into the toilet, flushing it away.

"Is it a bad cut?" asked Mary, soaping her cheeks.

"No," he said. He couldn't bear to look at them. He walked quickly into the hall.

"Bob, breakfast!"

"All right," he mumbled.

"*Bob*?"

"I'll be right down," he said.

Helen, Helen . . .

Robert Carter stood in front of the bedroom mirror looking at his body, a host of impenetrables rushing over him. Tonsils out, appendix out, dental work, vaccination, injections, blood tests, x-rays. The entire background against which he had acted out his seemingly mortal drama—a background of blood, tissue, muscles, glands and hormones, arteries, veins—

No answer. He dressed with quick, erratic motions, trying not to think. He took off the towel and placed a large Band-aid against the wound on his throat.

"Bob, come *on*!" she called.

He finished knotting his tie as he had knotted it thousands of times before. He was dressed now. He looked like a man. He stared at his reflection in the mirror and saw how exactly he looked like a man.

Bracing himself, he turned and went into the hall. He descended the stairs and walked across the dining room. He'd made up his mind. He wasn't going to tell her.

"There you are," she said. She looked him over. "Where did you cut yourself?"

"What?"

"The girls said you cut yourself. Where?"

"On my neck. It's fine now."

"Well, let me see."

"It's all right, Helen."

She peered at his neck, where the bandage was slightly visible above his shirt collar.

"It's still bleeding," she said.

Carter jolted. He reached up to touch his wound. The Bandaid was stained with a spot of oil. He looked back at Helen, startled. A second premonition came. He had to leave, *now*.

He left the kitchen and got his suit coat from the closet by the front door.

She'd seen blood.

His shoes made a fast, clicking sound on the sidewalk as he fled his house. It was a cold morning, gray and overcast. It was probably going to rain in a while. He shivered. He felt chilly. It was absurd now that he knew what he was; but he felt chilly.

She'd seen blood. Somehow, that terrified him even more than knowing what he was. That it was oil staining the bandage was painfully obvious. Blood didn't look like that, didn't smell like that. Yet she'd seen blood. *Why?*

Hatless, blond hair ruffling slightly in the breeze, Robert Carter walked along the street, trying to think. He was a robot; there was that to begin with. If there ever had been a human Robert Carter, he was now replaced. But why? *Why?*

He moved down the subway steps, lost in thought. People milled about him. People with explicable lives, people who knew that they were flesh and blood and did not have to think about it.

On the subway platform, he passed a newsstand and saw the headlines in a morning paper: THREE DIE IN HEAD-ON CRASH. There was a photograph—mangled automobiles, inert, partly covered bodies on a dark highway. Streams of blood. Carter thought, with a shudder, of himself lying in the photograph, a stream of oil running from his body.

He stood at the edge of the platform staring at the tracks. Was it possible that his human self *had* been replaced by a robot? Who would go to such trouble? And, having gone to it, who would allow it to be so easily discovered? A cut, a nick, a nosebleed even, and the fraud was revealed. Unless that blow on his head had jarred something loose. Maybe if he had cut himself without that blow, he would have seen only blood and tissue.

As he thought, unconsciously he took a penny from his trouser pocket and slipped it into a gum machine. He pulled at the knob and the gum thumped down. He had it half unwrapped before it struck him. Chew gum now? He grimaced, visualizing a turn of gears in his head, levers attached to curved bars attached to artificial teeth; all moving in response to a synaptic impulse.

He shoved the gum into his pocket. The station was trembling with the approach of a train. Carter's eyes turned to the left. Far in the distance, he saw the red and green eyes of the Manhattan express. He turned back front. Replaced when? Last night, the night before, last year? No, it was impossible to believe.

The train rushed by him with a blur of windows and doors. He felt the warmish, stale wind rush over him. He could smell it. His eyes blinked to avoid the swirl of dust. All this in seconds. As a machine, his reactions were so close to being human that it was incredible.

The train screeched to a halt in front of him. He moved over and entered the car with the pushing crowd. He stood by a pole, his left hand gripping it for balance. The doors slid shut again, the train rolled forward. Where was he going? he wondered suddenly. Surely not to work. Where then? To think, he told himself. He had to think.

That was when he found himself staring at a man standing near him.

The man had a bandage on his left hand and the bandage was stained with oil.

That sense of being frozen again—of his brain petrified by shock, his body still and numbed.

He wasn't the only one.

The neon sign above the door read EMERGENCY. Robert Carter's hand shook as he reached for the handle and pulled open the door.

It took no more than a moment to find out. There had been a traffic accident—a man driving to work, a flat tire, a truck. Robert Carter stood in the hallway staring in at the man on the table. He was being bandaged. There was a deep cut over his eye and oil was running down his cheek and dripping onto his suit.

"You'll have to go in the waiting room."

"What?" Carter started at the sound of the nurse's voice.

"I say you'll have to—"

She stopped as he turned away suddenly and pushed out into the April morning.

Carter walked along the sidewalk slowly, barely able to hear the sounds of the city.

There were other robots then—God only knew how many. They walked among men and were never known. Even if they were hurt they weren't known. That was the insane part. That man had been covered with oil. Yet no one had noticed it except him.

Robert Carter stopped. He felt so heavy. He had to sit down and rest a while.

The bar had only one customer, a man sitting at the far end of the counter, drinking beer and reading a newspaper. Carter pushed onto a leather stool and hooked his feet tiredly around its legs. He sat there, shoulders slumped, staring at the counter's dark, glossy wood.

Pain, confusion, dread and apprehension mixed and writhed in him. Was there a solution? Or was he just to wander like this, hopeless? Already it seemed a month since he'd left his house. But then it wasn't his house anymore.

Or was it? He sat up slowly. If there were others like him, could Helen and the girls be among that number? The idea repelled and appealed at once. He wanted them back desperately—yet how could he feel the same toward them if he knew that they, too, were wire and metal and electric current? How could he tell them about it since, if they were robots, they obviously didn't know it?

His left hand thumped down heavily on the bar. God, he was so tired. If only he could rest.

The bartender came out of the back room. "What'll it be?" he asked.

"Scotch on the rocks," said Robert Carter automatically.

Sitting alone and quiet as the bartender made the drink, it came to him. *How could he drink?* Liquid would rust metal, short out circuits. Carter sat there, tightening fearfully, watching the bartender pour. A wave of terror broke across him as the bartender came back and put the glass on the counter.

No, this wouldn't rust him. Not this.

Robert Carter shuddered and stared down into the glass while the bartender walked off to make change for a five-dollar bill. *Oil.* He felt like screaming. A glass of oil.

"*Oh, my God . . .*" Carter slipped off the stool and stumbled for the door.

Outside, the street seemed to move about him. What's happening to me? he thought. He leaned weakly against a plate-glass window, blinking dizzily.

His eyes focused. Inside the cafeteria, a man and woman were sitting, eating. Robert Carter gaped at them.

Plates of grease. Cups of oil.

People walked around him, making him an island in their swirling midst. How many of them? he thought. Dear God, *how many of them*?

What about agriculture? What about grain fields, vegetable patches, fruit orchards? What about beef and lamb and pork?

What about processing, canning, baking? No, he had to go back, to retrench, to recapture simple possibility. He'd struck his head and was losing contact with reality. Things were still as they had always been. It was him.

Robert Carter began to smell the city.

It was a smell of hot oils and machinery turning, the smell of a great, unseen factory. His head snapped around, his face a mask of terror. Dear God, *how many*? He tried to run but couldn't. He could hardly move at all.

Robert Carter cried out.

He was running down.

He moved across the hotel lobby very slowly, with a halting, mechanical motion.

"Room," he said.

The clerk eyed him suspiciously, this man with the ruffled hair, the strangely haunted look in his eyes. He was given a pen to sign the register.

Robert Carter, he wrote very slowly, as if he had forgotten how to spell it.

In the room, Carter locked the door and slumped down on the bed. He sat, staring at his hands. Running down like a clock. A clock that never knew its builder nor its fate.

One last possibility—wild, fantastic, yet all he could manage now.

Earth was being taken over, each person replaced by mechanical duplicates. Doctors would be first, undertakers, policemen, anyone who would come in contact with exposed bodies. And they would be conditioned to see nothing. He, as an accountant, would be high on the list. He was part of the basic commerce system. He was—

Robert Carter closed his eyes. How stupid, he thought. How stupid and impossible.

It took him minutes just to stand. Lethargically, he took out an envelope and a piece of paper from a desk drawer. For a moment his eye was caught by the Gideon Bible in the drawer. Written by robots? he thought. The idea repelled him. No, there must have been humans *then*. This had to be a contemporary horror.

He drew out his fountain pen and tried to write a letter to Helen. As he fumbled, he reached into his pocket for the gum. It was a habit. Just as he was going to put it in his mouth, he became conscious of it. It wasn't gum. It was a piece of solid grease.

It fell from his hand. The pen slipped from his failing grip and dropped to the rug, and he knew he wouldn't have the strength to pick it up again.

The gum. The drink in the bar. The food in the cafeteria. His eyes raised, impelled.

And what was beginning to rain down from the sky?

The truth crushed down on him.

Just before he fell, his staring gaze was fastened to the Bible once again. *And God said let us make man in our image,* he thought.

Then the darkness came.

ONE FOR THE BOOKS

When he woke up that morning, he could talk French.

There was no warning. At six-fifteen, the alarm went off as usual and he and his wife stirred. Fred reached out a sleep-deadened hand and shut off the bell. The room was still for a moment.

Then Eva pushed back the covers on her side and he pushed back the covers on his side. His vein-gnarled legs dropped over the side of the bed. He said, "*Bon matin*, Eva."

There was a slight pause.

"Wha'?" she asked.

"*Je dis bon matin*," he said.

There was a rustle of nightgown as she twisted around to squint at him. "*What'd* you say?"

"All I said was good—"

Fred Elderman stared back at his wife.

"What *did* I say?" he asked in a whisper.

"You said '*bone matinn*' or—"

"*Je dis bon matin. C'est un bon matin, n'est-ce pas?*"

The sound of his hand being clapped across his mouth was like that of a fast ball thumping in a catcher's mitt. Above the knuckle-ridged gag, his eyes were shocked.

"Fred, what *is* it?"

Slowly, the hand drew down from his lips.

"I dunno, Eva," he said, awed. Unconsciously, the hand reached up, one finger of it rubbing at his hair-ringed bald spot. "It sounds like some—some kind of foreign talk."

"But you don't know no foreign talk, Fred," she told him.

"That's just it."

They sat there looking at each other blankly. Fred glanced over at the clock.

"We better get dressed," he said.

While he was in the bathroom, she heard him singing, "*Elle fit un fromage, du lait de ses moutons, ron, ron, du lait de ses moutons,*" but she didn't dare call it to his attention while he was shaving.

Over breakfast coffee, he muttered something.

"What?" she asked before she could stop herself.

"*Je dis que veut dire ceci?*"

He heard the coffee go down her gulping throat.

"I mean," he said, looking dazed, "what does this mean?"

"Yes, what *does* it? You never talked no foreign language before."

"I *know* it," he said, toast suspended halfway to his open mouth. "What—what kind of language is it?"

"S-sounds t'me like French."

"*French?* I don't know no French."

She swallowed more coffee. "You do now," she said weakly.

He stared at the tablecloth.

"*Le diable s'en méle,*" he muttered.

Her voice rose. "Fred, *what?*"

His eyes were confused. "I said the devil has something to do with it."

"Fred, you're—"

She straightened up in the chair and took a deep breath. "Now," she said, "let's not profane, Fred. There has to be a good reason for this." No reply. "Well, *doesn't* there, Fred?"

"Sure, Eva. *Sure.* But—"

"No buts about it," she declared, plunging ahead as if she were afraid to stop. "Now is there any reason in this world why you should know how to talk French"—she snapped her thin fingers—"just like that?"

He shook his head vaguely.

"Well," she went on, wondering what to say next, "let's see then." They looked at each other in silence. "Say something," she decided. "Let's—" She groped for words. "Let's see what we . . . have here." Her voice died off.

"Say somethin'?"

"Yes," she said. "Go on."

"*Un gémissement se fit entendre. Les dogues se mettent à aboyer. Ces gants me vont bien. Il va sur les quinze ans—*"

"Fred?"

"*Il fit fabriquer une exacte représentation du monstre.*"

"Fred, hold on!" she cried, looking scared.

His voice broke off and he looked at her, blinking.

"What . . . what did you say this time, Fred?" she asked.

"I said—a moan was heard. His mastiffs began to bark. These gloves fit me. He will soon be fifteen years old and—"

"What?"

"And he had an exact copy of the monster made. *Sans même l'entamer.*"

"*Fred?*"

He looked ill. "Without even scratchin'," he said.

At that hour of the morning, the campus was quiet. The only classes that early were the two seven-thirty Economics lectures and they were held on the White Campus. Here on the Red there was no sound. In an hour the walks would be filled with chatting, laughing, loafer-clicking student hordes, but for now there was peace.

In far less than peace, Fred Elderman shuffled along the east side of the campus, headed for the administration building. Having left a confused Eva at home, he'd been trying to figure it out as he went to work.

What was it? When had it begun? *C'est une heure*, said his mind.

He shook his head angrily. This was terrible. He tried desperately to think of what could have happened, but he couldn't. It just didn't make sense. He was fifty-nine, a janitor at the university with no education to speak of, living a quiet, ordinary life. Then he woke up one morning speaking articulate French.

French.

He stopped a moment and stood in the frosty October wind, staring at the cupola of Jeramy Hall. He'd cleaned out the French office the night before. Could that have anything to do with—

No, that was ridiculous. He started off again, muttering under his breath—unconsciously. *"Je suis, tu es, il est, elle est, nous sommes, vous êtes—"*

At eight-ten, he entered the History Department office to repair a sink in the washroom. He worked on it for an hour and seven minutes, then put the tools back in the bag and walked out into the office.

"Mornin'," he said to the professor sitting at a desk.

"Good morning, Fred," said the professor.

Fred Elderman walked out into the hall thinking how remarkable it was that the income of Louis XVI, from the same type of taxes, exceeded that of Louis XV by 130 million livres and that the exports which had been 106 million in 1720 were 192 million in 1745 and—

He stopped in the hall, a stunned look on his lean face.

That morning, he had occasion to be in the offices of the Physics, the Chemistry, the English and the Art Departments.

The Windmill was a little tavern near Main Street. Fred went there Monday, Wednesday and Friday evenings to nurse a couple of draught beers and chat with his two friends—Harry Bullard, manager of Hogan's Bowling Alley, and Lou Peacock, postal worker and amateur gardener.

Stepping into the doorway of the dim-lit saloon that evening, Fred was heard—by an exiting patron—to murmur, *"Je connais tous ces braves gens,"* then look around with a guilty twitch of cheek. "I mean . . ." he muttered, but didn't finish.

Harry Bullard saw him first in the mirror. Twisting his head around on its fat column of neck, he said, "C'mon in, Fred, the whiskey's fine," then, to the bartender, "Draw one for the elder man," and chuckled.

Fred walked to the bar with the first smile he'd managed to summon that day. Peacock and Bullard greeted him and the bartender set down a brimming stein.

"What's new, Fred?" Harry asked.

Fred pressed his mustache between two foam-removing fingers.

"Not much," he said, still too uncertain to discuss it. Dinner with Eva had been a painful meal during which he'd eaten not only food but an endless and detailed running commentary on the Thirty Years War, the Magna Charta and boudoir information about Catherine the Great. He had been glad to retire from the house at seven-thirty, murmuring an unmanageable, "*Bon nuit, ma chère.*"

"What's new with you?" he asked Harry Bullard now.

"Well," Harry answered, "we been paintin' down at the alleys. You know, redecoratin'."

"That right?" Fred said. "When painting with colored beeswax was inconvenient, Greek and Roman easel painters used *tempera*—that is, colors fixed upon a wood or stucco base by means of such a medium as—"

He stopped. There was a bulging silence.

"Hanh?" Harry Bullard asked.

Fred swallowed nervously. "Nothing," he said hastily. "I was just—" He stared down into the tan depths of his beer. "Nothing," he repeated.

Bullard glanced at Peacock, who shrugged back.

"How are your hothouse flowers coming, Lou?" Fred inquired, to change the subject.

The small man nodded. "Fine. They're just fine."

"Good," said Fred, nodding, too. "*Vi sono pui di cinquante bastimenti in porto.*" He gritted his teeth and closed his eyes.

"What's that?" Lou asked, cupping one ear.

Fred coughed on his hastily swallowed beer. "Nothing," he said.

"No, what did ya say?" Harry persisted, the half-smile on his broad face indicating that he was ready to hear a good joke.

"I—I said there are more than fifty ships in the harbor," explained Fred morosely.

The smile faded. Harry looked blank.

"What harbor?" he asked.

Fred tried to sound casual. "I—it's just a joke I heard today. But I forgot the last line."

"Oh." Harry stared at Fred, then returned to his drink. "Yeah."

They were quiet a moment. Then Lou asked Fred, "Through for the day?"

"No. I have to clean up the Math office later."

Lou nodded. "That's too bad."

Fred squeezed more foam from his mustache. "Tell me something," he said, taking the plunge impulsively. "What would you think if you woke up one morning talking French?"

"Who did that?" asked Harry, squinting.

"Nobody," Fred said hurriedly. "Just . . . *supposing*, I mean. Supposing a man was to—well, to *know* things he never learned. You know what I mean? Just *know* them. As if they were always in his mind and he was seeing them for the first time."

"What kind o' things, Fred?" asked Lou.

"Oh . . . history. Different . . . languages. Things about . . . books and painting and . . . and atoms and—chemicals." His shrug was jerky and obvious. "Things like that."

"Don't get ya, buddy," Harry said, having given up any hopes that a joke was forthcoming.

"You mean he knows things he never learned?" Lou asked. "That it?"

There was something in both their voices—a doubting incredulity, a holding back, as if they feared to commit themselves, a suspicious reticence.

Fred sloughed it off. "I was just supposing. Forget it. It's not worth talking about."

He had only one beer that night, leaving early with the excuse that he had to clean the Mathematics office. And, all through the silent minutes that he swept and mopped and dusted, he kept trying to figure out what was happening to him.

He walked home in the chill of night to find Eva waiting for him in the kitchen.

"Coffee, Fred?" she offered.

"I'd like that," he said, nodding. She started to get up. "No, *s'accomadi, la prego*," he blurted.

She looked at him, grim-faced.

"I mean," he translated, "sit down, Eva. I can get it."

They sat there drinking coffee while he told her about his experiences.

"It's more than I can figure, Eva," he said. "It's . . . scary, in a way. I know so many things I never knew. I have no idea where they come from. Not the least idea." His lips pressed together. "But I *know* them," he said, "I certainly know them."

"More than just . . . French now?" she asked.

He nodded his head worriedly. "Lots more," he said. "Like—" He looked up from his cup. "Listen to this. Main progress in producing fast particles has been made by using relatively small voltages and repeated acceleration. In most of the instruments used, charged particles are driven round in circular or spiral orbits with the help of a—you listenin', Eva?"

He saw her Adam's apple move. "I'm listenin'," she said.

"—help of a magnetic field. The acceleration can be applied in different ways. In the so-called betatron of Kerst and Serber—"

"What does it *mean*, Fred?" she interrupted.

"I don't know," he said helplessly. "It's . . . just words in my head. I know what it means when I say something in a foreign tongue, but . . . this?"

She shivered, clasping at her forearms abruptly.

"It's not right," she said.

He frowned at her in silence for a long moment.

"What do you mean, Eva?" he asked then.

"I don't know, Fred," she said quietly and shook her head once, slowly. "I just don't know."

She woke up about midnight and heard him mumbling in his sleep.

"The natural logarithms of whole numbers from ten to two hundred.

"Number one—*zero*—two point three oh two six. *One*—two point three nine seven nine. *Two*—two point—"

"Fred, go t' *sleep*," she said, frowning nervously.

"—four eight four nine."

She prodded him with an elbow. "Go t'sleep, Fred."

"*Three*—two point—"

"Fred!"

"Huh?" He moaned and swallowed dryly, turned on his side.

In the darkness, she heard him shape the pillow with sleep-heavy hands.

"Fred?" she called softly.

He coughed. "What?"

"I think you better go t'Doctor Boone t'morra mornin'.'"

She heard him draw in a long breath, then let it filter out evenly until it was all gone.

"I think so, too," he said in a blurry voice.

On Friday morning, when he opened the door to the waiting room of Doctor William Boone, a draft of wind scattered papers from the nurse's desk.

"Oh," he said apologetically. "*Le chieggo scuse. Non ne val la pena.*"

Miss Agnes McCarthy had been Doctor Boone's receptionist-nurse for seven years and in that time she'd never heard Fred Elderman speak a single foreign word.

Thus she goggled at him, amazed. "What's that you said?" she asked.

Fred's smile was a nervous twitch of lips.

"Nothing," he said, "Miss."

Her returned smile was formal. "Oh." She cleared her throat. "I'm sorry the doctor couldn't see you yesterday."

"That's all right," he told her.

"He'll be ready in about ten minutes."

Twenty minutes later, Fred sat down beside Boone's desk and the heavy-set doctor leaned back in his chair with an, "Ailing, Fred?"

Fred explained the situation.

The doctor's cordial smile became, in order, amused, fixed, strained and finally nonexistent.

"This is really so?" he demanded.

Fred nodded with grim deliberation. "*Je me laisse conseiller.*"

Doctor Boone's heavy eyebrows lifted a noticeable jot. "French," he said. "What'd you say?"

Fred swallowed. "I said I'm willing to be advised."

"Son of a gun," intoned Doctor Boone, plucking at his lower lip. "*Son* of a gun." He got up and ran exploring hands over Fred's skull. "You haven't received a head blow lately, have you?"

"No," said Fred. "Nothing."

"Hmmm." Doctor Boone drew away his hands and let them

drop to his sides. "Well, no apparent bumps or cracks." He buzzed for Miss McCarthy. Then he said, "Well, let's take a try at the x-rays."

The x-rays revealed no break or blot.

The two men sat in the office, discussing it.

"Hard to believe," said the doctor, shaking his head. Fred sighed despondently. "Well, don't take on so," Bonne said. "It's nothing to be disturbed about. So you're a quiz kid, so what?"

Fred ran nervous fingers over his mustache. "But there's no sense to it. Why is it happening? What is it? The fact is, I'm a little scared."

"Nonsense, Fred. *Nonsense.* You're in good physical condition. That I guarantee."

"But what about my—" Fred hesitated "—my brain?"

Doctor Boone stuck out his lower lip in consoling derision, shaking his head. "I wouldn't worry about that, either." He slapped one palm on the desk top. "Let me think about it, Fred. Consult a few associates. You know—*analyze* it. Then I'll let you know. Fair enough?"

He walked Fred to the door.

"In the meantime," he prescribed, "no worrying about it. There isn't a thing to worry about."

His face as he dialed the phone a few minutes later was not unworried, however.

"Fetlock?" he said, getting his party. "Got a poser for you."

Habit more than thirst brought Fred to the Windmill that evening. Eva had wanted him to stay home and rest, assuming that his state was due to overwork; but Fred had insisted that it wasn't his health and left the house, just managing to muffle his *"Au revoir."*

He joined Harry Bullard and Lou Peacock at the bar and finished his first beer in a glum silence while Harry revealed why they shouldn't vote for Legislator Milford Carpenter.

"Tell ya the man's got a private line t'Moscow," he said. "A few men like that in office and we're in for it, take my word." He looked over at Fred staring into his beer. "What's with it, elder man?" he asked, clapping Fred on the shoulder.

Fred told them—as if he were telling about a disease he'd caught.

Lou Peacock looked incredulous. "So that's what you were talking about the other night!"

Fred nodded.

"You're not kiddin' us now?" Harry asked. "Y'know *everything*?"

"Just about," Fred admitted sadly.

A shrewd look overcame Harry's face.

"What if I ask ya somethin' ya *don't* know?"

"I'd be happy," Fred said in a despairing voice.

Harry beamed. "Okay. I won't ask ya about atoms nor chemicals nor anythin' like that. I'll just ask ya t'tell me about the country between my home town Au Sable and Tarva." He hit the bar with a contented slap.

Fred looked hopeful briefly, but then his face blanked and he said in an unhappy voice, "Betweeen Au Sable and Tarva, the route is through typical cut-over land that once was covered with virgin pine (*danger: deer on the highway*) and now has only second-growth oak, pine and poplar. For years after the decline of the lumber industry, picking huckleberries was one of the chief local occupations."

Harry gaped.

"Because the berries were known to grow in the wake of fires," Fred concluded, "residents deliberately set many fires that roared through the country."

"That's a damn dirty lie!" Harry said, chin trembling belligerently.

Fred looked at him in surprise.

"You shouldn't ought t'go around tellin' lies like that," Harry said. "You call that knowin' the countryside—telling *lies* about it?"

"Take it easy, Harry," Lou cautioned.

"Well," Harry said angrily, "he shouldn't ought to tell lies like that."

"I didn't say it," Fred answered hopelessly. "It's more as though I—I *read it off*."

"Yeah? Well . . ." Harry fingered his glass restlessly.

"You really know *everything*?" Lou asked, partly to ease the tension, partly because he was awed.

"I'm afraid so," Fred replied.

"You ain't just . . . playin' a trick?"

Fred shook his head. "No trick."

Lou Peacock looked small and intense. "What can you tell me," he asked in a back-alley voice, "about orange roses?"

The blank look crossed Fred's face again. Then he recited, "Orange is not a fundamental color but a blend of red and pink of varied intensity and yellow. There were very few orange roses prior to the Pernatia strain. All orange, apricot, chamois and coral roses finish with pink more or less accentuated. Some attain that lovely shade—*Cuisse de Nymphe émue.*"

Lou Peacock was open-mouthed. "Ain't that something?"

Harry Bullard blew out heavy breath. "What d'ya know about Carpenter?" he asked pugnaciously.

"Carpenter, Milford, born 1898 in Chicago, Illi—"

"Never mind," Harry cut in. "I ain't interested. He's a Commie; that's all I gotta know about him."

"The elements that go into a political campaign," Fred quoted helplessly, "are many—the personality of the candidates, the issues—if any—the attitude of the press, economic groups, traditions, the opinion polls, the—"

"I tell ya he's a Commie!" Harry declared, voice rising.

"You voted for him last election," Lou said. "As I re—"

"I did *not!*" snarled Harry, getting redder in the face.

The blank look appeared on Fred Elderman's face. "Remembering things that are not so is a kind of memory distortion that goes by several names such as *pathological lying* or *mythomania.*"

"You callin' me a liar, Fred?"

"It differs from ordinary lying in that the speaker comes to believe his own lies and—"

"Where did you get that black eye?" a shocked Eva asked Fred when he came into the kitchen later. "Have you been fighting at *your* age?"

Then she saw the look on his face and ran for the refrigerator.

She sat him on a chair and held a piece of beefsteak against his swelling eye while he related what had happened.

"He's a bully," she said. "A bully!"

"No, I don't blame him," Fred disagreed. "I insulted him. I don't even know what I'm saying any more. I'm—I'm all mixed up."

She looked down at his slumped form, an alarmed expression on her face. "When is Doctor Boone going to do something for you?"

"I don't know."

A half hour later, against Eva's wishes, he went to clean up the library with a fellow janitor; but the moment he entered the huge room, he gasped, put his heads to his temples and fell down on one knee, gasping, "My head! My *head*!"

It took a long while of sitting quietly in the downstairs hallway before the pain in his skull stopped. He sat there staring fixedly at the glossy tile floor, his head feeling as if it had just gone twenty-nine rounds with the heavy-weight champion of the world.

Fetlock came in the morning. Arthur B., forty-two, short and stocky, head of the Department of Psychological Sciences, he came bustling along the path in porkpie hat and checkered overcoat, jumped up on the porch, stepped across its worn boards and stabbed at the bell button. While he waited, he clapped leather-gloved hands together energetically and blew out breath clouds.

"Yes?" Eva asked when she opened the door.

Professor Fetlock explained his mission, not noticing how her face tightened with fright when he announced his field. Reassured that Doctor Boone had sent him, she led Fetlock up the carpeted steps, explaining, "He's still in bed. He had an attack last night."

"Oh?" said Arthur Fetlock.

When introductions had been made and he was alone with the janitor, Professor Fetlock fired a rapid series of questions. Fred Elderman, propped up with pillows, answered them as well as he could.

"This attack," said Fetlock, "what happened?"

"Don't know, Professor. Walked in the library and—well, it was as if a ton of cement hit me on the head. No—*in* my head."

"Amazing. And this knowledge you say you've acquired—are you conscious of an *increase* in it since your ill-fated visit to the library?"

Fed nodded. "I know more than ever."

The professor bounced the fingertips of both hands against each other. "A book on language by Pei. Section 9-B in the library, book number 429.2, if memory serves. Can you quote from it?"

Fred looked blank, but words followed almost immediately. "Leibnitz first advanced the theory that all language came not from a historically recorded source but from proto-speech. In some respects he was a precursor of—"

"Good, good," said Arthur Fetlock. "Apparently a case of spontaneous telepathic manifestations coupled with clair-voyance."

"Meaning?"

"Telepathy, Elderman. Telepathy! Seems every book or educated mind you come across, you pick clean of content. You worked in the French office, you spoke French. You worked in the Mathematics office, you quoted numbers, tables, axioms. Similarly with all other offices, subjects and individuals." He scowled, purse-lipped. "Ah, but why?"

"*Causa qua re*," muttered Fred.

A brief wry sound in Professor Fetlock's throat. "Yes, I wish I knew, too. However . . ." He leaned forward. "What's that?"

"How come I can learn so much?" Fred asked worriedly. "I mean—"

"No difficulty there," stated the stocky psychologist. "You see, no man ever utilized the full learning capacity of the brain. It still has an immense potential. Perhaps that's what's happening to you—you're realizing this potential."

"But how?"

"Spontaneously realized telepathy and clairvoyance plus in-finite retention and unlimited potential." He whistled softly. "Amazing. Positively amazing. Well, I must be going."

"But what'll I do?" Fred begged.

"Why, enjoy it," said the professor expansively. "It's a perfectly fantastic gift. Now look—if I were to gather together a group of faculty members, would you be willing to speak to them? Informally, of course."

"But—"

"They should be entranced, positively entranced. I must do a paper for the *Journal*."

"But what does it mean, Professor?" Fred Elderman asked, his voice shaking.

"Oh, we'll look into it, never fear. Really, this is revolutionary. An unparalleled phenomenon." He made a sound of delighted disbelief. "In-credible."

When Professor Fetlock had gone, Fred sat defeatedly in his bed. So there was nothing to be done—nothing but spout endless, inexplicable words and wonder into the nights what terrible thing was happening to him. Maybe the professor was excited; maybe it was exciting intellectual fare for outsiders. For him it was only grim and increasingly frightening business.

Why? Why? It was the question he could neither answer nor escape.

He was thinking that when Eva came in. He lifted his gaze as she crossed the room and sat down on the bed.

"What did he say?" she asked anxiously.

When he told her, her reaction was the same as his.

"That's all? Enjoy it?" She pressed her lips together in anger. "What's the matter with him? Why did Doctor Boone send him?"

He shook his head, without an answer.

There was such a look of confused fear on his face that she reached out her hand suddenly and touched his cheek. "Does your head hurt, dear?"

"It hurts inside," he said. "In my . . ." There was a clicking in his throat. "If one considers the brain as a tissue which is only moderately compressible, surrounded by two variable factors—the blood it contains and the spinal fluid which surrounds it and fills the ventricles inside the brain we have—"

He broke off spasmodically and sat there, quivering.

"God help us," she whispered.

"As Sextus Empiricus says in his *Arguments Against Belief in a God*, those who affirm, positively, that God exists cannot avoid falling into an impiety. For—"

"Fred, stop it!"

He sat looking at her dazedly.

"Fred, you don't . . . know what you're saying. Do you?"

"No. I never do. I just—Eva, what's going on!"

She held his hand tightly and stroked it. "It's all right, Fred. Please don't worry so."

But he did worry. For behind the complex knowledge that filled his mind, he was still the same man, simple, uncomprehending—and afraid.

Why was it happening?

It was as if, in some hideous way, he were a sponge filling more and more with knowledge and there would come a time when there was no room left and the sponge would explode.

Professor Fetlock stopped him in the hallway Monday morning. "Elderman, I've spoken to the members of the faculty and they're all as excited as I. Would this afternoon be too soon? I can get you excused from any work you may be required to do."

Fred looked bleakly at the professor's enthusiastic face. "It's all right."

"Splendid! Shall we say four-thirty then? My offices?"

"All right."

"And may I make a suggestion?" asked the professor. "I'd like you to tour the university—all of it."

When they separated, Fred went back down to the basement to put away his tools.

At four twenty-five, he pushed open the heavy door to the Department of Psychological Sciences. He stood there, waiting patiently, one hand on the knob, until someone in the large group of faculty members saw him. Professor Fetlock disengaged himself from the group and hurried over.

"Elderman," he said, "come in, come in."

"Professor, has Doctor Boone said anything more?" Fred insisted. "I mean about—"

"No, nothing. Never fear, we'll get to it. But come along. I want you to—Ladies and gentlemen, your attention, please!"

Fred was introduced to them, standing in their midst, trying to look at ease when his heart and nerves were pulsing with a nervous dread.

"And did you follow my suggestion," Fetlock asked loudly, "and tour all the departments in the university?"

"Yes . . . sir."

"Good, good." Professor Fetlock nodded emphatically. "That should complete the picture then. Imagine it, ladies and gentlemen—the sum total of knowledge in our entire university—all in the head of this one man!"

There were sounds of doubt from the faculty.

"No, no, I'm serious!" claimed Fetlock. "The proof of the pudding is quite ample. Ask away!"

Fred Elderman stood there in the momentary silence, thinking of what Professor Fetlock had said. The knowledge of an entire university in his head. That meant there was no more to be gotten here then.

What now?

Then the questions came—and the answers, dead-voiced and monotonous.

"What will happen to the sun in fifteen million years?"

"If the sun goes on radiating at its present rate for fifteen million years, its whole weight will be transformed into radiation."

"What is a root tone?"

"In harmonic units, the constituent tones seem to have unequal harmonic values. Some seem to be more important and dominate the sounding unity. These roots are—"

All the knowledge of an entire university in his head.

"The five orders of Roman architecture."

"Tuscan, Doric, Corinthian, Ionic, Composite. Tuscan being a simplified Doric, Doric retaining the triglyphs, Corinthian characterized by—"

No more knowledge there he didn't possess. His brain crammed with it. Why?

"Buffer capacity?"

"The buffer capacity of a solution may be defined as dx/dpH where dx is the small amount of strong acid or—"

Why?

"A moment ago. French."

"*Il n'y a qu'un instant.*"

Endless questions, increasingly excited until they were almost being shouted.

"What is literature involved with?"

"Literature is, of nature, involved with ideas because it deals with Man in society, which is to say that it deals with formulations, valuations and—"

Why?

"Rule for masthead lights on steam vessels?" A laugh.

"A steam vessel when under way shall carry (a) on or in front of the foremast or, if a vessel without a foremast, then in the forepart of the vessel, a bright, white light so constructed as to—"

No laughter. Questions.

"How would a three-stage rocket take off?"

"The three-stage rocket would take off vertically and be given a slight tilt in an easterly direction, Brennschluss taking place about—"

"Who was Count Bernadotte?"

"What are the by-products of oil?"

"Which city is—?"

"How can—?"

"What is—?"

"When did—?"

And when it was over and he had answered every question they asked, there was a great, heavy silence. He stood trembling and yet numb, beginning to get a final knowledge.

The phone rang then and made everyone start.

Professor Fetlock answered it. "For you, Elderman."

Fred walked over to the phone and picked up the receiver.

"Fred?" he heard Eva say.

"*Oui.*"

"What?"

He twitched. "I'm sorry, Eva. I mean yes, it's me."

He heard her swallowing on the other end of the line. "Fred, I . . . just wondered why you didn't come home, so I called your office and Charlie said—"

He told her about the meeting.

"Oh," she said. "Well, will you be—home for supper?"

The last knowledge was seeping, rising slowly.

"I'll try, Eva. I think so, yes."

"I been worried, Fred."

He smiled sadly. "Nothing to worry about, Eva."

Then the message sliced abruptly across his mind and he said, "Goodbye, Eva," and dropped the receiver. "I have to go," he told Fetlock and the others.

He didn't exactly hear what they said in return. The words, the transition from room to hall were blurred over by his sudden, concentrated need to get out on the campus.

The questioning faces were gone and he was hurrying down the hall on driven feet, his action as his speech had been— unmotivated, beyond understanding. Something drew him on. He had spoken without knowing why; now he rushed down the long hallway without knowing why.

He rushed across the lobby, gasping for breath. The message said, *Come. It's time.* These things, these many things—who would want to know them? These endless facts about all earthly knowledge.

Earthly knowledge . . .

As he came half tripping, half running down the building steps into the early darkness, he saw the flickering bluish-white light in the sky. It was aiming over the trees, the buildings, straight at him.

He stood petrified, staring at it, and knew exactly why he had acquired all the knowledge he had.

The blue-white light bore directly at him with a piercing, whining hum. Across the dark campus, a young girl screamed.

Life on the other planets, the last words crossed his mind, *is not only possibility but high probability.*

Then the light hit him and bounced straight back up to its source, like lightning streaking in reverse from lightning rod to storm cloud, leaving him in awful blackness.

They found the old man wandering across the campus grass like a somnambulant mute. They spoke to him, but his tongue was still. Finally, they were obliged to look in his wallet, where they found his name and address and took him home.

A year later, after learning to talk all over again, he said his first stumbling words. He said them one night to his wife when she found him in the bathroom holding a sponge in his hand.

"Fred, what are you doing?"

"*I been squeezed,*" he said.

NOW DIE IN IT

They were in the kitchen when the phone rang. Don was whipping cream. He stopped turning the rotary beater and looked over at his wife.

"Get it, will you, honey?" he asked.

"All right."

Betty walked into the dining room, drying her hands. She stopped by the phone table. "Don't make it into butter now," she called back.

"Aye, aye, sir."

Smiling a little, she picked up the receiver and pushed back her reddish-blonde hair with the earpiece.

"Hello," she said.

"Don Tyler there?" a man's voice asked.

"No," she said, "You must have the wrong number."

The man laughed unpleasantly. "No, I guess not," he said.

"What number are you calling?" Betty asked.

The man coughed loudly and Betty pulled the receiver away from her ear with a grimace.

"Listen," the man said, hoarsely, "I wanna talk to Don Tyler."

"I'm sorry but—"

"You married to him?" interrupted the man.

"Look here, if you—"

"I said I wanna talk t' Don." The man's voice rose in pitch and Betty heard a distinct break in it.

"Hold the line," she said, dumping the receiver unceremoniously on the table. She went back into the kitchen.

"Man says he wants Don," she said. "Don *Tyler* though."

"Oh?" Don grunted and started for the dining room. "Who is it?" he asked over his shoulder.

"I don't know," Betty said, starting to put cream on the chocolate pudding.

In the dining room she heard Don pick up the receiver and say hello. There was a moment's silence. She smoothed the cream over the surface of the glossy pudding.

"*What*!" Don's sudden cry made her start. She put down the cream bowl and went to the doorway. She looked at Don standing in the half-dark dining room, his face in a patch of light from the living-room lamp. His face was taut.

"Listen," he was saying. "I don't know what this is all about but—"

The man must have interrupted him. Betty saw Don's mouth twitch as he listened. His shoulders twisted.

"You're *crazy*!" he said suddenly, frowning. "I've never even *been* in Chicago!"

From where she stood, Betty could hear the angry sound of the man's voice over the phone. She moved into the dining room.

"Look," Don was explaining. "Look, get this straight, will you? My name is Martin, not Tyler. What are you—*listen*, I'm trying to tell you—"

The man cut him off again. Don drew in a ragged breath and gritted his teeth.

"*Look*," he said, sounding half-frightened now. "If this is a joke, I—"

Betty saw him wince as the phone clicked. He looked at the receiver incredulously, then put it down in its cradle and stared at it, his mouth slightly open.

"Don, what *is* it?"

He jumped at the sound of her voice. He turned and looked at her as she walked over and stood in front of him.

"Don?"

"I don't know," he muttered.

"Who *was* it?"

"I don't *know*, Betty," he said, his voice on edge.

"Well . . . what did he want?"

His face was blank as he answered her.

"He said he was going to kill me."

She picked up the towel with shaking fingers. "He said *what*?"

He looked at her without answering and their eyes held for a long, silent moment. Then he repeated it in a flat voice.

"But why, Don? *Why*?"

He shook his head slowly and swallowed.

"Do you think it's a joke?" she asked.

"He didn't sound like he was joking."

In the kitchen the clock buzzed once for eight-thirty. "We'd better call the police," Betty said.

He drew in a shaky breath.

"I guess so," he said, his voice worried and uncertain.

"Maybe it was one of the men from your office," she said, "You know they're always—"

She saw from the bleak expression on his face that she was wrong. She stood there restively, clutching the towel with numbed fingers. It seemed as if all the sounds in the house had stopped, as if everything were waiting.

"We'd better call the police," she said, her voice rising a little.

"Yes," he said.

"Well, *call* them," she said, nervously.

He seemed to snap out of it. He patted her on the shoulder and managed a thin smile.

"All right," he said. "Clear up the dishes. I'll call them."

At the kitchen door she turned back to face him. "You were never in Chicago, were you?" she asked.

"Of course not."

"I thought maybe you were there during the war."

"I was never there," he said.

She swallowed. "Well, be sure to tell them it's a mistake," she said. "Tell them the man asked for Tyler and your name is Martin. Don't forget to—"

"All right, Betty, all *right*."

"Sorry," she murmured and went back into the kitchen.

She heard his low voice in the dining room, then the receiver being put down. Footsteps; he came back into the kitchen.

"What did they say?" she asked.

"They said it was probably some crank."

"They're coming over though, aren't they?"

"Probably."

"Probably! Don, for God's sake—!" Her voice broke off in frightened exasperation.

"They'll come," he said then.

"That man said he was going to—"

"They'll *come*," he interrupted, almost angrily.

"I should hope so."

In the silence, he pulled down a towel from the rack and started drying glasses. She kept washing the dishes, rinsing them and standing them in the rack to dry.

"Do you want any pudding?" she asked.

He shook his head. She put the pudding bowl into the refrigerator, then turned, her hand still on the door handle and looked at him.

"Haven't you any idea who it might be?"

"I *said* I didn't," he answered.

Her mouth tightened. "Don't wake up Billy," she said, quietly.

He turned to face the cabinet and put glasses on the shelf.

"I'm sorry," he said. "I'm nervous. It isn't everyday that—" He broke off and started drying the dishes, wooden-like.

"It'll be all right, sweetheart," she said. "As long as you say the police are coming."

"Yeah," he said, without conviction.

She went back to her work and the only sound in the kitchen was that of dishes, glass and silverware being handled. Outside, a cold November wind blew across the house.

She gasped as Don put down a glass so hard it cracked. "What *is* it?" she asked.

"I just thought," he said, "that he might have been calling from the corner drug store."

She dried her hands automatically. "What are we going to do?" she asked. "What if the police don't come in time?"

She followed as he ran into the dining room. He started turning off the living room lamps and she turned and ran back, her nervous fingers pushing down the wall switch in the kitchen. The fluorescent tube went out and she stood there trembling in the dark kitchen until she heard him come back in.

"Call the police again," she said in a low, guarded voice as if the man were already lurking nearby.

"It wouldn't do any good," he answered, "They—"

"Try."

"Christ, the upstairs light!" he said.

He ran out of the kitchen and she heard him jumping up the carpeted steps. She moved into the dining room, legs trembling. Upstairs she heard Don close the door to Billy's room quietly. She hurried for the stairs.

She was about to start up when, suddenly, she heard Don's footsteps cease.

Someone was ringing the front doorbell.

He came down the stairs.

"Is it him? Do you think it's him?" she asked.

"I don't know." He stood beside her without moving.

"What if Billy wakes up?"

"What?"

"He'll cry if he wakes up. You know how afraid he is of the dark."

"I'll see who it is," Don said.

He moved silently across the living room rug and she followed a few feet, then stopped. He stood against the wall and looked out through the window curtains. Rays of light from the street lamp fell across the brick porch.

"Can you see?" she asked as quietly as she could. "Is it him?"

He took a heavy, shaking breath in the darkness. "It's him."

She stood in the middle of the living room and it seemed as if all the heat in the house had suddenly disappeared. She shuddered.

The doorbell kept ringing.

"Maybe it's the police," she said nervously.

"No. It's not."

They stood there silently a moment and the buzzing stopped.

"What are we going to *do*?" she asked.

He didn't answer.

"If we opened the door, wouldn't he——?" She heard the sound he made and didn't finish. "Why should he make such a mistake with *you*? Why?"

His breath sucked in. "Damn it," he muttered.

"What?"

He was already moving for the front door—and her mind was seared by the sudden thought—*it isn't locked.*

She watched Don stoop and take off his shoes. He moved quietly into the front hall. She closed her eyes and listened tensely. Didn't the man hear that slight clicking as Don turned the lock? Her throat moved convulsively. How did Don know it wasn't a detective? Would a man intent on murder ring the doorbell of the man he intended to——

Then she saw a dark figure standing at the front windows trying to look in, and froze where she stood.

Don came back from the hall. "I think he——" he began to say.

"*Shhh!*"

He stiffened and, as if he knew, turned his head quickly toward the living room window. It was so still that Betty heard his dry swallow distinctively.

Then the shadow moved away from the window and Betty realized that she'd been holding her breath. She let it escape, her chest shuddering as she exhaled.

"I'd better get my gun," Don said in a husky voice.

She started then. "Your——?"

"I hope it works. I haven't cleaned it in a long time."

Don pushed by her. She heard him bounding up the stairs. She stood paralyzed.

Upstairs, she heard Billy crying.

She backed out of the kitchen and felt her way to the stairs, her eyes always on the kitchen, in her ears the sound of the man trying to get in the house to kill Don.

At the top of the stairs, Don came around the wall edge and almost collided with her.

"What are you *doing*?" he snapped.

"I heard Billy crying."

She heard something snap in the darkness and realized that he'd set the hammer of his army automatic.

"Didn't you tell the police that he said he was going to *kill* you?"

"I told them."

"Well, where are they, then?"

Her words choked off. The man was breaking through a back window.

She stood mute, listening to the fragments of window spatter on the kitchen linoleum.

"*What are we going to do?*" Her whisper shook in the darkness.

He pulled away from her grip and moved down the stairs without a sound. She heard his shoeless feet pad cross the dining room rug. In the kitchen the man was clambering through the window. She gripped the banister until her hand hurt.

There was a rush of sight and sounds.

The kitchen light flickered on. Don leaped from the wall and pointed the gun at something in the kitchen. "Drop it!" he ordered. The house was filled with the roar of a gun and something crashed in the front room.

Then Betty sank down on the steps in a nerveless crouch as Don's pistol only clicked and she saw it drop from his hand. Between the banister posts she saw him standing in the light that flooded from the kitchen.

The man in the kitchen laughed.

"Got you," he said. "I got you now."

"No!" She didn't even realize that she'd cried out. All she knew was that Don was staring up at her, his white face helpless in the kitchen light. The man looked up at her.

"Turn on the light," the man told Don. His throat seemed clogged; all the words came out thick and indistinct.

The dining room light went on. Betty stared at a man with lank, black hair, white face, an unkempt tweed suit with an egg-spotted vest buttoned to the top. The dark revolver he held in a claw of hand.

"Come down here," he told her.

She went down the steps. The man backed into the kitchen, kicking aside Don's gun.

"Get in here, both of you," he ordered.

In the fluorescent light, the man's pocked face looked even whiter and grimier. His lips kept drawing back from his teeth as he sniffed. He kept clearing his throat.

"Well, I got you," he repeated.

"You don't understand," Betty was able to speak at last. "You've made a mistake. Our name is Martin, not Tyler."

The man paid no attention to her. He looked straight at Don.

"Thought you could change your name, I wouldn't find you, huh?" he said. His eyes glittered. He coughed once, his chest lurching, spots of red rising in his puffed-out cheeks.

"You've got the wrong man," Don said quietly. "My name is Martin."

"That's not what it was in the old days, is it?" the man said hoarsely.

Betty glanced at Don, saw his face go slack. Something cold gripped her insides.

"I don't know what you're talking about," Don said.

"Oh, don't you!" snarled the man. "It was okay so long as the riding was high, wasn't it, Donsy boy. Soon as things got hot you cut out quick enough, didn't you? Didn't you, you son-of-a—"

She didn't dare speak. Her eyes fled from the man's face to Don's and back again, her mind jumping in ten different directions at once. Why didn't Don *say* something?

"You know what they did t'us?" the man went on in a flat voice. "You know what they did? Sent us up for ten years. Ten years; *count* 'em." His smile was crooked. "But not you, Donsy boy. Not you."

"Don," Betty said. He didn't look at her.

"And you got married," said the man, the gun shaking in his hand. "You got *married*. Ain't that—"

A cough shook his body. For a second, his eyes filled with

tears and he stepped back quickly and banged against the table. Then, in an instant, he stood, legs wide apart, holding the gun out before him, rubbing the tears from his pale cheeks.

"*Get back*," he warned. They hadn't moved. His eyes widened, then his face grew suddenly taut. "Well, I'm gonna kill you," he said. "I'm gonna kill you."

"Mister, you got—" Don began.

"Shut up!" screamed the man.

Then he was quiet, his dark eyes peering toward the dining room, the stairs. He was listening to Billy crying again.

"You got a kid," the man said slowly.

"*No*." Betty said it suddenly. She stared at the impossible face of the impossible man who had just said he was going to kill her husband, who was asking with unholy interest about her son.

"This is gonna be a *pleasure*," said the man. "I'm gonna pay you back good for what you done t'me."

She saw Don's face whiten, heard his voice, frail and unbelieving. "What do you mean?"

"Get in the dining room," the man said.

They backed into the next room, their eyes never leaving the man's pock-marked face. Betty's heart thudded. She shivered without control at the sound of Billy's crying.

"You're not—"

"Get up the stairs." A violent cough shook the man.

Betty shuddered as Don's hand gripped her left arm. She glanced over at him dazedly but he didn't return her look. He was holding her back from the stairs.

"You're not going to hurt my boy," he said, his voice husky.

The man prodded with his gun and Don backed up a step. Betty moved beside him. They went up another step and with each upward movement, Betty felt waves of horror grow stronger in her.

"Simpson, kill *me*," Don begged suddenly. "Leave my boy alone."

Don knew his name. Betty slumped against the wall weakly with the knowledge that everything the man had said was true. True.

"I *swear* to you!" Don said.

"Swear!" the man shouted at him, "Twelve years I been after you. Ten in stir and two years running you down!"

Suddenly his face was convulsed with coughing; he shot out his left hand for the banister.

In the same second, Don leaped.

Betty felt a scream tear from her throat as the roar of the gun deafened her. She heard Don cry out in pain and watched in rigid horror as the two men grappled on the stairway just below her. She saw blood running down Don's shirt and splashing on the green-carpeted steps.

Her eyes grew wide as she watched the man's hate-tortured face grow hard, the flesh seeming to tighten as if drawn at the edges by screws. The two men made no sound, only gasped in each other's faces. Their hands, wrestling for the gun, were hidden from her.

Another deafening roar.

The two men stood straight, staring at each other. Then the man's mouth opened and spittle ran across his unshaven chin. He toppled backwards down the steps and landed in a crumpled heap on the landing. His dead eyes stared up at them.

For a long while, Betty stood quite still.

Then she left the room and went back into the hall, closing the door quietly behind her. She went to the bathroom and got the medical kit.

Don was sitting on a step halfway downstairs, his head propped on two blood-drained fists, his elbows resting on his knees. He didn't turn as she came down the steps.

She sat down beside him and drew a bandage tight around his shoulder and arm.

"Does it hurt?" she asked dully.

He shook his head.

"I wonder if the neighbors heard," she said.

"They must have," he said. "You'd better call the police."

Her fingers grew still on the bandage. "You didn't call them before, did you?"

"No."

He began to speak slowly, without looking at her.

"When I was just a kid," he said. "Eighteen, nineteen—I worked the rackets in Chicago." He looked down at the dead man. "Simpson was one of the guys I worked with. He was always hot-headed, maybe a little crazy."

His head fell forward. "Well, when the police caught up with us I . . ." He let out a slow, tired breath. "I got scared and ran. I didn't think then either. I was just a kid and I was scared. So I ran."

She looked at him thinking how strange it was to have been married nine years to a man she didn't know about.

"The rest is simple," he said. "I changed my name, I tried to live a decent life, an honest one. I tried to forget." He shook his head defeatedly. "I don't know how he found me." He swallowed. "It doesn't matter, really. You'd better call the police. Before somebody else does."

She finished the bandage and stood. She went down the steps, avoiding the sight of the man lying there with his blood-soaked chest.

She dialed the operator. "Police," she said and waited, looking up at Don's pale face looking at her between the posts of the banister. He looked like a frightened boy who'd been chased and punished and knew that he deserved it.

"Thirteenth precinct," said the man's voice on the phone.

"I'd like to report a shooting," Betty said.

The man took the address. Betty's eyes were on Don, on the look of resignation on his face.

"The man broke into our house," she said.

"No," Don said, "Tell them the truth."

"That's right," she said, "We never saw him before. I guess he was a burglar. Most of our lights were out. We were watching television. I guess he thought we weren't home."

Don sagged and closed his eyes as she told the police to bring a doctor. Then, after she hung up she stood looking down at him.

"All right," he murmured.

The blood started oozing through his bandage then and Betty went and got a clean towel from the linen closet. She went back and sat beside her husband and held the towel against his shoulder until the flow stopped. Then she got up, went to Billy's bedroom and rocked him gently in her arms.

Downstairs, Don waited quietly for the men to come and take away the body.

THE CONQUEROR

That afternoon in 1871, the stage to Grantville had only the
two of us as passengers, rocking and swaying in its dusty, hot
confines under the fiery Texas sun. The young man sat across
from me, one palm braced against the hard, dry leather of the
seat, the other holding on his lap a small black bag.

He was somewhere near nineteen or twenty. His build was
almost delicate. He was dressed in checkered flannel and wore
a dark tie with a stickpin in its center. You could tell he was a
city boy.

From the time we'd left Austin two hours before, I had been
wondering about the bag he carried so carefully in his lap. I
noticed that his light-blue eyes kept gazing down at it. Every
time they did, his thin-lipped mouth would twitch—whether
toward a smile or a grimace I couldn't tell. Another black bag,
slightly larger, was on the seat beside him, but to this he paid
little attention.

I'm an old man, and while not usually garrulous, I guess I do
like to seek out conversation. Just the same, I hadn't offered to
speak in the time we'd been fellow passengers, and neither had
he. For about an hour and a half I'd been trying to read the Austin paper, but now I laid it down beside me on the dusty seat. I
glanced down again at the small bag and noted how tightly his
slender fingers were clenched around the bone handle.

Frankly, I was curious. And maybe there was something in
the young man's face that reminded me of Lew or Tylan—my
sons. Anyhow, I picked up the newspaper and held it out to him.

"Care to read it?" I asked him above the din of the 24
pounding hoofs and the rattle and creak of the stage.

There was no smile on his face as he shook his head once. If anything, his mouth grew tighter until it was a line of almost bitter resolve. It is not often you see such an expression in the face of so young a man. It is too hard at that age to hold on to either bitterness or resolution, too easy to smile and laugh and soon forget the worst of evils. Maybe that was why the young man seemed so unusual to me.

"I'm through with it if you'd like," I said.

"No, thank you," he answered curtly.

"Interesting story here," I went on, unable to rein in a runaway tongue. "Some Mexican claims to have shot young Wesley Hardin."

The young man's eyes raised up a moment from his bag and looked at me intently. Then they lowered to the bag again.

"'Course I don't believe a word of it," I said. "The man's not born yet who'll put John Wesley away."

The young man did not choose to talk, I saw. I leaned back against the jolting seat and watched him as he studiously avoided my eyes.

Still I would not stop. What is this strange compulsion of old men to share themselves? Perhaps they fear to lose their last years in emptiness. "You must have gold in that bag," I said to him, "to guard it so zealously."

It was a smile he gave me now, though a mirthless one.

"No, not gold," the young man said, and as he finished saying so, I saw his lean throat move once nervously.

I smiled and struck in deeper the wedge of conversation.

"Going to Grantville?" I asked.

"Yes, I am," he said—and I suddenly knew from his voice that he was no Southern man.

I did not speak then. I turned my head away and looked out stiffly across the endless flat, watching through the choking haze of alkali dust, the bleached scrub which dotted the barren stretches. For a moment, I felt myself tightened with that rigidity we Southerners contracted in the presence of our conquerors.

But there is something stronger than pride, and that is loneliness. It was what made me look back to the young man and once more see in him something of my own two boys who gave their lives at Shiloh. I could not, deep in myself, hate the young man for being from a different part of our nation. Even then, imbued as I was with the stiff pride of the Confederate, I was not good at hating.

"Planning to live in Grantville?" I asked.

The young man's eyes glittered. "Just for a while," he said. His fingers grew yet tighter on the bag he held so firmly in his lap. Then he suddenly blurted, "You want to see what I have in—"

He stopped, his mouth tightening as if he were angry to have spoken.

I didn't know what to say to his impulsive, half-finished offer.

The young man very obviously clutched at my indecision and said, "Well, never mind—you wouldn't be interested."

And though I suppose I could have protested that I would, somehow I felt it would do no good.

The young man leaned back and braced himself again as the coach yawed up a rock-strewn incline. Hot, blunt waves of dust-laden wind poured through the open windows at my side. The young man had rolled down the curtains on his side shortly after we'd left Austin.

"Got business in our town?" I asked, after blowing dust from my nose and wiping it from around my eyes and mouth.

He leaned forward slightly. "You live in Grantville?" he asked loudly as overhead the driver, Jeb Knowles, shouted commands to his three teams and snapped the leather popper of his whip over their straining bodies.

I nodded. "Run a grocery there," I said, smiling at him. "Been visiting up North with my oldest—with my son."

He didn't seem to hear what I had said. Across his face a look as intent as any I have ever seen moved suddenly.

"Can you tell me something?" he began. "Who's the quickest pistolman in your town?"

The question startled me, because it seemed born of no idle curiosity. I could see that the young man was far more than ordinarily interested in my reply. His hands were clutching, bloodless, the handle of his small black bag.

"Pistolman?" I asked him.

"Yes. Who's the quickest in Grantville? Is it Hardi? Does he come there often? Or Longley. Do they come there?"

That was the moment I knew something was not quite right in that young man. For, when he spoke those words, his face was strained and eager beyond a natural eagerness.

"I'm afraid I don't know much about such things," I told him. "The town is rough enough; I'll be the first man to admit to that. But I go my own way and folks like me go theirs and we stay out of trouble."

"But what about Hardin?"

"I'm afraid I don't know about that either, young man," I said. "Though I do believe someone said he was in Kansas now."

The young man's face showed a keen and heartfelt disappointment.

"Oh," he said and sank back a little.

He looked up suddenly. "But there are pistolmen there," he said, "*dangerous* men?"

I looked at him for a moment, wishing, somehow, that I had kept to my paper and not let the garrulity of age get the better of me. "There are such men," I said stiffly, "wherever you look in our ravaged South."

"Is there a sheriff in Grantville?" the young man asked me then.

"There is," I said—but for some reason did not add that Sheriff Cleat was hardly more than a figurehead, a man who feared his own shadow and kept his appointment only because the county fathers were too far away to come and see for themselves what a futile job their appointee was doing.

I didn't tell the young man that. Vaguely uneasy, I told him nothing more at all and we were separated by silence again, me to my thoughts, he to his—whatever strange, twisted thoughts they were. He looked at his bag and fingered at the handle, and his narrow chest rose and fell with sudden lurches.

A creaking, a rattling, a blurred spinning of thick spokes. A shouting, a deafening clatter of hoofs in the dust. Over the far rise, the buildings of Grantville were clustered and waiting.

A young man was coming to town.

Grantville in the postwar period was typical of those Texas towns that struggled in the limbo between lawlessness and settlement. Into its dusty streets rode men tense with the anger of defeat. The very air seemed charged with their bitter resentments—resentments toward the occupying forces, toward the rabble-rousing carpetbaggers and, with that warped evaluation of the angry man, toward themselves and their own kind. Threatening death was everywhere, and the dust was often red with blood. In such a town I sold food to men who often died before their stomachs could digest it.

I did not see the young man for hours after Jeb braked up the stage before the Blue Buck Hotel. I saw him move across the ground and up the hotel porch steps, holding tightly to his two bags.

Then some old friends greeted me and I forgot him.

I chatted for a while and then I walked by the store. Things there were in good order. I commended Merton Winthrop, the young man I had entrusted the store to in my three weeks' absence, and then I went home, cleaned up, and put on fresh clothes.

I judge it was near four that afternoon when I pushed through the batwings of the Nellie Gold Saloon. I am not nor ever was a heavy drinking man, but I'd had for several years the pleasurable habit of sitting in the cool shadows of a corner table with a whiskey drink to sip. It was a way that I'd found for lingering over minutes.

That particular afternoon I had chatted for a while with George P. Shaughnessy, the afternoon bartender, then retired to my usual table to dream a few presupper dreams and listen to the idle buzz of conversations and the click of chips in the back-room poker game.

That was where I was when the young man entered.

In truth, when he first came in, I didn't recognize him. For what a strange, incredible altering in his dress and carriage! The city clothes were gone; instead of a flannel coat he wore a broadcloth shirt, pearl-buttoned; in place of flannel trousers there were dark, tight-fitting trousers whose calves plunged into glossy-high-heeled boots. On his head a broad-brimmed hat cast a shadow across his grimly set features.

His boot heels had clumped him almost to the bar before I recognized him, before I grew suddenly aware of what he had been keeping so guardedly in that small black bag.

Crossed on his narrow waist, riding low, a brace of gunbelts hung, sagging with the weight of two Colt .44s in their holsters.

I confess to staring at the transformation. Few men in Grantville wore two pistols, much less slender young city men just arrived in town.

In my mind, I heard again the questions he had put to me. I had to set my glass down for the sudden, unaccountable shaking of my hand.

The other customers of the Nellie Gold looked only briefly at the young man, then returned to their several attentions. George P. Shaughnessy looked up, smiling, gave the customary unnecessary wipe across the immaculate mahogany of the bar top, and asked the young man's pleasure.

"Whiskey," the young man said.

"Any special kind, now?" George asked.

"Any kind," the young man said, thumbing back his hat with studied carelessness.

It was when the amber fluid was almost to the glass top that the young man asked the question I had somehow known he would ask from the moment I had recognized him.

"Tell me, who's the quickest pistolman in town?"

George looked up. "I beg your pardon, mister?"

The young man repeated the question, his face emotionless.

"Now, what does a fine young fellow like you want to know that for?" George asked him in a fatherly way.

It was like the tightening of hide across a drum top the way the skin grew taut across the young man's cheeks.

"I asked you a question," he said with unpleasant flatness. "Answer it."

The two closest customers cut off their talking to observe. I felt my hands grow cold upon the table top. There was ruthlessness in the young man's voice.

But George's face still retained the bantering cast it almost always had.

"Are you going to answer my question?" the young man said, drawing back his hands and tensing them with light suggestiveness along the bar edge.

"What's your name, son?" George asked.

The young man's mouth grew hard and his eyes went cold beneath the shadowing brim of his hat. Then a calculating smile played thinly on his lips. "My name is Riker," he said as if somehow he expected this unknown name to strike terror into all our hearts.

"Well, young Mr. Riker, may I ask you why you want to know about the quickest pistolman in town?"

"Who *is* it?" There was no smile on Riker's lips now; it had faded quickly into that grim, unyielding line again. In back I noticed one of the three poker players peering across the top of half-doors into the main saloon.

"Well, now," George said, smiling, "There's Sheriff Cleat. I'd say that he's about—"

His face went slack. A pistol was pointing at his chest.

"Don't tell me lies," young Riker said in tightly restrained anger. "I know your sheriff is a yellow dog; a man at the hotel told me so. I want the *truth.*"

He emphasized the word again with a sudden thumbing back of hammer. George's face went white.

"Mr. Riker, you're making a very bad mistake," he said, then twitched back as the long pistol barrel jabbed into his chest.

Riker's mouth was twisted with fury. "Are you going to *tell* me?" he raged. His young voice cracked in the middle of the sentence like an adolescent's.

"Selkirk," George said quickly.

The young man drew back his pistol, another smile trembling for a moment on his lips. He threw across a nervous glance at where I sat but did not recognize me. Then his cold blue eyes were on George again.

"Selkirk," he repeated. "What's the first name?"

"Barth," George told him, his voice having neither anger nor fear.

"Barth Selkirk." The young man spoke the name as though to fix it in his mind. Then he leaned forward quickly, his nostrils flaring, the thin line of his mouth once more grown rigid.

"You tell him I want to kill him," he said. "Tell him I—" He swallowed hastily and jammed his lips together. "Tonight," he said then. "Right here. At eight o'clock." He shoved out the pistol barrel again. "You *tell* him," he commanded.

George said nothing and Riker backed away from the bar, glancing over his shoulder once to see where the doors were. As he retreated, the high heel at his right boot gave a little inward and he almost fell. As he staggered for balance, his pistol barrel pointed restlessly around the room, and in the rising color of his face, his eyes looked with nervous apprehension into every dark corner.

Then he was at the doors again, his chest rising and falling rapidly. Before our blinking eyes, the pistol seemed to leap back into its holster. Young Riker smiled uncertainly, obviously desperate to convey the impression that he was in full command of the moment.

"Tell him I don't like him," he said as if he were tossing out a casual reason for his intention to kill Selkirk. He swallowed again, lowering his chin a trifle to hide the movement of his throat.

"Tell him he's a dirty Rebel," he said in a breathless-sounding voice. "Tell him—tell him I'm a Yankee and I *hate* all Rebels!"

For another moment he stood before us in wavering defiance. Then suddenly he was gone.

George broke the spell. We heard the clink of glass on glass as he poured himself a drink. We watched him swallow it in a single gulp. "Young fool," he muttered.

I got up and went over to him.

"How do you like *that*?" he asked me, gesturing one big hand in the general direction of the doors.

"What are you going to do?" I asked him, conscious of the two men now sauntering with affected carelessness for the doors.

"What am I *supposed* to do?" George asked me. "Tell Selkirk, I guess."

I told George about my talk with young Riker and of his strange transformation from city boy to, apparently, self-appointed pistol killer.

"Well," George said when I was finished talking, "where does that leave me? I can't have a young idiot like that angry with me. Do you know his triggers were filed to a hair? Did you see the way he slung that Colt?" He shook his head. "He's a fool," he said. "But a dangerous fool—one that a man can't let himself take chances with."

"Don't tell Selkirk," I said. "I'll go to the sheriff and—"

George waved an open palm at me. "Don't joke now, John," he said. "You know Cleat hides his head under the pillow when there's shooting in the air."

"But this would be a slaughter, George," I said. "Selkirk is a hardened killer, you know that for a fact."

George eyed me curiously. "Why are you concerned about it?" he asked me.

"Because he's a boy," I said. "Because he doesn't know what he's doing."

George shrugged. "The boy came in and asked for it himself, didn't he?" he said. "Besides, even if I say nothing, Selkirk will hear about it, you can be sure of that. Those two who just went out—don't you think *they'll* spread the word?"

A grim smile raised Shaughnessy's lips. "The boy will get his fight," he said. "And may the Lord have mercy on his soul."

George was right. Word of the young stranger's challenge flew about the town as if the wind had blown it. And with the word, the threadbare symbol of our justice, Sheriff Cleat, sought the sanctuary of his house, having either scoffed at all storm warnings or ignored them in his practiced way.

But the storm *was* coming; everyone knew it. The people who had found some reason to bring them to the square—they knew it. The men thronging the Nellie Gold who seemed to have developed a thirst quite out of keeping with their normal desires—they knew it. Death is a fascinating lure to men who can stand aside and watch it operate on someone else.

I stationed myself near the entrance of the Nellie Gold, hoping that I might speak to young Riker, who had been in his hotel room all afternoon, alone.

At seven-thirty, Selkirk and his ruffian friends galloped to the hitching rack, tied up their snorting mounts, and went into the saloon. I heard the greetings offered them and their returning laughs and shouts. They were elated, all of them; that was not hard to see. Things had been dull for them in the past few months. Cleat had offered no resistance, only smiling fatuously to their bullying insults. And, in the absence of any other man willing to draw his pistol on Barth Selkirk, the days had dragged for him and for his gang, who thrived on violence. Gambling and drinking and the company of Grantville's lost women was not enough for these men. It was why they were all bubbling with excited anticipation that night.

While I stood waiting on the wooden sidewalk, endlessly drawing out my pocket watch, I heard the men shouting back and forth among themselves inside the saloon. But the deep, measured voice of Barth Selkirk I did not hear. He did not shout or laugh then or ever. It was why he hovered like a menacing wraith across our town. For he spoke his frightening logic with the thunder of his pistols and all men knew it.

Time was passing. It was the first time in my life that impending death had taken on such immediacy to me. My boys had died a thousand miles from me, falling while, oblivious, I sold flour to the blacksmith's wife. My wife had died slowly, passing in the peace of slumber, without a cry or a sob.

Yet now I was deeply in this fearful moment. Because I had spoken to young Riker, because—yes, I knew it now—he had reminded me of Lew, I now stood shivering in the darkness, my hands clammy in my coat pockets, in my stomach a hardening knot of dread.

And then my watch read eight. I looked up—and I heard his boots clumping on the wood in even, unhurried strides.

I stepped out from the shadows and moved toward him. The people in the square had grown suddenly quiet. I sensed men's eyes on me as I walked toward Riker's approaching form. It was, I knew, the distortion of nerves and darkness, but he seemed taller than before as he walked along with measured steps, his small hands swinging tensely at his sides.

I stopped before him. For a moment, he looked irritably confused. Then that smile that showed no humor flickered on his tightly drawn face.

"It's the grocery man," he said, his voice dry and brittle.

I swallowed the cold tightness in my throat. "Son, you're making a mistake," I said, "a very bad mistake."

"Get out of my way," he told me curtly, his eyes glancing over my shoulder at the saloon.

"Son, *believe* me. Barth Selkirk is too much for you to—"

In the dull glowing of saloon light, the eyes he turned on me were the blue of frozen, lifeless things. My voice broke off, and without another word, I stepped aside to let him pass. When a man sees in another man's eyes the insensible determination that I saw in Riker's, it is best to step aside. There are no words that will affect such men.

A moment more he looked at me and then, squaring his shoulders, he started walking again. He did not stop until he stood before the batwings of the Nellie Gold.

I moved closer, staring at the light and shadows of his face illuminated by the inside lamps. And it seemed as though, for a moment, the mask of relentless cruelty fell from his features to reveal stark terror.

But it was only a moment, and I could not be certain I had really seen it. Abruptly, the eyes caught fire again, the thin mouth tightened, and Riker shoved through the doors with one long stride.

There was silence, utter ringing silence in that room. Even the scuffing of my bootheels sounded very loud as I edged cautiously to the doors.

Then, as I reached them, there was that sudden rustling, thumping, jingling combination of sounds that indicated general withdrawal from the two opposing men.

I looked in carefully.

Riker stood erect, his back to me, looking toward the bar. It now stood deserted save for one man.

Barth Selkirk was a tall man who looked even taller because of the black he wore. His hair was long and blond; it hung in thick ringlets beneath his wide-brimmed hat. He wore his pistol low on his right hip, the butt reversed, the holster thronged tightly to his thigh. His face was long and tanned, his eyes as sky-blue as Riker's, his mouth a motionless line beneath the well-trimmed length of his mustaches.

I had never seen Abilene's Hickok, but the word had always been that Selkirk might have been his twin.

As the two eyed each other, it was as though every watching man in that room had ceased to function, their breaths frozen, their bodies petrified—only their eyes alive, shifting back and forth from man to man. It might have been a room of statues, so silently did each man stand.

Then I saw Selkirk's broad chest slowly expanding as it filled with air. And as it slowly sank, his deep voice broke the silence with the impact of a hammer blow on glass.

"Well?" he said and let his boot slide off the brass rail and thump down onto the floor.

An instant pause. Then, suddenly, a gasping in that room as if one man had gasped instead of all.

For Selkirk's fingers, barely to the butt of his pistol, had turned to stone as he gaped dumbly at the brace of Colts in Riker's hands.

"Why you dirty—" he began—and then his voice was lost in the deafening roar of pistol fire. His body was flung back against the bar edge as if a club had struck him in the chest. He held there for a moment, his face blank with astonishment. Then the second pistol kicked, thundering in Riker's hand, and Selkirk went down in a twisted heap.

I looked dazedly at Selkirk's still body, staring at the great gush of blood from his torn chest. Then, my eyes were on Riker again as he stood veiled in acrid smoke before the staring men.

I heard him swallow convulsively. "My name is Riker," he said, his voice trembling in spite of efforts to control it. "Remember that. *Riker*."

He backed off nervously, his left pistol holstered in a blur of movement, his right still pointed toward the crowd of men.

Then he was out of the saloon again, his face contorted with a mixture of fear and exultation as he turned and saw me standing there.

"Did you see it?" he asked me in a shaking voice. "Did you *see* it?"

I looked at him without a word as his head jerked to the side and he looked into the saloon again, his hands plummeting down like shot birds to his pistol butts.

Apparently, he saw no menace, for instantly his eyes were back on me again—excited, swollen-pupiled eyes.

"They won't forget me now, will they?" he said and swallowed. "They'll remember my name. They'll be afraid of it."

He started to walk past me, then twitched to the side and leaned, with a sudden weakness, against the saloon wall, his chest heaving with breath, his blue eyes jumping around feverishly. He kept gasping at the air as if he were choking.

He swallowed with difficulty. "Did you *see* it?" he asked me again, as if he were desperate to share his murderous triumph. "He didn't even get to *pull* his pistols—didn't even get to pull them." His lean chest shuddered with turbulent breath. "*That's* how," he gasped, "*that's* how to do it." Another gasp. "I showed them. I showed them all how to do it. I came from the city and I showed them how. I got the *best one* they had, the best one." His throat moved so quickly it made a dry, clicking sound. "I showed them," he muttered.

He looked around blinking. "Now I'll—"

He looked all around with frightened eyes, as if an army of silent killers were encircling him. His face went slack and he forced together his shaking lips.

"Get out of my way," he suddenly ordered and pushed me aside. I turned and watched him walking rapidly toward the hotel, looking to the sides and over his shoulder with quick jerks of his head, his hands half poised at his sides.

I tried to understand young Riker, but I couldn't. He was from the city; that I knew. Some city in the mass of cities had borne him. He had come to Grantville with the deliberate intention of singling out the fastest pistolman and killing him face to face. That made no sense to me. That seemed a purposeless desire.

Now what would he do? He had told me he was only going to be in Grantville for a while. Now that Selkirk was dead, that while was over.

Where would young Riker go next? And would the same scenes repeat themselves in the next town, and the next, and the next after that? The young city man arriving, changing outfits, asking for the most dangerous pistolman, meeting him—was that how it was going to be in every town? How long could such insanity last? How long before he met a man who would not lose the draw?

My mind was filled with these questions. But, over all, the single question—*Why?* Why was he doing this thing? What calculating madness had driven him from the city to seek out death in this strange land?

While I stood there wondering, Barth Selkirk's men carried out the blood-soaked body of their slain god and laid him carefully across his horse. I was so close to them I could see his blond hair ruffling slowly in the night wind and hear his life's blood spattering on the darkness of the street.

Then I saw the six men looking toward the Blue Buck Hotel, their eyes glinting vengefully in the light from the Nellie Gold, and I heard their voices talking low. No words came clear to me as they murmured among themselves, but from the way they kept looking toward the hotel I knew of what they spoke.

I drew back into the shadows again, thinking they might see me and carry their conversation elsewhere. I stood in the blackness watching. Somehow I knew exactly what they intended even before one of their shadowy group slapped a palm against his pistol butt and said distinctly, *"Come on."*

I saw them move away slowly, the six of them, their voices suddenly stilled, their eyes directed at the hotel they were walking toward.

Foolishness again; it is an old man's trademark. For, suddenly, I found myself stepping from the shadows and turning the corner of the saloon, then running down the alley between the Nellie Gold and Pike's Saddlery; rushing through the squares of light made by the saloon windows, then into darkness again. I had no idea why I was running. I seemed driven by an unseen force which clutched all reason from my mind but one thought—*warn him.*

My breath was quickly lost. I felt my coattails flapping like furious bird wings against my legs. Each thudding bootfall drove a mail-gloved fist against my heart.

I don't know how I beat them there, except that they were walking cautiously while I ran headlong along St. Vera street and hurried in the backway of the hotel. I rushed down the silent hallway, my bootheels thumping along the frayed rug.

Maxwell Tarrant was at the desk that night. He looked up with a start as I came running up to him.

"Why, Mr. Callaway," he said, "what are—?"

"Which room is Riker in?" I gasped.

"Riker?" young Tarrant asked me.

"*Quickly,* boy!" I cried and cast a frightened glance toward the entranceway as the jar of bootheels sounded on the porch steps.

"Room 27," young Tarrant said. I begged him to stall the men who were coming in for Riker, and rushed for the stairs.

I was barely to the second floor when I heard them in the lobby. I ran down the dimlit hall, and reaching Room 27, I rapped urgently on its thin door.

Inside, I heard a rustling sound, the sound of stockinged feet padding on the floor, then Riker's frail, trembling voice asking who it was.

"It's Callaway," I said, "the grocery man. Let me in, quickly. You're in danger."

"Get out of here," he ordered me, his voice sounding thinner yet.

"God help you, boy, prepare yourself," I told him breathlessly. "Selkirk's men are coming for you."

I heard his sharp, involuntary gasp. "*No,*" he said. "That isn't—" He drew in a rasping breath. "How *many?*" he asked me hollowly.

"Six," I said, and on the other side of the door I thought I heard a sob.

"That isn't fair!" he burst out then in angry fright. "It's not fair, six against one. It isn't *fair*!"

I stood there for another moment, staring at the door, imagining that twisted young man on the other side, sick with terror, his heart jolting like club beats in his chest, able to think of nothing but a moral quality those six men never knew.

"What am I going to *do*?" he suddenly implored me.

I had no answer. For, suddenly, I heard the thumping of their boots as they started up the stairs, and helpless in my age, I backed quickly from the door and scuttled, like the frightened thing I was, down the hall into the shadows there.

Like a dream it was, seeing those six grim-faced men come moving down the hall with a heavy trudging of boots, a thin jingling of spur rowels, in each of their hands a long Colt pistol. No, like a nightmare, not a dream. Knowing that these living creatures were headed for the room in which young Riker waited, I felt something sinking in my stomach, something cold and wrenching at my insides. Helpless I was; I never knew such helplessness. For no seeming reason, I suddenly saw my Lew inside that room, waiting to be killed. It made me tremble without the strength to stop.

Their boots halted. The six men ringed the door, three on one side, three on the other. Six young men, their faces tight with unyielding intention, their hands bloodless, so tightly did they hold their pistols.

The silence broke. "Come out of that room, you Yankee bastard!" one of them said loudly. He was Thomas Ashwood, a boy I'd once seen playing children's games in the streets of Grantville, a boy who had grown into the twisted man who now stood, gun in hand, all thoughts driven from his mind but thoughts of killing and revenge.

Silence for a moment.

"I said, *come out*!" Ashwood cried again, then jerked his body to the side as the hotel seemed to tremble with a deafening blast and one of the door panels exploded into jagged splinters.

As the slug gouged into papered plaster across the hall, Ash-wood fired his pistol twice into the door lock, the double flash of light splashing up his cheeks like lightning. My ears rang with the explosions as they echoed up and down the hall.

Another pistol shot roared inside the room. Ashwood kicked in the lock-splintered door and leaped out of my sight. The ear-shattering exchange of shots seemed to pin me to the wall.

Then, in a sudden silence, I heard young Riker cry out in a pitiful voice, "Don't shoot me any more!"

The next explosion hit me like a man's boot kicking at my stomach. I twitched back against the wall, my breath silenced, as I watched the other men run into the room and heard the crashing of their pistol fire.

It was over—all of it—in less than a minute. While I leaned weakly against the wall, hardly able to stand, my throat dry and tight, I saw two of Selkirk's men help the wounded Ash-wood down the hall, the other three walking behind, murmuring excitedly among themselves. One of them said, "We got him good."

In a moment, the sound of their boots was gone and I stood alone in the empty hallway, staring blankly at the mist of powder smoke that drifted slowly from the open room.

I do not remember how long I stood there, my stomach a grinding twist of sickness, my hands trembling and cold at my sides.

Only when young Tarrant appeared, white-faced and frightened at the head of the steps, did I find the strength to shuffle down the hall to Riker's room.

We found him lying in his blood, his pain-shocked eyes staring sightlessly at the ceiling, the two pistols still smoking in his rigid hands.

He was dressed in checkered flannel again, in white shirt and dark stockings. It was grotesque to see him lying there that way, his city clothes covered with blood, those long pistols in his still, white hands.

"Oh, God," young Tarrant said in a shocked whisper. "Why did they kill him?"

I shook my head and said nothing. I told young Tarrant to get the undertaker and said I would pay the costs. He was glad to leave.

I sat down on the bed, feeling very tired. I looked into young Riker's open bag and saw, inside, the shirts and underclothes, the ties and stockings.

It was in the bag I found the clippings and the diary.

The clippings were from Northern magazines and newspapers. They were about Hickok and Longley and Hardin and other famous pistol fighters of our territory. There were pencil marks drawn beneath certain sentences—such as *Wild Bill usually carries two derringers beneath his coat* and *Many a man has lost his life because of Hardin's so-called "border roll" trick.*

The diary completed the picture. It told of a twisted mind holding up as idols those men whose only talent was to kill. It told of a young city boy who bought himself pistols and practiced drawing them from their holsters until he was incredibly quick, until his drawing speed became coupled with an ability to strike any target instantly.

It told of a projected odyssey in which a city boy would make himself the most famous pistol fighter in the Southwest. It listed towns that this young man had meant to conquer.

Grantville was the first town on the list.

THE HOLIDAY MAN

"You'll be late," she said.

He leaned back tiredly in his chair.

"I know," he answered.

They were in the kitchen having breakfast. David hadn't eaten much. Mostly, he'd drunk black coffee and stared at the tablecloth. There were thin lines running through it that looked like intersecting highways.

"Well?" she said.

He shivered and took his eyes from the tablecloth.

"Yes," he said. "All right."

He kept sitting there.

"*David*," she said.

"I know, I know," he said, "I'll be late." He wasn't angry. There was no anger left in him.

"You certainly will," she said, buttering her toast. She spread on thick raspberry jam, then bit off a piece and chewed it cracklingly.

David got up and walked across the kitchen. At the door he stopped and turned. He stared at the back of her head.

"Why couldn't I?" he asked again.

"Because you can't," she said. "That's all."

"But *why*?"

"Because they need you," she said. "Because they pay you well and you couldn't do anything else. Isn't it obvious?"

"They could find someone else."

"Oh, stop it," she said. "You know they couldn't."

He closed his hands into fists. "Why should I be the one?" he asked.

She didn't answer. She sat eating her toast.

"Jean?"

"There's nothing more to say," she said, chewing. She turned around. "Now, will you go?" she said. "You shouldn't be late today."

David felt a chill in his flesh.

"No," he said, "not today."

He walked out of the kitchen and went upstairs. There, he brushed his teeth, polished his shoes and put on a tie. Before eight he was down again. He went into the kitchen.

"Goodbye," he said.

She tilted up her cheek for him and he kissed it. "Bye, dear," she said. "Have a—" She stopped abruptly.

" —nice day?" he finished for her. "Thank you." He turned away. "I'll have a lovely day."

Long ago he had stopped driving a car. Mornings he walked to the railroad station. He didn't even like to ride with someone else or take a bus.

At the station he stood outside on the platform waiting for the train. He had no newspaper. He never bought them any more. He didn't like to read the papers.

"Mornin', Garret."

He turned and saw Henry Coulter who also worked in the city. Coulter patted him on the back.

"Good morning," David said.

"How's it goin'?" Coulter asked.

"Fine. Thank you."

"Good. Lookin' forward to the Fourth?"

David swallowed. "Well . . ." he began.

"Myself, I'm takin' the family to the woods," said Coulter. "No lousy fireworks for us. Pilin' into the old bus and headin' out till the fireworks are over."

"Driving," said David.

"Yes, sir," said Coulter. "Far as we can."

It began by itself. No, he thought; not now. He forced it back into its darkness.

"—tising business," Coulter finished.

"What?" he asked.

"Said I trust things are goin' well in the advertising business."
David cleared his throat.

"Oh, yes," he said. "Fine." He always forgot about the lie
he'd told Coulter.

When the train arrived he sat in the No Smoking car, knowing that Coulter always smoked a cigar en route. He didn't
want to sit with Coulter. Not now.

All the way to the city he sat looking out the window. Mostly
he watched road and highway traffic; but, once, while the train
rattled over a bridge, he stared down at the mirrorlike surface of
a lake. Once he put his head back and looked up at the sun.

He was actually to the elevator when he stopped.

"Up?" said the man in the maroon uniform. He looked at
David steadily. "Up?" he said. Then he closed the rolling doors.

David stood motionless. People began to cluster around
him. In a moment, he turned and shouldered by them, pushing
through the revolving door. As he came out, the oven heat of
July surrounded him. He moved along the sidewalk like a man
asleep. On the next block he entered a bar.

Inside, it was cold and dim. There were no customers. Not
even the bartender was visible. David sank down in the shadow
of a booth and took his hat off. He leaned his head back and
closed his eyes.

He couldn't do it. He simply could not go up to his office.
No matter what Jean said, no matter what anyone said. He
clasped his hands on the table edge and squeezed them until
the fingers were pressed dry of blood. He just *wouldn't*.

"Help you?" asked a voice.

David opened his eyes. The bartender was standing by the
booth, looking down at him.

"Yes, uh . . . beer," he said. He hated beer but he knew he had
to buy something for the privilege of sitting in the chilly silence
undisturbed. He wouldn't drink it.

The bartender brought the beer and David paid for it. Then,
when the bartender had gone, he began to turn the glass slowly

on the table top. While he was doing this it began again. With a gasp, he pushed it away. No!—he told it, savagely.

In a while he got up and left the bar. It was past ten. That didn't matter of course. They knew he was always late. They knew he always tried to break away from it and never could.

His office was at the back of the suite, a small cubicle furnished only with a rug, sofa and a small desk on which lay pencils and white paper. It was all he needed. Once, he'd had a secretary but he hadn't liked the idea of her sitting outside the door and listening to him scream.

No one saw him enter. He let himself in from the hall through a private door. Inside, he relocked the door, then took off his suitcoat and laid it across the desk. It was stuffy in the office so he walked across the floor and pulled up the window.

Far below, the city moved. He stood watching it. How many of them? he thought.

Sighing heavily, he turned. Well, he was here. There was no point in hesitating any longer. He was committed now. The best thing was to get it over and clear out.

He drew the blinds, walked over to the couch and lay down. He fussed a little with the pillow, then stretched once and was still. Almost immediately, he felt his limbs going numb.

It began.

He did not stop it now. It trickled on his brain like melted ice. It rushed like winter wind. It spun like blizzard vapor. It leaped and ran and billowed and exploded and his mind was filled with it. He grew rigid and began to gasp, his chest twitching with breath, the beating of his heart a violent stagger. His hands drew in like white talons, clutching and scratching at the couch. He shivered and groaned and writhed. Finally he screamed. He screamed for a very long while.

When it was done, he lay limp and motionless on the couch, his eyes like balls of frozen glass. When he could, he raised his arm and looked at his wristwatch. It was almost two.

He struggled to his feet. His bones felt sheathed with lead but he managed to stumble to his desk and sit before it.

There he wrote on a sheet of paper and, when he was finished, slumped across the desk and fell into exhausted sleep.

Later, he woke up and took the sheet of paper to his superior, who, looking it over, nodded.

"Four hundred eighty-six, huh?" the superior said. "You're sure of that?"

"I'm sure," said David, quietly. "I watched every one." He didn't mention that Coulter and his family were among them.

"All right," said his superior. "Let's see now. Four hundred fifty-two from traffic accidents, eighteen from drowning, seven from sun-stroke, three from fireworks, six from miscellaneous causes."

Such as a little girl being burned to death, David thought. Such as a baby boy eating ant poison. Such as a woman being electrocuted; a man dying of snake bite.

"Well," his superior said, "let's make it—oh, four hundred and fifty. It's always impressive when more people die than we predict."

"Of course," David said.

The item was on the front page of all the newspapers that afternoon. While David was riding home the man in front of him turned to his neighbor and said, "What I'd like to know is—*how can they tell?*"

David got up and went back on the platform on the end of the car. Until he got off, he stood there listening to the train wheels and thinking about Labor Day.

NO SUCH THING AS A VAMPIRE

In the early autumn of the year 18—Madame Alexis Gheria
awoke one morning to a sense of utmost torpor. For more than a
minute, she lay inertly on her back, her dark eyes staring upward.
How wasted she felt. It seemed as if her limbs were sheathed in
lead. Perhaps she was ill, Petre must examine her and see.

Drawing in a faint breath, she pressed up slowly on an
elbow. As she did, her nightdress slid, rustling, to her waist.
How had it come unfastened? She wondered, looking down at
herself.

Quite suddenly, Madame Gheria began to scream.

In the breakfast room, Dr. Petre Gheria looked up, startled,
from his morning paper. In an instant, he had pushed his chair
back, slung his napkin on the table and was rushing for the hallway. He dashed across its carpeted breadth and mounted the
staircase two steps at a time.

It was a near hysterical Madame Gheria he found sitting on
the edge of her bed looking down in horror at her breasts. Across
the dilated whiteness of them, a smear of blood lay drying.

Dr. Gheria dismissed the upstairs maid, who stood frozen
in the open doorway, gaping at her mistress. He locked the
door and hurried to his wife.

"Petre!" she gasped.

"Gently." He helped her lie back across the blood-stained
pillow.

"Petre, what *is* it?" she begged.

"Lie still, my dear." His practiced hands moved in swift
search over her breasts. Suddenly, his breath choked off. Pressing aside her head, he stared down dumbly at the pinprick

lancinations on her neck, the ribbon of tacky blood that twisted downward from them.

"My *throat*," Alexis said.

"No, it's just a—" Dr. Gheria did not complete the sentence. He knew exactly what it was.

Madame Gheria began to tremble. "Oh, my God, my *God*," she said.

Dr. Gheria rose and foundered to the washbasin. Pouring in water, he returned to his wife and washed away the blood. The wound was clearly visible now—two tiny punctures close to the jugular. A grimacing Dr. Gheria touched the mounds of inflamed tissue in which they lay. As he did, his wife groaned terribly and turned her face away.

"Now listen to me," he said, his voice apparently calm. "We will not succumb, immediately, to superstition, do you hear? There are any number of—"

"I'm going to die," she said.

"Alexis, do you hear me?" He caught her harshly by the shoulders.

She turned her head and stared at him with vacant eyes. "You know what it is," she said.

Dr. Gheria swallowed. He could still taste coffee in his mouth.

"I know what it appears to be," he said, "and we shall—not ignore the possibility. However—"

"I'm going to die," she said.

"Alexis!" Dr. Gheria took her hand and gripped it fiercely. "*You shall not be taken from me*," he said.

Solta was a village of some thousand inhabitants situated in the foothills of Rumania's Bihor Mountains. It was a place of dark traditions. People, hearing the bay of distant wolves, would cross themselves without a thought. Children would gather garlic buds as other children gather flowers, bringing them home for the windows. On every door there was a painted cross, at every throat a metal one. Dread of the vampire's blighting was as normal as the dread of fatal sickness. It was always in the air.

Dr. Gheria thought about that as he bolted shut the windows of Alexis' room. Far off, molten twilight hung above the mountains. Soon it would be dark again. Soon the citizens of Solta would be barricaded in their garlic-reeking houses. He had no doubt that every soul of them knew exactly what had happened to his wife. Already the cook and upstairs maid were pleading for discharge. Only the inflexible discipline of the butler, Karel, kept them at their jobs. Soon, even that would not suffice. Before the horror of the vampire, reason fled.

He'd seen the evidence of it that very morning when he'd ordered Madame's room stripped to the walls and searched for rodents or venomous insects. The servants had moved about the room as if on a floor of eggs, their eyes more white than pupil, their fingers twitching constantly to their crosses. They had known full well no rodent or insects would be found. And Gheria had known it. Still, he'd raged at them for their timidity, succeeding only in frightening them further.

He turned from the window with a smile.

"There now," said he, "nothing alive will enter this room tonight."

He caught himself immediately, seeing the flare of terror in her eyes.

"Nothing at *all* will enter," he amended.

Alexis lay motionless on her bed, one pale hand at her breast, clutching at the worn silver cross she'd taken from her jewel box. She hadn't worn it since he'd given her the diamond-studded one when they were married. How typical of her village background that, in this moment of dread, she should seek protection from the unadorned cross of her church. She was such a child. Gheria smiled down gently at her.

"You won't be needing that, my dear," he said, "you'll be safe tonight."

Her fingers tightened on the crucifix.

"No, no, wear it if you will," he said. "I only meant that I'll be at your side all night."

"You'll stay with me?"

He sat on the bed and held her hand.

"Do you think I'd leave you for a moment?" he said.

Thirty minutes later, she was sleeping. Dr. Gheria drew a chair beside the bed and seated himself. Removing his glasses, he massaged the bridge of his nose with the thumb and forefinger of his left hand. Then, sighing, he began to watch his wife. How incredibly beautiful she was. Dr. Gheria's breath grew strained.

"There is no such thing as a vampire," he whispered to himself.

There was a distant pounding. Dr. Gheria muttered in his sleep, his fingers twitching. The pounding increased; an agitated voice came swirling from the darkness. "Doctor!" it called.

Gheria snapped awake. For a moment, he looked confusedly towards the locked door.

"Dr. Gheria?" demanded Karel.

"What?"

"Is everything all right?"

"Yes, everything is—"

Dr. Gheria cried out hoarsely, springing for the bed. Alexis' nightdress had been torn away again. A hideous dew of blood covered her chest and neck.

Karel shook his head.

"Bolted windows cannot hold away the creature, sir," he said.

He stood, tall and lean, beside the kitchen table on which lay the cluster of silver he'd been polishing when Gheria had entered.

"The creature has the power to make itself a vapor which can pass through any opening however small," he said.

"But the cross!" cried Gheria. "It was still at her throat—untouched! Except by—blood," he added in a sickened voice.

"This I cannot understand," said Karel, grimly. "The cross should have protected her."

"But why did I see nothing?"

"You were drugged by its mephitic presence," Karel said. "Count yourself fortunate that you were not also attacked."

"I do not count myself fortunate!" Dr. Gheria struck his

palm, a look of anguish on his face. "What am I to do, Karel?" he asked.

"Hang garlic," said the old man. "Hang it at the windows, at the doors. Let there be no opening unblocked by garlic."

Gheria nodded distractedly. "Never in my life have I seen this thing," he said, brokenly. "Now, my own wife—"

"I have seen it," said Karel. "I have, myself, put to its rest one of these monsters from the grave."

"The stake—?" Gheria looked revolted.

The old man nodded slowly.

Gheria swallowed. "Pray God you may put this one to rest as well," he said.

"Petre?"

She was weaker now, her voice a toneless murmur. Gheria bent over her. "Yes, my dear," he said.

"It will come again tonight," she said.

"No." He shook his head determinedly. "It cannot come. The garlic will repel it."

"My cross didn't," she said, "you didn't."

"The garlic will," he said. "And see?" He pointed at the bedside table. "I've had black coffee brought for me. I won't sleep tonight."

She closed her eyes, a look of pain across her sallow features.

"I don't want to die," she said. "Please don't let me die, Petre."

"You won't," he said. "I promise you; the monster shall be destroyed."

Alexis shuddered feebly. "But if there is no way, Petre," she murmured.

"There is always a way," he answered.

Outside the darkness, cold and heavy, pressed around the house. Dr. Gheria took his place beside the bed and began to wait. Within the hour, Alexis slipped into a heavy slumber. Gently, Dr. Gheria released her hand and poured himself a cup of steaming coffee. As he sipped it hotly, bitter, he looked around the room. Door locked, windows bolted, every opening sealed with garlic, the cross at Alexis' throat. He nodded slowly to himself. It will work, he thought. The monster would be thwarted.

He sat there, waiting, listening to his breath.

Dr. Gheria was at the door before the second knock.

"Michael!" He embraced the younger man. "Dear Michael, I was sure you'd come!"

Anxiously, he ushered Dr. Vares towards his study. Outside darkness was just falling.

"Where on earth are all the people of the village?" asked Vares. "I swear, I didn't see a soul as I rode in."

"Huddling, terror-stricken, in their houses," Gheria said, "and all my servants with them save for one."

"Who is that?"

"My butler, Karel," Gheria answered. "He didn't answer the door because he's sleeping. Poor fellow, he is very old and has been doing the work of five." He gripped Vares' arm. "Dear Michael," he said, "you have no idea how glad I am to see you."

Vares looked at him worriedly. "I came as soon as I received your message," he said.

"And I appreciate it," Gheria said. "I know how long and hard a ride it is from Cluj."

"What's wrong?" asked Vares. "Your letter only said—"

Quickly, Gheria told him what had happened in the past week.

"I tell you, Michael, I stumble at the brink of madness," he said. "Nothing works! Garlic, wolfsbane, crosses, mirrors, running water—useless! No, don't say it! This isn't superstition nor imagination! This is *happening*! A vampire is destroying her! Each day she sinks yet deeper into that—deadly torpor from which—"

Gheria clinched his hands. "And yet I cannot understand it."

"Come, sit, sit." Doctor Vares pressed the older man into a chair, grimacing at the pallor of him. Nervously, his fingers sought for Gheria's pulse beat.

"Never mind me," protested Gheria. "It's Alexis we must help." He pressed a sudden, trembling hand across his eyes. "Yet how?" he said.

He made no resistance as the younger man undid his collar and examined his neck.

"You, too," said Vares, sickened.

"What does that matter?" Gheria clutched at the younger man's hand. "My friend, my dearest friend," he said, "tell me that it is not I! Do *I* do this hideous thing to her?"

Vares looked confounded. "*You?*" he said. "But—"

"I know, I know," said Gheria. "I, myself, have been attacked. Yet nothing follows, Michael! What breed of horror is this which cannot be impeded? From what unholy place does it emerge? I've had the countryside examined foot by foot, every graveyard ransacked, every crypt inspected! There is no house within the village that has not yet been subjected to my search. I tell you, Michael, there is nothing! Yet, there is something—something which assaults us nightly, draining us of life. The village is engulfed by terror—and I as well! I never see this creature, never hear it! Yet, every morning, I find my beloved wife—"

Vares's face was drawn and pallid now. He stared intently at the older man.

"What am I to do, my friend?" pleaded Gheria. "How am I to save her?"

Vares had no answer.

"How long has she—been like this?" asked Vares. He could not remove his stricken gaze from the whiteness of Alexis' face.

"For many days," said Gheria. "The retrogression has been constant."

Dr. Vares put down Alexis' flaccid hand. "Why did you not tell me sooner?" he asked.

"I thought the matter could be handled," Gheria answered, faintly. "I know now that it—cannot."

Vares shuddered. "But, surely—" he began.

"There is nothing left to be done," said Gheria. "Everything has been tried, *everything*!" He stumbled to the window and stared out bleakly into the deepening night. "And now it comes again," he murmured, "and we are helpless before it."

"Not helpless, Petre." Vares forced a cheering smile to his lips and laid his hand upon the older man's shoulder. "I will watch her tonight."

"It's useless."

"Not at all, my friend," said Vares, nervously. "And now you must sleep."

"I will not leave her," said Gheria.

"But you need rest."

"I cannot leave," said Gheria. "I will not be separated from her."

Vares nodded. "Of course," he said. "We will share the hours of watching then."

Gheria sighed. "We can try," he said, but there was no sound of hope in his voice.

Some twenty minutes later, he returned with an urn of steaming coffee which was barely possible to smell through the heavy mist of garlic fumes which hung in the air. Trudging to the bed, Gheria set down the tray. Dr. Vares had drawn a chair up beside the bed.

"I'll watch first," he said. "You sleep, Petre."

"It would do no good to try," said Gheria. He held a cup beneath the spigot and the coffee gurgled out like smoking ebony.

"Thank you," murmured Vares as the cup was handed to him. Gheria nodded once and drew himself a cupful before he sat.

"I do not know what will happen to Solta if this creature is not destroyed," he said. "The people are paralyzed by terror."

"Has it—been elsewhere in the village?" Vares asked him.

Gheria sighed exhaustedly. "Why need it go elsewhere?" he said. "It is finding all it—craves within these walls." He stared despondently at Alexis. "When we are gone," he said, "it will go elsewhere. The people know that and are waiting for it."

Vares set down his cup and rubbed his eyes.

"It seems impossible," he said, "that we, practitioners of a science, should be unable to—"

"What can science effect against it?" said Gheria. "Science which will not even admit its existence? We could bring, into this very room, the foremost scientists of the world and they would say—my friends, you have been deluded. There is no vampire. All is mere trickery."

Gheria stopped and looked intently at the younger man. He said, "Michael?"

Vares' breath was slow and heavy. Putting down his cup of untouched coffee, Gheria stood and moved to where Vares sat slumped in his chair. He pressed back an eyelid, looked down briefly at the sightless pupil, then withdrew his hand. The drug was quick, he thought. And most effective. Vares would be insensible for more than time enough.

Moving to the closet, Gheria drew down his bag and carried it to the bed. He tore Alexis's nightdress from her upper body and, within seconds, had drawn another syringe full of her blood; this would be the last withdrawal, fortunately. Staunching the wound, he took the syringe to Vares and emptied it into the young man's mouth, smearing it across his lips and teeth.

That done, he strode to the door and unlocked it. Returning to Vares, he raised and carried him into the hall. Karel would not awaken; a small amount of opiate in his food had seen to that. Gheria labored down the steps beneath the weight of Vares' body. In the darkest corner of the cellar, a wooden casket waited for the younger man. There he would lie until the following morning when the distraught Dr. Petre Gheria would, with sudden inspiration, order Karel to search the attic and cellar on the remote, nay fantastic possibility that—

Ten minutes later, Gheria was back in the bedroom checking Alexis's pulse beat. It was active enough; she would survive. The pain and torturing horror she had undergone would be punishment enough for her. As for Vares—

Dr. Gheria smiled in pleasure for the first time since Alexis and he had returned from Cluj at the end of the summer. Dear spirits in heaven, would it not be sheer enchantment to watch old Karel drive a stake through Michael Vares' damned cuckolding heart!

BIG SURPRISE

Old Mr. Hawkins used to stand by his picket fence and call to the little boys when they were coming home from school.

"Lad!" he would call. "Come here, lad!"

Most of the little boys were afraid to go near him, so they laughed and made fun of him in voices that shook. Then they ran away and told their friends how brave they'd been. But once in a while a boy would go up to Mr. Hawkins when he called, and Mr. Hawkins would make his strange request.

> *Dig me a hole, he said,*
> *Winking his eyes,*
> *And you will find*
> *A big surprise.*

No one knew how long they'd heard the children chanting it. Sometimes the parents seemed to recall having heard it years ago.

Once a little boy started to dig the hole but he got tired after a while and he didn't find any big surprise. He was the only one who had ever tried—

One day Ernie Willaker was coming home from school with two of his friends. They walked on the other side of the street when they saw Mr. Hawkins in his front yard standing by the picket fence.

"Lad!" they heard him call. "Come here, lad!"

"He means you, Ernie," teased one of the boys.

"He does not," said Ernie.

Mr. Hawkins pointed a finger at Ernie. "Come here, lad!" he called.

Ernie glanced nervously at his friends.

"Go on," said one of them. "What're ya scared of?"

"Who's scared?" said Ernie. "My ma says I have to come home right after school is all."

"Yella," said his other friend. "You're scared of old man Hawkins."

"Who's scared!"

"Go *on*, then."

"Lad!" called Mr. Hawkins. "Come here, lad."

"Well." Ernie hesitated. "Don't go nowhere," he said.

"We won't. We'll stick around."

"Well—" Ernie braced himself and crossed the street, trying to look casual. He shifted his books to his left hand and brushed back his hair with his right. *Dig me a hole, he says,* muttered in his brain.

Ernie stepped up to the picket fence. "Yes, sir?" he asked.

"Come closer, lad," the old man said, his dark eyes shining. Ernie took a forward step.

"Now you aren't afraid of Mister Hawkins, are you?" said the old man winking.

"No, sir," Ernie said.

"Good," said the old man. "Now listen, lad. How would you like a big surprise?"

Ernie glanced across his shoulder. His friends were still there. He grinned at them. Suddenly he gasped as a gaunt hand clamped over his right arm. "Hey, leggo!" Ernie cried out.

"Take it easy, lad," soothed Mr. Hawkins. "No one's going to hurt you."

Ernie tugged. Tears sprang into his eyes as the old man drew him closer. From the corner of an eye Ernie saw his two friends running down the street.

"L-leggo," Ernie sobbed.

"Shortly," said the old man. "Now then, would you like a big surprise?"

"No-no, thanks, mister."

"Sure you would," said Mr. Hawkins. Ernie smelled his breath and tried to pull away, but Mr. Hawkins's grip was like iron.

"You know where Mr. Miller's field is?" asked Mr. Hawkins.

"Y-yeah."

"You know where the big oak tree is?"

"Yeah. Yeah, I know."

"You go to the oak tree in Mr. Miller's field. and face towards the church steeple. You understand?"

"Y-y-yeah."

The old man drew him closer. "You stand there and you walk ten paces. You understand? Ten paces."

"Yeah—"

"You walk ten paces and you dig down ten feet. *How many feet?*" He prodded Ernie's chest with a boney finger.

"T-ten," said Ernie.

"That's it," said the old man. "Face the steeple, walk ten paces, dig ten feet—and there you'll find a big surprise." He winked at Ernie. "Will you do it, lad?"

"I—yeah, sure. *Sure.*"

Mr. Hawkins let go and Ernie jumped away. His arm felt completely numb.

"Don't forget, now," the old man said.

Ernie whirled and ran down the street as fast as he could. He found his friends waiting at the corner.

"Did he try and murder you?" one of them whispered.

"Nanh," said Ernie. "He ain't so m-much."

"What'd he want?"

"What d'ya s'pose?"

They started down the street, all chanting it.

> *Dig me a hole, he said,*
> *Winking his eyes,*
> *And you will find*
> *big surprise.*

Every afternoon they went to Mr. Miller's field and sat under the big oak tree.

"You think there's somethin' down there really?"

"Nanh."

"What if there *was* though?"

"What?"

"Gold, maybe."

They talked about it every day, and every day they faced the steeple and walked ten paces. They stood on the spot and scuffed the earth with the tips of their sneakers.

"You s'pose there's gold down there really?"

"Why should he tell us?"

"Yeah, why not dig it up himself?"

"Because he's too old, stupid."

"Yeah? Well, if there's gold down there we split it three ways." They became more and more curious. At night they dreamed about gold. They wrote *gold* in their schoolbooks. They thought about all the things they could buy with gold. They started walking past Mr. Hawkins's house to see if he'd call them again and they could ask him if it was gold. But he never called them.

Then, one day, they were coming home from school and they saw Mr. Hawkins talking to another boy.

"He told us *we* could have the gold!" said Ernie.

"Yeah!" they stormed angrily. "Let's go!"

They ran to Ernie's house and Ernie went down to the cellar and got shovels. They ran up the street, over lots, across the dump, and into Mr. Miller's field. They stood under the oak tree, faced the steeple, and paced ten times.

"Dig," said Ernie.

Their shovels sank into the black earth. They dug without speaking, breath whistling through their nostrils. When the hole was about three feet deep, they rested.

"You think there's gold down there really?"

"I don't know but we're gonna find out before that other kid does."

"Yeah!"

"Hey, how we gonna get out if we dig ten feet?" one of them said.

"We'll cut out steps," said Ernie.

They started digging again. For over an hour they shoveled

out the cool, wormy earth and piled it high around the hole. It stained their clothes and their skin. When the hole was over their heads one of them went to get a pail and a rope. Ernie and the other boy kept digging and throwing the earth out of the hole. After a while the dirt rained back on their heads and they stopped. They sat on the damp earth wearily, waiting for the other boy to come back. Their hands and arms were brown with earth.

"How far're we down?" wondered the boy.

"Six feet," estimated Ernie.

The other boy came back and they started working again. They kept digging and digging until their bones ached.

"Aaah, the heck with it," said the boy who was pulling up the pail. "There ain't nothin' down there."

"He said ten feet," Ernie insisted.

"Well, I'm quittin'," said the boy.

"You're yella!"

"Tough," said the boy.

Ernie turned to the boy beside him. "You'll have to pull the dirt up," he said.

"Oh—okay," muttered the boy.

Ernie kept digging. When he looked up now, it seemed as if the sides of the hole were shaking and it was all going to cave in on him. He was trembling with fatigue.

"Come on," the other boy finally called down. "There ain't nothin' down there. You dug ten feet."

"Not yet," gasped Ernie.

"How deep ya goin', *China*?"

Ernie leaned against the side of the hole and gritted his teeth. A fat worm crawled out of the earth and tumbled to the bottom of the hole.

"I'm goin' home," said the other boy. "I'll catch it if I'm late for supper."

"You're yella too," said Ernie miserably.

"Aaaaah—*tough*."

Ernie twisted his shoulders painfully. "Well, the gold is all mine," he called up.

"There ain't no gold," said the other boy.

"Tie the rope to something so I can get out when I find *the gold*," said Ernie.

The boy snickered. He tied the rope to a bush and let it dangle down into the hole. Ernie looked up and saw the crooked rectangle of darkening sky. The boy's face appeared, looking down.

"You better not get stuck down there," he said.

"I ain't gettin' stuck." Ernie looked down angrily and drove the shovel into the ground. He could feel his friend's eyes on his back.

"Ain't you scared?" asked the other boy.

"What of?" snapped Ernie without looking up.

"I dunno," said the boy.

Ernie dug.

"Well," said the boy, "I'll see ya."

Ernie grunted. He heard the boy's footsteps move away. He looked around the hole and a faint whimper sounded in his throat. He felt cold.

"Well, I ain't leavin'," he mumbled. The gold was his. He wasn't going to leave it for that other kid.

He dug furiously, piling the dirt on the other side of the hole. It kept getting darker.

"A little more," he told himself, gasping. "Then I'm goin' home with the gold."

He stepped hard on the shovel and there was a hollow sound beneath him. Ernie felt a shudder running up his back. He forced himself to keep on digging. Will I give *them* the horse laugh, he thought. Will I give *them*—

He had uncovered part of a box—a long box. He stood there looking down at the wood and shivering. *And you will find*—

Quivering, Ernie stood on top of the box and stamped on it. A deeply hollow sound struck his ears. He dug away more earth and his shovel scraped on the ancient wood. He couldn't uncover the entire box—it was too long.

Then he saw that the box had a two-part cover and there was a clasp on each part.

Ernie clenched his teeth and struck the clasp with the edge of his shovel. Half of the cover opened.

Ernie screamed. He fell back against the earth wall and stared in voiceless horror at the man who was sitting up.

"Surprise!" said Mr. Hawkins.

A VISIT TO SANTA CLAUS

All the way across the dark parking lot, Richard kept sighing sulkily.

"All right, that's *e-nough*," Helen said to him when they reached the car. "We'll see him on Tuesday. How many times do I have to tell you?"

"Wanna see 'im *now*," Richard said, twitching with a sob.

Ken was reaching for the keys, trying not to drop the packages in his arms. "*Oh*," he said irritably, "I'll take him."

"What do you mean?" she asked, shifting her bundles and shivering in the cold wind that raced across the car-packed lot.

"I mean I'll take him now," he said, fumbling for the door lock.

"*Now?*" she asked. "It's too late now. Why didn't you take him while we were in the store? There was plenty of time then."

"So I'll take him now. What's the difference?"

"I wanna see *Sanna* Claus!" Richard broke in, looking intently at Helen. "Mama, I wanna see Sanna Claus *now*!"

"Not now, Richard," Helen said, shaking her head. She dumped her bundles on the front seat and straightened her arms with a groan. "That's *e-nough,* I said," she warned as Richard began whining again. "Mommy's too tired to walk all the way back to the store."

"You don't have to go," Ken told her, throwing his packages in beside hers. "I'll take him in myself." He turned on the light.

"Mama, *please*, Mama? *Please?*"

She made herself a place on the seat and sank down with a

weary grunt. He noticed the lock of unkempt brown hair dangling across her forehead, the caking dryness of her lipstick.

"Well, what made you change your mind now?" she asked tiredly. "I only asked you about a hundred times to take him while we were in the store."

"For God's sake, what's the difference?" he snapped. "Do you want to drive back here on Tuesday just to see Santa Claus?"

"No."

"Well, then . . ." He noticed the wrinkles in her stockings as she pulled her legs around and faced the front of the car. She looked old and sour in the dim light. It gave him an odd sensation in his stomach.

"*Please*, Mama?" Richard was begging as if Helen were all authority, Ken thought, as if *he*, the father, had no say at all. Well, that was probably the way it was.

Helen stared glumly at the windshield, then reached back and turned off the light. Two hours of being exposed to frantic Christmas shoppers, never-strained sales people, Richard's constant demands to see Santa Claus, and Ken's irritating refusals to take him had jaded her.

"And what am I supposed to do while you're gone?" she asked.

"It'll only be a few minutes, for God's sake," Ken answered. He'd been on hooks all night, either remote and uncommunicative or snapping nervously at her and Richard.

"Oh, go a-*head*," she said, arranging her coat over her legs, "and please hurry."

"*Sanna* Claus, *Sanna* Claus!" Richard shouted, tugging joyously at his father's topcoat.

"All right!" Ken flared. "Stop pulling at me, for God's sake!"

"Joy to the world. The Lord has come," Helen said, her sigh one of disgust.

"Yeah, sure," Ken said bitterly, grabbing at Richard's hand. "Come on."

Helen pulled the car door shut, and Ken noticed she didn't push down the button to lock it. She might though, after they'd gone. *The keys!*—the thought exploded suddenly, and he drove his hand into his topcoat pocket, his palsied fingers tightening over their cold metal. A dry swallow moved his throat and he sucked in cold air shakily, heartbeats thudding like a fist inside his chest. Take it easy, he told himself, just . . . take it easy.

He knew enough not to look back. It would be like taking one more look at a funeral. He stared up, deliberately, at the glittering neon wreath on the department store roof. He could barely feel Richard's hand on his. His other hand clutched at the keys in his pocket. He wouldn't look back, he—

"Ken!"

His body clamped in a spasmodic start as her voice rang out thinly in the huge lot. Automatically, he turned and saw her standing by the Ford, looking at them.

"Leave the keys!" she called. "I'll drive around to the front of the store so you don't have to walk all the way back here!"

He stared blankly at her, feeling the sudden cramped tightness of his stomach muscles.

"That's—" He cleared his throat, almost furiously. "It's not that far!" he called back.

He turned away before she could answer, noticing how Richard glanced at him. His heartbeat was like a club swung against the wall of his chest.

"Mama's calling," Richard said.

"You want to see Santa Claus or not?" Ken demanded sharply.

"Y-es."

"Then shut up!"

He swallowed again painfully and lengthened his stride. Why did *that* have to happen? A shudder ran down his back. He looked up at the neon wreath again, but he could still see Helen standing by the car in her green corduroy coat, one arm raised a little, her eyes on him. He could still hear her voice— *so you don't have to walk all the way back here!*—sounding thin and plaintive over the buffeting night wind.

He felt that wind chilling his cheeks now as his and Richard's shoes made a crisp, uneven sound on the gravel-strewn asphalt. Seventy yards, maybe it was seventy yards to the store. Was that the sound of their car door slamming shut? She was probably angry. If she pushed down the button, it would be harder to—

The man in the dark, sagging-brimmed hat stood at the end of the aisle. Ken pretended not to see him, but the air seemed rarefied suddenly, as though he were beyond atmosphere, trudging in an icy darkness that was nearly vacuum. It was the constriction around his heart that made him feel that way, the apparent inability of his lungs to hold in breath.

"Does Sanna Claus love me?" Richard asked.

Ken's chest labored with forced breathing. "Yes, yes," he said, "he—does." The man just stood there staring up at the sky, both hands deep in the pockets of his old checked overcoat, as if he were waiting for his wife to come out of the department store. But he wasn't. Ken's fingers grew rigid on the keys. His legs felt like heavy wood carrying him closer to the man.

I won't do it, he thought suddenly. He'd walk right by the man, take Richard to see Santa Claus, return to the car, go home, forget about it. He felt incapable and without strength. Helen alone in the Ford, sitting beside their Christmas packages, waiting for her husband and son to return. The thought sent strange electric pricklings through his body. I just won't do it. He heard the words as if someone were speaking them in his mind. I just won't—

His hand was growing cold and numb on the keys as, unconscious of it, he cut off the flow of blood to his fingers.

He *had* to do it; it was the only way. He wasn't going to return to the nerve-knotting frustration that was his present, the dreary expanse that was his future. Interior rages were poisoning him. For his own health it had to be done, for what was left of his life.

They reached the end of the aisle and walked past the man.

Richard cried, "Daddy, you dropped the keys!"

"Come on!" He pulled at Richard's hand, forcing himself not to look back over his shoulder.

"But you did, Daddy!"

"I said—!"

Ken's voice broke off abruptly as Richard pulled away from him and ran to where the ring of keys lay on the asphalt. He stared with helpless eyes at the man who hadn't budged from his place. The man appeared to shrug, but Ken couldn't see what his expression was beneath the wide hat brim.

Richard came running back with the keys. "Here, Daddy."

Ken slid them into his topcoat pocket with shaking fingers, a sick dismay twisting his insides. It won't work, he thought, feeling both an agony of disappointment and an agony of wrenching guilt.

"Say thank you," Richard said, taking his father's hand again.

Ken stood motionless in indecision, still holding on to the keys in his pocket. Empathic muscle tension pulled him toward the man, but he knew he couldn't go to him. Richard would see.

"Let's go, Daddy," Richard urged.

Ken turned away quickly, his face a painted mask as he started for the store. He felt dizzy, without feeling. It's over! He thought in bitter fury, *over*!

"Say thank you, Daddy."

"Will you—!" The sound of his voice startled him and he trapped the hysterical surge of words behind pressed, trembling lips. Richard was silent. He glanced cautiously at his taut-faced father.

They were halfway to the store entrance when the man in the checked overcoat brushed past Ken.

"Scuse it," muttered the man, and apparently by accident his arm brushed roughly against the pocket where the keys were, indicating that he wanted and was ready to receive them.

Then the man was past them, walking in jerky strides toward the store. Ken watched him go, feeling as if his head were being compressed between two hands, the palms contoured to his skull. It's not over, he thought. He didn't even know whether he was glad it wasn't. He saw the man stop and turn before one of the glass doors that flanked the revolving door. Now, he told himself, it has to be now. He took out the keys again.

"I wanna go that way, Daddy!" Richard was tugging him toward the revolving door which spun shoppers into the crowded din or out into the silent chill of night.

"It's too crowded," he heard himself say, but it was someone else speaking. It's my future, he kept thinking, my future.

"It's not crowded, Daddy!"

He didn't argue. He jerked Richard toward the side door. And as he pulled the door open with the keys in his hand, he felt them grabbed from his fingers.

Then, in a second, he and Richard were in the noisome brightness of the store, and it was done.

Ken didn't look over his shoulder, but he knew the man was walking back into the dark lot now, back toward the aisle where the Ford was parked.

For one horrible instant, he felt as if he were going to make an outcry. A great sickness rushed up through his body, and he almost yelled and dashed back into the night after the man. No, I've changed my mind; I don't want it done! In that instant, everything he hated about Helen and his life with her seemed to vanish, and all he could remember was that she was going to drive the car to the front of the store so he and Richard wouldn't have to walk back across the cold, wind-swept lot.

But then Richard had pulled him into the warmth and the noise and the milling press of shoppers and he was walking along dizzily, moving deeper into the store. Chimes were playing from the second-floor balcony—*Joy to the world, the Lord has come*. She'd said that. He felt dizzy and ill; sweat began trickling across his forehead. He couldn't go back now.

He stopped in the middle of the floor and leaned against a pillar, his legs feeling as if they'd turned to water. It's too late, he thought, too late. There was nothing he could do now.

"I wanna see Sanna Claus, Daddy."

Breath faltered through his parted lips. "Yes," he said, nodding feebly. "All right."

He tried to move along without thinking but found that impossible. His thoughts were flashing visual images. The man walking down the wide aisle toward the Ford. The man checking the miniature license plate on the key ring to make sure he got the right car. The man's face as it had been that night in the Main Street bar—thin, pale, corrupted. A whimper started in Ken's throat, but he cut it off. *Helen*, his thought said with anguish.

THIS WAY TO SANTA'S MAGIC HOUSE! He started numbly toward the door escalator, Richard skipping and wriggling beside him, whispering in breathless excitement, "*Sanna* Claus, *Sanna* Claus." What would Richard feel when his mother was—

All right!—he forced a strengthening rage through himself—if he had to think, he'd think about the future, not this. He hadn't planned all this just to collapse into useless infirmity when it came about. There was reason behind the act; it wasn't just a thoughtless viciousness.

They stepped onto the escalator. Richard's hand was tight in his, but he hardly felt it. South America and Rita—he'd think about that. Twenty-five thousand dollars insurance money; the girl he'd wanted at college and never stopped wanting; a future without the debasing struggle to stay one jump ahead of creditors. Freedom, simple pleasures and a relationship that wouldn't be eroded away by the abrasion of petty existence.

The up escalator angled past them, and Ken glanced at the shoppers' faces—tired, irritable, happy, blank. *It came upon a midnight clear,* the chimes began to play. He stared straight ahead, thinking about Rita and South America. Thinking about that made everything a lot easier.

Now the chimes faded and were swallowed in a raucous glee club blaring of "Jingle Bells." Richard began skipping excitedly as they stepped off the escalator, and Ken suddenly found himself thinking about Helen again. *Jingle all the way!*

"There 'e is!" Richard cried, pulling frantically. "There!"

"All right, all right!" Ken muttered under his breath as they moved toward the line that shuffled toward Santa's Magic House.

Had it happened yet? That contracting of stomach muscle again. Was the man in the car? Was Helen unconscious in back? Was the man driving across the lot toward dark side streets where he'd—?

Don't worry. The man's last words to him were like a flame searing his mind. *Don't worry. I'll make it look good.*

Look good, look good, look good, look good. The words thumped on in his thought as he and Richard moved slowly toward the house of Santa Claus. One hundred down, nine hundred to follow—the price of one medium-sized wife.

Ken shut his eyes suddenly and felt himself shivering as if it were cold in the store instead of unbearably stuffy. His head ached. Drops of sweat trickled down from his arm pits, feeling like insects on his flesh. It's too late, he thought, realizing that part of the tension he'd felt since entering the store had been the struggle with his impulse to rush back to the car to stop the man.

But, as you say—he heard a quiet voice whispering in his mind—it's too late.

"What shall I tell Sanna, Daddy?" Richard asked.

Ken looked down bleakly at his five-year-old son and thought, he'll be better off with Helen's mother—a lot better off. I can't—

"What shall I, Daddy?"

He tried to smile, and for a moment he even managed to visualize himself as a gallant man bearing up under a terrible burden that fate had put on his shoulders.

"Tell him—what you want for Christmas," he said. "Tell him you've been a—a good boy and . . . what you want for Christmas. That's all."

"But how?"

The vision had already faded; he knew exactly what he was and what he'd done.

"How should I know?" he snapped angrily. "Look, if you don't want to see him, you don't have to."

A man in front of them turned and shook his head at Ken with a wry smile that seemed to say, I know what you're going through, buddy. Ken's smile in return was little more than a slight, mirthless twitching of the lips. Oh, God, I've got to get out of here, he thought miserably. How can I stand here while—

Breath labored in his lungs. It was what he had to do. It was the plan and it had to be carried out. He wasn't going to spoil it now with stupid histrionics.

If only he could be with Rita, though, in his apartment,

beside her. But it was impossible. He'd settle for a drink, a stiff one. Anything to break the tension.

They pushed open the white gate and it set off a record of a man's booming laughter. Ken jumped and looked around. The laughter sounded insane to him. He tried not to listen, but it surrounded him, dinning in his ears.

Then the gate closed behind them and the laughter stopped. He heard a thin voice piping over the PA system, *I wiss you a mehwy Cwiss-muss an' a Happ-ee New Year.*

I'll make it look good.

Ken released Richard. He rubbed his damp palm against his coat. Richard tried to take his hand again, but Ken jerked his hand away so savagely that Richard looked frightened and puzzled.

No. No, I can't act this way, Ken heard the instruction in his mind. *Richard might be asked questions, questions like How did your daddy act when you were in the store together?* He took Richard's hand and managed to force a smile.

"Almost there," he said. The calmness of his voice shocked him. *I tell you I don't know how I lost the keys. I had them in my pocket when I went in the store; I'm sure of it. That's all I know. Arc you trying to imply that—?*

No! ALL WRONG. No matter what they intimated he must never let them know he understood. Shocked, dazed, hardly capable of coherence—that was the way he'd have to be. A man who had taken his son to see Santa Claus, who had been told the next day that they'd found his wife still in the car.

*I'll make it look—*Why couldn't he forget that!

The Santa Claus was sitting in a high-backed chair on the porch of the magic house—magic because it changed color every fifteen seconds. He was a fat, middle-aged man with a chuckling voice who held children on his lap a few moments, spoke the formula words, then put the children down, one peppermint stick richer, patted them on the rear and said goodbye and Merry Christmas.

When Richard came on the porch, Santa Claus picked him up and set him on his broad, red-knickered lap. Ken stood on the bottom step, feeling dizzy in the warmth of the store, staring, dull-eyed, at the red-rouged face, the dreadfully false whiskers.

"Well, sonny," said Santa Claus, "have you been a good boy this year?"

Richard tried to answer, but speech stuck in his throat. Ken saw him nod, flushing nervously. He'll be better off with Helen's mother. I can't do right by him. I'd just—

His eyes strained into focus on the red, whiskered face. "What?"

"I say has this boy been good this year?"

"Oh. Yes. *Yes*. Very good."

"Well," said Santa Claus, "old Santa is glad to hear that. Very glad. And what would you like for Christmas, sonny?"

Ken stood there, motionless, sweat soaking into his shirt while the faint voice of his son droned on endlessly, itemizing toys he wanted. The porch seemed to waver before his eyes. I'm sick, he thought. I've got to get out of here and get some fresh air. Helen, I'm sorry, I'm sorry. I . . . just couldn't do it any other way, don't you see?

Then Richard came down the steps with his peppermint stick, and they started toward the escalator.

"Sanna said I'll get ev'rything I ast," Richard told him.

Ken nodded jerkily, reaching into his suit coat pocket for a handkerchief. Maybe the people wouldn't think it was perspiration he was wiping from his cheeks. Maybe they'd think he was overcome with emotion because it was Christmas and he loved Christmas and that's why there were tears on his face.

"I'm gonna tell Mama," Richard said.

"Yes." His voice was barely audible. We'll go out and walk back to where the car was parked. We'll look around a while. Then I'll call the police.

"Yes," he said.

"What, Daddy?"

He shook his head. "Nothing."

The escalator lifted them toward the main floor. The glee club started singing "Jingle Bells" again. Ken stood behind Richard and stared down at his blond hair. This is the part that counts most, he told himself. What went before was just time consumption.

He'd have to act surprised on the telephone, irritated. A little concerned, maybe, but not too much. A man wouldn't panic under such circumstances. Normally, a man wouldn't conceive that his wife's disappearance meant—Behind them the recorded laughter boomed faintly over the glee club's singing.

He tried to erase his mind as if it were a blackboard, but words kept forming there. Be a little concerned, a little irritated, a—

—We're not implying anything Mister Burns. Abruptly, they were at him again. We're just saying that twenty-five thousand is a lot of insurance.

Look! His face tightened as he flared back at them. It's something we believe in, see? I'm insured for twenty-five thousand, too, you know. You forget that.

It was his biggest point. The insurance had been in effect less than a year, but at least they were both equally insured.

He scuffed his shoe toe at the top of the escalator and found himself back in the store again, walking beside his son toward the doors which would revolve them into the night. A thin current of air fluttered his trouser cuffs. He felt the chill on his ankles. We'll look around a while, then I'll—

It came over him. He didn't know how, but suddenly he couldn't leave the store. Suddenly he was standing in front of a counter, staring down intently at handkerchiefs and ties. He felt Richard's eyes on him and he was admonishing himself, I mustn't look upset! I didn't plan all this just to break down at the last minute!

Rita. South America. Money. It was good to think about the future. He'd known that all along, and yet he'd allowed himself to forget. The future was what was important, Rita and he together in South America.

There, that was better. He took in a long, faltering breath of warm air. The hands in his coat pockets unknotted.

"Come on," he said, and this time he was grimly pleased at the calmness of his voice. "Let's go."

As he took Richard's hand, the closing gong sounded above the organ playing "Silent Night, Holy Night." Perfect timing, he told himself. Nine p.m., Monday night. We'll go out to where the Ford was parked; then I'll call the police.

But should he call the police? A momentary touch of panic startled him. Wouldn't he, normally, think that maybe Helen had gotten angry and—

I thought she'd gotten angry and driven home without us. No, she's never done anything like it before. Anyway we went home by bus, my son and I, but my wife wasn't there. And I don't know where she is. Yes, I checked at her mother's house. No, that's our only relative in the city.

They had pushed through the doorway now and were back outside. Ken looked straight across the car-filled lot as they moved away from the store. He couldn't feel the grip of Richard's hand in his. All he could feel was his heartbeat, leaping— like something imprisoned—at the wall of his chest. Well, I wonder where Mother went, he imagined himself saying to Richard when they'd reach the place where the Ford had been parked. Where's Mama? Would be Richard's reply. Then there would be the wait, calling the police finally. No, she's never done anything like this, his mind ticked on, unbidden. I assumed she was angry and had gone home, but when my son and I got home she wasn't there.

For a moment, he thought that he had died, that his heart had ceased to beat. He felt as if he'd been turned to stone. The wind blew coldly into his stricken face.

"Come on, Daddy," Richard said, tugging at him.

He didn't move. He stood looking at the car, Helen sitting in it.

"I'm cold, Daddy."

He found himself walking, moving with a dazed, somnambulistic tread. Intelligence would not return to him. He could only stare at the car and at Helen and suffer a twisting sickness in his stomach. His head felt light and fragile, as if it were about to float off. Only the impact of his footsteps that jarred consciousness through him held the parts of his body together. His eyes were set unmovingly on the car. He knew a great, warm surge of relief. Helen was looking at him.

He pulled open the door.

"It's about *time* you got back," she said.

He couldn't speak. Trembling, he pushed the seat forward and Richard clambered into the back.

"Come on, come *on*. Let's get out of here," Helen said.

Ken slid his hand into his coat pocket and with the act remembered.

"Well?" she said.

"I—I—can't find the keys." He patted feebly at his pockets. "Had them with me when—"

"Oh, *no*." The lilt of her voice was weariness and disgust.

Ken swallowed.

"Well, where are they?" Helen asked. "I swear if your head weren't fastened to your shoulders—"

"I—I don't know," he said. "I—must have dropped them—somewhere."

"Well, go pick them *up* then," she snapped.

"Yes," he said, "yes." He pushed the door out almost desperately and stood in the cold air.

"I'll be right back," he said.

She didn't answer, but he could feel her hostility.

He shut the door and moved away from the car, his face beginning to harden. That bastard, taking his money and—!

He suddenly imagined himself trying to explain the lack of a hundred dollars in the checking account. She'd never believe that it had simply vanished. She'd investigate, find out about the cash he'd gotten, probe, demand. Oh, God, he thought, I'm done, I'm *done*.

He looked off, his eyes unseeing, fixed on the huge neon wreath on the roof of the store. In the middle of it, tall, white letters were blinking off and on. He focused on them suddenly. MERRY CHRISTMAS—darkness. MERRY CHRISTMAS—darkness. MERRY CHRISTMAS—darkness.

FINGER PRINTS

When I got on the bus, the two of them were sitting in the third row on the right-hand side. The small woman in the aisle seat was staring into her lap where her hands were resting limply. The other one was staring out the window. It was almost dark.

There were two empty seats across the aisle from them, so I put my suitcase up on the rack and sat down. The heavy door was pulled shut and the bus pulled out of the depot.

For awhile I contented myself with looking out the window and browsing through a magazine I'd brought with me.

Then I looked over at the two women.

The one on the aisle had dry, flat colored blonde hair. It looked like the wig from a doll that had fallen on the floor and gotten dusty. Her skin was tallow white and her face looked as if it had been formed of this tallow with two fingers, a pinch for the chin, one for the lips, one for the nose, one each for the ears, and finally two savage pokes for her beady eyes.

She was talking with her hands.

I had never seen that before. I'd read about it and I'd seen pictures of the various hand positions that deaf-mutes use for communication, but I'd never actually seen them used.

Her short, colorless fingers moved energetically in the air as though her mind were teeming with interesting things she must say and was afraid to lose. The hands contracted and expanded; they assumed a dozen different shapes in the space of a few moments. She drew the taut hand figures one over the other, pulling and squeezing out her deathly still monologue.

I looked at the other woman.

Her face was thin and weary. She was leaning back on the head rest with her eyes fixed dispassionately on her gesticulating companion. I had never seen such eyes before. They never moved; they were without a glimmer of life. She stared dully at the mute woman and kept nodding her head in an endless jerky motion as if it were on rockers.

Once in a while she'd try to turn away and look out the window or close her eyes. But the moment she did, the other woman would reach out her pudgy right hand and pluck at her dress, tugging at it until her companion was forced to look once more at the endless patterns of shapes created by the white hands.

To me it was phenomenal that it could be understood at all. The hands moved so quickly that I could hardly see them. They were a blur of agitating flesh. But the other woman kept nodding and nodding.

In her soundless way, the deaf-mute woman was a chatterbox.

She wouldn't stop moving her hands. She acted as though she had to keep it up at top speed or perish. It got to a point where I almost could hear what she was talking about, almost could imagine in my mind the splatter of insensate trivia and gossip.

Every once in a while, she seemed to come up with something very amusing to herself, so overpoweringly amusing that she would push her hands away quickly, palms out, as though physically repulsing this outstandingly funny bit of business, lest, in retaining it, she should destroy herself with hilarity.

I must have stared at them a long time, because suddenly they were conscious of it and the two of them were looking at me.

I don't know which of their looks was the more repelling.

The small deaf-mute woman looked at me with her eyes like hard black beads, her buttonlike nose twitching and her mouth arced into a dimpling bowlike smirk, and in her lap her white fingers plucked like leprous bird beaks at the skirt of her flowered dress. It was the look of a hideous life-sized doll somehow come to life.

The other woman's look was one of strange hunger.

Her dark-rimmed eyes ran over my face, then abruptly down over my body, and I saw the shallow rise of her breasts swell suddenly under her dark dress before I turned to the window.

I pretended to look out at the fields, but I could still feel the two of them looking at me steadily.

Then, from the corner of an eye I saw the deaf-mute woman throw up her hands again and begin weaving her silent tapestries of communication. After a few minutes I glanced over at them.

The gaunt woman was watching the hands again in stolid silence. Yes, she nodded wearily, yes, yes, yes.

I fell into a half-sleep, seeing the flashing hands, the rocking head. Yes, yes, yes . . . I woke up suddenly, feeling a furtive pluck of fingers on my jacket.

I looked up and saw the deaf-mute woman weaving in the aisle over me. She was tugging at my jacket, trying to pull me up. I stared up at her in sleepy bewilderment.

"What are you doing?" I whispered, forgetting that she couldn't hear.

She kept tugging resolutely and every time the bus passed a street lamp, I could see her pale white face and her dark eyes glittering like jewels set in the waxy flesh.

I had to get up. She kept pulling, and I was so sleepy I couldn't get my mind awake enough to combat her insistent efforts.

As I stood up in the aisle, she plumped down where I had been and drew up her feet so that she covered both seats. I stared down at her uncomprehendingly. Then, as she pretended to be suddenly asleep, I turned and looked at her companion.

She was sitting quietly, looking out the window.

With a lethargic movement I dropped down beside her. Seeing that she was not going to say anything I asked, "Why did your friend do that?"

She turned and looked at me. She was even more gaunt than I had thought. I saw her scrawny throat contract.

"It was her own idea," she said. "I didn't tell her to."

"What idea?" I asked.

She looked more closely at me, and again I saw that look of hunger. It was intense. It burned out from her like an arc of drawing flame. I felt my heart jolt.

"Are you sisters?" I asked for no other reason than to break the silence.

She didn't answer for a moment. Then her face grew tight.

"I'm her companion," she said. "I'm her paid companion."

"Oh," I said, "I guess it—" I forgot what I was going to say.

"You don't have to talk to me," she said. "It was her idea. I didn't tell her to."

We sat in awkward, painful silence, me looking at her groggily, her watching the dark streets pass by. Then she turned and her eyes glittered once from the light of a street lamp.

"She keeps talking all the time," she said.

"What?"

"She keeps talking all the time."

"That's funny," I said awkwardly, "to call it talking, I mean. I mean—"

"I don't see her mouth anymore," she said. "Her hands are her mouth. I can hear her talking with her hands. Her voice is like a squeaky machine." She drew in hurried breath. "God, how she talks," she said.

I sat without speaking, watching her face.

"I never talk," she said. "I'm with her all the time and we never talk because she can't. It's always quiet. I get surprised when I hear people really talking. I get surprised when I hear *myself* really talking. I forget how it is to talk. I feel like I'm going to forget everything I know about talking."

Her voice was jerky and rapid, of indefinite pitch. It plunged from a guttural croak to a thin falsetto, more so since she was trying to speak under her breath. There was mounting unrest in it, too, which I began to feel in myself, as though at any moment something in her was going to explode.

"She never lets me have any time to myself," she said. "She's always with me. I keep telling her I'm leaving. I can talk a little with my hands, too. I tell her I'm going to leave. And she cries and moans around and says she's going to kill herself if I go away. God, it's awful to watch her begging. It makes me sick.

"Then I feel sorry for her and I don't leave. And she's happy as a lark and her father gives me a raise and sends us on another trip to see some of her relatives. Her father hates her. He likes to get rid of her. I hate her, too. But it's like she has some power over us all. We can't argue with her. You can't yell with your hands. And it isn't enough for you to close your eyes and turn away so you can't see her hands anymore."

Her voice grew heavier and I noticed how she kept pressing her palms into her lap as she spoke. The more she pressed down against herself, the harder it was to keep my eyes off her hands. After a while I couldn't stop. Even when I knew she saw me looking I couldn't stop. It was like the complete abandon one feels in a dream, when any desire is allowable.

She kept on talking, her voice trembling a little as she spoke.

"She knows I want to get married," she said. "Any girl wants that. But she won't let me leave her. Her father pays me good and I don't know anything else. Besides, even when I hate her most, I feel sorry for her when she cries and begs. It's not like real crying and real begging. It's so quiet, and all you see are tears running down her cheeks. She keeps begging me until I stay."

Now I felt my own hands trembling in my lap. Somehow her words seemed to mean something more than they said on the surface. It seemed that what was coming grew more and more apparent. But I was hypnotized. With the lights flashing over us in the pitch blackness as the bus sped on through the night, it was like being inextricably bound in some insane nightmare.

"Once she said she'd get me a boyfriend," she said, and I shuddered. "I told her to stop making fun of me, but she said she'd get me a boyfriend. So when we went on a trip to Indianapolis, she went across the aisle in the bus and brought a sailor to talk to me. He was just a boy. He told me he was twenty, but I bet he was eighteen. He was nice though. He sat with me and we talked. At first I was embarrassed and I didn't know what to say. But he was nice, and it was nice talking to him except for *her* sitting across the way."

Instinctively I turned, but the deaf-mute woman seemed to be asleep. Yet I had the feeling that the moment I turned my back, her beady eyes popped open again and refocused on us. "Never mind her," said the woman beside me.

I turned back.

"Do you think it's wrong?" she said suddenly, and I shuddered again as her hot, damp hand closed over mine.

"I—I don't know."

"The sailor was so nice," she said in a heavy voice. "He was so nice. I don't care if she's watching. It doesn't matter, does it? It's dark and she can't really see. She can't hear anything."

I must have drawn back, because her fingers tightened on mine.

"I'm clean," she whined pathetically. "It's not all the time. I only did it with the sailor, I swear I only did. I'm not lying."

As she spoke more and more excitedly, her hand slipped off mine and dropped, quivering, on my leg. It made my stomach lurch. I couldn't move. I guess I didn't want to move. I was paralyzed by the sound of her thickening voice and the flaring sensation of her hand beginning to move over my leg, sensuously caressing.

"*Please*," she said, almost gasping the word.

I tried to say something but nothing came.

"I'm always alone," she said, starting in again. "She won't let me get married because she gets afraid and she doesn't want to let me leave her. It's all right, no one can see us."

Now she was clutching at my leg, digging her hand in fiercely. She put her other hand in my lap and as a blaze of light splashed over us, I saw her mouth as a dark gaping wound, her starved eyes shining.

"You have to," she said, moving closer.

Suddenly, she threw herself against me. Her mouth was burning hot, shaking under mine. Her breath was hot in my throat and her hands were wild and throbbing on my suddenly exposed flesh. Her frail, hot limbs seemed to wrap themselves around me again and again like writhing tentacles. The heat of her body blasted me into submission. I'll never know how the other passengers slept through it. But they didn't all sleep through it. One of them was watching.

Suddenly, the night had chilled; it was over, and she drew back quickly and her dress rustled angrily as she pulled it down like an outraged old lady who has inadvertently exposed her legs. She turned and looked out the window as if I wasn't there any longer. Stupidly, I watched her back rise and fall, feeling drained of strength, feeling as if my muscles had become fluid.

Then, shakily, I adjusted my clothing and struggled up into the aisle. Instantly, the deaf-mute woman jumped up and pushed past me roughly, wide awake. I caught a glimpse of her excited face as she moved.

As I slumped down on the other seat, I looked across the aisle again and saw her stubby white fingers grasping and fluttering, milking greedy questions from the air. And the gaunt woman was nodding and nodding and the deaf woman wouldn't let her turn away.

MUTE

The man in the dark raincoat arrived in German Corners at
two-thirty that Friday afternoon. He walked across the bus
station to a counter behind which a plump, gray-haired woman
was polishing glasses.

"Please," he said, "where might I find authority?"

The woman peered through rimless glasses at him. She saw
a man in his late thirties, a tall, good-looking man.

"Authority?" she asked.

"Yes—how do you say it? The constable? The—?"

"Sheriff?"

"Ah." The man smiled. "Of course. The sheriff. Where
might I find him?"

After being directed, he walked out of the building into the
overcast day. The threat of rain had been constant since he'd
woken up that morning as the bus was pulling over the mountains into Casca Valley. The man drew up his collar, then slid
both hands into the pockets of his raincoat and started briskly
down Main Street.

Really, he felt tremendously guilty for not having come
sooner; but there was so much to do, so many problems to
overcome with his own two children. Even knowing that
something was wrong with Holger and Fanny, he'd been unable to get away from Germany until now—almost a year
since they'd last heard from the Nielsens. It was a shame that
Holger had chosen such an out of the way place for his corner
of the four-sided experiment.

Professor Werner walked more quickly, anxious to find out

what had happened to the Nielsens and their son. Their progress with the boy had been phenomenal—really an inspiration to them all. Although, Werner felt, deep within himself, that something terrible had happened he hoped they were all alive and well. Yet, if they were, how to account for the long silence?

Werner shook his head worriedly. Could it have been the town? Elkenberg had been compelled to move several times in order to avoid the endless prying—sometimes innocent, more often malicious—into *his* work. Something similar might have happened to Nielsen. The workings of the small town composite mind could, sometimes, be a terrible thing.

The sheriff's office was in the middle of the next block. Werner strode more quickly along the narrow sidewalk, then pushed open the door and entered the large, warmly heated room.

"Yes?" the sheriff asked, looking up from his desk.

"I have come to inquire about a family," Werner said, "the name of Nielsen."

Sheriff Harry Wheeler looked blankly at the tall man.

Cora was pressing Paul's trousers when the call came. Setting the iron on its stand, she walked across the kitchen and lifted the receiver from the wall telephone.

"Yes?" she said.

"Cora, it's me."

Her face tightened. "Is something wrong, Harry?"

He was silent.

"Harry?"

"*The one from Germany is here.*"

Cora stood motionless, staring at the calendar on the wall, the numbers blurred before her eyes.

"Cora, did you hear me?"

She swallowed dryly. "Yes."

"I—I have to bring him out to the house," he said.

She closed her eyes.

"I know," she murmured and hung up.

Turning, she walked slowly to the window. It's going to rain, she thought. Nature was setting the scene well.

Abruptly, her eyes shut, her fingers drew in tautly, the nails digging at her palms.

"No." It was almost a gasp. *"No."*

After a few moments she opened her tear-glistening eyes and looked out fixedly at the road. She stood there numbly, thinking of the day the boy had come to her.

If the house hadn't burned in the middle of the night there might have been a chance. It was twenty-one miles from German Corners but the state highway ran fifteen of them and the last six—the six miles of dirt road that led north into the wood-sloped hills—might have been navigated had there been more time.

As it happened, the house was a night-lashing sheet of flame before Bernhard Klaus saw it.

Klaus and his family lived some five miles away on Skytouch Hill. He had gotten out of bed around one-thirty to get a drink of water. The window of the bathroom faced north and that was why, entering, Klaus saw the tiny flaring blaze out in the darkness.

"*Gott'n'immel*!" he slung startled words together and was out of the room before he'd finished. He thumped heavily down the carpeted steps, then, feeling at the wall for guidance, hurried for the living room.

"Fire at Nielsen house!" he gasped after agitated cranking had roused the night operator from her nap.

The hour, the remoteness, and one more thing doomed the house. German Corners had no official fire brigade. The security of its brick and timbered dwellings depended on voluntary effort. In the town itself this posed no serious problem. It was different with those houses in the outlying areas.

By the time Sheriff Wheeler had gathered five men and driven them to the fire in the ancient truck, the house was lost. While four of the six men pumped futile streams of water into the leaping, crackling inferno, Sheriff Wheeler and his deputy, Max Ederman, circuited the house.

There was no way in. They stood in back, raised arms warding off the singeing buffet of heat, grimacing at the blaze.

"They're done for!" Ederman yelled above the windswept roar.

Sheriff Wheeler looked sick. "The *boy*," he said but Ederman didn't hear.

Only a waterfall could have doused the burning of the old house. All the six men could do was prevent ignition of the woods that fringed the clearing. Their silent figures prowled the edges of the glowing aura, stamping out sparks, hosing out the occasional flare of bushes and tree foliage.

They found the boy just as the eastern hill peaks were being edged with gray morning.

Sheriff Wheeler was trying to get close enough to see into one of the side windows when he heard a shout. Turning, he ran towards the thick woods that sloped downwards a few dozen yards behind the house. Before he'd reached the underbrush, Tom Poulter emerged from them, his thin frame staggering beneath the weight of Paal Nielsen.

"Where'd you find him?" Wheeler asked, grabbing the boy's legs to ease weight from the older man's back.

"Down the hill," Poulter gasped. "Lyin' on the ground."

"Is he burned?"

"Don't look it. His pajamas ain't touched."

"Give him here," the sheriff said. He shifted Paal into his own strong arms and found two large, green-pupilled eyes staring blankly at him.

"You're awake," he said, surprised.

The boy kept staring at him without making a sound.

"You all right, son?" Wheeler asked. It might have been a statue he held, Paal's body was so inert, his expression so dumbly static.

"Let's get a blanket on him," the sheriff muttered aside and started for the truck. As he walked he noticed how the boy stared at the burning house now, a look of mask-like rigidity on his face.

"*Shock*," murmured Poulter and the sheriff nodded grimly.

They tried to put him down on the cab seat, a blanket over him but he kept sitting up, never speaking. The coffee Wheeler tried to give him dribbled from his lips and across his chin.

The two men stood beside the truck while Paal stared through the windshield at the burning house.

"Bad off," said Poulter. "Can't talk, cry nor nothing."

"He isn't burned," Wheeler said, perplexed. "How'd he get out of the house without getting burned?"

"Maybe his folks got out too," said Poulter.

"Where are they then?"

The older man shook his head. "Dunno, Harry."

"Well, I better take him home to Cora," the sheriff said. "Can't leave him sitting out here."

"Think I'd better go with you," Poulter said. "I have t' get the mail sorted for delivery."

"All right."

Wheeler told the other four men he'd bring back food and replacements in an hour or so. Then Poulter and he climbed into the cab beside Paal and he jabbed his boot toe on the starter. The engine coughed spasmodically, groaned over, then caught. The sheriff raced it until it was warm, then eased it into gear. The truck rolled off slowly down the dirt road that led to the highway.

Until the burning house was no longer visible, Paal stared out the back window, face still immobile. Then, slowly, he turned, the blanket slipping off his thin shoulders. Tom Poulter put it back over him.

"Warm enough?" he asked.

The silent boy looked at Poulter as if he'd never heard a human voice in his life.

As soon as she heard the truck turn off the road, Cora Wheeler's quick right hand moved along the stove-front switches. Before her husband's bootfalls sounded on the back porch steps, the bacon lay neatly in strips across the frying pan, white moons of pancake batter were browning on the griddle, and the already-brewed coffee was heating.

"Harry."

There was a sound of pitying distress in her voice as she saw the boy in his arms. She hurried across the kitchen.

"Let's get him to bed," Wheeler said. "I think maybe he's in shock."

The slender woman moved up the stairs on hurried feet, threw open the door of what had been David's room, and moved to the bed. When Wheeler passed through the doorway she had the covers peeled back and was plugging in an electric blanket.

"Is he hurt?" she asked.

"No." He put Paal down on the bed.

"Poor darling," she murmured, tucking in the bedclothes around the boy's frail body. "Poor little darling." She stroked back the soft blond hair from his forehead and smiled down at him.

"There now, go to sleep, dear. It's all right. Go to sleep."

Wheeler stood behind her and saw the seven-year-old boy staring up at Cora with that same dazed, lifeless expression. It hadn't changed once since Tom Poulter had brought him out of the woods.

The sheriff turned and went down to the kitchen. There he phoned for replacements, then turned the pancakes and bacon, and poured himself a cup of coffee. He was drinking it when Cora came down the back stairs and returned to the stove.

"Are his parents—?" she began.

"I don't know," Wheeler said, shaking his head. "We couldn't get near the house."

"But the boy—?"

"Tom Poulter found him outside."

"*Outside.*"

"We don't know how he got out," he said. "All we know's he was there."

His wife grew silent. She slid pancakes on a dish and put the dish in front of him. She put her hand on his shoulder.

"You look tired," she said. "Can you go to bed?"

"Later," he said.

She nodded, then, patting his shoulder, turned away. "The bacon will be done directly," she said.

He grunted. Then, as he poured maple syrup over the stack of cakes, he said, "I expect they are dead, Cora. It's an awful fire; still going when I left. Nothing we could do about it."

"That poor boy," she said.

She stood by the stove watching her husband eat wearily.

"I tried to get him to talk," she said, shaking her head, "but he never said a word."

"Never said a word to us either," he told her, "just stared."

He looked at the table, chewing thoughtfully.

"Like he doesn't even know how to talk," he said.

A little after ten that morning the waterfall came—a waterfall of rain—and the burning house sputtered and hissed into charred, smoke-fogged ruins.

Red-eyed and exhausted, Sheriff Wheeler sat motionless in the truck cab until the deluge had slackened. Then, with a chest-deep groan, he pushed open the door and slid to the ground. There, he raised the collar of his slicker and pulled down the wide-brimmed Stetson more tightly on his skull. He walked around to the back of the covered truck.

"Come on," he said, his voice hoarsely dry. He trudged through the clinging mud towards the house.

The front door still stood. Wheeler and the other men by-passed it and clambered over the collapsed living room wall. The sheriff felt thin waves of heat from the still-glowing timbers and the throat-clogging reek of wet, smoldering rugs and upholstery turned his edgy stomach.

He stepped across some half-burned books on the floor and the roasted bindings crackled beneath his tread. He kept moving, into the hall, breathing through gritted teeth, rain spattering off his shoulders and back. I hope they got out, he thought, I hope to God they got out.

They hadn't. They were still in their bed, no longer human, blackened to a hideous, joint-twisted crisp. Sheriff Wheeler's face was taut and pale as he looked down at them.

One of the men prodded a wet twig at something on the mattress.

"Pipe," Wheeler heard him say above the drum of rain. "Must have fell asleep smokin'."

"Get some blankets," Wheeler told them. "Put them in the back of the truck."

Two of the men turned away without a word and Wheeler heard them clump away over the rubble.

He was unable to take his eyes off Professor Holger Nielsen and his wife Fanny, scorched into grotesque mockeries of the handsome couple he remembered—the tall, big-framed Holger, calmly imperious; the slender, auburn-haired Fanny, her face a soft, rose-cheeked—

Abruptly, the sheriff turned and stumped from the room, almost tripping over a fallen beam.

The boy—what would happen to the boy now? That day was the first time Paal had ever left this house in his life. His parents were the fulcrum of his world; Wheeler knew that much. No wonder there had been that look of shocked incomprehension on Paal's face.

Yet how did he know his mother and father were dead?

As the sheriff crossed the living room, he saw one of the men looking at a partially charred book.

"Look at this," the man said, holding it out.

Wheeler glanced at it, his eyes catching the title: *The Unknown Mind.*

He turned away tensely. "Put it down!" he snapped, quitting the house with long, anxious strides. The memory of how the Nielsens looked went with him; and something else. A question.

How did Paal get out of the house?

Paal woke up.

For a long moment he stared up at the formless shadows that danced and fluttered across the ceiling. It was raining out. The wind was rustling tree boughs outside the window, causing shadow movements in this strange room. Paal lay motionless in the warm center of the bed, air crisp in his lungs, cold against his pale cheeks.

Where were they? Paal closed his eyes and tried to sense their presence. They weren't in the house. Where then? Where were his mother and father?

Hands of my mother. Paal washed his mind clean of all but

the trigger symbol. They rested on the ebony velvet of his concentration—pale, lovely hands, soft to touch and be touched by, the mechanism that could raise his mind to the needed level of clarity.

In his own home it would be unnecessary. His own home was filled with the sense of them. Each object touched by them possessed a power to bring their minds close. The very air seemed charged with their consciousness, filled with a constancy of attention.

Not here. He needed to lift himself above the alien drag of here.

Therefore, I am convinced that each child is born with this instinctive ability. Words given to him by his father appearing again like dew-jewelled spider web across the fingers of his mother's hands. He stripped it off. The hands were free again, stroking slowly at the darkness of his mental focus. His eyes were shut; a tracery of lines and ridges scarred his brow, his tightened jaw was bloodless. The level of awareness, like waters, rose.

His senses rose along, unbidden.

Sound revealed its woven maze—the rushing, thudding, drumming, dripping rain; the tangled knit of winds through air and tree and gabled eave; the crackling settle of the house; each whispering transience of process.

Sense of smell expanded to a cloud of brain-filling odors—wood and wool, damp brick and dust and sweet starched linens. Beneath his tensing fingers weave became apparent—coolness and warmth, the weight of covers, the delicate, skin-scarring press of rumpled sheet. In his mouth the taste of cold air, old house. Of sight, only the hands.

Silence; lack of response. He'd never had to wait so long for answers before. Usually, they flooded on him easily. His mother's hands grew clearer. They pulsed with life. Unknown, he climbed beyond. *This bottom level sets the stage for more important phenomena.* Words of his father. He'd never gone above that bottom level until now.

Up, up. Like cool hands drawing him to rarified heights.

Tendrils of acute consciousness rose towards the peak, searching desperately for a holding place. The hands began breaking into clouds. The clouds dispersed.

It seemed he floated towards the blackened tangle of his home, rain a glistening lace before his eyes. He saw the front door standing, waiting for his hand. The house drew closer. It was engulfed in licking mists. Closer, closer—

Paal, no.

His body shuddered on the bed. Ice frosted his brain. The house fled suddenly, bearing with itself a horrid image of two black figures lying on—

Paal jolted up, staring and rigid. Awareness maelstromed into its hiding place. One thing alone remained. He knew that they were gone. He knew that they had guided him, sleeping, from the house.

Even as they burned.

That night they knew he couldn't speak.

There was no reason for it, they thought. His tongue was there, his throat looked healthy. Wheeler looked into his opened mouth and saw that. But Paal did not speak.

"So *that's* what it was," the sheriff said, shaking his head gravely. It was near eleven. Paal was asleep again.

"What's that, Harry?" asked Cora, brushing her dark blonde hair in front of the dressing table mirror.

"Those times when Miss Frank and I tried to get the Nielsens to start the boy in school." He hung his pants across the chair back. "The answer was always no. Now I see why."

She glanced up at his reflection. "There must be something wrong with him, Harry," she said.

"Well, we can have Doc Steiger look at him but I don't think so."

"But they were college people," she argued. "There was no earthly reason why they shouldn't teach him how to talk. Unless there was some reason he *couldn't.*"

Wheeler shook his head again.

"They were strange people, Cora," he said. "Hardly spoke a

word themselves. As if they were too good for talking—or something." He grunted disgustedly. "No wonder they didn't want that boy to school."

He sank down on the bed with a groan and shucked off boots and calf-high stockings. "What a day," he muttered.

"You didn't find anything at the house?"

"Nothing. No identification papers at all. The house is burned to a cinder. Nothing but a pile of books and they don't lead us anywhere."

"Isn't there any way?"

"The Nielsens never had a charge account in town. And they weren't even citizens so the professor wasn't registered for the draft."

"Oh." Cora looked a moment at her face reflected in the oval mirror. Then her gaze lowered to the photograph on the dressing table—David as he was when he was nine. The Nielsen boy looked a great deal like David, she thought. Same height and build. Maybe David's hair had been a trifle darker but—

"What's to be done with him?" she asked.

"Couldn't say, Cora," he answered. "We have to wait till the end of the month, I guess. Tom Poulter says the Nielsens got three letters the end of every month. Come from Europe, he said. We'll just have to wait for them, then write back to the addresses on them. Maybe the boy has relations over there."

"Europe," she said, almost to herself. "That far away."

Her husband grunted, then pulled the covers back and sank down heavily on the mattress.

"Tired," he muttered.

He stared at the ceiling. "Come to bed," he said.

"In a little while."

She sat there brushing distractedly at her hair until the sound of his snoring broke the silence. Then, quietly, she rose and moved across the hall.

There was a river of moonlight across the bed. It flowed over Paal's small, motionless hands. Cora stood in the shadows a long time looking at the hands. For a moment she thought it was David in his bed again.

It was the sound.

Like endless club strokes across his vivid mind, it pulsed and throbbed into him in an endless, garbled din. He sensed it was communication of a sort but it hurt his ears and chained awareness and locked incoming thoughts behind dense, impassable walls.

Sometimes, in an infrequent moment of silence he would sense a fissure in the walls and, for that fleeting moment, catch hold of fragments—like an animal snatching scraps of food before the trap jaws clash together.

But then the sound would start again, rising and falling in rhythmless beat, jarring and grating, rubbing at the live, glistening surface of comprehension until it was dry and aching and confused.

"Paal," she said.

A week had passed; another week would pass before the letters came.

"Paal, didn't they ever talk to you? Paal?"

Fists striking at delicate acuteness. Hands squeezing sensitivity from the vibrant ganglia of his mind.

"Paal, don't you know your name? Paal? *Paal.*"

There was nothing physically wrong with him. Doctor Steiger had made sure of it. There was no reason for him not to talk.

"We'll teach you, Paal. It's all right, darling. We'll teach you." Like knife strokes across the weave of consciousness. *"Paal. Paal."*

Paal. It was himself; he sensed that much. But it was different in the ears, a dead, depressive sound standing alone and drab, without the host of linked associations that existed in his mind. In thought, his name was more than letters. It was *him,* every facet of his person and its meaning to himself, his mother and his father, to his life. When they had summoned him or thought his name it had been more than just the small hard core which sound made of it. It had been everything interwoven in a flash of knowing, unhampered by sound.

"Paal, don't you understand? It's your name. Paal Nielsen. Don't you understand?"

Drumming, pounding at raw sensitivity. Paal. The sound kicking at him. *Paal. Paal.* Trying to dislodge his grip and fling him into the maw of sound.

"Paal. *Try*, Paal. Say it after me. Pa-al. *Pa-al.*"

Twisting away, he would run from her in panic and she would follow him to where he cowered by the bed of her son.

Then, for long moments, there would be peace. She would hold him in her arms and, as if she understood, would not speak. There would be stillness and no pounding clash of sound against his mind. She would stroke his hair and kiss away sobless tears. He would lie against the warmth of her, his mind, like a timid animal, emerging from its hiding place again—to sense a flow of understanding from this woman. Feeling that needed no sound.

Love—wordless, unencumbered, and beautiful.

Sheriff Wheeler was just leaving the house that morning when the phone rang. He stood in the front hallway, waiting until Cora picked it up.

"Harry!" He heard her call. "Are you gone yet?"

He came back into the kitchen and took the receiver from her. "Wheeler," he said into it.

"Tom Poulter, Harry," the postmaster said. "Them letters is in."

"Be right there," Wheeler said and hung up.

"The letters?" his wife asked.

Wheeler nodded.

"*Oh,*" she murmured so that he barely heard her.

When Wheeler entered the post office twenty minutes later, Poulter slid the three letters across the counter. The sheriff picked them up.

"Switzerland," he read the postmarks, "Sweden, Germany."

"That's the lot," Poulter said, "like always. On the thirtieth of the month."

"Can't open them, I suppose," Wheeler said.

"Y'know I'd say yes if I could, Harry," Poulter answered. "But law's law. You know that. I got t'send them back unopened. That's the law."

"All right." Wheeler took out his pen and copied down the return addresses in his pad. He pushed the letters back. "Thanks."

When he got home at four that afternoon, Cora was in the front room with Paal. There was a look of confused emotion on Paal's face—a desire to please coupled with a frightened need to flee the disconcertion of sound. He sat beside her on the couch looking as if he were about to cry.

"Oh *Paal*," she said as Wheeler entered. She put her arms around the trembling boy. "There's nothing to be afraid of, darling."

She saw her husband.

"What did they *do* to him?" she asked, unhappily.

He shook his head. "Don't know," he said. "He should have been put in school though."

"We can't very well put him in school when he's like *this*," she said.

"We can't put him anywhere till we see what's what," Wheeler said. "I'll write those people tonight."

In the silence, Paal felt a sudden burst of emotion in the woman and he looked up quickly at her stricken face.

Pain. He felt it pour from her like blood from a mortal wound.

And while they ate supper in an almost silence, Paal kept sensing tragic sadness in the woman. It seemed he heard sobbing in a distant place. As the silence continued he began to get momentary flashes of remembrance in her pain-opened mind. He saw the face of another boy. Only it swirled and faded and there was *his* face in her thoughts. The two faces, like contesting wraiths, lay and overlay upon each other as if fighting for the dominance of her mind.

All fleeing, locked abruptly behind black doors as she said, "You have to write to them, I suppose."

"You know I do, Cora," Wheeler said.

Silence. Pain again. And when she tucked him into bed, he

looked at her with such soft, apparent pity on his face that she turned quickly from the bed and he could feel the waves of sorrow break across his mind until her footsteps could no longer be heard. And, even then, like the faint fluttering of bird wings in the night, he felt her pitiable despair moving in the house.

"What are you writing?" she asked.

Wheeler looked over from his desk as midnight chimed its seventh stroke in the hall. Cora came walking across the room and set the tray down at his elbow. The steamy fragrance of freshly brewed coffee filled his nostrils as he reached for the pot.

"Just telling them the situation," he said, "about the fire, the Nielsens dying. Asking them if they're related to the boy or know any of his relations over there."

"And what if his relations don't do any better than his parents?"

"Now, Cora," he said, pouring cream, "I thought we'd already discussed that. It's not our business."

She pressed pale lips together.

"A frightened child *is* my business," she said angrily. "Maybe you—"

She broke off as he looked up at her patiently, no argument in his expression.

"*Well,*" she said, turning from him, "it's true."

"It's not our business, Cora." He didn't see the tremor of her lips.

"So he'll just go on not talking, I suppose! Being afraid of shadows!"

She whirled. "It's *criminal*!" she cried, love and anger bursting from her in a twisted mixture.

"It's got to be done, Cora," he said quietly. "It's our duty."

"*Duty.*" She echoed it with an empty lifelessness in her voice.

She didn't sleep. The liquid flutter of Harry's snoring in her ears, she lay staring at the jump of shadows on the ceiling, a scene enacted in her mind.

A summer's afternoon; the back doorbell ringing. Men standing on the porch, John Carpenter among them, a blanket-covered stillness weighing down his arms, a blank look on his face. In the silence, a drip of water on the sunbaked boards—slowly, unsteadily, like the beats of a dying heart. *He was swimming in the lake, Miz Wheeler and—*

She shuddered on the bed as she had shuddered then—numbly, mutely. The hands beside her were a crumpled whiteness, twisted by remembered anguish. All these years waiting, waiting for a child to bring life into her house again.

At breakfast she was hollow-eyed and drawn. She moved about the kitchen with a willful tread, sliding eggs and pancakes on her husband's plate, pouring coffee, never speaking once.

Then he had kissed her goodbye and she was standing at the living room window watching him trudge down the path to the car. Long after he'd gone, staring at the three envelopes he'd stuck into the side clip of the mailbox.

When Paal came downstairs he smiled at her. She kissed his cheek, then stood behind him, wordless and watching, while he drank his orange juice. The way he sat, the way he held his glass; it was so like—

While Paal ate his cereal she went out to the mailbox and got the three letters, replacing them with three of her own—just in case her husband ever asked the mailman if he'd picked up three letters at their house that morning.

While Paal was eating his eggs, she went down into the cellar and threw the letters into the furnace. The one to Switzerland burned, then the ones to Germany and Sweden. She stirred them with a poker until the pieces broke and disappeared like black confetti in the flames.

Weeks passed: and, with every day, the service of his mind grew weaker.

"Paal, dear, don't you understand?" The patient, loving voice of the woman he needed but feared. "Won't you say it once for me? Just for me? *Paal?*"

He knew there was only love in her but sound would destroy him. It would chain his thoughts—like putting shackles on the wind.

"Would you like to go to school, Paal? Would you? *School?*" Her face a mask of worried devotion.

"Try to talk, Paal. Just *try*."

He fought it off with mounting fear. Silence would bring him scraps of meaning from her mind. Then sound returned and grossed each meaning with unwieldy flesh. Meanings joined with sounds. The links formed quickly, frighteningly. He struggled against them. Sounds could cover fragile, darting symbols with a hideous, restraining dough, dough that would be baked in ovens of articulation, then chopped into the stunted lengths of words.

Afraid of the woman, yet wanting to be near the warmth of her, protected by her arms. Like a pendulum he swung from dread to need and back to dread again.

And still the sounds kept shearing at his mind.

"We can't wait any longer to hear from them," Harry said. "He'll have to go to school, that's all."

"No," she said.

He put down his newspaper and looked across the living room at her. She kept her eyes on the movements of her knitting needles.

"What do you mean, no?" he asked, irritably. "Every time I mention school you say no. Why *shouldn't* he go to school?"

The needles stopped and were lowered to her lap. Cora stared at them.

"I don't know," she said, "it's just that—" A sigh emptied from her. "I don't know," she said.

"He'll start on Monday," Harry said.

"But he's frightened," she said.

"Sure he's frightened. You'd be frightened too if you couldn't talk and everybody around you was talking. He needs education, that's all."

"But he's not *ignorant*, Harry. I—I swear he understands me sometimes. *Without* talking."

"*How*?"

"I don't know. But—well, the Nielsens weren't stupid people. They wouldn't just *refuse* to teach him."

"Well, whatever they taught him," Harry said, picking up his paper, "it sure doesn't show."

When they asked Miss Edna Frank over that afternoon to meet the boy she was determined to be impartial.

That Paal Nielsen had been reared in miserable fashion was beyond cavil, but the maiden teacher had decided not to allow the knowledge to affect her attitude. The boy needed understanding. The cruel mistreatment of his parents had to be undone and Miss Frank had elected herself to the office.

Striding with a resolute quickness down German Corners' main artery, she recalled that scene in the Nielsen house when she and Sheriff Wheeler had tried to persuade them to enter Paal in school.

And such a smugness in their faces, thought Miss Frank, remembering. Such a polite disdain. *We do not wish our boy in school*, she heard Professor Nielsen's words again. Just like that, Miss Frank recalled. Arrogant as you please. *We do not wish*—Disgusting attitude.

Well, at least the boy was out of it now. The fire was probably the blessing of his life, she thought.

"We wrote to them four, five weeks ago," the sheriff explained, "and we haven't gotten an answer yet. We can't just let the boy go on the way he is. He needs schooling."

"He most certainly does," agreed Miss Frank, her pale features drawn into their usual sum of unyielding dogmatism. There was a wisp of mustache on her upper lip, her chin came almost to a point. On Halloween the children of German Corners watched the sky above her house.

"He's very shy," Cora said, sensing that harshness in the middle-aged teacher. "He'll be terribly frightened. He'll need a lot of understanding."

"He shall receive it," Miss Frank declared. "But let's see the boy."

Cora led Paal down the steps speaking to him softly. "Don't be afraid, darling. There's nothing to be afraid of."

Paal entered the room and looked into the eyes of Miss Edna Frank.

Only Cora felt the stiffening of his body—as though, instead of the gaunt virgin, he had looked into the petrifying gaze of the Medusa. Miss Frank and the sheriff did not catch the flare of iris in his bright, green eyes, the minute twitching at one corner of his mouth. None of them could sense the leap of panic in his mind.

Miss Frank sat smiling, holding out her hand.

"Come here, child," she said and, for a moment, the gates slammed shut and hid away the writhing shimmer.

"Come on, darling," Cora said, "Miss Frank is here to help you." She led him forward, feeling beneath her fingers the shuddering of terror in him.

Silence again. And, in the moment of it, Paal felt as though he were walking into a century-sealed tomb. Dead winds gushed out upon him, creatures of frustration slithered on his heart, strange flying jealousies and hates rushed by—all obscured by clouds of twisted memory. It was the purgatory that his father had pictured to him once in telling him of myth and legend. This was no legend though.

Her touch was cool and dry. Dark wrenching terrors ran down her veins and poured into him. Inaudibly, the fragment of a scream tightened his throat. Their eyes met again and Paal saw that, for a second, the woman seemed to know that he was looking at her brain.

Then she spoke and he was free again, limp and staring.

"I think we'll get along just fine," she said.

Maelstrom!

He lurched back on his heels and fell against the sheriff's wife.

All the way across the grounds, it had been growing, growing—as if he were a Geiger counter moving towards some fantastic pulsing strata of atomic force. Closer, yet closer, the delicate controls within him stirring, glowing, trembling, reacting with increasing violence to the nearness of power. Even though his sensitivity had been weakened by over three months of sound he felt this now, strongly. As though he walked into a center of vitality.

It was *the young.*

Then the door opened, the voices stopped, and all of it rushed through him like a vast, electric current—all wild and unharnessed. He clung to her, fingers rigid in her skirt, eyes widened, quick breaths falling from his parted lips. His gaze moved shakily across the rows of staring children faces and waves of distorted energies kept bounding out from them in a snarled, uncontrolled network.

Miss Frank scraped back her chair, stepped down from her six-inch eminence and started down the aisle towards them.

"Good morning," she said, crisply. "We're just about to start our classes for the day."

"I—do hope everything will be all right," Cora said. She glanced down. Paal was looking at the class through a welling haze of tears. "Oh, *Paal*." She leaned over and ran her fingers through his blond hair, a worried look on her face. "Paal, don't be afraid, dear," she whispered.

He looked at her blankly.

"Darling, there's nothing to be—"

"Now just you leave him here," Miss Frank broke in, putting her hand on Paal's shoulder. She ignored the shudder that rippled through him. "He'll be right at home in no time, Mrs. Wheeler. But you've got to leave him by himself."

"Oh, but—" Cora started.

"No, believe me, it's the only way," Miss Frank insisted. "As long as you stay he'll be upset. Believe me. I've seen such things before."

At first he wouldn't let go of Cora but clung to her as the one familiar thing in this whirlpool of frightening newness. It was only when Miss Frank's hard, thin hands held him back that Cora backed off slowly, anxiously, closing the door and cutting off from Paal the sight of her soft pity.

He stood there trembling, incapable of uttering a single word to ask for help. Confused, his mind sent out tenuous shoots of communication but in the undisciplined tangle they were broken off and lost. He drew back quickly and tried, in vain, to cut himself off. All he could manage to do was let the torrent of needling thoughts continue unopposed until they had become a numbing, meaningless surge.

"Now, Paal," he heard Miss Frank's voice and looked up gingerly at her. The hand drew him from the door. *"Come along."*

He didn't understand the words but the brittle sound of them was clear enough, the flow of irrational animosity from her was unmistakable. He stumbled along at her side, threading a thin path of consciousness through the living undergrowth of young, untrained minds; the strange admixture of them with their retention of born sensitivity overlaid with the dulling coat of formal inculcation.

She brought him to the front of the room and stood him there, his chest laboring for breath as if the feelings around him were hands pushing and constraining on his body.

"This is Paal Nielsen, class," Miss Frank announced, and sound drew a momentary blade across the stunted weave of thoughts. "We're going to have to be very patient with him. You see his mother and father never taught him how to talk."

She looked down at him as a prosecuting lawyer might gaze upon exhibit A.

"He can't understand a word of English," she said.

Silence a moment, writhing. Miss Frank tightened her grip on his shoulder.

"Well, we'll help him learn, won't we, class?"

Faint mutterings arose from them; one thin, piping. "Yes, Miss Frank."

"Now, Paal," she said. He didn't turn. She shook his shoulder. "Paal," she said.

He looked at her.

"Can you say your name?" she asked. "Paal? Paal Nielsen? Go ahead. Say your name."

Her fingers drew in like talons.

"Say it. Paal. Pa-al."

He sobbed. Miss Frank released her hand.

"You'll learn," she said calmly.

It was not encouragement.

He sat in the middle of it like hooked bait in a current that swirled with devouring mouths, mouths from which endlessly came mind-deadening sounds.

"This is a boat. A boat sails on the water. The men who live on the boat are called sailors."

And, in the primer, the words about the boat printed under a picture of one.

Paal remembered a picture his father had shown him once. It had been a picture of a boat too; but his father had not spoken futile words about the boat. His father had created about the picture every sight and sound heir to it. Great blue rising swells of tide. Gray-green mountain waves, their white tops lashing. Storm winds whistling through the rigging of a bucking, surging, shuddering vessel. The quiet majesty of an ocean sunset, joining, with a scarlet seal, sea and sky.

"This is a farm. Men grow food on the farm. The men who grow food are called farmers."

Words. Empty, with no power to convey the moist, warm feel of earth. The sound of grain fields rustling in the wind like golden seas. The sight of sun setting on a red barn wall. The smell of soft lea winds carrying, from afar, the delicate clank of cowbells.

"This is a forest. A forest is made of trees."

No sense of presence in those black, dogmatic symbols whether sounded or looked upon. No sound of winds rushing like eternal rivers through the high green canopies. No smell of pine and birch, oak and maple and hemlock. No feel of treading on the century-thick carpet of leafy forest floors.

Words. Blunt, sawed-off lengths of hemmed-in meaning; incapable of evocation, of expansion. Black figures on white. This is a cat. This is a dog. Cat, dog. This is a man. This is a woman. Man, woman. Car. Horse. Tree. Desk. Children. Each word a trap, stalking his mind. A snare set to enclose fluid and unbounded comprehension.

Every day she stood him on the platform.

"Paal," she would say, pointing at him. "Paal. Say it. Paal."

He couldn't. He stared at her, too intelligent not to make the connection, too much afraid to seek further.

"Paal," A boney finger prodding at his chest. "Paal. Paal. *Paal.*"

He fought it. He had to fight it. He blanked his gaze and saw nothing of the room around him, concentrating only on

his mother's hands. He knew it was a battle. Like a jelling
of sickness, he had felt each new encroachment on his sensitivity.

"You're not listening, Paal Nielsen!" Miss Frank would accuse, shaking him. "You're a stubborn, ungrateful boy. Don't
you want to be like *other* children?"

Staring eyes; and her thin, never-to-be-kissed lips stirring,
pressing in.

"Sit down," she's say. He didn't move. She'd move him off
the platform with rigid fingers.

"Sit *down*," she'd say as if talking to a mulish puppy.

Every day.

She was awake in an instant; in another instant, on her feet
and hurrying across the darkness of the room. Behind her,
Harry slept with laboring breaths. She shut away the sound
and let her hand slip off the door knob as she started across
the hall.

"*Darling.*"

He was standing by the window, looking out. As she spoke,
he whirled and, in the faint illumination of the night light, she
could see the terror written on his face.

"Darling, come to bed." She led him there and tucked him
in, then sat beside him, holding his thin, cold hands.

"What is it, dear?"

He looked at her with wide, pained eyes.

"*Oh—*" She bent over and pressed her warm cheek to his.
"What are you afraid of?"

In the dark silence it seemed as if a vision of the schoolroom
and Miss Frank standing in it crossed her mind.

"Is it the school?" she asked, thinking it only an idea which
had occurred to her.

The answer was in his face.

"But school is nothing to be afraid of, darling," she said.
"You—"

She saw tears welling in his eyes, and abruptly she drew him
up and held him tightly against herself. *Don't be afraid*, she

thought. *Darling, please don't be afraid. I'm here and I love you just as much as they did. I love you even more—*

Paal drew back. He stared at her as if he didn't understand.

As the car pulled up in back of the house, Werner saw a woman turn away from the kitchen window.

"If we'd only heard from you," said Wheeler, "but there was never a word. You can't blame us for adopting the boy. We did what we thought was best."

Werner nodded with short, distracted movements of his head.

"I understand," he said quietly. "We received no letters however."

They sat in the car in silence, Werner staring through the windshield, Wheeler looking at his hands.

Holger and Fanny *dead*, Werner was thinking. A horrible discovery to make. The boy exposed to the cruel blunderings of people who did not understand. That was, in a way, even more horrible.

Wheeler was thinking of those letters and of Cora. He should have written again. Still, those letters should have reached Europe. Was it possible they were all missent?

"Well," he said, finally, "you'll—want to see the boy."

"Yes," said Werner.

The two men pushed open the car doors and got out. They walked across the backyard and up the wooden porch steps. Have you taught him how to speak?—Werner almost said but couldn't bring himself to ask. The concept of a boy like Paal exposed to the blunt, deadening forces of usual speech was something he felt uncomfortable thinking about.

"I'll get my wife," said Wheeler. "The living room's in there."

After the sheriff had gone up the back stairs, Werner walked slowly through the hall and into the front room. There he took off his raincoat and hat and dropped them over the back of a wooden chair. Upstairs he could hear the faint sound of voices—a man and woman. The woman sounded upset.

When he heard footsteps, he turned from the window.

The sheriff's wife entered beside her husband. She was

smiling politely, but Werner knew she wasn't happy to see him there.

"Please sit down," she said.

He waited until she was in a chair, then settled down on the couch.

"What is it you want?" asked Mrs. Wheeler.

"Did your husband tell you—?"

"He told me who you were," she interrupted, "but not why you want to see Paul."

"Paul?" asked Werner, surprised.

"We—" Her hands sought out each other nervously. "—We changed it to Paul. It—seemed more appropriate. For a Wheeler, I mean."

"I see." Werner nodded politely.

Silence.

"Well," Werner said then, "you wish to know why I am here to see—the boy. I will explain as briefly as possible.

"Ten years ago, in Heidelbert, four married couples—the Elkenbergs, the Kalders, the Nielsens, and my wife and I— decided to try an experiment on our children—some not yet born. An experiment of the mind.

"We had accepted, you see, the proposition that ancient man, deprived of the dubious benefit of language, had been telepathic."

Cora started in her chair.

"Further," Werner went on, not noticing, "that the basic organic source of this ability is still functioning though no longer made use of—a sort of ethereal tonsil, a higher appendix—not used but neither useless.

"So we began our work, each searching for physiological facts while, at the same time, developing the ability in our children. Monthly correspondence was exchanged, a systematic methodology of training was arrived at slowly. Eventually, we planned to establish a colony with the grown children, a colony to be gradually consolidated until these abilities would become second nature to its members.

"Paal is one of these children."

Wheeler looked almost dazed.

"This is a *fact?*" he asked.

"A fact," said Werner.

Cora sat numbly in her chair staring at the tall German. She was thinking about the way Paal seemed to understand her without words. Thinking of his fear of the school and Miss Frank. Thinking of how many times she had woken up and gone to him even though he didn't make a sound.

"What?" she asked, looking up as Werner spoke.

"I say—may I see the boy now?"

"He's in school," she said. "He'll be home in—"

She stopped as a look of almost revulsion crossed Werner's face.

"*School?*" he asked.

"Paal Nielsen, stand."

The young boy slid from his seat and stood beside the desk. Miss Frank gestured to him once and, more like an old man than a boy, he trudged up to the platform and stood beside her as he always did.

"Straighten up," Miss Frank demanded. "Shoulders back."

The shoulders moved, the back grew flat.

"What's your name?" asked Miss Frank.

The boy pressed his lips together slightly. His swallowing made a dry, rattling noise.

"*What is your name?*"

Silence in the classroom except for the restive stirring of the young. Erratic currents of their thought deflected off him like random winds.

"*Your name,*" she said.

He made no reply.

The virgin teacher looked at him and, in the moment that she did, through her mind ran memories of her childhood. Of her gaunt, mania-driven mother keeping her for hours at a time in the darkened front parlor, sitting at the great round table, her fingers arched over the smoothly worn ouija board— making her try to communicate with her dead father.

Memories of those terrible years were still with her—always with her. Her minor sensitivity being abused and twisted into knots until she hated every single thing about perception. Perception was an evil, full of suffering and anguish.

The boy must be freed of it.

"Class," she said, "I want you all to think of Paal's name." (This was his name no matter what Mrs. Wheeler chose to call him.) "Just think of it. Don't say it. Just think: Paal, Paal, Paal. When I count three. Do you understand?"

They stared at her, some nodding. "*Yes,* Miss Frank," piped up her only faithful.

"All right," she said, "One—two—*three.*"

It flung into his mind like the blast of a hurricane, pounding and tearing at his hold on wordless sensitivity. He trembled on the platform, his mouth fallen ajar.

The blast grew stronger, all the power of the young directed into a single, irresistible force. Paal, *Paal, PAAL*!! It screamed into the tissues of his brain.

Until, at the very peak of it, when he thought his head would explode, it was all cut away by the voice of Miss Frank scalpelling into his mind.

"Say it! Paal!"

"Here he comes," said Cora. She turned from the window. "Before he gets here, I want to apologize for my rudeness."

"Not at all," said Werner, distractedly, "I understand perfectly. Naturally, you would think that I had come to take the boy away. As I have said, however, I have no legal powers over him—being no relation. I simply want to see him as the child of my two colleagues—whose shocking death I have only now learned of."

He saw the woman's throat move and picked out the leap of guilty panic in her mind. She had destroyed the letters her husband wrote. Werner knew it instantly but said nothing. He sensed that the husband also knew it; she would have enough trouble as it was.

They heard Paal's footsteps on the bottom step of the front porch.

"I *will* take him out of school," Cora said.

"Perhaps not," said Werner, looking towards the door. In spite of everything he felt his heartbeat quicken, felt the fingers of his left hand twitch in his lap. Without a word, he sent out the message. It was a greeting the four couples had decided on; a sort of password.

Telepathy, he thought, *is the communication of impressions of any kind from one mind to another independently of the recognized channels of sense.*

Werner sent it twice before the front door opened.

Paal stood there, motionless.

Werner saw recognition in his eyes, but, in the boy's mind, was only confused uncertainty. The misted vision of Werner's face crossed it. In his mind, all the people had existed—Werner, Elkenberg, Kalder, all their children. But now it was locked up and hard to capture. The face disappeared.

"Paul, this is Mister Werner," Cora said.

Werner did not speak. He sent the message out again—with such force that Paal could not possibly miss it. He saw a look of uncomprehending dismay creep across the boy's features, as if Paal suspected that something was happening yet could not imagine what.

The boy's face grew more confused. Cora's eyes moved concernedly from him to Werner and back again. Why didn't Werner speak? She started to say something, then remembered what the German had said.

"Say, what—?" Wheeler began until Cora waved her hand and stopped him.

Paal, think!—Werner thought desperately—*Where is your mind?*

Suddenly, there was a great, wracking sob in the boy's throat and chest. Werner shuddered.

"My name is Paal," the boy said.

The voice made Werner's flesh crawl. It was unfinished, like a puppet voice, thin, wavering, and brittle.

"My name is Paal."

He couldn't stop saying it. It was as if he were whipping himself on, knowing what had happened and trying to suffer as much as possible with the knowledge.

"My name is Paal. My name is Paal." An endless, frightening babble; in it, a panic-stricken boy seeking out an unknown power which had been torn from him.

"My name is Paal." Even held tightly in Cora's arms, he said it. "My name is Paal." Angrily, pitiably, endlessly. *"My name is Paal. My name is Paal."*

Werner closed his eyes.

Lost.

Wheeler offered to take him back to the bus station, but Werner told him he'd rather walk. He said goodbye to the sheriff and asked him to relay his regrets to Mrs. Wheeler, who had taken the sobbing boy up to his room.

Now, in the beginning fall of a fine, mistlike rain, Werner walked away from the house, from Paal.

It was not something easily judged, he was thinking. There was no right and wrong of it. Definitely, it was not a case of evil versus good. Mrs. Wheeler, the sheriff, the boy's teacher, the people of German Corners—they had, probably, all meant well. Understandably, they had been outraged at the idea of a seven-year-old boy not having been taught to speak by his parents. Their actions were, in light of that, justifiable and good.

It was simply that, so often, evil could come of misguided good.

No, it was better left as it was. To take Paal back to Europe—back to the others—would be a mistake. He could if he wanted to; all the couples had exchanged papers giving each other the right to take over rearing of the children should anything happen to the parents. But it would only confuse Paal further. He had been a trained sensitive, not a born one. Although, by the principle they all worked on, all children were born with the atavistic ability to telepath, it was so easy to lose, so difficult to recapture.

Werner shook his head. It was a pity. The boy was without his parents, without his talent, even without his name.

He had lost everything.

Well, perhaps, not everything.

As he walked, Werner sent his mind back to the house to

discover them standing at the window of Paal's room, watching sunset cast its fiery light on German Corners. Paal was clinging to the sheriff's wife, his cheek pressed to her side. The final terror of losing his awareness had not faded but there was something else counterbalancing it. Something Cora Wheeler sensed yet did not fully realize.

Paal's parents had not loved him. Werner knew this. Caught up in the fascination of their work they had not had the time to love him as a child. Kind, yes, affectionate, always; still, they had regarded Paal as their experiment in flesh.

Which was why Cora Wheeler's love was, in part, as strange a thing to Paal as all the crushing horrors of speech. It would not remain so. For, in that moment when the last of his gift had fled, leaving his mind a naked rawness, she had been there with her love, to soothe away the pain. And always would be there.

"Did you find who you were looking for?" the gray-haired woman at the counter asked Werner as she served him coffee.

"Yes. Thank you," he said.

"Where was he?" asked the woman.

Werner smiled.

"At home," he said.

SHOCK WAVE

"I tell you there's something wrong with her," said Mr. Moffat.

Cousin Wendall reached for the sugar bowl.

"Then they're right," he said. He spooned the sugar into his coffee.

"They are *not*," said Mr. Moffat, sharply. "They most certainly are *not*."

"If she isn't working," Wendall said.

"She *was* working until just a month or so ago," said Mr. Moffat. "She was working *fine* when they decided to replace her the first of the year."

His fingers, pale and yellowed, lay tensely on the table. His eggs and coffee were untouched and cold before him.

"Why are you so upset?" asked Wendall. "She's just an organ."

"*She is more*," Mr. Moffat said. "She was in before the church was even finished. Eighty years she's been there. *Eighty*."

"That's pretty long," said Wendall, crunching jelly-smeared toast. "Maybe too long."

"There's nothing wrong with her," defended Mr. Moffat. "Leastwise, there never was before. That's why I want you to sit in the loft with me this morning."

"How come you haven't had an organ man look at her?" Wendall asked.

"He'd just agree with the rest of them," said Mr. Moffat, sourly. "He'd just say she's too old, too worn."

"Maybe she is," said Wendall.

"*She is not*." Mr. Moffat trembled fitfully.

"Well, I don't know," said Wendall, "she's pretty old though."

"She worked fine before," said Mr. Moffat. He stared into the blackness of his coffee. "The gall of them," he muttered. "Planning to get rid of her. The *gall*."

He closed his eyes.

"Maybe she knows," he said.

The clock-like tapping of his heels perforated the stillness in the lobby.

"This way," Mr. Moffat said.

Wendall pushed open the arm-thick door and the two men spiraled up the marble staircase. On the second floor, Mr. Moffat shifted the briefcase to his other hand and searched his keyring. He unlocked the door and they entered the musty darkness of the loft. They moved through the silence, two faint, echoing sounds.

"Over here," said Mr. Moffat.

"Yes, I see," said Wendall.

The old man sank down on the glass-smooth bench and turned the small lamp on. A wedge of bulb light forced aside the shadows.

"Think the sun'll show?" asked Wendall.

"Don't know," said Mr. Moffat.

He unlocked and rattled up the organ's rib-skinned top, then raised the music rack. He pushed the finger-worn switch across its slot.

In the brick room to their right there was a sudden hum, a mounting rush of energy. The air-gauge needle quivered across its dial.

"She's alive now," Mr. Moffat said.

Wendall grunted in amusement and walked across the loft. The old man followed.

"What do you think?" he asked inside the brick room.

Wendall shrugged.

"Can't tell," he said. He looked at the turning of the motor. "Single-phase induction," he said. "Runs by magnetism."

He listened. "Sounds all right to me," he said.

He walked across the small room.

"What's this?" he asked, pointing.

"Relay machines," said Mr. Moffat. "Keep the channels filled with wind."

"And this is the fan?" asked Wendall.

The old man nodded.

"Mmm-hmm." Wendall turned. "Looks all right to me," he said.

They stood outside looking up at the pipes. Above the glossy wood of the enclosure box, they stood like giant pencils painted gold.

"Big," said Wendall.

"She's *beautiful*," said Mr. Moffat.

"Let's hear her," Wendall said.

They walked back to the keyboards and Mr. Moffat sat before them. He pulled out a stop and pressed a key into its bed.

A single tone poured out into the shadowed air. The old man pressed a volume pedal and the note grew louder. It pierced the air, tone and overtones bouncing off the church dome like diamonds hurled from a sling.

Suddenly, the old man raised his hand.

"*Did you hear?*" he asked.

"Hear what?"

"It *trembled*," Mr. Moffat said.

As people entered the church, Mr. Moffat was playing Bach's chorale-prelude *Aus der Tiefe rufe ich (From the Depths, I cry)*. His fingers moved certainly on the manual keys, his sprinkling shoes walked a dance across the pedals; and the air was rich with moving sound.

Wendall leaned over to whisper, "There's the sun."

Above the old man's gray-wreathed pate, the sunlight came filtering through the stained-glass window. It passed across the rack of pipes with a mistlike radiance.

Wendall leaned over again.

"Sounds all right to me," he said.

"*Wait*," said Mr. Moffat.

Wendall grunted. Stepping to the loft edge, he looked down at the nave. The three-aisled flow of people was branching off into rows. The echoing of their movements scaled up like insect scratchings. Wendall watched them as they settled in the brown-wood pews. Above and all about them moved the organ's music.

"*Sssst.*"

Wendall turned and moved back to his cousin.

"What is it?" he asked.

"*Listen.*" Wendall cocked his head.

"Can't hear anything but the organ and the motor," he said.

"That's *it*," the old man whispered. "*You're not supposed to hear the motor.*"

Wendall shrugged. "So?" he said.

The old man wet his lips. "I think it's starting," he murmured.

Below, the lobby doors were being shut. Mr. Moffat's gaze fluttered to his watch propped against the music rack, thence to the pulpit where the Reverend had appeared. He made of the chorale-prelude's final chord a shimmering pyramid of sound, paused, then modulated, *mezzo forte,* to the key of G. He played the opening phrase of the Doxology.

Below, the Reverend stretched out his hands, palms up, and the congregation took its feet with a rustling and crackling. An instant of silence filled the church. Then the singing began.

Mr. Moffat led them through the hymn, his right hand pacing off the simple route. In the third phrase an adjoining key moved down with the one he pressed and an alien dissonance blurred the chord. The old man's fingers twitched; the dissonance faded.

"*Praise Father, Son and Holy Ghost.*"

The people capped their singing with a lingering Amen. Mr. Moffat's fingers lifted from the manuals, he switched the motor off, the nave remurmured with the crackling rustle and the dark-robed Reverend raised his hands to grip the pulpit railing.

"Dear Heavenly Father," he said, "we, Thy children, meet with Thee today in reverent communion."

Up in the loft, a bass note shuddered faintly.

Mr. Moffat hitched up, gasping. His gaze jumped to the switch (off), to the air-gauge needle (motionless), toward the motor room (still).

"*You heard that?*" he whispered.

"Seems like I did," said Wendall.

"*Seems?*" said Mr. Moffat tensely.

"Well . . ." Wendall reached over to flick a nail against the air dial. Nothing happened. Grunting, he turned and started toward the motor room. Mr. Moffat rose and tiptoed after him.

"Looks dead to me," said Wendall.

"*I hope so,*" Mr. Moffat answered. He felt his hands begin to shake.

The offertory should not be obtrusive but form a staidly moving background for the clink of coins and whispering of bills. Mr. Moffat knew this well. No man put holy tribute to music more properly than he.

Yet, that morning . . .

The discords surely were not his. Mistakes were rare for Mr. Moffat. The keys resisting, throbbing beneath his touch like things alive; was that imagined? Cords thinned to fleshless octaves, then, moments later, thick with sound; was it he? The old man sat, rigid, hearing the music stir unevenly in the air. Ever since the Responsive Reading had ended and he'd turned the organ on again, it seemed to possess almost a willful action.

Mr. Moffat turned to whisper to his cousin.

Suddenly, the needle of the other gauge jumped from *mezzo* to *forte* and the volume flared. The old man felt his stomach muscles clamped. His pale hands jerked from the keys and, for a second, there was only the muffled sound of usher's feet and money falling into baskets.

Then Mr. Moffat's hands returned and the offertory murmured once again, refined and inconspicuous. The old man noticed, below, faces turning, tilting upward curiously and a jaded pressing rolled in his lips.

"Listen," Wendall said when the collection was over, "how do you *know* it isn't you?"

"Because it isn't," the old man whispered back. "It's *her.*"

"That's crazy," Wendall answered. "Without you playing, she's just a contraption."

"No," said Mr. Moffat, shaking his head. "No. She's more."

"Listen," Wendall said, "you said you were bothered because they're getting rid of her."

The old man grunted.

"So," said Wendall, "I think you're doing these things yourself, unconscious-like."

The old man thought about it. Certainly, she was an instrument; he knew that. Her soundings were governed by his feet and fingers, weren't they? Without them, she was, as Wendall had said, a contraption. Pipes and levers and static rows of keys; knobs without function, arm-long pedals and pressuring air.

"Well, what do you think?" asked Wendall.

Mr. Moffat looked down at the nave.

"Time for the Benediction," he said.

In the middle of the Benediction postlude, the *swell to great* stop pushed out and, before Mr. Moffat's jabbing hand had shoved it in again, the air resounded with a thundering of horns, the church air was gorged with swollen, trembling sound.

"*It wasn't me,*" he whispered when the postlude was over, "*I saw it move by itself.*"

"Didn't see it," Wendall said.

Mr. Moffat looked below where the Reverend had begun to read the words of the next hymn.

"*We've got to stop the service,*" he whispered in a shaking voice.

"We can't do that," said Wendall.

"But something's going to happen, I know it," the old man said.

"What can happen?" Wendall scoffed. "A few bad notes is all."

The old man sat tensely, staring at the keys. In his lap his hands wrung silently together. Then, as the Reverend finished reading, Mr. Moffat played the opening phrase of the hymn. The congregation rose and, following that instant's silence, began to sing.

This time no one noticed but Mr. Moffat.

Organ tone possesses what is called "inertia," an impersonal character. The organist cannot change this tonal quality; it is inviolate.

Yet, Mr. Moffat clearly heard, reflected in the music, his

own disquiet. Hearing it sent chills of prescience down his spine. For thirty years he had been organist here. He knew the workings of the organ better than any man. Its pressures and reactions were in the memory of his touch.

That morning, it was a strange machine he played on.

A machine whose motor, when the hymn was ended, would not stop.

"Switch it off again," Wendall told him.

"I *did*," the old man whispered frightenedly.

"*Try it again.*"

Mr. Moffat pushed the switch. The motor kept running. He pushed the switch again. The motor kept running. He clenched his teeth and pushed the switch a seventh time.

The motor stopped.

"*I don't like it,*" said Mr. Moffat faintly.

"Listen, I've seen this before," said Wendall. "When you push the switch across the slot, it pushes a copper contact across some porcelain. That's what joins the wires so the current can flow.

"Well, you push that switch enough times, it'll leave a copper residue on the porcelain so's the current can move across it. Even when the switch is off. I've seen it before."

The old man shook his head.

"She *knows*," he said.

"That's *crazy*," Wendall said.

"*Is it?*"

They were in the motor room. Below, the Reverend was delivering his sermon.

"Sure it is," said Wendall. "She's an organ, not a person."

"I don't know any more," said Mr. Moffat hollowly.

"Listen," Wendall said, "you want to know what it probably is?"

"She knows they want her out of here," the old man said. "That's what it is."

"Oh, come on," said Wendall, twisting impatiently, "I'll tell you what it is. This is an old church—and this old organ's been shaking the walls for eighty years. Eighty years of that and walls are going to start warping, floors are going to start settling. And when the floor settles, this motor here starts tilting and wires go and there's arcing."

"Arcing?"

"Yes," said Wendall. "Electricity jumping across gaps."

"I don't see," said Mr. Moffat.

"All this here extra electricity gets into the motor," Wendall said. "There's electromagnets in these relay machines. Put more electricity into them, there'll be more force. Enough to cause those things to happen maybe."

"Even if it's so," said Mr. Moffat, "Why is she fighting me?"

"Oh, stop talking like that," said Wendall.

"But I know," the old man said, "I *feel*."

"It needs repairing is all," said Wendall. "Come on, let's go outside. It's hot in here."

Back on his bench, Mr. Moffat sat motionless, staring at the keyboard steps.

Was it true, he wondered, that everything was as Wendall had said—partly due to faulty mechanics, partly due to him? He mustn't jump to rash conclusions if this were so. Certainly, Wendall's explanations made sense.

Mr. Moffat felt a tingling in his head. He twisted slightly, grimacing.

Yet, there were these things which happened: the keys going down by themselves, the stop pushing out, the volume flaring, the sound of emotion in what should be emotionless. Was this mechanical defect; or was this defect on his part? It seemed impossible.

The prickling stir did not abate. It mounted like a flame. A restless murmur fluttered in the old man's throat. Beside him, on the bench, his fingers twitched.

Still, things might not be so simple, he thought. Who could say conclusively that the organ was nothing but inanimate machinery? Even if what Wendall had said were true, wasn't it feasible that these very factors might have given strange comprehension to the organ? Tilting floors and ruptured wires and arcing and overcharged electromagnets—mightn't these have bestowed cognizance?

Mr. Moffat sighed and straightened up. Instantly, his breath was stopped.

The nave was blurred before his eyes. It quivered like a gelatinous haze. The congregation had been melted, run together. They were welded substance in his sight. A cough he heard was hollow detonation miles away. He tried to move but couldn't. Paralyzed, he sat there.

And it came.

It was not thought in words so much as raw sensation. It pulsed and tremored in his mind electrically. *Fear—Dread—Hatred*—all cruelly unmistakable.

Mr. Moffat shuddered on the bench. Of himself, there remained only enough to think, in horror—*She does know!* The rest was lost beneath overcoming power. It rose up higher, filling him with black contemplations. The church was gone, the congregation gone, the Reverend and Wendall gone. The old man pendulumed above a bottomless pit while fear and hatred, like dark winds, tore at him possessively.

"Hey, what's wrong?"

Wendall's urgent whisper jarred him back. Mr. Moffat blinked.

"What happened?" he asked.

"You were turning on the organ."

"Turning on—?"

"And *smiling*," Wendall said.

There was a trembling sound in Mr. Moffat's throat. Suddenly, he was aware of the Reverend's voice reading the words of the final hymn.

"*No*," he murmured.

"What is it?" Wendall asked.

"*I can't turn her on.*"

"What do you mean?"

"*I can't.*"

"Why?"

"I don't know. I just—"

The old man felt his breath thinned as, below, the Reverend ceased to speak and looked up, waiting. No, thought Mr. Moffat. No, I *mustn't*. Premonition clamped a frozen hand on him. He felt a scream rising in his throat as he watched his hand reach forward and push the switch.

The motor started.

Mr. Moffat began to play. Rather, the organ seemed to play, pushing up or drawing down his fingers at its will. Amorphous panic churned the old man's insides. He felt an overpowering urge to switch the organ off and flee.

He played on.

He started as the singing began. Below, armied in their pews, the people sang, elbow to elbow, the wine-red hymnals in their hands.

"*No,*" gasped Mr. Moffat.

Wendall didn't hear him. The old man sat staring as the pressure rose. He watched the needle of the volume gauge move past *mezzo* toward *forte*. A dry whimper filled his throat. No, please, he thought, *please.*

Abruptly, the *swell to great* stop slid out like the head of some emerging serpent. Mr. Moffat thumbed it in desperately. The *swell unison* button stirred. The old man held it in; he felt it throbbing at his finger pad. A dew of sweat broke out across his brow. He glanced below and saw the people squinting up at him. His eyes fled to the volume needle as it shook toward *grand crescendo.*

"Wendall, try to—!"

There was no time to finish. The *swell to great stop* slithered out again, the air ballooned with sound. Mr. Moffat jabbed it back. He felt keys and pedals dropping in their beds. Suddenly, the *swell unison* button was out. A peal of unchecked clamor filled the church. No time to speak.

The organ was alive.

He gasped as Wendall reached over to jab a hand across the switch. Nothing happened. Wendall cursed and worked the switch back and forth. The motor kept on running.

Now pressure found its peak, each pipe shuddering with storm winds. Tones and overtones flooded out in a paroxysm of sound. The hymn fell mangled underneath the weight of hostile chords.

"Hurry!" Mr. Moffat cried.

"It won't go off!" Wendall shouted back.

Once more, the *swell to great* stop jumped forward. Coupled with the volume pedal, it clubbed the walls with dissonance. Mr. Moffat lunged for it. Freed, the *swell unison* button jerked out again. The raging sound grew thicker yet. It was a howling giant shouldering the church.

Grand crescendo. Slow vibrations filled the floors and walls.

Suddenly, Wendall was leaping to the rail and shouting, "Out! Get Out!"

Bound in panic, Mr. Moffat pressed at the switch again and again; but the loft still shook beneath him. The organ still galed out music that was no longer music but attacking sound.

"Get out!" Wendall shouted at the congregation. *"Hurry!"*

The windows went first.

They exploded from their frames as though cannon shells had pierced them. A hail of shattered rainbow showered on the congregation. Women shrieked, their voices pricking at the music's vast ascension. People lurched from their pews. Sound flooded at the walls in tidelike waves, breaking and receding.

The chandeliers went off like crystal bombs.

"Hurry!" Wendall yelled.

Mr. Moffat couldn't move. He sat staring blankly at the manual keys as they fell like toppling dominoes. He listened to the screaming of the organ.

Wendall grabbed his arm and pulled him off the bench. Above them, two last windows were disintegrated into clouds of glass. Beneath their feet, they felt the massive shudder of the church.

"*No!*" The old man's voice was inaudible; but his intent was clear as he pulled his hand from Wendall's and stumbled backward toward the railing.

"*Are you crazy?*" Wendall leaped forward and grabbed the old man brutally. They spun around in battle. Below, the aisles were swollen. The congregation was a fear-mad boil of exodus.

"Let me go!" screamed Mr. Moffat, his face a bloodless mask. "I have to stay!"

"No, you don't!" Wendall shouted. He grabbed the old man

bodily and dragged him from the loft. The storming dissonance rushed after them on the staircase, drowning out the
old man's voice.

"You don't understand!" screamed Mr. Moffat. "*I have to
stay!*"

Up in the trembling loft, the organ played alone, its stops all
out, its volume pedals down, its motor spinning, its bellows
shuddering, its pipe mouths bellowing and shrieking.

Suddenly, a wall cracked open. Arch frames twisted, grinding stone on stone. A jagged block of plaster crumbled off the
dome, falling to the pews in a cloud of white dust. The floors
vibrated.

Now the congregation flooded from the doors like water.
Behind their screaming, shoving ranks, a window frame broke
loose and somersaulted to the floor. Another crack ran crazily
down a wall. The air swam thick with plaster dust.

Bricks began to fall.

Out on the sidewalk, Mr. Moffat stood motionless staring
at the church with empty eyes.

He was the one. How could he have failed to know it? His
fear, his dread, his hatred. His fear of being also scrapped, replaced; his dread of being shut out from the things he loved
and needed; his hatred of a world that had no use for aged
things.

It had been he who turned the overcharged organ into a maniac machine.

Now, the last of the congregation was out. Inside the first
wall collapsed.

It fell in a clamorous rain of brick and wood and plaster.
Beams tottered like trees, then fell quickly, smashing down the
pews like sledges. The chandeliers tore loose, adding their ex-
plosive crash to the din.

Then, up in the loft, the bass notes began.

The notes were so low they had no audible pitch. They were
vibrations in the air. Mechanically, the pedals fell, piling up a
mountainous chord. It was the roar of some titanic animal, the
thundering of a hundred, storm-tossed oceans, the earth
sprung open to swallow every life. Floors buckled, walls caved

in with crumbling roars. The dome hung for an instant, then rushed down and mangled half the nave. A monstrous cloud of plaster and mortar dust enveloped everything. Within its swimming opacity, the church, with a crackling, splintering, crashing, thundering explosion, went down.

Later, the old man stumbled dazedly across the sunlit ruins and heard the organ breathing like some unseen beast dying in an ancient forest.

The stories in this volume were first published
in magazines and books as follows:

Alfred Hitchcock's Mystery Magazine: "A Visit to Santa Claus"
(as "I'll Make It Look Good" under the name Logan Swanson)

Amazing Stories: "The Last Day"

Beyond Fantasy Fiction: "Long Distance Call"
(as "Sorry, Right Number")

Bluebook: "The Conqueror"

Ed Bain's Mystery Book: "Day of Reckoning" (as "The Faces")

Ellery Queen's Mystery Magazine: "Big Surprise"
(as "What Was in the Box?")

Fantastic Story Magazine: "Death Ship"

Fifteen Detective Stories: "Dying Room Only"

Galaxy Science Fiction: "Shipshape Home," "Third from the Sun,"
"One for the Books"

Gamma: "Deus Ex Machina," "Shock Wave" (as "Crescendo")

Imagination: "Blood Son" (as "Drink My Red Blood . . .")

The Magazine of Fantasy & Science Fiction: "Born of Man and
Woman," "Dress of White Silk," "The Funeral," "Holiday Man"

Mystery Tales: "Now Die In It"

Playboy: "Prey," "Button, Button," "Duel,"
"No Such Thing as a Vampire"

Startling Stories: "Witch War"

Alone By Night, edited by Michael Congdon and Don Congdon
(Ballantine Books, 1962): "Nightmare at 20,000 Feet"

Dark Forces, edited by Kirby McCauley (The Viking Press, 1980):
"Where There's a Will," written with Richard Christian Matheson

The Fiend in You, edited by Charles Beaumont
(Ballantine Books, 1962): "Fingerprints," "Mute"

Masques V, edited by J. N. Williamson and Gary Braunbeck
(Gauntlet Press, 2006): "Haircut"

Matheson Uncollected: Volume One (Gauntlet Press, 2008):
"Counterfeit Bills," "Man with a Club," "The Prisoner"

Star Science Fiction Stories, no. 3, edited by Frederik Pohl
(Ballantine Books, 1954): "Dance of the Dead"

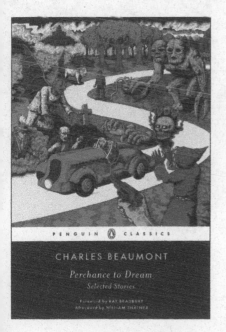